STATE OF DECAY & RUIN

PEGGY MARTINEZ

A PERMUTED PRESS book

ISBN (trade paperback): 978-1-61868-533-9
ISBN (eBook): 978-1-61868-534-6

PERMUTED
PRESS

STATE OF DECAY
BOOK ONE

To live without hope is to cease to live.
~Fyodor Dostoevsky

Prelude

Despite what you've been told, the Apocalypse doesn't begin with fire raining down from the heavens, nor does it begin with the human race falling down on their faces in supplication before a triumphant god. No, the sounds of the Apocalypse are much more terrifying than that, and I should know, I've heard them, and hearing the world tumble into chaos around me is not something I'll ever forget.

The first sounds were just a buzzing really, a buzzing of the television newscast in the background of our house, like so many other homes in America. Just the news playing in another room while we all went on about our day-to-day lives. The reports were of something happening far off—not to us—so it didn't worry anyone all that much. The sound of reporters and mainstream media feeding us all a bunch of hoopla to keep the masses entertained and calm when they should have been telling everyone what was really going on and how to protect themselves and their families. And my family, like most others in the world, fed into their lies and sat idly by while an epidemic swept through the world when we were all sleeping in our beds, assured of one thing: we were too advanced a people, too evolved a species, to ever tumble into a dark age of death, destruction, and chaos.

Oh, how the mighty and powerful fall.

Have you ever heard the sounds of mass hysteria or the sounds of a Boeing 767 plummeting from the sky to crash land in your neighborhood? It isn't a pleasant sound. There is a deafening roar as the plane falls from the sky and lands on top of houses you had walked past only the afternoon before, an explosion so loud, you swear you'd never hear again. And then the screaming. Dear God, sometimes when I close my eyes, I can still hear the screaming. Even to this day, when my adrenaline's pumping, when I find myself in a tight spot, or I know I'm *this* close to dying, there is a flashback of that sound, a sadistic mix of tearing, screeching metal, and gut-wrenching screams that make me dizzy from the high pitched wail echoing inside my skull.

And then there are the sounds that don't make sense to you, the ones you can't place... the ones that your brain can't comprehend, even if everything is playing out right before your eyes in all its Technicolor glory.

The First Day

Go get the handgun. Go get the handgun. GO GET THE HANDGUN.
What my dad had said while he ran through our front door was playing over and over again inside my head, like a scratched up CD that couldn't get past the deep gouge in its surface.

My dad was rushing through the house, hollering for me to get a bag together and to be ready to leave when he gave the word. He ran out the front door toward the wreckage to search for survivors. That's who my dad was, a hero. I could hear my own labored breathing—harsh to my ears—as I hurried to my room and grabbed my beat up, army green backpack and shoved random stuff inside of it, not really seeing what I was doing, not really paying attention to whatever crap I was packing. I threw a black tank top over the blue one I was already wearing, discarded my Cookie Monster pajama bottoms in favor of black cargo pants, and made sure to yank on my most worn-in black combat boots, lacing them up quickly.

"I'll be right back, don't worry. Everything will be fine, Mel. Go get the handgun and bullets and put them in your bag." That's what he had said. Did he know something was going to happen or was he just taking a precaution with all the chaos surrounding us at that moment? Didn't matter. I ran to my dad's room and unlocked the gun case stowed in his closet, and made sure to do exactly what he told me. My dad had been an officer in the Army for over twenty-five years and I knew he wouldn't have told me to get the gun if he didn't honestly believe there was some kind of threat looming. I found a camouflage rucksack, what my dad referred to as his "bug out bag", in the bottom of his closet. After making sure the safety was on and the gun was loaded, I stuffed it and all the ammo I could find in the bag and then headed to the kitchen.

I grabbed everything I thought that my dad would have told me to. Bottles of water, beef jerky, granola bars, cracker packs, a bag of apples, and a pack we always had ready in a closet for when we went camping, which was often. The screams from outside were getting louder, which only intensified the ache pounding through my head. I stood in the middle of our living room with no idea what to do next. I wanted to drop everything and run to help my dad, but I knew that wasn't the smart thing to do. I stood rooted to the spot, listening to screams and the wail of sirens in the distance.

I'm not sure how long I stood in the living room, wondering if I should go in search of my dad or hang tight like he'd told me to. I quite clearly remember the uneasiness worming its way into the pit of my stomach, the prickly sensation at the back of my neck, and the sense of dread settling around me like a thick fog. When my mother was alive, she used to tell me that I had a sixth sense about me, that all the women in her family did, but I never really put any real stock into what she was saying. After all, what good is it to have any extra "senses" if they didn't help you out in any way? Regardless, something was shimmering right out of focus, something niggling in the back of my mind that things were never going to be the same, that after that night my world would forever be changed. I can see that now, but back then, I was still a naïve teenager, not realizing things bigger than the plane crash were happening, not understanding that I should have been wondering *why* the plane had crashed in the first place. Instead, I was too busy wondering how long it would take for everything to get cleaned up, how my neighbors were, and when things would be getting back to normal.

When my dad swung open the front door early in the morning, I had dozed off on the couch with my backpack still on and the rucksack sitting on the coffee table in front of me. My dad looked around the house, his eyes slightly out of focus, as if he wasn't really seeing anything around him.

"Dad?" I whispered gently. His head swung around and his eyes met mine, and I knew right then that he'd seen some horrific things through the night. I just didn't know *how* horrific.

"Mel, get the keys to the jeep and put your bags inside. Get in and wait for me, I'm going to grab my gun and then we'll leave." His jaw clenched and his hand balled tightly into a fist.

"I've got the gun, Dad, it's in my bag, just like you told me." I picked up the rucksack and walked around the coffee table to stand in front of him. His eyes hardened and he strode past me, toward the back of the house.

"Not that gun, baby girl," he murmured harshly under his breath. I knew my dad owned other guns, guns he didn't normally use for protection. He collected guns and used them at shooting ranges and for hunting, and some he still had from his Army days. I knew those days haunted him and I knew he wouldn't be bringing those guns out unless something was seriously wrong. I wiped my damp palms on my pants and ran to the kitchen to grab the keys out of the cookie jar and then went into the garage to put the bags in the back seat. When my dad came back out he was wearing full Army camo and was carrying a very large duffel bag and his sniper rifle over his shoulder. I swallowed back the fear and apprehension clawing its way up my throat and climbed into the passenger seat of our jeep. My dad put his bag in the back seat and then brought his rifle in the front with him. He started up the vehicle and then just sat there, staring blankly into the windshield for a few seconds before he spoke.

"There's something going on. I'm not sure what exactly, but it's serious, Melody." He glanced over at me. I swallowed and licked my suddenly dry lips. I could see the fear behind his eyes and if my dad was scared. I really didn't want to contemplate what could be happening. "Where's the gun I told you to grab?" he asked gruffly.

"In the back," I answered. He reached into the back seat and pulled the rucksack onto his lap. When he pulled out the handgun his face was a mask of stone, his years of Army training taking over, and I was actually relieved to see it. This was the version of my dad I could handle in the face of whatever was going on. His finger clicked off the safety and he checked the gun over, nodding in approval that it was loaded. He pulled two extra magazines out of the bag and handed them to me. After he threw the bag back into the back of the jeep, he clenched his jaw and turned to me.

"Keep the safety off. Keep your gun where you can have easy access to it, and be careful. You've been handling guns for a long time and I know you'll act responsibly. I can't take you out of this house without knowing you are fully armed. If anything were to happen to me…"

"Daddy, I—"

He held up a hand and turned to face me. His face was granite, his eyes hard and unyielding. "If anything were to happen to me, you'd have a good chance to survive. I've taught you how to shoot, how to take care of yourself, everything I know. Don't trust anyone and always remember, survival means being smart. Acting rashly is what gets people killed."

I blinked furiously, trying to keep the threatening tears from spilling over. What was he saying? What was going on beyond the plane crash in our neighborhood? I swallowed hard and nodded my head sharply as I looked my father in the eye.

"I'll remember, Daddy," I promised. My dad's eyes softened a fraction and his hand cupped my cheek gently before he handed me the Colt 1911 handgun and a black leg holster. I took the gun with a shaking hand and attached it to my right leg while my dad backed the jeep out of the garage. The moment we pulled out onto our cul-de-sac, I was immediately, unequivocally sure that my life as I knew it was over.

My first real glimpse of my neighborhood in the early morning light took my breath away and left a gaping hole in the center of my chest. Over half of the houses in my line of vision had been completely demolished, fires burned in every direction, and debris littered the entire area. We moved slowly down the street, trying to avoid chunks of metal and wandering people. Mr. Howe, from a street over, was sitting on the edge of our sidewalk, still wearing his pajamas and missing a shoe. His face was blackened and smudged with what looked like soot, and blood had dripped down his face and splattered all over his white tee shirt from a large wound on his head. He was staring off into the distance like he was waiting for something to happen. I didn't see his wife or daughter anywhere and I suddenly didn't want to know why that was. There were a dozen or more people, some hurt more badly than others, some not hurt at all, but they all were either screaming and crying or completely emotionless. In the far distance, I heard a *rat-tat-tat* and the only thing I could think was, *Why would there be shooting at a plane crash site?*

A shiver slithered down my spine.

"Should we be leaving?" I asked my dad. "We could stay and help out everyone. They're our neighbors, our friends," I pleaded. My dad's hands clenched the steering wheel as he drove off the street to avoid a large piece of debris in the middle of the road before driving out of our cul-de-sac.

"We *have* to leave. We have to get out of here and get to the base." I searched his face, wondering why he wanted us to get to a military base. Surely we could go after we helped our neighborhood.

"Why, Dad? What's going on? I need to know. I need to be prepared."

My dad pulled our jeep onto a main road that would lead into our local, small town of Midtown, North Carolina. We had barely been residents of Midtown for a month and yet we'd come to love the small town and gorgeous forest areas since my dad had retired from service. I tried to relax back into my seat, but my body was tense, my mind racing a hundred miles a minute. When my dad finally spoke, I flinched at the invasion of my inner turmoil.

"There have been reports... reports that most civilians were not supposed to hear. *I* wouldn't have heard, except some of the officers from the base were helping with the wounded at the crash site and recognized me and broke protocol to tell me." He ran a hand roughly over his face and shook his head. "I didn't believe it completely, but if you had seen the look on their faces, *you* wouldn't have doubted them. I realize that now. And then when the bodies—the bodies that weren't incinerated in the explosion or the crash—began... *twitching*..." My dad swallowed loudly and then cleared his throat. My hand spasmed around the door handle and I tightened my grip, preparing myself for whatever he was about to say.

"At first, even after what the soldiers told me, I thought that they had somehow survived, somehow pulled through. I ran to the person nearest to me who was making horrible gurgling sounds and writhing around on the ground like a wild person and tried to pull them from the wreckage, only to have a soldier come up behind me and point-blank shoot the survivor right between the eyes."

I gasped, unable to control the spurt of emotion. My dad's story was far from finished.

"I screamed at the soldier and got in his face, telling him he was a disgrace to America, but then all of a sudden, like a demented orchestra, bodies were thrashing around, and the moaning... God, the moaning and gurgling. Soldiers started shooting, and I *still* didn't understand. It wasn't until a volunteer who had been helping us with survivors through the early morning hours ran over and knelt beside one of the bodies right next to me to help them... and the body—the thing—sank its teeth into the volunteer's neck and blood sprayed from his carotid artery, did I finally get it through my skull. We weren't dealing with survivors, we were dealing with monsters. Monsters who lived inside of dead bodies."

My dad drove for a few minutes in silence and I tried to digest everything he had just told me. The government obviously knew something, but the general public had no idea what was going on. The dead were somehow reviving and killing humans. It all sounded so surreal, so completely insane, that if anyone else had told me, there was no way in hell I would have believed them. But my dad was the strongest and most down to earth person I'd ever met. There was no way he'd be exaggerating or could have mistaken something so serious as this. He may not know everything, but he knew enough to realize the shit was about to hit the fan and we needed to get to the best place possible if we were going to be safe. Unfortunately for us, we didn't realize the extent to which the problem had spread.

I pulled my cellphone out of my pocket and tried to send my best friend back in our hometown a text. It wouldn't go through. I hadn't seen Jess since my dad moved us away right after I'd graduated over a month ago. He felt we needed a change of scenery after all that we had been through the past year, and while I didn't want to leave Jess, I had agreed with him. Jessica had gotten me through so much and I could only hope she would be okay. My mind drifted back.

"Come on, Mel, you know you want to." I threw a fry at Jess and

smirked when she ducked to dodge the greasy bomb sailing her way. I did want to go, but that was beside the point. She didn't let up. "You know what they're playing, don't you?" she asked in a sing-song voice. The old movie theater in town was playing Benny & Joon, one of my all-time favorite movies, for their Thursday Throwback feature show. All that awesomeness for a throwback ticket price of one dollar. "You probably also know Miguel will be there too, right?" My eyes widened and Jessica giggled. I hadn't known that. All that sexiness and he'd be going to watch a chick flick? Swoon.

"I'd love to, Jess, but I probably shouldn't tonight," I said with a sigh. "I have tons of homework to catch up on and I'm supposed to spend some quality time with my dad making fun of Jerry Springer reruns." I laughed when Jess choked and ranted because I'd used the terms "quality time" and "Jerry Springer" in the same sentence. When it came down to it, though, Jess didn't push. She never did. She knew my real reason for not going out, but she understood that I didn't want to talk about it, and that made her the best friend in the world. My mom's surgery had failed and her brain tumor was more aggressive than ever and I spent all of my free time with her.

"Well, don't blame me if Miguel has a hard time keeping his hands to himself. I am pretty fabulous, you know." She flipped her long, blonde hair and winked at me.

.⟨.

God, I hoped she was going to be safe.

"Jesus," my dad muttered as we drove into town. I snapped out of my memories, sat up, and placed a hand on the gun strapped to my leg. The scene we drove into was so unbelievable that I was sure I was either having some sort of out-of-body experience, or that we had somehow driven onto the set of a horror film. Fires burned everywhere, people ran and screamed, some were bashing in store front windows, and mixed in with it all was tumultuous violence and the stench of death. Bodies lay haphazardly on sidewalks and out in the middle of the street, people fought off humans with eerie, vacant eyes, blood clotted around their mouths, and ripped skin hanging from their teeth while they tore into the remains of their victims.

"Dad?" I whispered, swallowing the bile in my throat.

"Hold on, Mel. We are going to get out of here."

I gazed straight ahead and tried to block out all the violence and gore surrounding me, tried to see how my dad was going to get us out of the center of town. The streets were becoming more and more congested and I couldn't help but feel panic starting to claw at my chest. My dad gunned the gas and we had to weave dangerously through the streets, trying to get free of the madness. If we could just get off of the main drag in town, and make it to the main highway, we'd have a straight shot to the Army base. A woman ran out in the road and my dad swerved hard to the left. I screamed and grabbed the door handle, holding on for dear life. We missed the woman only by a few inches. My dad swerved again, this time trying to miss one of the lumbering corpses, but the jeep swiped him, causing the corpse to fly back in the street. I glanced back and saw the body get up like nothing had happened, and then attack the woman we had missed a few seconds earlier. My hand immediately went to my gun while we were speeding away and yet I couldn't do anything. I had never felt so utterly wretched as I did driving out of that city and not doing a damned thing to help anyone. I could only hope help—in the form of police or military—would be on their way as soon as possible.

"How did this happen?" I asked after we were a few miles out of the city.

"I don't know, but I am going to find out," my dad promised vehemently.

The following hours of my memory aren't much more than extremely realistic screen shots in my mind. I think I prefer it that way, glad that my mind chooses to try and protect me from the horrors of that first day.

The day that my old life ended.

My dad was flipping through radio channels, finding none that were broadcasting anything about what was happening, and cursing under his breath, I remember that. I remember him saying we couldn't be more than twenty minutes from the base and the next thing I remember was a flash. Not a flash of light, just a flash of red... a red shirt. The next thing I knew the whole world was spinning. The whole world was red.

"Melody? Melody, are you okay?" Dad's voice sounded so far away. My eyes cracked open and I saw his concerned face close to mine. "Thank God." His voice echoed around me, like we had somehow ended up in a tunnel.

Blackness.

An annoying dinging replaced my dad's voice. My eyes fluttered open again. I reached up to touch my head. It felt abnormally inflated and my hand felt light and detached from the rest of my body. When I brought it back in front of me I saw that it was covered in blood. I was suddenly drowned in sounds... everything came rushing back so fast that I nearly passed out from the sensory overload. I gazed around myself and realized I was alone in the jeep and my dad's door was standing wide open. The dinging noise.

I must have hit my head on the dashboard, I thought, stumbling out of the jeep and into the damp grass. Where was my dad? My hand rested on my gun as I made my way around to the back of the jeep, barely taking note that the front end of our vehicle was wrapped around a small tree.

I spotted my dad hunched over a body several yards away. I started to walk that way, but before I could make it, a large figure shuffled from behind an overturned Impala and fell on top of my dad. I screamed out, my voice cutting through the morning like a wayward piece of shrapnel finding its mark. My dad moved quickly, but not before the large dead man sunk his teeth into his shoulder. I grabbed my gun and ran to help him, but in my absolute terror, I didn't notice the small figure lunging for me.

The next thing I remembered was landing on the pavement with an *umph* and my gun hitting the ground about a foot away from me, and *way* too far away from dad. I looked up into the crazed, colorless eyes of a little girl about seven or eight years old, with blonde pigtails and gnashing teeth. I held onto the girl's neck and used all my strength to keep her teeth from getting too close to my face. It wasn't easy, she was a lot stronger than any normal seven year old should have been. I turned my head and reached frantically for my gun. My arm trembled with the effort it took to hold the little demon off of me as I strained to reach the handle of my handgun. When my fingers wrapped around the butt of the gun, I caught a glimpse of my dad wrestling with the huge monster on top of him. He bellowed out his anger and pain as the man ripped into the soft flesh of his neck.

"Dad, no!" I screamed, tears coursing down my face. I brought my gun up with my free hand and pointed it right in the face of the miniature monster on top of me. Even then, my hand wavered, my trigger finger stiffened. She was a little girl, someone's baby, still wearing hair bows and a Disney Princess tee shirt.

"Take the shot." I turned my head and found my dad's eyes narrowed on me, his words coming out in wet gasps. "Take… the… fucking… head… shot, Mel. You… will… live, baby girl." I turned and put the gun up to the little girl's head and pulled the trigger. I sobbed, closing my eyes. The little body fell limply on me and blood and brain matter and miniscule chunks of skull pelted my face.

I don't remember much else of what happened, none of the details, thankfully. I do know that my gun was missing three bullets when I was lucid enough to check later. I not only killed a little girl that day, I also put down her dad, and my own father before his body ever had a chance to change. It was the only thing I could for him, the only way I could think to let him die with his dignity. He deserved that at the very least.

I grabbed my backpack and the rucksack out of the back of the jeep and added a few of my dad's weapons and ammo to the bag I had packed. I ran into the tree line of the woods on the side of the road that we had been driving on. I walked without stopping, without thinking, and I walked with my eyes on the road, making sure I wouldn't run into more dead, also trying to avoid running into any living people. I knew without a shadow of doubt that I would have been an easy target for people trying to survive. A teenage girl carrying supplies and weapons. I was a sitting duck in a world gone crazy. My only goal was to survive. And to survive meant getting to the Army base.

I heard the gunfire before I saw the base. Hell, I heard the screams and the groans before I saw the base. When I was finally close enough to see it from the cover of the woods, I realized with a sinking heart that there would be no survival and no safe haven there. The Army base was overrun with dead and dying. I sat my rucksack down on the ground and then stood there listening to the deafening sounds of chaos all around me. What was I supposed to do? What would my Dad have done? A tear tracked down my cheek and I quickly wiped it away and clenched my fist. There would be time for that later. Right then I had to make a decision. Acting rashly could get me killed. I breathed deeply through my nose, picked my bag up off the forest floor, and turned to move deeper into the woods, away from the base, away from the roads, and away from everything.

I wasn't sure what I was going to do in the long run, but I did know one thing. I was going to live. If I had to, I'd taking the fucking head shot over and over again. You better bet your sweet ass, I wasn't going down without fight.

I was going to survive.

Seventy-Two Hours Later

I could almost pretend everything was normal. If I closed my eyes tight enough and long enough I could imagine my dad was just gone to catch us some fish for dinner and we were on a normal father-daughter camping trip, like always. My reality was too harsh. The reality was that my dad was gone and that fucking hurt like someone had stuck a knife up under my breast bone and was twisting it harder and plunging it deeper every second. The pain took my breath away and I was reminded of my loss every time I tried to breathe in. Something had broken off inside me and I wasn't sure it could ever be repaired.

I sat on my bedroll and looked over all the supplies I'd carried out to the woods in my rucksack. It wasn't a lot, but I had a feeling it was a ton more than a lot of other people ended up with three days ago. Most importantly, I was checking for the things I was most in danger of running out of, and the things I didn't have. Where food was concerned, I was doing pretty well. My dad had seven MREs, Meals Ready-to-Eat, in the rucksack, and I had added a box of granola bars, a bag of apples, crackers, peanut butter, beef jerky, and a few other odds and ends to the bags before we left. If I was very frugal, I was pretty positive I could last at the very least three to four weeks on the supplies I had, and that didn't include any fish I might catch.

I bit my lip and sorted through the rest of my supplies: small first aid kit, flash light with batteries, waterproof matches, a can of lighter fluid, a collapsible fishing pole, and miscellaneous personal hygiene supplies. I had four water bottles on me, two were empty and two were full. I could simply refill the bottles, since I'd already scouted a water source, but it would be easier if I had a jug or two.

I paced around the place I'd claimed my own and then glanced up into the blue sky above my head. The first forty-eight hours that I'd kept moving further and further into the woods, I'd heard the sound of helicopters flying overhead several times. Once I started to second guess myself and wonder if I should head back into town, that maybe I had overreacted and things were already getting better. I had a feeling deep down that the best thing for me to do was to keep moving and to get as far away as possible from any other humans—dead or alive. I squatted down again and ran a hand over my weary eyes.

"Daddy, what should I do?" I whispered. A tear tracked down my cheek, followed by another and then another. Pretty soon the floodgate that I'd kept so diligently locked for the past three days came crashing open and I sunk to the ground and *unraveled.*

.:.

It wasn't until the next morning that I had the will to pull myself off of my bedroll and make my way over to the stream to wash off. I changed my top and threw my two tank tops on the ground. I'd burn those. Even if I could get all the blood and other bits that had seeped in and dried for three days straight after that first night, I'd never be able to wear them again.

I packed away all my things except for a small pack of essentials— those I put into a smaller, lighter weight backpack that I'd take with me into town. I found a spot under thick foliage and hid all my things and then took the time to brush the ground with branches to make my little camping spot less conspicuous. When I was finished, I checked my pack one last time and made sure I had my weapons on me. Along with my handgun strapped to my leg, and my dad's M4 across my back, I added a twelve inch recon knife. The blade was wicked sharp and deadly, and just the thing to have if you found yourself in a tight spot, but didn't want to make too much noise. I sat down and pulled out some beef jerky and a power bar. It was going to be a long hike. I wanted to see what had happened in the past several days, but I also had to make sure I had made the right choice. Not only that, I needed to do one other thing, something personal. I finished off my breakfast and filled my water bottles. This was going to suck on so many levels. I grabbed my backpack and made my way back to the place of nightmares and monsters.

.:.

The edge of the woods came faster than I thought possible. I'm sure it had taken the same amount of time to leave my campsite that it did for me to get to it, but when I was heading toward chaos and death, I sincerely wished it would have taken a lot longer. The two day hike had passed in a blur. I exited the woods several miles south of where I'd entered them near the Army base. I'd made sure to give the place that my dad had died a wide berth and found myself probably a mile south of the spot where his body still lay, close to the jeep where it was wrapped around the tree we had hit. I walked along the road staying close to the edge of the woods just in case I had to duck and cover or make a run for it. Plus, the trees made me feel safer, like I didn't stand out like a sore thumb. I walked for several hours before I knew I would be coming up on Midtown.

It took me several pep talks before I was actually able to run across the highway and duck behind an Ace Hardware store skirting the edge of town. It was early morning and the sun was beginning to rise and shine its rays on everything, living and dead, in town.

The scent of the dead slapped me in the face like an oversaturated blanket of smog. I gasped and choked, trying to breathe in through my mouth instead of my nose, but breathing through my mouth only made it worse. Have you ever tasted the scent of rot and decay on the back of your tongue? It's no palate pleaser, that's for sure. And let's not mention the amount of gnats a person can consume in a single inhale. Bleck!

With my heart pounding frantically in my chest I made my way slowly around the building until I was sure I could make a run for the shadow of another building. I kept that up for the next thirty minutes, ducking, hiding, and darting to the back of buildings, from shadow to shadow, until I was closer to the main part of town. When I finally reached the center of town, I knew things were even worse than I imagined and that I had been right to take sanctuary in the woods.

I'd just pressed myself against the wall of a Starbucks, the only one in town, when a wave of zombies decided to come lurching into view. I'd see the dead before, the ones that we drove by from the safety of our jeep, the one that killed my dad, and the little girl who had attacked me that first day. However, nothing had prepared me for the sight of so many corpses walking down the street in the middle of broad daylight. I squeezed myself tightly against the brick wall behind me, trying to make myself as small as possible. I held my breath and cursed my heart for pounding so loudly in my chest, sure it would draw their attention to me.

A dozen or more of them shuffled past the front of the store moaning and making gurgling noises that had the hairs on the back of my neck standing on end. Even more disturbing was the normalcy of their appearance. Zombie movies featured the undead wearing clothing that was shredded and either gray, tan, or some varying shade of dirt. The undead *were* dirty, their clothing *was* torn in some places, yet underneath the bloodstains and the gore was the clothing of your everyday, average American—bright and cheery clothing made macabre by the things that wore them and the current state of the world. The colors were now harsh and surreal, giving them a creepy IT circus-y freak show feel. A woman who struggled to move along with the others was wearing a bright purple tank top and a jean skirt, a man wearing khakis and a light blue button up shirt walked close to her, and the children—dear God, the children—they were the worst. Some wore pajamas with happy cartoon characters depicted on them, but Elmo didn't look quite as endearing when he was covered in leftover bits of human flesh from the zombie kid's most recent meal. I shuddered and shrunk further into my hiding spot.

After the last zombie had gone by and several minutes had passed, I stepped closer to the front of the building to see what had become of the main street leading into and out of town. The word *apocalypse* came to mind immediately, though even that word was too tame of a description for what I saw. Smoke rose from a pile of bodies close by, cars and debris lined the streets, decomposing bodies, stripped of almost everything except the bones, lay scattered about. Splashes of dark reddish-brown muck and blood splattered the street, the sidewalk, cars, storefronts, and to top it all off—walking corpses were *everywhere*. There was no way any living could be left in the town. It had been infested with the undead.

I found myself in a conundrum. I was in the middle of town with zombies crawling all over the place. I didn't know which way to turn. I knew at least a dozen zombies had gone back the way I had just come from and I knew if I got cornered by that many of them, I'd be a goner. I didn't know what move to make next. I glanced around the streets at the cars that littered the roads. Most of them probably had a full tank of gas and keys left inside. People were caught off guard, they'd had no idea what to expect. They weren't even warned. The only problem was the zombies. It would be impossible for me to get to a car without being seen. Not only that, but I might choose a car that happened to not have keys in the ignition and I had no idea how to hotwire a car. I'd be trapped in a car with zombies gnashing their teeth to get to me. I crouched down and tried to formulate a plan.

I happened to glance up and catch a reflection of myself in the glass of a window across the street. I could barely make out my own shape. I also happened to notice the reflection of the Starbucks I was hiding next to, and it had its entire front window busted out. It was then that an insane, makeshift plan tickled the back of my mind. With my mind made up, I got up and edged around the building just enough to see if I had a chance. I glanced up and down the road and counted over fifty lumbering dead before I gave up counting and rounded it up to seventy-five to be safe. I calculated everything I had on me and knew I'd be pushing my luck to carry out my idea and I knew that if I survived, I'd have to catch quite a few lucky breaks. Still, I decided it was my best option.

When I was fairly certain most of the zombies were unaware of my presence, I swallowed the huge lump of fear threatening to choke me and ran around the building out into the open and jumped into the busted out window of the Starbucks. I immediately flattened myself against the inner wall and held my breath. My heart was pounding so hard, I could feel the vein in my temple throbbing wildly, and I was concerned it was about to burst from the pressure. When I'd entered the store, my boots crunched the broken glass and I could swear the sound echoed into the furthest reaches of outer space. A minute passed and then several, before I exhaled a relieved breath. Looked like I'd live to see my plan through. Oh joy.

I glanced around the interior of the store and felt a tinge of remorse for what I was about to do. I remembered when my dad and I had just moved into this town a few weeks back. The Starbucks was brand spanking new and it was a source of pride for the locals; they had recently opened their first Starbucks in one of the renovated storefront spaces, a true testament to the fact that the town was growing. The building was ancient just like the town and I had loved the old world feel of it the second we stepped inside. My dad had done some work on his laptop that day while he drank a latte with a double shot of espresso and I had plugged in my iPod and sat near him and people watched through the large glass window up front. I sipped my iced caramel coffee. It had been a good day.

Fortunately for me, I also had paid attention to the tour they had given us and knew that this particular store had a second story storage attic and had a place with a ladder you could climb and exit out to the roof. I was banking on the fact that if the Starbucks had that feature, maybe several of the other old storefronts would as well.

I moved slowly along the edge of the store until I reached the front counter. I slid my backpack off and sat it on the counter as quietly as possible. I pulled out the bottle of lighter fluid I'd brought with me and grimaced when I realized how badly this whole thing could go, but there was no backing out now. I opened the lighter fluid and started soaking the walls and tables and floors thoroughly. I crept up to the front of the store and made sure I sprayed a line of the fluid out onto the side walk in front of the store too. I took a wad of paper towels from a dispenser on the floor and twisted them tightly into a nice, thick rope then used the remaining lighter fluid to soak the rope. I was pulling out my boxes of ammo when I realized how badly I had to go to the bathroom. Even during a zombie outbreak, when you had to go, you had to go. I shoved all my stuff back into my bag and carefully made my way back into the two stall women's bathroom in the store. The bathroom looked eerily normal. It was still spotless and there was absolutely none of the carnage that waited right outside the doors. It was a little potty room utopia. I hurried up and did my business, afraid to dawdle too long and make some dire mistake. I grabbed two rolls of toilet paper and stuffed them into my bag. I was pretty sure I'd be needing them once I made back to my new home in the woods.

I'd relaxed after making it into town safely, let down my guard once I'd infiltrated the freaking Starbucks successfully and I almost paid for it with my life. I'd just come out of the bathroom, feeling sorry that I couldn't simply live in the immaculate bathroom forever, when I headed around the counter to go into the back room. The zombie had probably been there the whole time and I'd never noticed him. As I pushed through the swinging door to go into the back room the zombie lunged for me. I didn't have time to scream, I didn't have time to dodge the attack, yet somehow I managed to lift the backpack I was carrying in my arms just enough that when the zombie tried to sink his teeth into my chest, he got a mouthful of my canvas backpack instead.

The back of my head ricocheted off of the swinging door as the zombie knocked me back and landed on top of me. His weight slammed the breath out of my lungs and when I tried to suck in a much-needed inhalation of air, I got the undiluted version of zombie B.O. I swung out wildly, trying to knock the zombie off of me, to get free of the dead body that pinned me down. The zombie wasn't going to give up easily though, he was like a mindless animal, aware his next meal had just walked right into his lair. I grabbed my backpack with my right arm and shoved with all my might, kicking up with my feet at the same time to try and dislodge the putrid scented zombie from my body. The backpack hit the zombie directly in the face and I heard a bone crack in his nose. Momentarily stunned, it loosened his grip on me and I took advantage by kicking out once again and heaving my body upward as hard as possible.

The zombie rolled off of me and I crawled over frantically toward the recon knife that I'd dropped during the chaos, closed my fist around it, and turned, still on my knees. Just then the zombie lunged off the ground toward me again. Out of reflex, I thrust my knife out and caught the animated corpse right in the larynx. Unfortunately, that didn't kill *or* stop him. I pulled my knife out with my right hand and swung my backpack with my left, knocking the zombie over again. The zombie rolled over he immediately came at me wildly, his movement more frantic. This time when I thrust my knife, it went right into his left eye and poked out of the back of his skull. The zombie stilled, blood and other rank fluids oozing out of his mouth, neck, and eye. As soon as I yanked my knife free the second time and the zombie fell with a *splat* into its own juices, I vomited and dry heaved until my stomach was completely empty.

I wiped my mouth off and got up on shaky legs, resting my

forehead on a large wall of boxes for a moment while I got my breathing back under control. When I stepped back again, I blinked in surprise. What were the odds? There were boxes and boxes of Starbucks VIA Ready Brew stacked on top of each other, and right in front of my face was the caramel flavored ones. Those were my favorites. I snatched a box off of the shelf and used my smaller knife to tear open the box. I snatched a fifty count bag out and shoved it into my pack. I snagged a bag of the Strawberry lemonade refreshers. I figured I deserved it, especially since the zombie that had nearly taken me out was still wearing a Starbucks employee apron. I'm pretty sure I could have sued under normal circumstances. A small, hysterical laugh burst through my lips. No time to crack up now, I needed to get a move on. I didn't want to get stuck in town when the sun went down. I shivered and closed up my bag, heading to the back of the store, this time keeping an eye out for any more zombiefied baristas.

There was an old set of stairs in the very back of the store with a sign that read "Employees Only". I pulled it open and went up onto the second floor. The room was large and housed a ton of boxes. I made my way over to what looked like a trap door leading up to the roof, pulled on a cord hanging from the ceiling, and a set of stairs folded down. When I made it out onto the roof I knelt down and then slowly made my way over to the front of the roof that overlooked the center of town. From my vantage point on the roof, I could see that my earlier zombie estimation had been a little off. If I had to guess, I'd have said there were definitely closer to a hundred zombies that I could see. No telling how many were inside of buildings or outside of my view.

I sat my bag down and pulled out the boxes of ammo I had in my pack. I had around a hundred rounds for my M4 rifle and a lot less for my handgun. I took out my handgun and added three more bullets to the chamber. I'd forgotten all about reloading it after I'd used it that first day. That could have gotten me killed. I sat the handgun down and loaded the M4. When I was ready, I laid down on the roof on my stomach, propped the rifle up, and peered through the scope. I lined my shot up with the head of a zombie directly in the center of town. I sucked in a breath and pulled the trigger. The shot hit him in the shoulder and he barely flinched from the impact. It did begin stirring trouble down below. The zombies all took notice and they all started to twitch and lurch a little bit more.

I lined the shot up again and sucked in a breath, and just before I pulled the trigger I heard the gentle voice my dad used to use when we went target practicing together.

"*Don't suck in your breath, Mel. Relax and breathe in slowly. Then, as you exhale, release the bullet with your trigger finger. Let it be a part of you, an extension of you and your actions and you won't miss."*

I could almost feel his hand on my shoulder. When I pulled the trigger the second time, my bullet struck true and the zombie dropped. So did the next twenty.

I'd already blasted through four twenty-round magazines before I realized how many more zombies had shown up on the streets in front of me when they'd heard all the commotion. I picked up my last magazine and loaded the M4, taking a glance around at my handiwork. The streets were literally covered in bodies—finally, truly dead. Some had fallen on top of each other, creating piles of the undead. For every ten I had taken out, two more had walked out into the open, which meant I had over forty zombies—that I could see—and only twenty bullets left. I needed to make each one count and I still didn't like the odds. When the final body dropped to the ground, I counted exactly twenty-three zombies left. Time for part two of my genius plan. I crawled back over to the roof opening that led back into the store and made my way back down to the interior of the store.

I headed straight for the front store window, trying not to think too much about what I was about to do. I stepped halfway out of the storefront window and checked out the street. The closest zombie was several stores down and the furthest was quite a bit farther. I wasn't sure how fast a zombie could move or run, so my next move was foolish at best. I pulled the small hunting knife out of my pocket and slid it across my left palm, hissing as the stinging brought tears to my eyes. I jumped out of the store window and stood directly in the middle of the street and squeezed my hand into a tight fist, causing my blood to drip onto the asphalt.

"Hey you bunch of ugly fuckers!" I yelled. The world's best movie director couldn't have choreographed the scene any better. The zombies turned as one, their heads all swiveled in my direction like they had been attached by an invisible force. The hairs on my arms stood on end. "Yeah, you! Come get some, bitches!" I shouted, backing up. The zombies had already begun to shamble-run towards me. The promise of fresh meat and blood was too strong an enticement to keep them standing still. I swear to God I wanted to run, instead I stood my ground. I'll forever have nightmares of standing in the middle of that ruined street as I watched over twenty monsters with crazed eyes and gnashing teeth come toward me. When the closest zombie was within a dozen feet of me, I turned and ran back into Starbucks. At this point, I knew I had to get back to the roof without delay or I was dead.

The second I cleared the window seal, I slipped. I vividly recall thinking "Aww, hell!" I scrambled off of my knees and pulled a piece of glass out of my palm. I had made it around the counter when I heard the first zombies fall into the front of the store.

To close, too close, too close!

I kept moving, even when I heard the sound of glass crunching beneath the feet of a bunch of zombies, I kept moving to the back of the store. I wiped my palms all over the door that led to the second floor and then slammed it shut. By the time I was halfway across the second floor, I heard the thumps and moans of the zombies right outside the door. I sprinted for the stairs and made sure to pull them up after me when I cleared the roof. I had no idea if a zombie could open a door or climb stairs or not, and I didn't really want to find out.

With a shaking hand, I pulled out my box of waterproof matches and walked over to the edge of the roof. There were zombies clamoring to get into the store directly below me.

Jesus, I thought, *I sure would hate to fall into that.*

I struck a match and stood close to the edge of the wall and let it drop. Nothing happened. I wiped my damp palms on my pants and struck another one; it too fizzled out before it hit the ground. I had been pretty sure that would have worked, so when I had to pick up the napkin rope I had drenched in lighter fluid, I was feeling a little frantic. This *had* to work, it was my last resort. I took out a match, licked my dry lips, and lit it. The rope it burst into flames and I screeched, barely holding onto the edge of it. I held it over the edge of the roof for a second longer and then let it go with a prayer. The flaming napkin rope hit the sidewalk right next to a zombie, and at first nothing happened. I was just about to give up and go on with the third part of my plan when the flames from the napkin caught the line of lighter fluid I'd sprayed out onto the sidewalk.

A line of fire flew into the store. I waited several breathless moments to see if my plan had been a success and then smoke and flames shot from the front of the store. I squealed out loud like a lunatic. I ran over to where I had sat my backpack and jerked it on. My adrenaline was kicking and I was charged and ready to get the next part of my plan over with. My mouth felt dry when I thought about what I was about to do. I walked over to the edge of the building and once again peered over to the roof of the building next to the one I was standing on. It was totally doable, but that didn't make my fear any less real. Two stories was a long way to drop when you had nothing but pavement, fire, and zombies to break your fall. I backed up several feet and tried to ignore the sounds of popping glass and zombies moaning in the distance. I had already put my knife away. If running with scissors was bad for your health, I'm pretty sure jumping from one rooftop to another with a twelve inch blade in your hand would've been downright lethal.

"I can do this. I can do this. I *have* to do this," I chanted to myself. I ran full out, my legs pumping as hard as my heart and then I screamed like a girl and catapulted myself off of the roof. I made it with a hysterical giggle and plenty of room to spare. I got up and brushed myself off and then, while I still had the nerve, jumped over to the next building, and then one more, before I stopped. The roof of the next building was too far away. I ran over to the front edge of the roof and looked back towards the Starbucks. Flames and smoke were still pouring out of the building, and to my horror, so were zombies. Zombies are terrifying. Zombies lit up like the human torch? They were *petrifying*. I stood there in a shocked stupor before I physically shook myself and ran to the trap door on the roof.

I pushed on the trap door, but it didn't budge; I slammed my fists on it, and yet it didn't open. I could feel that the wood was old, though, that it might give if I could put enough pressure on it. I stepped back and brought my boot down with all my might on the outer edge of the boards. The vibrations of my stomp jarred my leg and my hips, and clattered my teeth together. I slammed my foot down again and again until my entire leg was numb from the strain. The boards creaked and groaned, but didn't break. As a last ditch effort, I stood completely on the door with both feet and then with all my body weight poised above the entry, I jumped up and came back down with all my might. The plywood broke and I fell through the opening with a resounding *CRASH*!

Lucky for me, my backpack broke my fall, though I thought I had died from the jarring impact alone that knocked the air completely from my lungs. Unfortunately for me, I brought a piece of the wood with me when I fell. When I was able to move, I sat up and reached for the six inch long piece of wood sticking out of my right thigh. I shimmied out of my backpack and pulled out the small first aid kit. I opened up some gauze and medical tape and then unscrewed the small bottle that had been labeled "rubbing alcohol". With the gauze in my mouth and the alcohol in my left hand, I took a deep breath, jerked out the piece of wood, and poured the liquid on the wound. I almost blacked out from the pain. When I could see past my agony, I pressed the gauze to the wound and then tightly secured the gauze in place by wrapping medical tape all the way around my leg.

I shoved everything back in my bag and stood up carefully. The leg was sore, but not bad enough to hinder my movements too much. I had lost precious time breaking into the building and getting hurt. I clutched my recon blade in my left hand and my handgun in my right.

It was time to move. I made my way down the rickety stairs and cautiously pushed the door open. I wasn't even sure which store I was in. I didn't know the town all that well. I walked out and immediately knew where I was—Midtown Antiques and Collectibles. The back part of the store was a disaster and the front part of the store was worse. The good thing? I didn't run into any zombie antique dealers.

The vehicle that I had my eye on from the roof of Starbucks sat parked in front of the shop across the road from where I now stood. The odd thing about the antique shop was that none of the windows had been busted out, so I felt a tiny bit safer than I had at Starbucks. I was going to have to make a run for the SUV and hope that I was right about the keys being left in the ignition. I tightened my grip on my gun and knife and jerked the door open... and *froze*. I hadn't noticed as I stood in the store that above the door there was a large bell attached, so that when people entered, the store owner would hear them from the back room. I had just rung the fucking dinner bell. And sure enough, from the right side of the building came two zombies and from the left came one zombie lit up like a flamethrower. I ran.

I made it across the street quickly and when I glanced into the window I saw the keys dangling in the ignition. I grabbed the door handle only to find it locked. Right about that time, the first zombie caught up with me.

I screeched and aimed for the head, and pulled the trigger. The zombie fell backward immediately and I pointed my gun at the backseat window and shot. Another zombie lunged for me with his mouth already opened wide. I stumbled back slightly and I pulled the trigger, catching the zombie point-blank in the face, dropping it. I shoved my arm impossibly far into the window to try and get the locks open, not caring that my arm was getting all scraped and cut up in the process. I was reaching as far as I could, my heart likely to explode out of my chest at any second because I saw zombie-torch-dude coming up on me in my peripheral vision. My finger skimmed the button and I heard all the locks pop open. I swung open the door and skidded inside just as the zombie-on-fire crashed into the door and pounded his fists against my window. Each thump against the window pounded through my skull; each fist that smashed against the glass left behind chunks of melted and charred skin and bloody smears.

The engine turned over on the first try and I could have cried from pure relief. I slammed the vehicle into drive and pressed the gas like my life depended on it, which it did. Not even the blast of Justin Bieber's *Baby* coming through the speaker system could wipe the smile off my face. No, I turned the volume up full blast, held on tightly to the steering wheel and navigated around as many obstacles as possible, even running over bodies if I had to, laughing the whole time with tears streaming down my face. I glanced in the rearview mirror when I was almost all the way out of the roughest part of town and saw at least two dozen bodies lurching out of alleyways and out into the open. Several of them were on fire. I might not have cleaned out all the zombies in town, but I sure as hell put a dent in their numbers before I left.

*

I took the time to pull over and load more bullets into my gun before I drove into my old neighborhood. Well, neighborhood didn't really fit any longer. *Warzone* seemed much more appropriate. Everything I could see was completely destroyed from the huge airplane that fell from the sky and landed in my residential neighborhood. The burnt trees and houses looked like a group of tornadoes made of lava had touched down and leveled everything in their path. Anxiety pitted the center of my stomach as I pulled in front of my house. I cut off the engine and stepped out of my commandeered vehicle, shoving the keys into my pocket. A zombie lumbered around the side of my neighbor's house when I shut the door. With a jolt, I recognized Mr. Howe, still wearing his pajamas and only one shoe, just like I'd last seen him.

I swallowed back tears and stuffed my gun into the holster on my leg. He moved quickly until he was right on top of me. I lashed out and drove my blade right into his forehead. He jerked and then stilled, his body dropping to the ground.

"Sorry, Mr. Howe," I whispered. I glanced around hastily and then ran to the front door of my house. The door had been kicked in. I swallowed back my anger and entered the front room with my gun drawn. I made my way from room to room and realized they had only been after food and supplies.

Even knowing the house was clear, I knew I couldn't dawdle too long. I needed to get what I came for and then leave. I headed back to my dad's room and sat down on his bed. I picked up his pillow and held it to my nose, inhaling the scent that clung to his pillowcase. I closed my eyes and hugged the pillow to me like a lifeline. After I sat there for much too long, I stood up and gathered the things I'd come for. I went into the kitchen and grabbed a large black garbage bag and started in my father's room. I added my dad's pillow and a sturdy sheet and blanket to the bag first, followed by the last five MREs that were left in a box under his bed. I took out all the ammunition that was left in a storage bin under the bed and added it to the bag as well. I was relieved to find more ammo for the rifle.

Next, I went into my room and glanced around. This was going to be the last time I would be back here for a long time—maybe ever. I grabbed my iPod out of my desk drawer and shoved it into the bag. I knew it was fully charged, so I still had a little playtime left on it. I swung open my closet and thanked the heavens above I had never been a girly-girl. I'd insisted, even when my dad protested, that my clothes and shoes be practical and even border on boyish. Since I was about to turn eighteen, he'd given up on trying to get me to wear any pink. I think he had finally realized what a waste of time it was. I added a week's worth of undergarments, socks, and one set of flannel pajamas to the bag. Next I added every single tank top I owned and then half a dozen tee shirts, two pairs of jeans, two pairs of dark cargo pants, and three long-sleeved thermal shirts and leggings. The small, compact bundle would've made my dad proud.

I grabbed my dad's dog tags and my mom's locket off of my dresser and hung them around my neck, glad to have my most prized possessions with me again. I glanced around my room once again before I walked out. I snagged a picture of my dad and me off of my desk and one of my mom and threw them in too. Nothing else meant anything to me, and anything else would have been a burden to carry.

When I went into the bathroom I simply raked everything I thought might be useful into the bag: Tylenol, cold medicine, rubbing alcohol, more first aid supplies, toothpaste, lotion, lip glosses, two towels and washcloths. In the kitchen I grabbed Ziploc bags and two empty water jugs. By the time I was done, my bag was bulging. I only had two more items I needed. I headed to the garage and found what I was looking for.

When I left the house I had to move fast, even with everything I was carrying with me. Three zombies were heading for me when I came around the corner and reached the SUV. I threw my huge sack into the back and then jumped into the driver's seat before the zombies made it to me.

I started the car, threw the Justin Bieber CD out of the window, shoved my own Flyleaf CD into the player, rolled down my window, and waited for the zombies to get in range. Then, just as the words "fully alive" blasted through my speakers, I put the three zombies down. I drove out of my old neighborhood, determined to make it back to the cover of the woods before it got dark.

.⸱.

When I pulled the SUV off the road, I was dreading getting out of it. My heart was pounding and I was sweating before I stepped out of the vehicle. I walked to the back and took the shovel out, making my way over to an all-too-familiar wreck site. I pushed everything that I did after that to the back of my mind. I had to, or I would have never been able to go through with it. When I was done, I sunk to the ground and wept until I couldn't weep anymore. I now had my dad's wallet and wedding band in my pocket, and once he was buried inside the tree line where we had crashed, I felt a sense of relief and calm wash over me. He would have been proud of me.

I wiped my eyes and got back into the SUV. I found a spot about a half mile down the road where I could drive the SUV into the woods. I went as far back as I dared and parked it in an area that was surrounded by thick foliage. I pocketed the keys and then grabbed the huge bag out of the back of the vehicle and also grabbed the tent I'd picked up out of the garage. It was a nice one, not too big, but most importantly, it would keep my safer from the elements. I exited the woods and stepped onto the road, peering over to the place where I had parked. I couldn't see the SUV and I sighed in relief. The vehicle could come in handy later on, so long as no one siphoned all the gas out of the tank.

I took a deep breath and made my way across the street, then stepped into the forest. I immediately relaxed, back in my element, and happy to be alive. I set out at a slow and steady pace, feeling the day's events weighing heavily on me, and the bag I carried slowed me down even more. I pulled out my iPod and allowed myself the luxury of one song while I made my way deeper and deeper into the forest. I played Pink's *Beam Me Up* and tuned everything else out.

With each step I took, the carnage and decay of the new world slipped further away from me. I put one foot in front of the other, each beautifully sung word cleansing a tiny piece of my soul until the uncertainty of my tomorrow didn't feel quite so unbearable.

Two Years After the World Went to Shit

The dead never sleep. They don't have to, they never get tired. They just keep going and going, like some sicko's version of an Energizer bunny. They do, however, have times when they shut down and stand idle for whatever reason. Don't get me wrong, you make too much noise or run in front of them, whether they've been like that for hours or months, they'll snap out of it in a flash and try to make you their next meal. Me? I don't plan on being anyone's meal anytime soon, so I kept my eyes alert and my footsteps quiet as I entered the military base.

It had been a little over two years since I had last seen the base, and with what I'd witnessed that day, I still hadn't expected the level of carnage and destruction I now found. In the cities, yes. But at a government Army base? I figured they would have been better prepared to deal with everything that went down. I guess no one could've been prepared for people—civilians and soldiers alike—dying and then coming back as mindless monsters, hungry for human flesh and blood.

I don't know what drove me out of the woods this time. I had been living in the forest by myself for the past two years and had only come out a handful of times to scavenge for supplies and to try and assess what kind of shape the world around me was in. This time I really didn't need supplies and it was pretty damn obvious the world had gone to Hell in a hand basket, and yet here I was making my way into a very dangerous situation. Of course, anywhere I went could now be considered a high risk since everywhere I turned I could run into one of the zombies lumbering around aimlessly. I think more than anything else I was just *ready*. Really ready to find out what was going on *elsewhere* in the world. Was the government completely shut down? Were there safe zones? Exactly what did happen two years ago to cause this fucked up mess? I had asked myself these questions over and over again the past months and had even gone so far as to pack up all my gear to make my way back to civilization a few times, but each time I stopped myself, came up with an excuse to hold out, to live the best way I could alone in the woods. To survive. It wasn't until a few days ago that I realized my dad wanted me to survive, yet survival meant so much more than just being alive. Survival meant adapting and moving forward. I'd survived, however, I wasn't living or adapting. I'd become stagnant.

So, here I was out of my element, trying to find some answers. I was feeling way too exposed out in the open. I'd gotten used to being cloaked and hidden in the woods. Now I felt naked and vulnerable with nothing around me as camouflage. I was no longer used to my old surroundings—civilization. The sounds of the dead shuffling around and moaning in the receding shadows caused a fine mist of sweat to break out on my upper lip as I pressed my back up against the checkpoint building leading into the Army base. Decaying bodies that had been left out in the elements since that first day were everywhere. Some hung out of vehicles, some littered the street and walkways, and others were mostly hidden in grass and weeds, strangled and overtaken by nature run amok. Between the decaying bodies that had been taken out with a bullet to the brain or a knife thrust through the cerebral cortex and the bloated, rotting flesh of the corpses that still lumbered around in search of their next meal, the air was oppressive and stank of things worse than death.

I tightened the cloth that covered my nose and mouth, repositioned my dad's M4 rifle on my back, and gripped my recon blade tightly in my right hand, slipping from shadow to shadow, avoiding detection by the zombies. My feet were light and sure as I made my way onto the base. Months and months in the woods had made me more careful, more alert to my surroundings and any sounds that I might make. I was making pretty good time moving stealthily along the perimeter of the property and kept the building I was headed for in my peripheral vision. I ducked and dodged my way past at least a dozen staggering zombies and was feeling pretty great about myself when I dipped behind a jeep to avoid a cluster of zombies standing in front of the building I needed to get into.

I lunged quickly to keep from being seen and brought my booted foot directly down into the chest cavity of a legless corpse. Unfortunately, the corpse was of the squishy, animated variety and the forward momentum of my boot, combined with all my body weight, caused the chest of the zombie to give beneath me like an engorged, overripe melon. Blood, putrid fluids, and skin burst from the zombie and exploded all over my leg. I barely reigned in a scream and kept my stomach contents down. Even with my foot crushing its rib cage and squishing its guts all over the place, the zombie lurched forward, its mouth snapping open with a gurgle. The promise of fresh meat had landed in its lap. Literally. I whipped my arm out, my hand still clutching the recon blade, and drove the sharpened point directly through its eye socket. The zombie's jaw wrenched open one last time and fetid-smelling fluids seeped out of its mouth and eye. I crouched and placed my goo covered boot on the head of the zombie to extract my blade.

"Shit," I whispered under my breath. The zombies in front of the building were all kind of standing there, some of them standing pretty still, some of them wavering back and forth as if they would topple over at any moment. I could have used my rifle to clear my way, however, I didn't want to make too much noise, drawing more zombies to the area, making my escape when I was ready to leave harder than it needed to be. I counted about five zombies and figured there had to be two or three more I couldn't see from my vantage point. The toxic fumes of the corpse I was almost kneeling in were beginning to burn my nostrils and make my eyes water. I was beyond ready to move. My dad's words echoed in the back of my mind and I took a moment to try and remember his voice.

Acting rashly is what gets people killed.

I duck-walked to the back of the jeep to see if I could find what I was looking for. I lucked out and found several large rocks within arm's reach. I gathered them up and went back to where I could see my targets the best. When I was sure I could pull off my plan, I reared back my arm and launched a rock at a zombie a little ways off from the rest of the group that was standing in between me and the building. The rock missed by several feet, but the zombie jerked at the sound of the rock landing near him. I had his attention. I picked up another large rock and launched it at the zombies nearest to the first one I'd aimed at. They both gnashed their teeth and moved toward the sound of the rock hitting the pavement. The three zombies looked so utterly confused that I almost laughed. For my idea to work, I'd have to launch another rock further than all the rest and hit a cracked window I'd spotted on another building across the way. I swung my arm with all my might and heaved a large rock through the air. The rock bounded off the building a foot away from the window. The zombies barely noticed. I grabbed another stone, this one a bit smaller, and took careful aim before I chucked it with all my strength. The rock glided through the air and hit the window dead-center. The shattering glass echoed all across the base, raising the hairs on my arms and drawing the attention of every zombie in the area, including my little trio of friends.

Several of the zombies started in the direction of the noise and a few others followed behind those that were on the move, sensing their interest. I took my window of opportunity and sprinted from my hiding place when the zombies were turned in the other direction. About halfway to my goal, two of them stopped mid-stride and turned back when they saw my movement. I raised my knife as I ran and met the first one head on. The zombie was so bloated that its skin looked almost translucent. It was kind of rubberized, with deep blue veins bulging in contrast to its pasty white skin. My knife caught the uniform-wearing zombie just above the collarbone and slid into its neck without much effort, but got stuck at the spine. My speed when I hit the zombie, drove us both to the ground with me on top. I pushed down with both hands on the hilt of my knife until I heard the crack of the spine and the head lobbed off to the side, only skin keeping it attached to the body.

My hands were still shaking when I jumped off of the corpse beneath me and ran for the building again. The second zombie was further away and was moving in a slow, lurching motion towards me. I was only fifty feet away from the doors when it caught up with me. When the zombie reached me, I realized why it moved so much slower than some of the others. Its leg had been almost completely eaten away, and all that remained was shredded fabric from its pants leg and splintered bones poking through a thin, flapping layer of decomposing skin. The zombie had no chance. My knife slid through its forehead and poked through the back of its skull without any resistance.

I reached for the door and had a moment's pause when I realized I had no idea what lay on the other side. As far as I knew, it could have been completely filled with zombies. From the corner of my eye I saw several shambling corpses hobble around the corner of the building and just like that, my mind was made up for me. I pushed into the building holding my breath, hoping against hope that I hadn't made a fatal error.

Just Me and Bobby McGee

I knelt inside with my back to the door and surveyed the room I'd entered, dust motes flying all around me. I let out a relieved breath when I wasn't immediately attacked by an entrapped zombie horde. I reached back and untied the cloth I'd secured around my face and took an unsteady breath in. The air was stale and thick with dust, but was surprisingly devoid of rot and decay. I stuffed the cloth into a pocket and moved slowly away from the door. The room looked like people had left in a hurry. Papers were scattered about, office chairs were knocked over, and tables, cabinets, and other various items lay broken and strewn about. I made my way around the large room, checking out several smaller offices off of the main room for zombie loners. The whole room appeared to be completely zombie free and abandoned. Something sparked in the back of my mind and I couldn't help wonder how, with all the chaos surrounding the base, the room was completely free of any dead bodies. Maybe at first they'd secured this building and everyone who turned or died had already left the building when it had happened. It didn't fit right, though. Something felt *off*. I spied a larger office in the back of the room and headed for it.

The office was clear of dead bodies and I was somewhat disappointed. I shook my head. The "norm" these days was death and corpses, and anything other than that made me squirm with uneasiness and suspicion. I made my way around the huge desk, sat down in the dust caked, black leather chair, and set my knife on top of it. The chair, which had sat unused for so long, squeaked beneath my weight and I froze, the sound overly harsh to my ears in the small space. I sat rigidly at first, my body not used to sitting anywhere other than the forest floor, but I soon relaxed back into the seat. Such small things meant so much now. After indulging myself for a moment or two, I sat up straighter in my seat and decided to see if I could find anything useful in the office.

I reached out and picked up a small frame that sat on the corner of the desk and wiped the glass with the edge of my palm. A man with laughing eyes smiled at me from the photo. He was decked out in his dress blues and a young woman with long blonde hair, wearing a mint colored sundress hugged his arm, resting her head on his shoulder. They were a beautiful couple. I remembered my dad dressed in his fancy uniform when we headed out to one of his officer's balls when I was sixteen. I'd laughed and tried to get him to change his mind about taking me as his date, but his eyes twinkled when he handed me a corsage. *Are you kidding me? I'll be the luckiest guy at the ball*, he had said with a wink. I knew he was just trying to make me forget that I'd been stood up for my junior year prom. I loved my dad all the more after that night.

I gently set the picture back down where I'd found it on the desk, blinked back tears, and got to work. I searched through all the papers that were scattered on the desk, pulled file folders out of drawers and discarded the majority of them because they had nothing to do with what had happened two years ago. I found a whole lot of nothing. I grabbed the wastebasket and emptied it out on the desk, un-crumpling several sheets of paper. Random messages, random papers. I found a sheet of paper with the words "infected", "shoot to kill", and "no known cure" scribbled on it like someone had hastily written down the notes with a slightly trembling hand. I slammed the paper down on the desk and walked around it with my hands on my hips. What exactly had I thought I was going to find in the office of the officer in charge of some random Army base in North Carolina? A detailed explanation of what had happened the days leading up to the dead taking over the world? I snorted in disbelief at my stupidity. I walked over to the blinds covering the window and peeked through a slat, barely bending it, and noted how the sun was beginning to sink behind the tree line. I needed to head back to my little spot in the woods, maybe rethink what I could do—what I *should* do.

I was standing in the center of the generously sized office when something else struck me as odd. Aside from the fact that there were no dead or undead in the entire office building, and even though the office I was sitting in must have belonged to whoever was in charge of the base, the office was still abnormally large. There was one thing I remembered from all the bases my dad had taken me to visit; of all the admirals' and sergeants' offices I ever saw, the Army didn't do large or fancy when it came to work spaces. I twirled around slowly and took in the office with a new perspective. The room was easily two times larger than any other office I'd ever been in, and I'd been in several. I furrowed my brow, wondering why I was wasting time thinking about it, why it even mattered, yet I couldn't shake that odd feeling that I was missing something. I walked over to the far wall. The entire wall was one huge, built-in bookshelf. I ran my finger along the spines of the books, my brain still not quite knowing where I was going with my thoughts, when I shrugged and wiped a bead of sweat from my forehead. When I spied a copy of *Watership Down* on the top shelf, I stretched up on my tiptoes to grab it to take back with me to camp.

"Keep your hands up. Don't move," a voice said gruffly from behind me. It had been so long since I'd heard a voice, so long since anyone had spoken to me, I couldn't help it, I gasped and swung around in utter shock. "I said not to fucking move," the man growled, pointing his rifle in my face.

My hand immediately twitched and made a move to grab for my gun. I barely stopped myself. It wouldn't do any good, he would shoot me before I ever touched the gun strapped to my leg. Fuck! I'd been so careless.

"Turn back around and put your hands up on the bookshelf," he barked. I swallowed slowly and turned, taking care not to make any more sudden movements. When I placed both my hands on the shelves in front of me, the man walked over and placed the tip of his gun on the back of my neck. My legs quivered in outrage and humiliation.

"Give me your weapons," he ordered. I stiffened and a real thread of fear slid through me. He nudged me with the rifle and repeated his command.

"Fuck you," I whispered hoarsely. It was barely audible.

"What was that?" he asked, incredulity coloring his voice.

I swallowed and cleared my throat. "I said, fuck you. I'm not giving up my weapons," I growled.

The man stood still for only a moment before he leaned in and whispered harshly into my ear. "Little girl, you have *no* choice, you realize that, right? You can die with your misguided sense of pride, or you can give me your weapons, and *maybe* live to see another day."

Unexpectedly, tears threatened. I had only cried three times over the past two years—once the day after my dad died, once after I'd buried him, and once after a particularly harrowing trip into town to scavenge for supplies. I had to do horrible things that day and saw even worse things before I made it back to the cover of my camp. I wasn't about to allow this douchebag to make me cry. I gritted my teeth and grunted my surrender.

I reached down with my right hand and very carefully unstrapped the holster that held my handgun.

"That's it... nice and easy," the man muttered.

I lifted my hand and held it out to the guy with the gun pointed at my neck.

"Now unhook the M4," he said. I clenched my jaw and once again removed my weapon with slow and methodical precision. I had more weapons back at camp, but it pissed me off that if I were to get out of this alive, some asshole with a G.I. Joe complex was going to be walking around with my dad's weapons.

"Any more weapons on you?" he asked, with almost a relieved grunt.

"The recon blade on the desk. That's it," I lied smoothly. No need for him to know about the small blade strapped to my thigh beneath my loose cargo pants. If he patted me down he'd find it, but I was going to take my chances. I heard him walk over to the desk and retrieve my knife from its surface. I seethed. I loved that blade.

Moaning and growls, too close by for comfort, echoed in the room around us. I flinched and reached for my gun before I realized I didn't have it on me. It was the first time in over two years it wasn't strapped to my leg.

"Don't worry, they just passed by the window," the guy said in a semi-whisper close to my ear. "Put your hands behind your back," he ordered.

My entire body tensed, but with no other choice, I complied. Ropes bound my wrists behind me and the next thing I knew black fabric was secured tightly around my eyes, blindfolding me. Pure, unadulterated fear crashed through me and a spike of adrenaline coursed through my veins. I threw my head back and made a last ditch effort to wrench myself free. Maybe I would get lucky and the asswipe would be smart enough not to take a shot and call down all the zombies on top of us. In my head, the idea was so much smarter than in reality. Here I was with my hands tied behind my back, blindfolded, and virtually weaponless, making a run for it... to where? Out into the nest of zombies lurking right outside?

"*Shit.*"

I heard the muffled curse come from behind me just before I was knocked to the ground with my captor landing on top of me. I tried bucking, kneeing, biting, and head butting before I started to feel the strain on my muscles. The guy was no lightweight and he was using his entire body to try and wrestle me to the floor. I grunted when he finally managed to flip me over and put his knee in the center of my back. All the air in my lungs left in me in a *whoosh*.

"What the hell is *wrong* with you?" the man huffed in between pants. "You are fucking crazy."

"You ain't seen crazy yet," I snarled.

He leaned more of his weight on me and breathed next to my face. "If you try that again or keeping making so much goddamn noise, I am going feed you to the zombies myself, you understand?"

I tried to smirk and blow off his threat, but that was hard to do since my cheek was squished into the dirty floor. Instead, I nodded sharply. "Good. Now I'm going to help you up. Don't try anything stupid."

When he pulled me off the ground, he snagged me by my arm and brought me close to him with a gun pressed into my side. We started walking and I could only assume it was back into the main area of desks and offices. After a few minutes of being pushed, pulled, and prodded into different directions, and yet never leaving the building, I wondered if we were going in circles.

"This the only way you could get a date? Tying up girls and making them play some twisted version of musical chairs with you?" I hissed between my teeth. "You hear music in your mind? Or little voices, maybe?" I smirked.

The guy tugged roughly on my arm and then we stopped. "You are such a pain in the ass, you know that?" he snarled. "No way in hell I'd take you on a date, even if voices told me to."

I felt him move around me while I stood there thinking what else to say, trying to keep him talking, and wondering what he had planned for me. He grunted, and then I heard a click, followed by a scraping sound.

"Move slowly forward to the stairs. We're going down." He gave me a small shove and I barely kept my balance.

"As soon as I get my hands untied, I'm going fuck you up," I whispered fiercely. My stomach bubbled and roiled in a sickening dread. Going down? Where the hell was he taking me? His chuckle did nothing to alleviate my fears. I took a tentative step forward and found the first step down. My captor kept a grip on my arm as we made our way lower and lower. My heart beat faster with every step we took and it was by sheer willpower alone that I didn't whimper in fear of the unknown.

"Alright, stop right there for now," he said. I heard him open something on a wall nearby and it sounded like he was pushing some sort of buttons. A beep echoed in my brain and it took me a very long moment to recognize the sound. Clangs and clicks, followed by the loud screech of metal directly in front of us, overwhelmed me and I stumbled slightly, my legs wobbling in shock and anxiety. My captor, almost gently, put an arm around me to keep me standing. A gust of air fanned my face and a sound I never thought I'd hear again besieged me—the sound of a lot of living humans—talking. The sounds came to an abrupt halt as my captor, with his arms still around me, walked us forward. More clicks and clangs followed our entry and the metal door behind us swung shut.

"What's going on, Jude?" a low, rumbling voice spoke out.

"Found her snooping through things on the base, Sir," he answered from next to me. I turned my head in the direction of the sound of several people whispering among themselves and strained to hear everything I could.

"Well, for Christ's sake, untie her already," he barked.

Jude, presumably the name of my captor, jumped to do what he was told. My blindfold came off first and I blinked several times, trying to adjust my eyes to the unfamiliar, overly-bright florescent lighting hanging overhead. My hands were untied and I rubbed the raw spots around my wrists.

"Am I a prisoner?" I asked sharply, staring directly into the eyes of the man who I assumed to be the group's leader. He was probably in his mid-thirties and he regarded me with interest, a hint of amusement shining in his blue eyes.

"Prisoner? Not at all. I'm sorry if you were under that impression," he said apologetically.

"What impression was I supposed to be under when Jude here stole my weapons, tied me up, and blindfolded me? That I was an honored guest?" I sneered.

The guy lifted a brow, but didn't apologize for anything. "We have to be careful. You've seen how it is up there yourself, you surely know that the zombies aren't the only threat we face now," he said. Though I wanted to remain angry, I couldn't. These people *did* have to be careful.

"I understand," I grumbled. "That doesn't mean I don't want my father's weapons back or that I'm not pissed off."

He cracked a huge grin and walked over to me. I took a step back and he stopped where he was.

"How many are in your group?" he asked quietly. "We could offer them a place here too."

I shook my head and clenched my jaw. "It's only me," I mumbled. A shadow fell across his eyes, a shadow of understanding and loss.

"How long ago did they die?" he asked gently.

I raised my eyes to meet his direct, probing blue stare. "I've been alone since the first day."

His eyes widened fractionally before he looked at me like he wanted to study me under a microscope. "What's your name, girl?" he asked.

I stiffened and squared my shoulders. "Melody Carter, daughter of Major John M. Carter of the United States Army," I answered proudly.

The man held his hand out to me. "Nice to meet you, Melody."

I smiled and went to stick my hand out until I realized I was still caked in all kind of gore and stench. I glanced up from my hand to the face of the man now looking at me curiously. I held my hands up and shrugged.

"Nice to meet you, Major, but you probably should hold off on that handshake for now." I grimaced when I realized how much of a mess I really was. I seriously stunk. His eyes widened and it was my turn to smirk. "I saw the picture on your desk," I mentioned by way of explanation. He was the same man in dress blues I'd seen earlier, but he looked like he had aged ten years instead of two. The major's smile vanished and his eyes frosted over. I knew that look; I'd felt the emotion behind it too. Heartache and loss. I met his eyes and nodded my head once, my eyes mirroring his own burning gaze. He nodded back stiffly and cleared his throat.

"Jude," he barked. Jude stiffened next to me. "Take our guest to one of the empty rooms and show her where she can go to get cleaned up," he ordered, then turned around, dismissing me.

"I have questions, Major," I interjected, my hand clenched at my side. Who cared about getting clean when these people might be able to answer some of my questions? "I'm sure you do, but they can wait a few more hours. Besides, you smell like you've been rolling around in zombie guts," he grimaced. Jude chuckled before the major and I both gave him a death stare. I was clenching my jaw so hard it ached.

"Fine," I muttered.

The major turned on his heel. I glanced over at Jude and put my hands on my hips. He returned my stare with a smirk and I made my personal mission to knock that smirk off of his face just one time.

"Follow me," he said stiffly. He turned on his heel and strode briskly across the room. I followed, taking in my surroundings. The common room was large and there were probably twenty people milling about doing various tasks. Some looked like officials or military personnel and a few looked like civilians. The room had several hallways leading off of it, one in the direction the major had gone, one that Jude had taken, which I could only assume led to sleeping quarters, and one leading off in a different direction. I had to jog to catch up to Jude.

I glanced at Jude from the corner of my eye as we walked down a long corridor. His jaw was clenched and his eyes hooded while he led me along. He looked angry; maybe he was upset he'd gotten the babysitting gig. I smiled at that. The jackass deserved *so* much worse. We rounded a corner and he stopped outside of a door at the very end of the hallway. He opened the door and motioned for me to go inside. I walked in and turned around in a circle. The room was sparsely furnished with a cot and a single chest of drawers. A small table and chair acted as a desk area and there was one tiny closet. It looked like the Ritz Carlton in my eyes.

"Alright, let me show you where you can shower and then I'll get out of here."

I picked my jaw up off of the floor at the promise of a shower and Jude was striding down the hall and around the corner. I barely registered the number of my room—107—then ran to catch up with him.

The shower area was as glorious as the room. I stood in the doorway staring at the showers, afraid to move and break the illusion. Jude snorted and pushed past me to open a closet at the end of the room where rows of identical pants and tops hung. Towels were also stacked on the top shelf.

"Leave your clothes next to the door and someone will pick them up for you." And just like that, he was gone. I smiled and ran over to the closet. I swear to God, it felt like I was staring at the clearance rack at the mall. It was heaven. I grabbed a soft V-neck tee shirt and a pair of pants that resembled yoga pants with wide legs and a drawstring waist, but made of a sturdier material, and inhaled the scent of them through my nostrils. They even smelled fresh and clean. Like a bullet out of a gun, I yanked off my filthy clothes and made a run for the shower stall. I wouldn't have cared if twenty people were there to watch, or if I had to shower with others, I was not going to miss every blessed second of running water I could soak up before I got yanked back to reality. I set my clean clothing, towel, and the knife no one had found on me on a bench outside of the stall before jumping into the shower and turning the knobs. I was expecting the cold, but I still shivered when it spurted out. I turned it up full blast and much to my shock, the water was hot.

"Thank you, Jesus," I moaned when the water cascaded over me. I don't know how long I stood like that, but I know my fingers were pruning up before I had the sense to snap out of my ecstasy and use the small bar of soap and bottle of shampoo to actually wash my body and hair. I scrubbed every nook and cranny of my body, spending extra time to work some conditioner into my mass of tangles. My little bubble of vacation burst abruptly when I heard a sound right outside of the shower area. Someone was right around the corner where the towels and clothes were kept. I left the water running and tiptoed out of the shower to grab my knife off of the bench. Something shuffled and I heard the sound of a gun being loaded, the unmistakable sound of a magazine being slid into place. Maybe if I acted quickly, I'd still hold the thread of surprise. With that thought in mind, I ran around the wall with a scream of rage. No way in hell I was going to die in a shower after surviving alone in the woods for over two years.

I rushed my attacker, brandishing my eight inch blade like it was a butcher knife. Jude stood there in such shock that when I had rushed him, he froze. When I collided with him, the gun was flung from his grasp. Much like with the zombie I'd taken down earlier, my momentum knocked us both off of our feet, with me landing on top of Jude with a loud and painful *thud*. Unlike the zombie takedown, I didn't drive my blade into Jude's neck like I had the corpse, but I did bring it close enough to his jugular that if he even spoke too loudly he would have been choking on his own blood.

I sat on top of his body, my knife to his neck, and my face directly above his. His light brown eyes were wide and shocked; he still hadn't had time to get pissed off yet. But it didn't take long.

"What the fuck is *wrong* with you?" he hissed through his teeth. I tightened my grip on my knife and he immediately stiffened and then relaxed a fraction.

"Maybe you should tell me why you were sneaking around with a gun while you thought I was defenseless," I countered. My hair was still wet and it was dripping all around me, soaking through Jude's white tee shirt. His eyes flashed angrily and he clenched his jaw, causing a muscle to tic in his cheek.

"You think I'd sneak up and shoot an unarmed, *naked* girl in the shower?" he growled. "What kind of man do you think I am?"

"I'm sure I don't know," I said casually. "Oh! Wait, I *do* know." I leaned forward until I was able to whisper in his ear. "You're the type of guy that would tie a girl up, take away all her weapons, making her defenseless, and blindfold her during a zombie apocalypse." I leaned back a fraction. "What were you doing then, Jude?" I asked.

"I was going to escort you back to your room, but you were still in the shower, so I was just going to leave your weapons here for you and come back later," he said on an exhale, too tired to care if I'd cut his throat. I blinked and then pulled back my knife a little. "I was doing my job out there, Melody," he sighed. I blinked again and realized how grossly I'd misread the situation.

"Shit," I whispered, and removed my knife from Jude's throat. Then it really hit me, I was friggin' *nude* and sprawled on top of him. No matter what I did next, I'd show how much of an idiot I was. Jude must have realized where my thoughts had led me, because the biggest grin I'd ever seen spread across his face. *Fuck.* I raised my chin and removed my naked self from Jude's now-soaked body, straightened myself out, and stood in front of him without any—well, not *too much*—shame.

He got up off of the floor and probed his neck with his fingers. I hadn't broken the skin. I wanted to run for cover, to shield my body from Jude's now hungry gaze, but I wanted to look tough a whole lot more, so I stood my ground.

"I'll be ready in a minute, but I think I can find my way to my room," I said hoarsely. A slow, devastatingly handsome smile lit up his face and I could feel myself blush. It ticked me off. I marched forward and pushed him out of the room. "Get out, before I cut your throat for the fun of it," I snarled. I felt the vibration beneath my hand when he chuckled. When he was out the door, I turned to shut it. Jude stuck his foot in the crack of the door and pushed it back open.

"Melody," he murmured. I shivered slightly at the sound of my name rolling off the tip of his tongue. *Damn.* "I am sorry about all that upstairs. I had to think about everyone's safety down here first," he said sincerely, then grinned wildly again. "Though, I gotta say... this..." he gestured to my body, "this made it all worthwhile."

I could feel my face flaming. He smiled at me again, his eyes scorching every part of my body and I realized for the first time since he'd stuck a gun in my face, exactly how sexy Jude was. If I had met him under different circumstances, back before the end of the world, I would have been *itching* to run my fingers through his short, dark brown hair, to taste his sensual lips... but this wasn't under normal circumstances and I wasn't a naïve little girl anymore. I smiled widely at Jude then and the change in his face was instantaneous. His pupils dilated and his hand came up to push a strand of my black hair out of my face. I opened the door just a little wider and then put a hand on his rock-hard abs and gave a little push. He stumbled a step back out of the doorway.

When my fist flew, he never saw it coming. His head jerked back and he sprawled on his ass, blood spurting from his nose.

"Apology accepted," I said. I slammed the door and locked it.

I considered it not only a payback for terrifying me and stripping me of all my defenses, but also a lesson for the future: *Never let your guard down during a zombie apocalypse.*

Guys, sex, and love were a thing of the past. Besides, I'd take a zombie showdown any day of the week. Lucky for me, there was a plethora of them waiting for me to kick their undead asses. And I planned to do just that.

Life Sucks & Then You Die ...
If You're Lucky

My breath fanned out before me in a cloud of frigid air. I inhaled sharply and my lungs inflated painfully from the freezing cold. I pressed my back against the trunk of a tree that I'd ducked behind. All around me I heard sounds, sounds I hadn't heard only a few moments before. Groans, shuffling, and the telltale gurgling of the undead surrounding me in the forest. I wiggled my fingers that held my blade in a death grip. Even with the gloves on, they were stiff and nearly frozen. How far was I from my campsite? Half a mile? Maybe less. Which put these zombies wandering in the woods further out than any had been in over five months. I'd been foolish to think the cold would slow them down or keep them out of the woods. I just felt so fucking tired all the time. I was always looking over my shoulder, always sleeping just enough to keep me going another day, afraid to sleep too long or too deeply and wake up with a zombie tearing into my throat.

I pulled my gun out of my holster and considered waiting until I knew how many I was up against, or at least what my odds were, but I had stood still for too long. I was worried my reflexes would be slow from standing in the same position in the freezing cold for too long. I released a slow breath and watched the snow flurries floating all around me. I wiggled my fingers once more, trying to bring some warmth back to them before I made my move. The zombies' movements grew so loud and harsh in the otherwise quiet forest that my head started to pound. I shook my head roughly, feeling disoriented and panicked. A branch snapped close by and I immediately swiveled in that direction with my gun pointed out in front of me. The wet gurgle of a fresh zombie came from directly behind me. A drop of sweat trickled down the side of my face as an icy finger of dread danced up my spine.

I cried out and swung around, my numb finger already pulling the trigger. The snow floated around me in a hazy mist, everything slowed and went silent. I could hear my heartbeat pounding in slow motion; I could hear the gun cock back and the explosion of the bullet leaving my weapon. I could hear... my father's voice. *Melody*? He stood there with his hand outstretched toward me, his eyes wide in shock and hurt just before the bullet entered his forehead and a spray of dark red blood coated the fresh fallen snow at his feet.

"Noooooo!" I screamed out as his body fell slowly to the ground. My voice echoed all around me, filling the forest up with the sound of my utter anguish, the sound of my heart being torn from my chest.

I sprung forward, my hand immediately reaching for my knife under my pillow. My heart was thumping erratically and sweat had soaked through my tee shirt. I wiped my hair from my face and glanced around, trying to remember where I was. The previous day came back to me in bits and pieces and I gradually regained my senses. I was in an underground safe house at the army base. I pushed my knife back under my pillow and swung my legs over the side of my little cot. It had been a long time since I'd had a nightmare and the images of what I'd dreamt were still flashing behind my eyelids. I pulled my hair back and tied it in a ponytail and then dropped to the ground next to my borrowed bed.

One, *two*, *three*, I chanted under my breath. I did my pushups, pushing myself until my arms were quivering from exhaustion. Even then I couldn't completely erase the images that were burned into my mind. I rolled over onto my back and placed my knees together with my feet flat on the floor. I did sit ups until I couldn't crawl back up onto the bed. Didn't matter, I wasn't used to sleeping on anything other than the ground anymore anyway. I dragged my blanket and pillow to the floor and then tucked my knife back beneath my pillow. I lay there for several hours, staring up at the ceiling before I decided to get up to find the major to get some answers.

I needed to get my mind off of my nightmares and off of my memories. Going down that road would only make me lose my mind, and losing your mind in the middle of a zombie apocalypse is highly discouraged. Well, losing your mind at any time is probably a bad idea, but doing so when you could have your insides ripped out by your next-door-neighbor-turned-flesh-eating-zombie would definitely suck.

You're THAT Girl!

When I made my way to the tiny mess hall, I was surprised to find it already inhabited by several people. I scarcely paid them any attention though, not with the yummy smells coming from the kitchen area. I strode over to the table where several bowls of piping hot oatmeal topped with cinnamon and raisins sat. I glanced up and met a pair of warm dark brown eyes belonging to an older woman who was setting out spoons and napkins. I glanced down at the bowls and then back up at the woman. She smiled broadly and motioned for me to take one. I smiled my thanks, grabbed a bowl, and made my way over to a table furthest away from the other six or seven people enjoying their breakfast. My position also allowed me to see the entire room from where I sat. I scooped up a spoonful of oatmeal and blew on it a few times then stuck the yummy stickiness in my mouth. That's all it took. I was in heaven. I had just shoveled more oatmeal into my pie-hole and was nearly vibrating with happiness when a shadow fell over me and a voice cut into my haze of euphoria.

"You almost look like a regular person when you're eating."

My back stiffened and I glanced up into his cocky face. I grinned and scooped another bite of my breakfast.

"You almost look like a regular person too, Jude," I said. "Well, a normal person with one hell of a shiner." I continued to eat, hoping Jude would take a hint. He sat down across from me at the table instead.

"Most people would think you don't like me, but I've got a theory," he said around a mouthful of oatmeal. This guy just wouldn't go away.

"A theory?" I asked.

He nodded his head, oblivious to my death stare. "Yup. See, I think you have some kind of post-zombie-apocalypse-stress-disorder or something, and you've regressed back to your childhood." He winked and took another bite.

I crossed my arms across my chest and decided to do exactly what he wanted me to. "Oh really? Regressed how?" I asked, knowing I was egging him on in his little fantasy, but I had to know what his puny brain had concocted. He looked over at me and shrugged.

"Back to the days where tugging on braids and hitting someone meant you really had a crush on them. Do you like me? Check yes-or-no type of stuff." He tsked as if he felt sorry for me and then grinned widely when my mouth dropped open again.

"Jude, you are such a jacka—"

"It *is* you!" a voice screeched, reverberating through the room. I flinched and had already risen halfway from my chair, grabbing for my gun before I realized what I was doing. Jude had stood too, his eyes studying me, his jaw set, wondering what I was about to do. I relaxed and breathed in deeply just as a tall, gangly boy of about fourteen strode up to our table. His eyes were wide with wonder, making me nervous. I sat back down and Jude followed suit, his eyes never leaving mine.

"Sorry, you must have the wrong person," I said sharply. "I don't know a lot of people around here."

"No, I'm positive it's you," the boy gushed, his eyes wide and his smile huge. "I'll never forget that day as long as I live. You freaking cleared out over a hundred zombies singlehandedly. You even set some on fire!"

My eyes widened and I stuttered a few times, but the kid kept on talking.

"You took out dozens and dozens, like it was just another day on the job for you. At first we didn't know who was shooting, but then you came down and walked right out onto the street like you weren't scared of anything, yelling 'Come get some, bitches!' I swear to God, we all about crapped our pants when you lit the old Starbucks and the zombies on fire."

I swallowed a lump in my throat and glanced up at Jude. He was studying me intently, his eyes searching mine for answers I didn't really have while the boy told his story for the whole mess hall to hear.

"We thought maybe you didn't make it after that, but then you busted through the doors a few buildings down and barely escaped from that zombie all lit up like a bonfire! Then we heard you laughing when you turned the music up. You drove over a few more zombies on your way out of town." His eyes were shining, remembering the day with all its ugly details. "You almost cleared out the whole town. You made it possible for my family and a few other people to get out of the town." I shook my head, knowing where he was going with his speech. "You saved our lives. You're a hero."

I stood abruptly and grabbed my bowl off of the table. "I'm no hero, kid," I said harshly.

His eyes widened and he backed up a step. "You are. I'd be dead right now if it weren't for you," he said vehemently.

I got up close to him and looked him in the eye. "How many of you escaped after that?"

"There were about a dozen of us."

I clenched my jaw and looked down at the ground. *Only a dozen?* "And how many did you have with you before I came that day?" I spat. I knew I was being unreasonable, too harsh, but I couldn't help myself.

The boy's eyes shuttered and pain flashed behind them. He looked at the ground as he spoke. "About fifty."

"And how many are with you out of the twelve survivors from that day?" I asked, softly now. He shook his head and his fists balled tightly at his sides. "How many?" I pushed mercilessly.

"Eight," he murmured.

My stomach knotted and I finally met the kid's stare. "I'm no fucking hero, kid. If I were, I'd have come sooner and stayed longer."

He shook his head, but I just walked away. I set my bowl in the dirty dish bin, aware that the eyes of everyone in the room were on me as I marched from the mess hall. I was halfway down the long corridor when Jude caught up with me.

"That was a bit harsh, don't you think, Melody?"

I stopped mid-stride and whirled around to face him. "That's none of your business, Jude," I hissed.

He raised his hands in the air in surrender and smiled. I frowned. This guy was worse than any chick with his mood swings.

"Most girls like to be idolized," he pushed.

I rolled my eyes and started walking again. "I'm not most girls."

"That's the understatement of the century," he laughed. I cut my eyes over to him and found that Jude was even more devastatingly handsome when he laughed. He grinned when he caught me looking at him. *Jerk.* "Anyway, I'm supposed to deliver you to Major Tillman," he said seriously.

"Perfect," I answered, and quickened my stride. My steps faltered when I realized Jude had stopped in the middle of the hallway.

"He's *this* way," he said, pointing in the opposite direction. I set my jaw and barely restrained my temper when I heard him chuckle under his breath. We went to meet the guy I'd been wanting to talk to all along, the guy I seriously hoped could give me some answers.

Ain't That Some Shit

Jude led me back through the room we had first come into the day before and then into a large meeting room that looked like it was being used as a central command center. Major Tillman was speaking to a young Hispanic man dressed in camouflage, similar to what Jude was wearing. His eyes flicked over me dismissively when we entered the room. The major stepped forward and held his hand out to me.

"Now that we can be officially introduced, I'm Major Tillman." I shook his hand and smiled at the major. He motioned to the man beside him. "This is Manuel, he'll be joining us today." I grasped the man's hand in mine and murmured my *nice-to-meet-you's*.

"Major, I really appreciate the shower and the room. It has been a long time since I've had either and they were a welcomed luxury."

His smile was genuine and warm. "I'm just sorry we hadn't run into you sooner, we would have gladly offered you a place here with us a long time ago."

I shook my head, remembering everything that I'd been through in the past two years. It hadn't been easy, in fact at times I thought I wasn't going to make it. Other times, I wanted to lay down and give up, but I didn't, and I was stronger for that reason.

"I appreciate that, Major, but I did alright and I don't think I'd change the last two years even if I could. My father taught me well and I have learned a lot about survival and killing zombies over the past two years."

The major stared at me a few moments, studying my face before he smiled again and held his hand out to an empty chair. "You're an extraordinary young woman, Melody," the major said. "Please have a seat. We have a lot to talk about, and I'm sure you have a ton of questions you're just dying to ask me."

I took a seat, so did the major, Jude, and Manuel.

"How many people do you have here, Major?" I asked after a moment. "We are responsible for nearly a hundred people. Seventy-six are civilians and twenty-two are Army," he said.

I was a bit surprised, I hadn't realized there were quite that many humans left in the area. Even more surprising was the ratio. I would have thought the majority of people left would have been military, but with only twenty-two soldiers, more than three quarters of the survivors were civilians. I didn't like that at all.

"How did the civilians find their way here?" I asked. They couldn't have found their way easily, unless they stupidly believed, like I had, that the base would have provided some sort of safe haven that first day. Even then, their odds weren't very good.

"Some are family members of soldiers. Jude and Manuel also lead a team out often to search for survivors," he answered. I glanced over at Jude, and then to Manuel. They both certainly looked capable of running those kinds of dangerous missions. I was still impressed. It would be nearly impossible to locate survivors, but to actually lead them back to the base without getting the entire group killed, well, those weren't odds I'd ever bet on. I took a deep breath and searched the major's face for answers.

"How did it happen?" I asked, my eyes wide. I knew my question sounded like a plea, like I wanted to believe someone had all the answers and that they would be able to tell me they were working on a plan, that the world would be on the way to getting back to normal before we knew it. The major's eyes held mine, but I didn't find any reassurances in them. Instead, I found despair and resignation. I shook my head, a jerky movement of denial.

The major told me everything he knew about what had happened a little over two years ago, what had happened to change the world forever and plunge my life into loneliness and darkness. When he was done relating to me what he knew, I sat there in stunned silence trying to process everything I'd heard. I kept trying to wrap my brain around the fact that it all boiled down to *technology*. Technology was what had spread the infection. I stood abruptly, causing Jude and Manuel to flinch in their seats. Only the major sat unmoving. I held up a finger. I really needed a moment to process.

Technology and the Peace Corps. Seriously? Apparently, Patient 001, as the military had dubbed him, was a retired military officer who was about to go on a trip he had been planning for over a year with the Peace Corps when he found out he had cancer. He decided to put off his treatment, knowing if he went through chemotherapy first, he wouldn't be fit enough to make the trip. Ironically enough, he trudged into the innermost depths of the African jungle to help distribute medical supplies and clean drinking water to the remote tribes, when he somehow ingested a rare parasite. The parasite was passed into his bloodstream where it nestled itself into the wall of an artery and it hatched eggs, then the parasites fed off of its host's internal organs. For ten days, Patient 001 was sick with what he thought was a stomach virus. He decided to cut his trip short and come home, assuming his cancer was preventing him from keeping anything he ate or drank down. The day he landed back in the U.S., Patient 001 called his doctor and rescheduled his chemotherapy for the next day.

The scientists and doctors most educated guess was that Patient 001 was carrying millions of microscopic parasites by the time he went through his first injections of chemotherapy. In the depths of the jungle the parasite might have killed its host over the course of several years. It had never before been exposed to any radiation or electromagnetic chaos, it had never been transported to a place where technology emanated from every single person, every single building, and every single street corner. Once the parasite had been exposed to the chemo, it mutated inside its host. Though the parasite had to be ingested before, now it could excrete itself through its host's sweat glands, through skin and hair follicles, and it was most concentrated in saliva. The parasites became more aggressive and every single person or object Patient 001 had any sort of contact with immediately became infected.

Instead of years, Patient 001 lived exactly one week. Unfortunately, the mutated parasites were able to live outside of his body for forty-eight hours until they found a new host. Forty-eight hours is a long time. When Patient 001 finally died, he had unknowingly spread the parasites all over Chicago. Every person he came in contact with and everything he had touched in those seven days had carried the parasites to hundreds and hundreds of hosts, who in turn carried them to thousands. Forty-eight hours of passing the mutated virus from person to person. A forty-eight hour window in which the parasite was able to be passed on by almost any means. The infected were dead within twenty-four hours, instead of the week it took to kill the original host.

At first officials and the CDC had no idea what was causing the hundreds of deaths that had already begun spreading to other cities and countries. Fortunately, the parasites, not only charged by the chemo, but also receiving a boost from the electromagnetic pulses in the city, could only survive while their host was alive. Unfortunately for the rest of us, once the host died the parasites were able to act as a stimuli in the corpses' brainstem, causing the host to "reanimate" and take on the parasite's lust for flesh and blood. The only thing lost in the reanimation process was how the parasite was able to transfer from one host to another. The corpses no longer sneezed, produced sweat, or any other bodily functions, other than saliva. Even though the parasites were concentrated in the zombie's saliva, the zombie had to bite into flesh and excrete saliva directly into the bloodstream of a victim for the parasite to infect someone and take on a new host.

My head swam with all the information I'd just been told. By the time the plane had crashed in our backyard, the parasites had spread beyond what anyone could have ever imagined or controlled, killing their hosts and then taking them over when they were dead. Now all that was left was millions of parasite-animated corpses who lusted for the flesh and blood of the few remaining uninfected humans.

"How bad is it out there?" I asked. I knew he understood what I meant. How bad off was the human race? How bad had it gotten while I was hiding in the forest and fighting to survive for the past two years?

"From the last we heard from anyone else, it was estimated that over eighty-two percent of the human population was killed or infected with the organ eating parasite," he said with a weary sigh.

My hand flew to my chest. *Eighty-two percent*? That meant that out of a hundred people, eighty-two were either dead or zombies now. Good God. What did that put the death toll at in the United States alone? Two hundred million? Two hundred and fifty million? The numbers were staggering. My legs wobbled slightly and I sank back down into my seat.

"Is there some kind of government in place?" I asked.

The major's jaw clenched and his eyes hardened. "We are no longer sure. We were receiving and sending communications to the base out of Charlotte, but the last we heard from them was over two months ago."

I glanced between the major's frowning face and the bleak faces on the two soldiers sitting in front of me. This wasn't good. "How often did you usually hear from them?"

It was Manuel who answered me. "We normally meet their person halfway and exchange information and supplies once every two weeks," he explained in clipped, official tones. "Our man has been at the rendezvous point three times in the past months, but theirs never appeared."

Something had happened, and if I knew anything at all, I knew it couldn't be anything good.

"We are going to send a small team into Charlotte. The city, from what our contact told us, is completely overrun by the undead, but we have to see what is going on. They were our only link to anything on the outside of here." His eyes frosted over and he stood abruptly, causing Jude and Manuel to jump from their seats. I got to my feet belatedly. "We are running out of supplies and we are starting to run low on ammunition. We were not prepared to be underground for this long. At the very least, our team will need to see what is going on at that base and then scout for supplies to bring back here. Then we'll be able to decide what we should do next for the good of the group." He ran a hand over his clean shaven face and sighed.

I swallowed and stood rigidly in front of Major Tillman. "I'd like to be part of the team that goes to Charlotte, Major."

Something that sounded suspiciously like a snort came from across the table. I ground my teeth together to keep from snapping at the meatheads there.

"Look, I appreciate that you are a tough young woman who has done rather well taking care of herself in the worst of situations, but I can't send you into a city that is overrun. You're not military and I couldn't send you with a clear conscience," he explained.

I gave the major a small smile that was not really meant to reassure anyone of anything and placed my hands on my hips. "Major, I appreciate the concern, but my daddy made sure I could shoot better than any man in this room on their best day. I could kill both of your men right now without them even realizing I'd made a move for my gun." Major Tillman stiffened slightly, his eyes narrowing. "I haven't just *survived*, I've taken out *hundreds* of zombies, looted for food and supplies in neighboring towns, and lived in the woods attuned to my own surroundings for two *years*." I let my words sink in the room for a moment before continuing on. "Name one soldier under your command who has done the same," I challenged. His eyes glanced over at his men, before coming back to rest on me. "I'd be an *asset* to this mission, Sir," I clipped.

He scrutinized my face, studying me until I felt twitchy under his scrutiny. He nodded once and turned to face Jude and Manuel.

"Looks like you've gained another team member, Agent Harrison," he said with a wry smile.

I blinked at him in surprise. *Agent?*

Jude crossed his arms over his chest and a smirk worked its way across his handsome face. "Guess I have," he answered coolly, his eyes pinning me with their intensity.

I swallowed and glanced over at Manuel. His eyes watched me, but they, unlike Jude's, gave nothing away. I was suddenly unsure of myself, but very sure of one thing, neither of them were your ordinary soldier.

Aww crap.

After You

At exactly 0700 hours, I was standing awkwardly in the main common area with Jude, Manuel, and three other guys. I'd put my own clothing back on since someone had freshly laundered and left them in my room the night before. My gun was strapped to my leg, my knife was in hand, and my rifle was slung across my back. It felt good to get moving. I was already feeling a little twitchy from being underground for over twenty-four hours. Safe, but twitchy.

"Alright, everyone, let's get going." Jude's eyes locked onto mine as the men filed pass him and he crooked his finger at me. I bit back a remark as I made my way over to him. "Listen, Melody. I know you are pretty much a soldier like any of my other men." My jaw unlocked and I barely held it in place. He was... *complimenting* me? He ran a hand over his face and met my gaze with one of steel. "You're tough. I have no doubt about that. But, you were also all alone and taking care of only yourself for the last two years. I need you to do exactly what I tell you without hesitation."

He held up a hand when my mouth flew open. I snapped it shut and tightened my grip on my knife. "Your actions won't only affect you when you step out those doors this time. Everything you do—or don't do—could cost me the life of one of my men. I'm not asking you. I'm *telling* you," he said with all the authority of someone who was used to having people snap at attention when he entered a room. "If you can't follow my orders once you step out those doors, just say the word and you stay here." His deadly serious eyes never left mine. "Are we clear?" he asked. I took a breath and nodded sharply. "Good. Now let's go."

I followed him through the door without a backward glance at the only safety I'd felt in a very, very long time.

We moved up a flight of stairs in silence and when we stepped out of the darkness, we were back in the large office I had been searching before. Jude pushed in a lever that caused the bookcase to swing back into place and hide the secret passageway. It was all so very government spy-like, that I almost giggled despite the fact that I was once again topside with parasite infested zombies looming right outside of the office building. That wiped the grin off of my face.

I glanced around the room and into the faces of five of the most dangerous looking men I'd ever encountered. Manuel was there wearing an army green tee shirt and camouflage pants with tons of pockets and a backpack, which held essentials, just like everyone else. My black tank top and camouflage pants almost matched. I looked like one of the guys. I felt a small smile lift the corners of my lips. A tall black man with an American flag tattooed on the side of his neck smiled widely at me. I grinned back and gave him a thumbs up. Manuel glanced up and made some motion toward the heavens like he was still trying to figure out how they'd gotten stuck with me. Jude motioned to two guys I didn't know and then we were all silently moving through the building with them taking point.

I could tell immediately that the men were used to the way we were going. They were probably some of the same men who went to the rendezvous point twice a month. That made me breathe a little easier. When we approached the front doors of the building, everyone stopped and waited for Jude to give the signal to go on. He glanced through the blinds on the window and held up four fingers and pointed to the left. He held up three more and pointed to the right. Seven zombies total in his line of sight between us and the building we were headed into. All of the men were so still, I could barely make out that they were breathing while we waited for him to give the signal. My heart pounded loudly and I adjusted my grip on my knife. Jude pointed to the huge, red-bearded man in the front and before I could blink, we were all running through the front door and back out into our new world of death and decay.

Zombies were on us before we made it a quarter of the way across the open asphalt. One by one and faster than I ever thought possible, the men dropped nine corpses like that were swatting away flies and without using a single bullet. The stench of the putrid bodies, hot and bloated by the summer sun, slapped me in the face and I barely held down the contents of my stomach. No matter how many times I'd been up close and personal with the zombies, no matter how many times I would have to stick my knife into the skull of the undead until rotten fluids seeped out, I'd never get used to the reek.

I stepped over bodies and we all kept moving, and then entered another building as easily as we had exited the last one. Jude and the men spread out and searched the large shed-like space. It was secure. Jude walked to a side door and we all followed suit. When I approached, he motioned me over to him.

"Right outside this door is a large SUV, fully gassed up and ready for us to go. We need to move fast, slide into the vehicle and keep sliding to make room for everyone." His eyes held mine. I nodded my understanding and he addressed the group. "Manuel will drive, so he goes first with Big Ben riding shotgun. Next will be Zach, Ghost, Melody, and then me bringing up the rear." Everyone nodded curtly.

I glanced at the door and realized we would be running blind. No windows were on this side of the building, so we'd literally not have any idea what was waiting for us. I wiped my sweaty palms on my pants and reached for my gun. Jude's hand stopped mine and I lifted my eyes to his. He shook his head and I stiffened under his grip. His hand tightened around mine. I set my jaw and relaxed my stance.

Fine, no guns, I thought. I raised a brow and he removed his hand from mine.

Jude walked over to the door and held up a hand that started the countdown to three. *One... two... three!* He pushed the door open and Manuel rushed through it with the red-bearded dude I could now assume was Big Ben following closely behind. I heard moans and grunts of engagement just before I cleared the doorway with Jude on my heels, making sure he secured the door behind us. In my peripheral vision I saw that Big Ben had the front passenger side door open and was sliding in behind Manuel when several zombies shambled around the side of the building to join the noise that several others were making as they attacked Zach and Ghost.

I ran toward the trio of zombies closing in on Ghost, intent on helping him when he let out a muted war cry and launched himself at the two furthest away from me. When I reached him, he had already taken down two of the zombies. I came up behind the zombie who had his sights set on the tall soldier. I dove, slashing the backs of the leg muscles of the rather huge monster. The knife went in smoothly and cut all the way to the bone, causing the zombie to fall backwards when his legs couldn't hold him up any longer. As soon as he fell, I shoved my knife deep into his forehead. A shadow fell over me and I spun, bringing my knife up into a defensive move, pulling back just in time to keep from pushing the blade into Jude's back. I wasn't used to having humans around me in the midst of fighting the undead. Jude swiped his blade across the throat of a zombie to his left and in one smooth movement, shoved it into the eye of a second zombie on his right. I finished off the one who was now missing most of its throat.

"Move, Melody!" Jude barked from beside me.

I jumped to my feet and ran to the SUV, following behind Ghost's disappearing feet. I scrambled across the seat quickly so I could to make room for Jude, which put me right on top of Ghost. Jude was right behind me and I never felt more relieved than I did when I heard the door slam shut behind him. Manuel gunned the gas.

"Booyah!" I shouted with a fist pump when we cleared the front gate area. I glanced around at the men in the silent truck and immediately felt foolish. "Too girly?" I asked seriously. Ghost started laughing and the deep rumbling made me grin and immediately reminded me that I was sitting in his lap. "Sorry, Ghost, I didn't mean to squish you," I mumbled, scrambling off of him.

"Hey, no hurry, you were okay right where you were." His voice was deep and I could hear a grin in it as he spoke. My cheeks warmed, which only made Ghost chuckle more. "Just a joke, Jude," he said with a smirk and a shrug.

I glanced over at Jude who was staring daggers at Ghost. I ignored both of them and leaned forward until I was hanging in between the two front seats and pulled back the center console, hoping to find something good.

"Melody, what are you doing?" Jude asked, sounding exasperated. I ignored him and kept searching.

"Aha!" I squealed. I pulled my prize out of its sleeve and leaned forward far enough to shove it into the player. I pushed a button and when the familiar sounds of Bob Marley's *Three Little Birds* blasted through the speaker system, I sat back with a small sigh of satisfaction. Ghost flashed me a sad smile, but I could feel the tension seeping out of the vehicle as we drove out of town.

Don't Worry About a Thing

We drove for about an hour, and I watched our progress through the window until I couldn't stomach what I saw any longer. The world was something I didn't recognize. I had kept myself mostly safe for two long years. It wasn't easy, but a lot of what kept me alive had to do with the simple fact that not only was I a little more prepared than the average citizen, but I'd also gotten to know almost every inch of the two local towns and every mile of the woods that I'd camped in. The woods were mine. I knew them almost as well in the pitch black of night as I did in the noonday sun. I had learned my surroundings like someone who might not have ever planned on leaving the area for the rest of their lives.

I sat there while a world full of death, destruction, and chaos passed by my window.

I realized with sudden clarity that I had sealed myself off from the outside world, convinced deep down that if I didn't know what was happening outside of my own personal hell, then maybe—just maybe—it wasn't really that bad in other places. I hadn't realized until I was leaving the area I knew so well that I'd convinced myself deep in my own subconscious that when I did finally leave, I'd be walking into some sort of safe haven, someplace *better* and maybe even *untouched* by all the death, loneliness, and despair that I'd been shrouded in for two years. The realization made my stomach revolt.

"Melody? Are you okay?" Jude's voice sounded concerned, but I couldn't answer him. I couldn't get past the pain in my chest and the ringing in my ears.

"Manuel, can you pull over?" I gasped in a breath and fuzzy splotches of gray danced in front of my eyes. A gush of wind hit me in the face as Jude pulled me from the truck and shook me gently.

"Melody? Breathe, sweetheart. Ah, hell, this is going to piss you off," he muttered. A brisk smack across my face brought Jude's concerned eyes into focus and a stinging along my cheekbone. I grabbed a handful of his tee shirt and jerked him a bit closer. I gasped in a huge breath of air into my lungs. I still felt dizzy.

"I didn't realize..." My eyes started to water and I blinked furiously until my head cleared. Jude's hand cupped the back of my head and his fingers massaged into my neck. "I don't know why I didn't expect it. I'm sorry."

Jude shushed me gently and kept rubbing my neck. "Don't apologize, Melody. I would have been more worried about you if all of this *didn't* affect you," he said gruffly.

I nodded once and took another long, cleansing breath before I was steady. I glanced up and realized Big Ben had been standing nearby as lookout. I let out a tiny not-so-sane giggle and looked up into Jude's questioning gaze.

"Didn't mean to go all girly on you at the wrong time." I stepped back from the circle of Jude's arms. "But if you ever slap me again, I'll kick your ass right in front of your men."

I heard what sounded suspiciously like a snort come from Big Ben. I jumped back into the SUV, extremely grateful none of the men acted like anything out of the ordinary had happened when we pulled back onto the highway to Hell.

.⋰.

It took us over two hours to drive to the halfway point about forty miles outside of Charlotte, North Carolina. Dodging wreckage, abandoned vehicles, and zombies made traveling take a lot longer than it used to. It felt like we were evading landmines, but instead of bombs we were trying to avoid becoming surrounded by the undead or stuck in a tight spot with nowhere to run if we had to. When Manuel pulled up to the back entrance of the rendezvous point I sat there for a second, wondering if the guys were just yanking my chain.

"You've got to be freaking kidding me," I mumbled when Manuel killed the engine.

I glanced out the window and only noticed two straggler zombies in the area, easy enough to take care of. Maybe the guys had a point. Looting a local Toy-R-Us would have been low on a priority list for people trying to survive in a zombie-riddled world. Fewer people looting in the area and the store equaled fewer zombies to worry about when meeting with other survivors.

"Ghost, Big Ben, you two take care of our decomposing friends while Manuel, Melody, and I secure the building. Join us inside after you scout the perimeter." Both men nodded briskly before opening their doors and sprinting toward the zombies who had already started heading our way. "Alright, let's move," Jude barked.

We entered through the back door of the building, our weapons ready and our movements almost synchronized. When the door shut behind us, it took a few moments for my eyes to adjust to the unlit interior of the store. The store had been ransacked and the interior smelled musty and unused, but at least we weren't overpowered by the stench of death and decay that was now common in most stores and populated areas. Still, being inside of a toy store tore the scab off of my freshly wounded heart and a tiny cry of distress left my lips before I could prevent it. Death and devastation consumed everything, and those bitches never skipped over children and innocents. No one was safe from their fury.

"Melody?" Manuel asked in a whisper. I swallowed back my fear and sadness and focused on the task at hand.

"I'm good," I whispered back. We all separated and searched the store for any broken doors or windows, and of course for any zombies. I made my way up and down each isle with my handgun drawn and an unreasonable fear that someone was going to be hiding under a shelf saying *"they all float down here"* and grab my leg. What? Zombies I could handle. Killer clowns? Hell no!

We all met each other near the door of the manager's office, where they would have all normally exchanged info with the men from the Charlotte base. Once supplies were exchanged, they would have gone back to their bases and met again two weeks later. That had been the routine until over two months ago when the other soldiers stopped showing.

"Everything clear?"

Both Manuel and I nodded and Jude opened the door to the office. The smell hit us before we took a single step inside. I gagged and yanked my knife from my sheath. Jude and Manuel spread out, but both seemed instantly aware where the other was so they could watch their backs.

"*Christo*," Manuel muttered. His stance changed and he lowered his arm slightly. Jude took a small flashlight from his pocket and flashed it to the corner of the room. There sat a corpse, twice dead and covered in maggots and flies. I gagged and stepped back out of the doorway to take a deep breath. When I returned to the office, Manuel and Jude were standing near the corpse, inspecting what was left of the body with the flashlight.

"Soldier. Probably from Charlotte," Manuel said. "No way to tell how long he's been here, but can't be longer than a month, since we were here thirty-four days ago." He pointed at the corpse's hand, still holding a handgun. "Looks like he was bitten and knew what was coming, so he took his own life."

Jude let out a string of obscenities that in other circumstances would have made me raise an eyebrow, but in this instance, I wholeheartedly agreed.

"So, the question is, why was he here after all this time, and most importantly, why was he alone?" Jude wondered out loud. "Maybe he wasn't alone. Maybe he had other men with him, but they left him once he became infected?" I offered up.

Manuel snorted.

Jude shook his head, his lips in a grim line. "No, if he had men, they wouldn't have left him even if he was infected. No man left behind. They would have taken care of the situation for him, not left him here to do it himself and then rot in this office. No way," Jude stated as fact.

"Okay, so he came alone. Why would he risk coming all this way alone to see if you guys would be here?" I asked to no one in particular.

"He needed help," Manuel said.

"Something was wrong," Jude agreed.

I shivered. That couldn't be good. I glanced back over at the body and cringed at the carnage. Blood and brain matter had been blown all over the desk area and wall behind the soldier when blew his brains out to avoid becoming one of the undead. I frowned and stepped closer to the body against my own will.

"Flash that light over there." I pointed to the desk behind the body. "There. What's that?" I asked breathlessly.

Manuel reached over and grabbed a piece of paper that had been pinned to the corkboard and splattered with gore. He handed it to Jude, who held the paper out and used the flashlight to try and make out what it said through the dark splatters.

Jude read the words out loud. I sucked in a breath and stepped back out of the room, the heat was stifling and the odor was overpowering. What the hell did *Germain* mean? Was it the soldier's name? The name of someone at the base? The rest I understood well enough. The Charlotte base had been taken over. But by who? It specifically said *under siege*, not *overrun*. Not good at all. Jude and Manuel came out of the office as Ghost and Big Ben joined us in the hallway, and Jude related everything to the two soldiers.

"So, what's the plan now?" I asked.

The men all looked at Jude. His fist tightened around the letter he still gripped in his hand and his eyes hardened when he spoke.

"You are all going to go scout for supplies locally and then head back to base. I'm going to Charlotte."

I wasn't the only person who had a problem with that order.

"No way," I argued.

"You're crazy, bro. Ain't no way I'm letting you go and get yourself killed," Manuel said stepping closer to Jude.

"You'll all do what I say," Jude barked gruffly.

"Like hell I will," Manuel ground out, his eyes daring Jude to try and make him. "We've been through too much for you to act all macho, pulling rank, and sending me home like a little bitch," he spat.

Jude grabbed Manuel by his shirt and slammed him up against the wall so fast I let out a yelp.

"Jude, don't," Ghost said, his hand gripping Jude's shoulder tightly to keep him from putting more pressure on Manuel's throat. Jude loosened his grip just enough to let Manuel breathe, but his face was still inches from Manuel's.

"I will not guide you all into an overrun city now that I know our contacts there have been overtaken, probably by some sort of militia. I don't know what we'd find and I won't be responsible for leading you all to your deaths, or worse, to your un-deaths." The muscle in Jude's neck thumped wildly and his eyes bore into Manuel's. "You will take everyone back to camp. Am I clear?" he snapped. Manuel stared him down for several seconds, his eyes glinting dangerously, before he nodded his agreement. "Good," Jude breathed before letting him go.

"So, Captain so-freaking-sure-of-himself, what is your plan if you get into Charlotte safely?" I snapped, drawing Jude's attention back to me. He stared at me, a muscle in his cheek twitching. I crossed my arms over my chest, waiting.

Jude sighed and ran a hand roughly over his face. "I'll dress down into civilian clothes and try to get into the base and see what I can find out. Like, how many soldiers are there, if there are any civilians being held captive, that sort of thing." I shook my head and smiled. Jude shot a questioning look at me and then over at Ghost, who was also grinning from ear to ear. "What?" he snapped.

"I hate to break it to you, Jude, but you could wear a pink tutu and call yourself the Tooth Fairy, but everyone will know you're military. Changing out of those camo pants and taking off all that gear sure as hell won't make a difference," I said, smirking when the guys chuckled. "I'd make you as a soldier in a crowd in a heartbeat and I'm not even military. I bet your first word was "hooah", wasn't it?" Jude continued to scowl at me, but I pushed on, hoping to get my point across. "I could go with you," I offered.

"No fucking way, Melody," Jude growled.

"Now listen, Jude," I chided and held up a hand. "Think about it, a single guy looking like you do would draw attention immediately. They would peg you as military, or at the very least, a threat, before you stepped a foot in the door. But if a civilian *couple* just happen to be needing shelter, well, we would be able to fly under the radar a little easier, since there would be no way I could be military," I said coaxingly. Jude's mouth swung open, but Big Ben cut in.

"She's got a point, Jude," he grumbled. "You'd be a lot less suspicious as a couple and you'd also have someone there to watch your back." Jude narrowed his eyes at the big man, but Ben only shrugged. He'd said his two cents.

"I agree," Manuel mumbled.

"Aww, hell. Not you too," Jude said with a throw of his arm.

Manuel stared at Jude for a moment before answering. "If one of us can't go with you, she'd be the next best thing. She couldn't have survived alone like she did without having to be one tough little bitch," Manuel said with grudging admiration. I smiled my thanks at him, even though he had just called me a bitch.

Jude paced back and forth for several moments before he sighed heavily and turned to face us. "Okay, she comes with me," he agreed. "We'll eat here and then Melody and I will head south on foot, while you all take the vehicle and head into the town west of here to scavenge for the most necessary supplies and head back to the base by dark." The men all nodded their heads. "Good. We'll rendezvous back here in one week at 0800 hours."

We all sat in the toy store together and ate lunch in relative silence, thinking about everything that could go wrong in the next several hours and over the next several days.

When it was time to go our separate ways, I had to stop myself from giving each of the guys a hug. Apparently my girliness showed itself at the worst times. I opted, instead, for handshakes all around.

"Alright, you guys head out first and we'll follow in a few minutes," Jude said. Manuel held my gaze and I nodded at him in silent communication. I would do my best to watch Jude's back and bring him back safely. It was an odd feeling to think I was going to be responsible for someone else's safety besides my own for once. It wasn't an entirely pleasant feeling.

"One week at 0800 hours," Manuel said, clasping Jude's arm.

"One week at 0800 hours," he confirmed.

And just like that, we were alone and without a vehicle in the middle of an abandoned Toys-R-Us with an uncertain future sprawled out before us.

Road to Charlotte

We were walking down the highway side-by-side, both of us hot and sweaty from keeping to a brisk pace for over three hours.

"How long do you think it will take us to get to Charlotte on foot?" I asked.

"Best guess would be about ten hours of uninterrupted walking, but if I take in consideration stopping for breaks and light meals and that I have a civilian with me, I'd say at least twelve hours."

I glanced up at the sky and frowned. If that was the case, then we would walking once darkness fell.

Jude noticed my look and smirked. "Don't worry, I don't plan on walking in the darkness. We'll walk until it begins to get dark and then we'll try to find a secure location to sleep until early morning," he explained. So far we'd lucked out and had only run into small clusters of zombies on our walk. If nothing else, Jude and I made a very effective zombie elimination team. He moved opposite me, his body attuned to my movements as we took on several zombies at once. It was uncanny, and also very reassuring. If we didn't get cornered or overrun by too many, we were virtually unstoppable.

We slowly approached a particularly cluttered part of highway, instantly on the alert for zombies and other hazards. I instinctually moved toward Jude, finding comfort in the fact that I knew he would have my back no matter how hairy any situation got. We passed several cars with their doors standing open wide, abandoned by whoever had initially inhabited them to travel on foot. Cars and trucks were all parked haphazardly along the stretch of highway bumper-to-bumper. The eerie lineup caused the hairs on my neck to prickle in uneasiness. Ahead of us by about half a mile, I could see a huge semi-truck turned over on its side and sprawled across the highway with several vehicles rammed into and around it, imagining with severe clarity how the scene must have unfolded during the accident. People in a panic, trying to drive their families out of whatever town or city they'd fled from only to watch helplessly as the huge eighteen wheeler lost control, either by accident, or the result of the virus, and flip over, causing a massive pileup on the southbound highway.

My hand ran along the side of an empty minivan. Had the van held a family with little children? I didn't peer into the window to find out. I didn't want to know. Had zombies immediately attacked this area during the traffic backup, or did the people get away on foot? No way to know. I blew out a weary breath and moved along with Jude, who was as silent as death beside me.

When we finally made it to the semi, I shivered. Not a single zombie so far and for that, I was grateful. Jude caught my eye and we both smiled at each other; the worst of this stretch was over. We headed around the back end of the semi, glad to get out of the jumbled graveyard of vehicles. The moment we cleared the bumper, we both knew what a mistake it had been to think we'd lucked out. Luck never was a friend of mine.

Nearly a dozen zombies in different states of decay were standing near the overturned truck in their trademark shutdown mode. When we stepped into their line of vision, they all snapped out of it and turned to face us.

"This is going to be fun," Jude muttered out of the side of his mouth. A strangled giggle escaped my lips. Fun, yeah, that's what we'd call it. "Try not to use your gun if at all possible and stay close to me," Jude said, his eyes hardening. I nodded, unable to form any words.

We moved quickly, slashing and hacking our way through engorged flesh and bone like a couple of macabre butchers. Six overly ripe corpses hit the pavement with a splat before we had made it a dozen feet. Bile rose in the back of my throat as the putrid aroma of rotting flesh and rancid fluids tickled the roof of my mouth and coated my taste buds. I drew back my arm and shoved my blade through the eye socket of a short and impossibly thin zombie, ignoring the fact that it was wearing a jean skirt, Hello Kitty tee, and had probably been someone's teen daughter.

After she fell, another zombie, faster and much fatter, took her place. It grabbed out to snatch my arm, trying to sink its rotting teeth into it. I used the zombie's own forward momentum, snagging it by the coat sleeve, and pulling it so hard that it stumbled and fell to the pavement when I swiveled out of the way. I stomped with all my might into the zombie's face, feeling its skull give way beneath my booted foot until there was nothing but putrefied mush squished into the pavement. I was so busy making sure the zombie on the ground didn't get back up, that I missed the one who had come up behind me in the chaos. I turned swiftly only to come face-to-face with a zombie so swollen with fluids and rot that it could have been someone's sick portrayal of zombies immortalized as a wax figurine. Its eyes were so unnervingly opaque that I had no idea how it could see. Its skin glistened in the sunlight, white and waxy, and stretched so tautly across the corpse's liquefied insides that I was surprised into immobility.

The undead man didn't hesitate like I did, however. His hunger for human flesh motivated him to try with all his might to rip into me. Surprised by his speed, I jumped back, only to slip on the mess of zombie goo I'd made and land on my ass right in the middle of it, losing my knife in the process. I moved fast, scrambling backward to get away, but the zombie was already on top of me. I fumbled for my gun, trying to get it free with my hand covered in slimy zombie insides, but I wasn't fast enough. I lunged back again, just as the zombie's mouth opened and a gurgle of sour zombie breath coated my shoulder. A scream clawed its way up my throat and the zombie stilled for a fraction of a second with his mouth hanging open before a fountain of blood and mushy zombie innards spewed forth with a *pop*, coating every inch of me from the neck down. In shock, I looked up into the face of the zombie, barely noting the long blade poking through his eye inches away from me.

"Are you alright?" Jude pushed the grotesquely bloated body to the side and held out a hand. I grabbed onto it and let him pull me from the pile of muck. "Were you bit?" he asked, searching my face. I shook my head, and glanced around at the bodies strewn all over the place. I felt lightheaded, slowly raising my hands up in front of myself. I looked at the gore and guts coating my arms in a detached sort of fascination.

"We should probably get moving, Melody," Jude said gently.

I bobbed my head again, never taking my eyes off of my arms. I turned slowly and glanced back at the mess I was sitting in and realized how very close I'd been to getting killed. My head began to buzz and I pitched forward and vomited until my stomach hurt from the pain of it. Jude rubbed my back the entire time, but I didn't hear whatever it was he was murmuring. When nothing was left except a headache, Jude helped me to my feet. He held my blade out to me and I muttered my thanks. We both started walking again, glad to put the semi and all its newly redecorated scenery behind us.

"I need to find somewhere to try and get cleaned up," I said once we were half an hour further down the road.

Jude nodded, glancing at the mess that was caked all over me. "We should take a short rest anyway. We only have another hour or two before we should start searching for a place to hole up for the night. There is a small town up an exit that we'll head for. Hopefully it won't be overrun by zombies or any of the violent groups of survivors I've run into in the past," he said. "Let's stop over there." He pointed over to what looked like it had once been one of those roadside produce stands.

I picked up my pace to keep up with him. When we were pretty sure it was safe, we walked around to the back of the stand where there was shade and set our backpacks down.

"Here," Jude said.

I glanced up from my intense hand-scrubbing with half a bottle of sanitizer and took a men's white tank top from Jude with a frown. "Are you sure?" I asked him. Jude gave me a look and then jerked the bottle of sanitizer out of my hand. "Hey!" I protested.

"Take off your shirt," Jude ordered.

"Excuse me?" I asked incredulously.

Jude clucked his tongue and then sighed. "Listen, that sanitizer isn't going to help get all that nasty crap off of you," he said. "Take off your shirt and I'll help you clean off with some water, then you can put on the tank top."

I shut my mouth and frowned.

"Believe me, Melody, I want you clean more than you do. No offense, but you smell like shit." He held up a hand and shrugged as if he were merely stating facts.

He was right, of course, my own stench was making me want to throw up again. I *had* to get clean.

"Besides," he said with a wicked glint in his eye, "it's not like I haven't seen you naked before."

My face flamed and he chuckled. I really didn't have a choice; I needed his help to get just a little clean. I pulled my shirt up, realizing right away that it had pretty much adhered itself to my skin as it dried when we were walking. *Just freaking great.* I yanked it roughly away from my skin and then pulled it slowly over my head, trying not to get any chunks or dried flakes of zombie guts in my hair.

Jude took a cloth and a bottle of water out of his pack. He poured water over my hands and I rubbed them together and then over my arms. He poured a stream of water on the back and front of my neck and I shivered when his hand gently washed my neck and shoulder area. I didn't dare look him in the eyes as he helped me get clean. I would have probably died in mortification. When he poured water over my chest, thankfully letting me wash myself there, he shifted away from me a tiny bit. My sad gray bra was thoroughly soaked, but at least it was still wearable for the time being. Jude held out the small cloth to me silently. I glanced up at him from beneath my lashes and saw a look of tenderness and longing flash across his face before he caught me looking. The look was quickly replaced by a smirk and a cool, detached gaze.

"You know, this could almost be one of my fantasies, if I could just focus on the wet tee shirt contest part of my fantasy and forget the puddle of zombie guts," he mentioned casually.

I rolled my eyes and dried off best I could then yanked Jude's white tank top over my head. It was too big, but it would work. On the plus side it didn't reek of noxious zombie guts; on the downside, it smelled of Jude.

Welcome to Pineville

We walked several miles until we found an exit leading into a small podunk, town named Pineville. We moved silently through the quiet town, and I couldn't help but have a flashback to the day I'd done the same when I had made my way back into Midtown a few days after my dad was killed. This town felt the same except it was quieter and there were a ton of decomposing bodies in cars, bodies in the streets, and an overall feeling of entering the twilight zone. I was not feeling very welcome in Pineville.

"Where are all the zombies?" I asked from where we were ducked behind a car parked on the side of a burned-out gas station.

"Are you complaining about not finding any?" Jude asked.

"I think it's kind of odd we haven't seen a single walking corpse in the entire town," I said uneasily.

Jude nodded and then glanced at the sky. "Let's find a place for the night. We'll get out of here at first light," he said.

Sounded good to me. I would be glad to leave Pineville far behind us.

"There," I said. "That's where we should stay." I pointed my finger at the building a little ways down from us and Jude smiled broadly when he saw it.

"It's perfect," he agreed. "Let's go."

We approached the used bookstore stealthily, waiting for something, anything really, to happen. When nothing did, we found a back entrance and entered the building warily. The place was a mess. Old blood was smeared across a wall and splattered the old wooden floorboards, but the tiny bookstore was mostly clean and the windows were already boarded up. It was uninhabited, and more importantly, not likely to be raided by anyone looking to scavenge for supplies. We secured the doors then went to work making the room as fortified and safe as possible before we settled in for the night. It wasn't long before the room was too dark to work in. Jude pulled three small candles out of his pack and put them on top of an overturned bookcase close to the ancient looking brown sofa we'd been ecstatic to find in the store.

It's the little things that cause excitement now.

Jude walked over to the front door and checked the area for the tenth time. We'd pushed a large bookshelf up against the door to be extra careful, but he still checked everything several times more before he came over and plopped down on the sofa next to me.

"I figure we have about six hours of walking ahead of us tomorrow," Jude said. "That's if we don't run into any more major problems."

I unstrapped my gun and set it on the floor close by, along with my backpack and other weapons. I didn't dare take my boots off.

"Oh, I forgot!" I jumped off the sofa and pulled my treasure out of my backpack. "Look at what I found," I said with a huge grin.

Jude smiled and reached out, taking a can from me. One bottle of water, one can of Coke, and one bag of Skittles.

"Where'd you find this?" he asked.

"In a mini fridge under the cash register," I answered. I popped the top to the Coke and sighed at the familiar sound. Jude started laughing when I moaned after taking a tiny sip. I held it out to him and he hesitated a second before taking the drink from me.

"I don't have cooties, *Agent*," I said sarcastically.

Jude snorted and took a sip of the Coke. "Mmm, I miss that," he said in appreciation.

I grinned and nudged my shoulder into his. "This is your lucky day. I don't share my Skittles with just any guy," I said jokingly.

I handed him all the green and orange Skittles and Jude's smile grew wicked. "Glad to hear it, Mel."

His voice was husky and I refused to look at him. I couldn't, not with the way things were. I didn't want to set myself up for more heartache. We finished sharing the soda and candy in silence. It wasn't awkward though, it felt companionable, and I was glad to have someone with me in the darkness for once.

Jude shifted and sat forward. "We should probably get some rest," he said.

I nodded, already yawning behind my hand. "How should we do this?" I asked.

He glanced over at me and winked. I snorted and rolled my eyes, which only made him grin wider.

"I'll take the floor, you can have the couch," he said after a moment.

"That hardly seems fair to you," I remarked.

Jude took one of the throw pillows and situated it just right before laying back on the couch in a half-sitting position. He crooked his finger at me. His eyes were half laughing, half mocking. *Jerk.* His eyes widened when I shifted my body and fit myself sideways into the crook of his arm, my head resting on his chest, my arm flung across his waist. His laugh rumbled his chest, which heated up my cheeks.

"You are full of surprises, Melody Carter," he murmured against the top of my head.

"What about you, Jude? What's your story?" I asked. "Where were you when all the crap hit the fan?"

Jude shifted beneath me and sighed. "If I told you, I'd have to kill you," he muttered.

I snorted. "How old are you?"

"I recently turned twenty-five," he answered.

"Old man," I joked.

He huffed. "And how old are you, Melody? About twenty-two?" he asked.

"I'll be *twenty* very soon," I answered.

"Oh shit, you're just a baby," he gasped, sounding horrified.

I smiled against his chest. Let him chew on that for a while.

"Sometimes I feel so much older," I whispered seriously.

Jude's arm tightened around me. He was quiet for several moments. "I was waiting for my fiancé at the airport the night everything went crazy," he said sadly.

"I'm sorry, Jude," I said gently.

"It's okay. Sometimes it seems like so long ago now." He sighed deeply. "We should get some sleep."

I nodded. "Goodnight, Jude."

"Goodnight, Mel."

My eyelids grew heavy and I was almost immediately lulled to sleep by Jude's warm embrace and his rhythmic heartbeat.

"Melody."

I groaned and turned over, pulling myself tighter into a ball.

"Melody, we need to get moving."

Jude's voice snapped me out of my left over sleep and I sprung from the couch.

"Easy," he whispered. "Everything's okay."

I pushed my hair back out of my face and glanced up at Jude standing next to the couch. He looked... different. I blinked and rubbed my eyes.

"Am I dreaming?"

Jude sighed and threw a wad of clothing on my lap. "Get dressed, smart ass. I hope I was right with the sizes," he said. I finally noticed what he'd handed me. A pair of jeans, a dark green tee shirt with the Green Lantern insignia on the front, and a... bra? I blushed. Jude raked his hands through his hair. "I thought you might need a new one after getting drenched in zombie juices yesterday, so I went scavenging for us," he muttered by way of explanation. His eyes were looking everywhere but at me. He was embarrassed.

How cute.

"Thank you," I said sincerely.

He nodded and walked around toward the back of the room. "I'll wait over here for you."

I got dressed, more than a little surprised that everything fit me well, including the cute, pale blue bra. I got my backpack and met Jude a moment later. He had traded his Army pants and tee for a pair of blue jeans and a black tee shirt. He almost looked normal, in a smoking hot sort of way.

"You realize once we make it to Charlotte, we will probably die," Jude mentioned as he turned to me.

My jaw tightened and I looked at him, searching his eyes. "I'm not going to let that happen," I answered truthfully.

Jude's eyes sparkled and his mouth turned up in a crooked grin. "I didn't think you would." He nodded his head over his shoulder and stepped closer to me. "There's four undead right outside we'll have to go through to get out of here," he said.

I reached for my knife, but Jude grabbed my hand and pulled me against his chest. My eyes immediately sought his.

"Don't hit me, but there's something I've been meaning to do," he muttered just before his lips crashed down to mine.

I stiffened in shock, but that didn't last long, not with Jude working wicked black magic on my lips. I melted into him, my hand going up to wrap around the back of his neck, to pull him closer. When he was done, he pulled back slowly, his eyes glazed with passion, both of us breathing hard.

"If I die now, I'll die a happy man," he whispered against my temple, placing a gentle kiss there. He stepped back and left me standing there in a bit of a daze. "You ready to kill some zombies?" he asked after a second.

Zombies? Sure, what the hell. Get kissed senseless and then take on some undead. All in a normal day. I picked up my knife, hefting its familiar weight in my hand. I felt anticipation rise.

"What do you think?" I asked with a cocky grin.

"Let's do this." Jude threw the door open and we both rushed out.

The zombies never had a chance.

We Ain't in Kansas Anymore

The zombie activity grew increasingly more pronounced the closer we came to the Charlotte city limits. We had probably killed over two dozen zombies since we left Pineville in the early morning hours, no groups larger than four or five though, so they were dispatched easily enough between the two of us. We passed a larger group of zombies about an hour outside of Charlotte, avoiding them by keeping our movements as quiet as possible and ducking behind a myriad of abandoned vehicles on the road leading out of Charlotte, a sinister reminder that we were definitely headed the wrong direction. Smarter people would have turned back at that point.

The coup de grâce should have been the smell, the overwhelming, choking smog of death and putrefaction emanating from the city. If that didn't deter people from entering Charlotte, the sounds should have. The noise coming from the city at first sounded like a single sound, unified, like an enormous white noise emitter. When we got closer to the city, we realized that what we were hearing was the sounds of thousands of shuffling feet, thousands of undead mouths open in death screams, only to exude rattling moans and gurgles. It was a terrifying and sobering realization.

"So, what's the plan?" I asked once we made it past another large group of wandering zombies just inside of the city limits.

Jude crouched down beside me and ran a hand through his hair. "I'm not sure, Mel. Maybe this was a bad idea. I don't want to get you killed on a mission that is doomed to failure." He sighed and rammed his knife into the ground between his feet. "How the fuck can anyone be living in *that*?" he asked, his eyes searching mine. I'd been thinking the same thing, but I didn't want to be the one to say it.

"Where's the base supposed to be located?" I asked instead.

"Not far from here, but it might as well be miles with all these undead fuckers walking around." His eyes searched the area around us, making sure we weren't going to be spotted. "Jesus, the sound alone would have driven me insane a long time ago."

I agreed. There had to be a somewhat safe way to enter the base, or they would have tried to move the survivors from there a long time back. Of course, even if we did happen to make it to the base, who was to say the people there would even let us in? For all we knew, they'd leave us out in the open and ring a dinner bell for the zombies.

"We have to try," I said after a moment. Jude's jaw tightened and he jerked his knife out of the ground. "Even if there is only the slimmest chance that there are soldiers or civilian survivors there being held captive, we have to try and help them. My dad would have helped them." I lifted my chin. "I have to try," I said resolutely.

Jude nodded, but he didn't like it. "Alright, G. I. Jane." Jude chuckled under his breath when I punched him in the arm. "Let's go and try not to get killed, okay?"

"I'll do my best, Agent."

"The building is supposed to be exactly half a mile that way," Jude said, pointing into the city. I poked my head over the hood of the car we were squatted behind and winced. Right into the center of a mess of zombies. Vehicles were bumper to bumper as far as the eye could see, on every street, bodies lay strewn all over the place, and zombies walked in between it all, some of them shoulder-to-shoulder with what looked like hundreds of their undead brethren. The further you looked into the city, the denser the zombie population became.

"The secret base is located beneath an old toy factory there."

What was with all the secret locations and toys? I grimaced. Creepy. "So, what's the plan again?"

"Run like hell?" Jude suggested. "You see how they're clustered?" I asked, squinting against the sun.

Jude nodded. "Some are in small groups or loners, but most of them are clustered in larger groups of twenty or more," he said.

I shook my head and pointed at the group closest to us. "Yeah, but do you see *where* the larger groups are clustered?" I asked.

Jude looked from group to group, his forehead crinkling in thought. His eyes widened fractionally. "They're grouped together in the shadiest areas," he murmured thoughtfully. He moved to the other end of the vehicle and searched over the trunk of the vehicle, scoping out the area. "We might have a better chance if we can find areas like that one." He pointed to a long spot of road and abandoned cars where only a few straggler zombies milled about in the heat of the day. "If we can move quickly, kill quickly, and get really fucking lucky, we might be able to make it to the factory by keeping to the sunniest areas."

I nodded my head. It was the best plan we had. I joined Jude at the back of the car and peeked over to the spot we were going to be running for. There were still half a dozen zombies between us and the first stretch of zombie-free zones. Not only that, once the zombies in the shade caught sight of us, being in the sunlight wouldn't save us. We had to move fast, and there would be no room for error.

Jude held up a hand, counted down from three, and we took off. My heart tripped out a frantic beat, the noise of the zombies in the city drowned out by the blood rushing in my ears as we began our dangerous game of Russian roulette with zombies instead of bullets. Jude ran ahead of me, his knife finding the skull of a lumbering zombie halfway to the first patch of sunlight. Two more came after him and we both drove our knives into their skulls before resuming our sprint across the road, weaving between cars and bodies. I didn't dare look behind me as we ran, I couldn't risk taking my eyes off of where we were going and I didn't really want to know if any zombies were already following us.

Jude jumped up onto the top of a small car and landed on the other side to take down a female zombie who looked like it hadn't fed since she'd been turned. I jumped up too, but my foot got caught halfway across. I landed hard on the roof, wondering how in the hell I'd gotten tripped up. I hadn't. A zombie who must have been nearby or in the car had grabbed my leg and was pulling me with the strength of a linebacker toward him, his mouth open with slushy green juices oozing down the front of his torn and tattered button up shirt. I raised my free foot and kicked him in the face three times with my boot, hearing bones crunch and rotten flesh squish, before his hold on me lessened. When he let go, I nearly screamed when Jude grabbed me by my arms to pull me the rest of the way across the little car.

"Are you done playing with the nice zombie?" Jude asked, breathing hard.

I snorted and we took off running once again. We ran full out, only pausing when a zombie got in our way. *Run. Kill. Run. Kill.* We were moving along quickly, but we were still pretty far from our destination. Jude drove his knife across the throat of a zombie while I rammed mine into the skull of one of his buddies. Another zombie materialized from behind a van and made his way toward Jude. I opened my mouth to tell him to watch out when, like out of a scene from a horror movie, zombies poured out from behind the van. Jude swiveled and his eyes widened. I kicked the zombie off of my blade and stabbed one close to me in the back of the neck. Jude sliced into a zombie and removed his knife just in time to ram it into the eye of another one. I made it to his side in time for us to find ourselves being corralled by a dozen or more of the menacing creatures.

"Jude! On top of the cars!" I shouted.

He slid his knife across the throat of two zombies and then pushed a huge one into four more closing in on us. "Go!" he shouted.

I jumped at his command and propelled myself up on the hood of a rusty blue car. Jude shoved his knife into the skull of another zombie and I kicked one coming up behind him in the face, caving in its mushy face.

"Jude, now!" I screamed. I ran, jumping from hood to bumper, hoping Jude was right behind me. I couldn't stop, couldn't glance back, afraid I'd lose my footing and land on the ground at the feet of the zombie horde. I could hear the zombies, their tormented sounds getting closer, their shuffling growing louder as they worked themselves into a frenzy at the prospect of a fresh midday meal.

Up ahead, I saw a large, rundown, factory and nearly wept from the sight. My elation was grounded though, when I realized the entire perimeter of the factory was closed off by a high chain link fence with barbed wire gracing the top. I came to a spot in my car jumping where I wouldn't be able to make the next jump. When I got to it, I jumped down to the asphalt and looked back, glad to find Jude only a car jump behind me. His eyes scanned the factory and I knew the moment his eyes found what I had. The absolute devastation was plain to read on his face.

"Keep moving, Mel!" Jude shouted as he jumped down from the car.

I kept the gate to the factory in my line of vision, praying to God we'd be able to find a way in. I cleared the corner of the only building left between us and the factory, my legs trembling from the pace we'd run at, when a zombie flew out of nowhere and knocked me to the ground. I scrambled back, pulling my gun out of its sheath on my leg. I held the tiny zombie off of me, but didn't realize for a few precious seconds that I'd begun crying when I realized that the zombie now trying to tear my throat out was a toddler, no older than three or four when he'd been turned. His body was a grotesque reminder of everything that was wrong in my new world, of everything that I'd tried to block from my mind and memories the last two years. The tiny tot-zombie gnashed his teeth in agitation and hunger, straining against my hold. I lifted my gun and a sob escaped my throat. The zombie was ripped off me while I lay there, useless for the first time in a very long time. I turned my head when Jude put the undead child down. He pulled me to my feet and shook me.

"Are you okay?" I nodded. "Good, cause we have problems," Jude said, grabbing my hand and jerking me toward the fence. We landed against the shut gate, hoping the chains would be faulty, or someone would come out of nowhere and let us in. Instead, just around the corner, in an alleyway we couldn't have seen from the direction we'd come from, dozens upon dozens of zombies stood in a silent stupor in the shade of the building. Their rattling breaths and moans were the only things that gave them away.

"Oh shit," I whispered.

"Yeah, that about sums it up," Jude whispered back. I pulled my gun out and put my knife in my left hand. "Melody, move quietly and slowly. See the side of the fence down that alleyway behind us?"

I nodded, my breathing growing labored as I realized exactly how far up a creek we really were. And now it looked like were going to try and get into the factory perimeter through a side gate. Of course, the gate was down a little alleyway, which would make us cornered if the gate didn't open there. We didn't even have to make the choice. Dozens of zombies approached the area from where we had run and their frenzied noise and movement immediately roused the slumbering zombies in the shadow-darkened alleyway.

"Move!" Jude yelled.

I ran full out, my legs pumping for everything I was worth, one hand gripping my blade, the other gripping my handgun. We ran up against the smaller gate and rebounded off of it. *Locked.*

I turned in time to see my greatest nightmare come to visit me in broad daylight. Zombies poured into the alleyway, blocking our only escape and our only hope.

"I'm sorry, Mel," Jude said, pulling his gun off of his back.

"Don't be," I said, blinking back my tears. "The kiss wasn't that bad," I said with a grin.

Jude snorted, shook his head, and then propped his gun up on his shoulder. I began squeezing off rounds, standing next to Jude as he made head shots one after another. Ten, twenty, thirty, undead dropped before us, but they seemed to multiply rather than diminish in numbers. When my gun was empty, I dropped it and pulled my knife out in front of me, waiting. It wasn't long before the zombies advanced further and Jude dropped his empty gun next to mine.

If anything would be said of us when we were gone, it would have been that we went out kicking undead ass and not caring about taking names. As a team we were something beautifully terrifying to behold. I lost count of how many face, necks, and skulls my blade sliced through. Eventually my arm was numb of feeling and I only slashed out purely out of habit. I couldn't feel where my blade ended and my arm began. The pile of undead in front of us grew large and somewhere in the back of my addled mind, I wondered if we would become buried beneath the rotting corpses and smothered to death rather than getting bitten. Wouldn't that just suck? About that time I started laughing. Jude jumped beside me, the sound foreign and out of place in our world of slicing and dicing.

I dropped a zombie, and two more took its place before me. My chest hurt, my arms hurt, and I was so tired. We were fighting a fruitless war and we both knew it. Out of some perverse sense of preservation I had kept fighting this long, but I didn't want to fight anymore. I glanced over and out of the corner of my eye, I saw Jude still fighting, his arm moving so lightning fast I could barely make it out, his face that of an avenging angel, and I was instantly sorry we didn't have more time. I sliced through the forehead of a girl in front of me and then... I stopped. I watched in some sort of sick fascination as two zombies bumbled over the mound of bodies in front of me. I put my knife back in my boot.

"Melody! What the fuck are you doing?" Jude screamed at me, his voice full of terror. I blinked back tears, but I didn't look at him. I couldn't. I closed my eyes.

"I'm sorry, Daddy," I whispered. I'd been a survivor long enough.

Will the Real Germain Please Step Forward?

When arms wrapped around me, I felt peace wash over me. I'd done enough, hadn't I? Arms banded about my waist and jerked me back. I felt myself being pulled and I heard Jude yelling, but no bites were forthcoming. When the shots came, I opened my eyes and found I was on the other side of the fence. Men in Army fatigues had Jude on the ground, his face was in the gravel and his eyes bore into mine accusingly. I went to move, but my arms had been pulled behind me by a large guy who was holding me in place. More shots echoed behind me.

"Let me go!" I said. "I need to check on him."

The guy behind me snorted and held my arms tighter.

"Let's get them inside, before these zombies work themselves into more of a frenzy," someone ordered from next to me.

"You don't have to treat us like criminals," I snarled. The man who held me pulled me closer to his body and I immediately stiffened in his grasp.

"Sweetheart, no offense, but we don't know you and you have to be cleared of any bites before we let you free of restraints. Just be glad I know how to treat a lady and didn't put cuffs on you like we did your boyfriend over there." His southern twang caressed my cheek and I shied away from his proximity, though I didn't think he was trying to intimidate me. He was only stating facts. I nodded my understanding. "That's a good girl," he said approvingly.

"Good girl, my ass," I muttered beneath my breath. I thought I heard the musclehead behind me chuckle, but I couldn't be sure. I was still so weak-kneed from our run, almost death, and prompt rescue that I probably would have fallen into a heap on the ground if the guy behind me wasn't holding me up as we walked into the factory.

The inside of the factory was exactly what I imagined it would be—creepy. Unused machines sat collecting dust while broken parts of toys littered the floor and work spaces. Besides toy clowns scaring the bejeesus out of me, old dolls were a close second. Walking through an abandoned room with doll parts everywhere was going to seriously take some major therapy. I chuckled and everyone around me tensed up. Wow, these guys needed to lighten up a bit. We were led into the back of the factory and then into what I could only imagine had been used as a cleaning supply storage room. In the back of the room a door opened and we were shuffled down a flight of stairs where we waited while a large door was unlocked. Down another flight of stairs the next room opened up into a large holding area. A holding area with a few cells and two small, windowless rooms, that is.

"Put him in that room, the girl in the other."

Jude's eyes met mine and I tried to smile reassuringly, but my heart was nearly pounding out of my chest. I didn't have my gun and I was pretty sure my knife had been taken the second we were pulled into the fenced in area outside. I'd never felt so vulnerable. Jude was shoved into a room and I heard someone grunt out an order for him to strip down. I swallowed back the fear rising in my throat and only barely kept from panicking. The large guy I'd yet to see led me into the room and turned on a light hanging from the ceiling by a cord. The light swayed back and forth, illuminating a chair and a drain in the floor, along with a hose hanging on the far wall.

"This should be interesting," someone said from the doorway. I shivered involuntarily and the man behind me stiffened.

"What should be?" he snapped at the two men standing there with their eyes on me.

"Oh, come on, Tex. You're not going to keep all that to yourself are you?" The guys leered from where they stood and I could feel the shame of what they were insinuating wash over me. I also felt Tex vibrating in barely-repressed anger near me.

"Get the fuck out," he growled over my shoulder. I shivered and a tiny sound of fear escaped my lips. One guy turned and left immediately, but a tall, pale skinned guy with shaggy blond hair curled his lip and stood there a moment longer, staring daggers at us before muttering curses beneath his breath. Tex let go of my arms and walked over to the door to lock it. He ran a hand through his dark brown hair before turning back to me. His eyes found mine and they looked apologetic, but I still didn't trust him, not even a little.

"Look, I'm sorry about this, but it needs to be done." He walked over and stood in front of me. "Please strip down to your bra and panties." I flinched and he sighed. "I really am sorry. But believe me, it's better me than one of those other guys. I won't hurt you. I just need to run some water over you and make sure you haven't been bitten before we take you any further into the compound," he explained. I stared at him a moment longer and then glanced over at the door. "They won't be coming in. I don't think any of them would hurt you, but taking advantage of your situation doesn't sit right with me. We don't get many women coming into the city."

I grabbed the hem of my shirt. *Get it over quickly. Don't think about it.* He was right, it could have been a lot worse, especially if that slimy-eyed guy had been the one in the room with me. I was shocked and grateful when Tex turned around to give me some semblance of privacy. I pulled my dirty, gore-splattered shirt over my head and then unbuttoned my jeans with shaking fingers. I moaned from the stiffness in my arm when I picked up my clothing from the floor and Tex swung around, his eyes wide and his hand going to his gun. I froze and tried to smile, but failed miserably.

"Sorry, my arm feels like hell right now," I said.

His body relaxed a bit and he let out a breath. "I thought there for a minute…"

"Sorry," I said peevishly. He grinned and I found myself smiling back at a guy I didn't know while standing in a bare room in my underwear, covered in filth and rot. I straightened fully and set my clothing on the only chair in the small room. I walked toward the center of the room and met Tex's eyes.

He walked over and removed the hose from the wall and turned it on. "Please hold your arms out. We'll start there," he said.

I nodded and did what I was told. The water was frigid and I gasped when it hit my skin.

"Sorry," he murmured. He grasped my arm and ran his rough palms up and down my arms, rubbing away the muck to find clean skin beneath. His eyes searched my arms and then my hands for any broken skin. He inspected my hands, running his fingers over my right palm gently. "You've roughened your right palm from using your knife and gun often," he said.

"I have taken care of myself for a long time now," I answered.

He smiled with a look of admiration. "This is going to be cold," he said by way of apology. Then he held the hose over my head.

I squealed. "Holy shit, that's freezing!" I gasped. He chuckled and let the stream of water run over me to wash away the worst of the gunk that coated me. Pretty soon the water felt good. "I'm pretty sure I have zombie in my hair," I said. Tex laughed loudly, making me jump. I opened my eyes and met his shining ones.

"Nothing sexier than zombie chunks in a girl's hair," he said with a wink. I laughed and did my best to get it all out. "Here, let me." His hands ran through my hair and he felt my scalp, I assumed to check for lacerations.

"If you had some soap and shampoo, I just might marry you," I said with a laugh. Tex stiffened and I was sorry for saying something so stupid to someone I didn't know. "I was joking," I said.

Tex smiled sadly and then ran his hands along my shoulders and back, and then had me lift my legs to check for bites on either one. "Looks like you're good to go," he said after a moment. He walked over to a cabinet and pulled out a towel, white tee, and drawstring pants that would barely fit me. He grabbed my filthy clothes off of the chair. "I'll be sure you get these back," he promised. "Go ahead and dry off and get dressed," he said, showing his back to me once again.

I dried off and got dressed, wondering if I should push my luck and ask Tex about what was going on in the compound. Would he tell me anything? I wasn't sure, and though he seemed like a decent guy, I still couldn't trust him quite yet.

"You're not old enough to be military, but the way you handled yourself out there..." Tex trailed off and I froze. I was tying the pants around my waist.

Keep to the truth as much as possible, I reminded myself.

"My dad was military. He taught me well," I said after a moment.

Tex nodded his head, accepting that. It was the truth after all.

"And your friend out there?" he asked. My heart sped up. Tex turned to face me, his eyes assessing and searching my face.

"Jude? Jude was army for two years before the outbreak," I answered with a shrug. That was the story we had come up with. It was believable; saying Jude wasn't military at all simply wouldn't fly. He *was* a soldier and anyone would be able to see that. We only had to make them think he had nothing to do with any military anymore. Tex stared at me a moment longer the turned and put a hand on the doorknob.

"What's your name?" he asked with his back to me.

"Melody."

"Let's go, Melody. Hope you're ready for this," he muttered cryptically. I followed Tex back out into the hallway. Jude was there wearing the same nondescript clothing I was, though his pants fit him better than mine did. He strode to my side, his eyes never leaving Tex's.

"You okay?" he asked harshly. I nodded and moved closer to him. Jude turned to face Tex and they squared off, each one sizing each other up, Jude clearly making it known I was off limits and he better not have tried anything. Jude looked ready to rip Tex's head off, but Tex just stood there, his bulk speaking for him, his eyes bored with Jude's show. I put a hand on Jude's arm and squeezed.

"I'm fine, Jude. He didn't hurt me or get out of line," I whispered. His arm stiffened beneath my touch and then his entire body relaxed, but just barely.

"If you're ready now?" Tex drawled. He walked to another door.

Jude reached an arm around my waist and pulled me closer to his side. "We need to talk," he whispered next to my ear and I nodded.

We trailed behind Tex into the compound, walking through a series of corridors with metal, industrial-looking doors until we came up to a large door that Tex had to open with a series of numbers entered into a keypad, much like the smaller underground base we'd come from. The door opened and I was once again bombarded by the beautiful sound of living, breathing humans instead of death gurgles.

We entered on a small metal platform above a large, open room filled with people. A metal staircase led down into the room. The four other men made their way down the stairs and Jude stepped forward, a look of surprise on his face, reflecting my own. There had to be close to a hundred people in this room alone. How many did the compound hold then? Two hundred? More? How many prisoners did they hold and where? My mind spun in twenty different directions. Tex came up close to me and leaned in to whisper a warning near my ear.

"Be careful, Melody. Don't ask too many questions and keep a low profile," he whispered then stepped back. Jude turned around and eyed Tex, who was now a foot away and whistling a little tune.

"Well, how about we get you folks a little food?" Tex drawled. He walked toward the stairs.

We followed him down the stairs, noting how everyone got quiet when we approached. They must not have had many newcomers. Where they were located, I wasn't surprised one little bit. This place took "keep your enemy close" to a whole new level. We followed behind Tex across the room and down a hall to enter another large room, their mess hall. Another thirty people were in the mess hall eating and joking around when we entered, it didn't take me long to realize how few women or children were living in the compound. I probably passed five in the common area, two were eating lunch, and four working in the kitchen area. A short, blading guy wearing glasses came up to our group.

"Germain wants to see you," he said in clipped tones, his eyes barely flicking over to me and Jude. I glanced up at Jude, but he gave nothing away. Tex eyed me before pointing over to the line for food.

"They will take care of you there. I'll be back to show you both around as soon as I can." He nodded at us both then headed back through the door with the little guy trying to keep pace with his long, sure strides.

"Let's grab some food," Jude said without looking at me. I knew without looking up that almost every single eye in the room was on us. Jesus, it felt like high school all over again. A woman who looked to be in her mid-forties handed us a tray and I only *just* kept myself from hugging her. Our trays each had a small pile of white rice with a ladle of piping hot canned beef stew poured on top. There was a fresh mini bread roll and a cookie with it. I smiled widely at the woman and she smiled back, aware of how much such a simple meal could mean to someone.

We sat in the back of the room and I opted to sit in front of Jude instead of next to him, even though that put my back to the exit and almost everyone in the room. Jude looked at me curiously, but didn't remark on it. We dug into our food, grateful for the warmth and the mutual silence. I moaned when I bit into my peanut butter cookie. Jude's eyes met mine and I steeled myself. He was pissed.

"Jude, I—" He held up a hand and I stopped mid-sentence.

His eyes bore into mine, intense and hurt. "You gave up, Mel," he said so low I could barely hear the words. "You were just going to stand there and let those fuckers have you."

My eyes closed and a fist squeezed around my heart. He was right, of course. I *did* give up and I hadn't given a second thought to how that would affect him. I had been selfish.

"I'm so sorry, Jude. I was being a selfish bitch," I whispered thickly. I met his eyes and sat up straighter in my seat. "It won't happen again."

"You better fucking believe it won't," he said angrily.

I reached my hand out tentatively and placed it on top of his. When he didn't jerk his hand back, I gave his a squeeze. "Is that an order, Agent?" I whispered, my eyes wide to keep from crying.

Jude's intense stare took my breath away. "Damn straight, woman."

I rolled my eyes at that and pulled back to finish off my cookie. When I eyeballed Jude's cookie he sighed and broke it in half, offering me the bigger part. I grinned and took it before he changed his mind. He just chuckled and shook his head, muttering something about *females* and *driving him insane*.

"Looks like *Germain* is someone in charge," I said, biting into the cookie.

"Yes, no telling who this guy is or how in the world he could have taken the base," he said with his eyes on his plate. "Look at this place, it had to have been damn near impossible to break into. But to take it over completely?" Jude shook his head and clenched his jaw. "It had to be someone already here, someone they wouldn't suspect." He met my eyes. *A traitor.* Someone dangerous and maybe even unstable.

"We need to find out if there are any prisoners," I said in a whisper.

"They won't trust me, hell, they already hate me." I flinched. He said it so certainly.

"Why do you say that?" I asked, perplexed. "Maybe they'll want to recruit you or something."

Jude smiled, but it wasn't a pleasant one. "I know because I have something almost every man in this place already wants for himself," he said caustically.

My mouth popped open to ask him what in the hell he could possibly have when it struck me with the force of a small hurricane. *Me.* Sweet baby Jesus. I was a hot commodity. I fidgeted in my seat and barely restrained myself from glancing behind me to see if all the eyes I'd felt on my back were still there or not.

"Exactly," he said through gritted teeth. "I didn't think this through well enough." He hand ran over his face and I could tell for the second time that day he was truly worried for my safety.

"Maybe I can use it to our advantage," I said gently. Jude drew back, his eyes going wide. "Not like *that*," I said. Jeepers. "I meant that maybe I could get some information from some of the guys, maybe from Tex." Jude's eyes hardened and his fist tightened on the table. I spoke hurriedly. "It's just that he was respectful in a situation that could've been very bad, Jude. I don't think he'd intentionally hurt anyone, so he might be our best bet."

"Alright, but be careful and if you feel even a little uneasy, just forget it. It isn't worth your life. Nothing is." He waited for my response and breathed a sigh of relief when I nodded my agreement.

We finished our lunch and left the mess hall to go to the common room and walk the halls. An armed guard followed us several steps back though. Jude put a hand on my back and steered me into the common room and over to a small seating area. There was a teen boy, a woman with curly, brown hair—probably in her late twenties, and a small girl with strawberry-blonde hair sitting there. The little girl was playing with a doll on the floor and the teen looked extremely bored. They all eyed us warily when we sat down in their area.

I glanced around the room, taking note of the sixty or so people walking around, playing games, or otherwise entertaining themselves. I also took note of several people who looked a little bit too interested in Jude and me. I stood up and stretched after twenty minutes of inactivity and pointed to a bookshelf across the room when Jude glanced up at me.

"I'll be right back. I'm just going to check out what they have to read," I said with a smile. The bookshelf didn't have much in the way of novels, but it did have the entire Harry Potter series. I picked up the first book and remembered the day my mom had bought me the entire collector's set for Christmas one year. I smiled to myself and thumbed through the first few pages.

"Hey, sweet thang, how 'bout you come over here and play a few games with me and my friends," a guttural voice came from directly behind me and my good memories immediately vanished into a wisp of thin air. I glanced over my shoulder at Jude, who had already risen halfway out of his seat, and shook my head. His eyes flared in anger, but he sat back down. I didn't look at the guy who spoke to me.

"I'd rather not," I said indifferently. A few catcalls and guys laughing at their friend's rebuff made the guy bolder.

"You think you're too good for me or something?" he hissed.

"Not at all," I said with a shrug. "I'm just not interested."

A hand gripped my shoulder and spun me around. The guy pushed me up against the bookshelf with a hand around my throat and brought his face close to mine. "You don't know what you're missing, little girl," he said against my cheek, his foul breath fanning my face. An armed guard came up next to us and put a hand on the man's arm.

"Back off, man, she's off limits," he said, sounding slightly panicked, slightly scared.

I wondered for only a second exactly who he was afraid of, but it was of no consequence. I pushed myself into the guy, catching him off guard when my body crashed flush into his own, knocking him back a step. What he and the guard failed to see soon enough was my hand darting out and snatching the ten inch blade from the guard's leg. By the time either of them had time to react, I had already swept the septic-breathed dude's legs out from under him and rode his body to the ground with the blade pressing directly into the hollow of his throat. The guard let out a surprised gasp and that only made me smile. I pressed the blade into his throat enough to draw a line of blood. He whimpered, his eyes wide. The entire room was deathly silent.

"You don't seem to know how to take *no* for an answer," I hissed down at the guy I was perched on top of. "Guys like you would be behind bars right now, away from the rest of society and such. But things are pretty fucked up right now, so worthless pieces of shit like you think you're above the law, huh?" I pressed my knife down a little more. The guy didn't dare breathe too deeply. "Maybe I should drive this into your throat right now. I'm sure it would go in as easily as it does one of the hundreds of undead I've taken out. Maybe easier." I smiled, letting the jerk see in my eyes that I meant exactly what I said. "I'd be doing what's left of society a favor," I said, pretending to mull it over.

"Melody, don't." It was Tex. I didn't look up or acknowledge him. I leaned down and brought my mouth up close to the guy's ear to whisper. "I swear to God and on all that is holy, if I ever hear of you hurting someone, or even looking sideways at some helpless woman or girl, I will fucking find you and cut your throat without even blinking. You understand me?" When he squeaked a very tiny "yes" as an answer I snatched the knife from his throat and removed myself from his prone body in one smooth movement. I held the knife out to the guard and turned to face Tex. Jude was standing there too, like a large storm cloud about ready to rain down a torrent of booming lightning.

"So much for keeping a low profile," Tex muttered with a sigh. "Follow me. Germain wants to see you both."

Tex strode off, leaving Jude and I scrambling to keep up. So much for stealth. It looked like we were going to be led straight to Germain himself. Time to meet the man who overthrew the secret Charlotte Army base.

The layout of the base was much like the one close to Midtown, but it was a lot larger and a bit more complicated with extra corridors and blocked off spaces. Too much for me to memorize as we strode briskly by.

"So, this Germain, he some kind of leader or something here?" I asked Tex nonchalantly.

He laughed loudly and turned to wink at me. "Something like that," he answered without really answering.

I turned and caught Jude looking at me; his expression matched my own. What on earth was going on around here? We stopped in front of a door that had a guard posted outside of it. When we approached the guard moved to the side for Tex and the rest of us to pass through. Tex was important. Good to know.

We entered a large room that looked like a meeting room with a huge table in its center. At the head of the table there sat a man with a shaved head and a goatee who watched us enter with hooded eyes. I could tell immediately he was someone in charge, someone who commanded authority. I did a quick search around the table and room. There were five other people in the room seated and standing close to the man sitting at the head of the table. Four men and one young woman. I didn't pay them much mind, I wanted to find out about Germain.

"Melody Carter," the man intoned from where he sat. I raised my chin and met his steely, blue gaze. "What are you and this Army man, Jude, doing here in Charlotte?" he asked, getting straight to the point.

"I have family and friends in Charlotte," I said truthfully. I *did* have friends in Charlotte a long time ago. "I needed to see if anyone was left, if we could find any of them."

"Why wait so long?" he asked. "Why wait two years after the outbreak if you were so concerned?"

"I lived by myself in the woods for almost two years before I met Jude." I motioned toward Jude and he put an arm across my shoulders. "I didn't think I could do it by myself. With him, I thought maybe I would have a chance. But the city was worse than I ever imagined."

A chuckle came from the young woman standing close to Germain.

Jude's arm tightened on my shoulder. Something niggled the back of my mind, something I should have noticed earlier. I sucked in a breath.

"How did you know my last name?" I snapped. Jude's entire body became rigid beside me. "I only told Tex my first name, but you called me by my last name as well." I narrowed my eyes at the man whose face hadn't shown a single ounce of emotion or surprise.

"Ah, Mel, you always were a smart one." The feminine voice rang out clearly through the room from the young woman, who now moved directly behind the man I'd been speaking with. She placed a hand on the back of his chair. "Do you know who I am?" she asked with a smile that didn't reach her eyes. "Surely, I've not changed so much that you wouldn't recognize your best friend," she said with a wicked gleam in her eye.

"Oh my God! Jess?" The room spun slightly. Jude put his arm around my waist to keep me upright. I stared with undisguised shock. It *was* her. Her long, straight blonde hair had been chopped short and spiked up on the top of her head and she had several ear piercings. Her arms were more muscular and her face was hard. She had traded in her pink designer clothing and heels for a black button up shirt and black leather pants. She'd changed so much that I could barely see the old Jess at all in the young woman standing before me.

Then my mind caught up with everything. *Germain*. Germain wasn't a first name, it was a last name. Jessica Germain. *Jesus, Mary, and Joseph*. Jessica was the leader of an underground militia.

My laughter, bordering on hysteria, echoed throughout the room. Jude and Tex glanced at each other and then at me, clearly at a loss. I laughed so hard I cried. I laughed until my sides cramped.

What has the world fucking come to?

If You Don't Know Me by Now

Jessica's eyes bore into mine, her jaw clenched, and it appeared by sheer will alone that she didn't launch herself across the room to choke the life out of me. My shock wore off halfway through my bout of hysteria and then the numbness and betrayal set in. Still, Jessica didn't necessarily know that we had come to Charlotte to seek out the leader of the underground militia. I could still hope that she had been forced into the role she was playing.

"I never thought I'd see you again," I said into the oppressive silence as I met her gaze. Her eyes were cold and calculating and I struggled to find the smallest indication that the girl I once knew was still there somewhere.

"I'm sure you didn't," she answered with a smile that exposed all her teeth. "I, however, figured *you* would still be alive." "Did you?" I asked interestedly.

"Of course I did. You were a better shot than any soldier when you were sixteen. You *thrived* on all the stuff your dad taught you." I flinched at the mention of my dad. Her mouth settled into a straight line. "He's dead then?" I nodded, a quick, jerky movement. She shrugged. "What did the fucking Army do for any of them in the end?" she spat. I could feel her hate in that moment. It radiated from her, her body nearly vibrating with the force of it.

"Not a whole of anything," I agreed. Her eyes met mine and she seemed to be searching for something there. "Your family?" I gently inquired. A flicker of pain was blinked away and replaced with rage. A white-hot rage so intense and all-consuming that it terrified me.

"My entire family is dead." Her words cut through the room, her voice like a whip. Her dad, a retired Army officer like my dad, her mom, and her six year old little brother Jeremiah, all dead.

I swallowed back tears and gulped. "I'm sorry, Jess," I said gently.

"Don't be," she snapped. "You're not the one to blame. And I go by *Germain* now." She shook her head once and flapped a hand dismissively through the air in front of her. "It was a long time ago now anyway." She stepped right in front of me and Jude as she spoke, but her eyes were fastened on Jude. "Why are you here, Melody?" she asked.

I stiffened. "Like I said—"

"And don't give me any of that *I had family and friends I was so worried about* bullshit you were trying to feed us earlier either," she snapped.

I shrugged, trying to think quickly on my feet. Jessica had always been intuitive and very smart. I couldn't pull off much of a lie without her sniffing it out. So I didn't over think it, instead I went with my gut.

"Jude and I ran across a guy—half dead—that kept mumbling about a base in Charlotte beneath a toy factory. He kept repeating over and over... *Need help. Soldiers need help.*" Jessica's eyes narrowed as I went on, pretending not to notice. "We figured the base might have been overrun by zombies, that maybe people, probably soldiers, were trapped down here, so we decided to come and see if we could be of any help." I glanced around the room. "We were obviously not needed. You're all doing fine here."

"Yes we are, aren't we?" she murmured, her eyes searching my face.

"Where are all the soldiers? Who's in charge?" I asked innocently. I watched her face carefully. She gave nothing away.

"Most are dead. Some are here in another part of the base." She walked back to the head of the table and stood beside the man seated there. "And to answer your other question, Jim here is in charge." I met the icy stare of the dark-skinned man seated there and shivered slightly. His gaze was *unsettling*. But there was something in the way Jessica held herself, the way she dismissed him a little too easily. Ole dead-eye-Jim might have been the original leader of this little group of usurpers, but I was very sure that the person who now ran things from her shotgun spot next to Jim was Jessica Germain.

"So, what happens next?" I asked. "Now that we know the base isn't overrun and that everything is fine here?" I looked at Jessica, but it was Jim who spoke this time. Evidently Jessica was done talking.

"What would you like to happen?" he asked as if we were having a normal social visit between friends. I glanced over at Jude and his eyes looked a little less confused than they had before. Things were starting to click into place for him.

"We'd like to stay on for a little while, if that's okay. We've been traveling and fighting zombies for a while and could use a few days to recover before we move on." Jude placed a hand on the back of my neck and squeezed. I smiled at him and nodded. He'd interjected just the right amount of *asking permission* and *exhaustion* into his question to sound believable. "That is if you wouldn't mind two more mouths to feed for that long."

"We'd be glad to pull our weight while we're here," I added.

Jessica and Jim both stared at us for a moment, making my insides all jittery.

"We'd be glad to have you for a few days," Jim said finally. "You might even think about staying on permanently after you've seen how things are here," he added with a small smile. His eyes, however, matched neither his words nor his smile. Jude's hand tensed behind my neck and we both smiled back pleasantly.

"We appreciate the invitation and the hospitality," Jude said through his forced smile.

Jim nodded graciously and then motioned toward Tex. "Show them to a room. We'll all talk again tomorrow at the *assembly*," he said, his eyes shining and his mouth turned up in the first true smile we'd seen. It was... *disturbing*.

Effectively dismissed, we followed Tex back through the door and out into an empty hallway. None of us said a single thing while we walked through the compound. My mind was still trying to catch up to the day's events and my body was plain tired. Tex opened a door and motioned for us to enter. The next thing I knew Jude was standing in front of me and pulling me into his arms. I stiffened at first and glanced toward the door. Tex was already gone and the door was closed. How long had I zoned out? I relaxed and leaned into Jude, allowing myself the comfort of his arms.

"I don't understand. She's not the same person I knew. She's cold and calculating. I don't know her anymore," I whispered against his chest.

"The last two years have changed people, Mel, and not for the better."

I knew what he said was true, but could the last two years have wiped out everything I knew of Jessica? Could she have changed so very much that I wouldn't be able to get through to her or be able to reason with her? I was going to find out one way or another. I was sure of that at least.

"That Jim guy creeped me out. Something about him just isn't right and they both are hiding things," Jude said.

I nodded in agreement. Something was definitely going on here besides the obvious.

"We need to find out where she's holding the soldiers or if they are even still alive," Jude said.

Could Jessica have killed them all or kept them prisoner? Why would she do such a thing? They probably could have just stayed as guests with the soldiers in charge. So why the power move? It didn't make sense unless Jim had her brainwashed. Maybe he had taken advantage of her emotional state and used her to take over the compound. I shook my head. So many questions and no answers.

"This is all kinds of fucked up," I murmured.

"Yes it is and I, for one, am hoping to learn something at this *assembly* of theirs tomorrow." He pulled me toward the full sized cot. "For now we need to get some rest. You're dead on your feet and I'm not much better."

I had no idea how he thought I'd be able to actually sleep with everything scrambling my mind, but I guessed it wouldn't hurt to stretch out for a bit. I groaned and sat down on the bed. I hadn't realized how bad my arms and legs were hurting from our day's activities. We both kicked our shoes off and without the tiniest bit of hesitation, Jude crawled into the bed and I spread out next to him. I fell asleep almost immediately.

No Paddles Available

I awoke in a panic, my mind fuzzy, and in unfamiliar surroundings, trying to remember where I was and what had happened the previous day. Once everything came back to me in all its awesomeness, I instantly wished I could simply forget it all again, just erase everything from my overflowing reserve of horrific memories. I couldn't though, not yet. I needed to find out what was going on at the base and I was still clinging to a faint hope that things weren't what they appeared when it came to Jessica. No matter how bad it appeared, she had been my best friend and until proven otherwise, I was going to give her the benefit of the doubt. I had to believe she wasn't responsible, that she was in over her head and I could somehow talk some sense into her.

The bed beside me was empty. I made myself as presentable as possible, which meant throwing my hair back in a ponytail and scrubbing my face, before heading out the door to find Jude to see what he might have found out. Unfortunately, the previous night was a blur in my mind after learning that Jessica was still alive, making my memories of walking to our room unreliable at best. A few minutes later and I'd become utterly turned around.

I came around a corner and spotted a door that I didn't remember seeing the day before. From the looks of the locks on the outside, only people with special access could get through it, unless shooting the locks off or a using a small, handy-dandy bomb was an option. It wasn't. I knew immediately that I wanted to get inside that room. I glanced around the corner from where I stood and took a deep breath to run across the hall and get a closer look at the impenetrable door. When I moved away from the wall, a large hand covered my mouth and an arm grabbed me about the middle, pulling me back against a body. I was yanked backwards and even though I tried to put up a fight, I knew it was useless. The arms about me were thick and muscular and all I could do was fight the panic rising up to choke me as I was pulled back into a dark room, my captor never loosening his grip or his determination. Still, I wiggled and bucked, trying to get free.

"Damn, woman, take a second and chill the hell out." My entire body froze when I recognized the familiar southern twang. *Tex*. "Relax, I'm going to take my hand off your mouth. I'm not going to hurt you. I just need to talk to you," he said. "You understand?" I nodded and he slowly removed his hand from my mouth.

"You can let go of me now, asshole," I snarled.

"If you insist, sweetheart," he said with a small chuckle. He stepped back and released me. I spun around and found I could barely make out his features in the dark room.

"If this is the only way you can get a chick to talk to you, you have issues, Tex," I said, my hands on my hips. "Scaring the crap out of a woman will not likely get you on their sweet side," I snapped. I couldn't see his face clearly, but I could feel his gaze on me, his carefree, laughing demeanor gone. I didn't need to see him well to know he was serious and staring at me intently, his eyes probably sharper than mine and searching my face as I stood toe-to-toe with him in the tiny, dark room. I swallowed in the darkness, feeling my heart rate pick up. Tension made breathing in the small space almost impossible.

"If I wanted on your sweet side, you would know it, Melody," he said gruffly. His hand came up and gently caressed the side of my face. For some reason unknown to me, I allowed it. "I don't normally have to kidnap women to get their attention." I smiled at that. No doubt Tex would normally have women lined up at his door. He was handsome in a good-ole-boy sort of way and all that southern charm would be an extra bonus in his favor. No, I seriously doubted Tex ever had any problems in the love and sex department.

"What do you need to talk to me about then, that I rate a kidnapping?" I asked with a smirk. A single word wiped the smile of my face.

"Germain," he answered.

"What about her?"

"I know she was once your friend. You need to understand that *that time* might as well have been a different lifetime. Even another dimension." I shook my head, closing my eyes and bowing my head. I didn't want to hear this. "She's done things..." He stopped and cleared his throat. "She's killed soldiers, had people killed, even had people thrown out into the city for whatever reason. Let go right out in the middle of all the undead without even a knife."

Why? I didn't understand it. *Why*? We had all lost loved ones, been through things humans should never have to endure. Why had it changed *her* so much?

"I don't understand what happened to her. You never knew her from before. If you had, you would understand why I can't believe that she is responsible for all this. Her daddy was military just like mine." I put a hand over my chest and pressed lightly over the pain radiating from my heart.

Tex put a hand on my shoulder. "I knew Jessica's dad," he said so softly I didn't think I'd heard him correctly.

"How?" "I was in my third year in the Army and had just moved to the base when the outbreak happened. I'd met and worked with Sgt. Germain several times the week before. When the crap hit the fan, I happened to be on base working."

A chill worked its way up my spine, making me shiver slightly. Tex's voice came out monotone, his way of telling the story while trying to stay removed from the emotion of it all. Another chill swept my body and Tex absentmindedly rubbed his hand up and down my arm to soothe himself as he spoke.

"I had no way to get to my wife. She called me and said she was holed up with her parents, but I knew deep down they wouldn't be safe there. I tried, God knows I did, but it was impossible. It wasn't until much later that I was able to get to their place." His voice shook slightly. "It was much too late then. The Germains were also off base at the time. Everything was in chaos here and all around the globe. Cities were trying to evacuate, only clogging all the exits out of the city and making it impossible for survivors to get free. There was no real protocol with how to deal with an outbreak on that scale. No protocol except one: Don't let anyone in; don't let anyone out, not even military."

I sucked in a breath through my teeth. *No one in and no one out.* Dear God.

"The Germains, like a lot of other military families, did what they thought was best. They headed toward their base and expected to be allowed sanctuary for their family. They were, after all, military. Instead, they found locked gates and changed passcodes." My head buzzed and my eyelids fluttered shut as he spoke, his hand still stroking my arm in a gentle motion. "Jessica blames the military for the death of her entire family. If they had been let through, if they had allowed them in, they would probably still be alive today. Instead, she had to not only watch her family die at the hands of the undead, but she also had to take down her own little brother and survive out in the infested and overrun city for over a year by herself."

I gasped. Now I could see it. Jessica had so much hurt, so much loss, and so much *blame*. Now it all had come to a head. A head of pure, undiluted rage. She was a ticking time bomb. She was dangerous.

"How do you know all that about Jessica?" I asked wearily.

"About six months ago we had heard through some of our scouts that there was a group out in the city that was planning a takeover, planning to try and take the base here. We didn't really believe it was possible, of course. We're well fortified and you've seen what it is like outside of the fences. Even if a group made it past the horde of zombies, we'd have seen them coming a mile away." I nodded. That's what I didn't understand. How had it been possible for any sized group to take over the base? "My commanding officer sent me to see what I could find out."

I gasped. They sent him out into the city? I could feel Tex's smile more than see it.

"Don't worry, sweetheart, I'm good at scouting, even in the middle of hordes of zombies. Anyway, I found my way into Jessica's little ragtag group. At that time, they only had about twenty-five people and I was quick to dismiss Jim and his followers as not having a chance in hell at taking the base. I was about to make my way back when I spotted Jessica coming back from a supply run. She looked so different, but I immediately recognized her. I spoke to her often over the next few weeks and when I thought I could trust her, I asked her to come back to the base with me." He shook his head and ran a hand through his hair, sighing deeply. "I guess I just thought maybe if I could save her, then I could let go of some of the guilt for failing everyone else. You know? *Just a little.* Instead of helping an innocent young woman, I ended up bringing the leader of the group right into the middle of the base. I didn't suspect her, no one did. Not until it was too late and she had snuck her entire group into the base and took it over in the middle of the night."

"Why are you telling me all this?"

"I wasn't born yesterday, Melody. I know you and Jude ain't here because you heard some dying soldier mumble vaguely about the base needing help." When I opened my mouth to protest, Tex cut me off. "And if *I* know something sounds hinky with your story, then you bet your sweet little ass that Jessica Germain suspects something ain't quite right." My mouth snapped shut and I took a step back, weighing my options. I really didn't *have* any options. I was going to have to trust Tex.

"Shit," I muttered beneath my breath.

"Shit creek. No paddle," Tex agreed.

"If you're really so trustworthy, tell me how many people she has here against their will and where she's keeping them." I took a deep breath and waited, hoping I hadn't grossly misread Tex.

"By my count, she has around twenty soldiers held prisoner," Tex answered after a moment. I breathed out a nervous breath. "However, freeing them from the place she has them is impossible. She has them guarded by several armed men twenty-four hours a day," he said. "Don't you think I've tried to get into the holding cells? That I would do everything in my power to set them free if I could?" He ran a hand through his hair roughly. "She doesn't truly trust anyone. I've spent the past several months trying to convince her that I'm on her team, that she can trust me. She will never trust me though. I'm military after all."

I placed a hand on his arm and squeezed gently. "You couldn't have known what she was planning, Tex," I said gently. "You aren't the only one who was fooled by her. Any other soldier would have done exactly what you did. She is at fault, not you."

He put a hand over mine and stood still for a moment, our breathing the only sound in the tiny room. "Thank you, Melody. I wish I could believe that."

"So what am I going to do to get these people free?" I whispered.

Tex chuckled. "You don't give up, do you?" he asked wryly.

"Not if I can help it," I answered with a grin.

"I've heard that Jim and Germain have something *special* in store for you and Jude later today at the assembly." A shiver ran down my spine. Tex rubbed the back of his neck and mumbled something beneath his breath. "You and your boy toy are going to have a very small window of time to get to the prisoners and then get out of the base. I have no idea how y'all will be able to survive once you're out of the base, but with a big enough diversion I can at least get you something of a head start. That's the best I can do." My mouth popped open to ask the hundred and one questions swirling around in my mind when I heard Tex mumbling beneath his breath once again. "Aww, the hell with it, I probably won't live past today anyway," he growled.

His arms came around me and crushed me to his chest as his hand cupped my neck and angled my head back to gain access to my lips. And man, oh, man did he ever gain access. My head spun from his assault on my mouth. I should have pushed him away. He would have stopped and I *knew* he would. But I couldn't think through the sweet, thick, haze of euphoria that I was hopelessly lost in. About the time I came to my senses, he pulled back and stepped away from me. I raised my eyes to Tex's.

"Tex, I—"

He held up a hand and brushed a wayward strand of my hair out of my eyes. "Don't. I had to. Life is too fragile—too short—nowadays to live with regret. And if I die today, I'll die without any after that kiss." I gulped, breathless and unable to articulate any response. I mean, what does a girl say to something like that? "I'll do what I can for you, so keep your eyes and ears ready for my distraction." He put a hand on the door handle.

"Wait. How am I supposed to know what your distraction is?" I asked.

He opened the door a crack and glanced back at me over his

shoulder. A smile spread across his face and he winked at me. "Oh, you'll know it when you see it, sweetheart," he said and went through the door, closing it behind him.

I waited several minutes after he left, trying to calm my heartbeat and my nerves before exiting the small supply closet. It wasn't until I was back out in the hallway that I remembered that I was lost.

"Damn," I muttered as I took off down a halfway familiar looking hallway.

Plan? What Plan?

Several strings of curse words later, I found myself back in the common area of the base, the place quite abandoned compared to the day before. A few people loitered here and there, but mostly it was empty. I was standing in the doorway, trying to decide where I should go and what I should do when Jude came striding down the opposite corridor with a murderous look on his face. Two of the six people in the common area saw him coming and scooted out of his way, sensing his mood well before he even got close to them. I didn't blame them; he looked capable of mass murder in that moment. When he finally noticed me standing across the room, his body visibly unwound just enough to allow the entire room to take a much needed breath of relief.

"What's up?" I asked.

"I'm feeling really twitchy. The guards here won't give me any of my weapons. Not even a knife." His eyes met mine and I could see that his pupils were slightly dilated. I nodded in understanding. I kept finding myself reaching for the hilt of my knife and it was a horrible feeling to be without any means of self-defense after living and fighting for your life every day for over two years. Yeah, I knew exactly how he felt. "I don't care how secure this base is, I want to be able to defend myself if necessary," he said. I reached out and put a hand on his arm. His eyes found mine again and his shoulders relaxed another fraction.

"We need to talk," I said, discreetly glancing around the room.

He nodded and led me off to another hallway. "Let's go grab a bagged lunch and talk back in the room," he suggested.

We got the lunches and left the mess hall as quickly as we entered it, both of us deep in our own thoughts. I was also in awe of how easily Jude had already memorized the layout of the base. It was completely unfair. I sat on the bed while Jude sat on the floor with his back against a wall in our room and polished off our light meals.

"So, what have you found out?" I asked around a mouthful of peanuts.

"You want the bad news or the worst news first?" he asked, taking a swig of water.

"Give me the bad," I answered with a frown.

"Well, it looks like however many soldiers are left, they are kept literally under lock and key twenty-four hours a day. Add to that several guards and it would be next to impossible to free them," he sighed in exasperation. His eyes met mine and I nodded. "You knew that much?" he asked, a bit surprised.

"I did. And there are maybe twenty soldiers left now."

Jude whistled. "Even if we were able to free them, we don't know what kind of shape they're in or how in the world we would be able to get them through the zombie hordes outside. If we made it that far."

I grimaced. It sounded even worse once I thought it through for the fifth time.

"If that's the bad news, what's the worst?" I asked.

"Jim and Jessica have something in store for us this afternoon, something we should probably worry about since it takes place during this *assembly* of theirs. At least, that's what my source said." His jaw clenched and then he glanced up at me. "Holy shit. You knew that too," he said in outrage.

I shrugged. "I'd heard something like that," I answered. "I also heard that they are probably onto us and don't plan on letting us get out of here in one piece. And in addition to that, Jessica Germain is more monster than human now, and she was the one who slipped into the base with only the intent to let her group in while everyone was asleep, that she hates anyone and everything military, and that she gets off on banishing people weaponless into the zombie infested city streets when they cross her." I took a deep breath and let my head fall back on the wall behind me.

What was the point of surviving if you lose your humanity in the process? What did everything matter if we only let ourselves turn into a different breed of monster?

"What do you plan on doing, then?" Jude asked gently. "About Germain, I mean? I know you two were close not so very long ago."

God, could it have been only a little less than three years ago that we were both in high school and giggling over hot guys and the shallowness of half the senior class girls? It felt like a lifetime ago. It felt like someone else's life. I didn't know this version of Jessica. She was a stranger to me in this new world surrounded by the dead and dying.

"I'll do what I have to do," I said after a moment. I sat up straighter and caught Jude's eye. "I'm going to kill Jessica Germain."

Jude's eyes searched mine and his mouth set into a grim line. "I hope it doesn't come to that, Mel."

"I hope it doesn't either."

"So what's the plan?" he asked, and when I looked at him curiously, he asked, "What?" with a crooked grin. "You know more than I do."

I smiled, despite myself. "Well, I'm not really sure. We are supposed to have some help," I said.

The smile disappeared from Jude's face instantly. "Help," he stated. Not really a question.

I swallowed and pushed ahead, blurting out most of what happened with Tex, but leaving out a few little details of a certain toe-curling kiss that probably should never have happened.

"So, yeah, help." I let out a long breath after my tale while Jude digested everything I'd told him.

"So we're not only supposed to trust him, but also just wait for his signal, his big distraction." His words dripped with sarcasm. I opened my mouth, but he was quick to cut me off. "Oh! Don't let me forget, we also have *no idea* what this distraction is supposed to be or if it will even work. *That* is our plan?" His eyes cut into mine, asking me if I heard what I'd just said.

I admit, it sounded lame, but what choice did we have?

"It's the *only* plan, Jude. What else can we do?" I asked. "Do you have any other ideas?"

His jaw clenched and he stood, striding back and forth in the room, running a hand through his hair in frustration.

"I don't. But surely we could come up with something. Anything. The guy probably just wants to get in your pants."

I gasped and bounded off the bed to stand directly in front of him. "That was uncalled for, Jude," I snapped.

Jude's gaze pierced me, searching my face. His eyes widened and his mouth settled into a straight line. "The son of a bitch made a move on you," he gritted out.

My face flamed, but I shook my head. "That has nothing to do with me trusting him or the fact that this is the only course of action we can take," I said calmly.

"The hell it doesn't. It's pretty hard to mistrust a guy who has his tongue in your mouth and his hand down your panties," Jude said in disgust.

I don't remember actually making a decision to get pissed off, but I guess my hand made it for me. The sound of my palm striking Jude across the cheek echoed in the room and jerked his head to the side. We both stood there with barely a foot of space between us, our chests heaving. My palm was stinging and I imagined Jude's cheek was smarting like a bitch. And just like that, the wind left my sails in one strong *whoosh*.

"I'm sorry, I shouldn't have—" My words were cut off, my breath robbed from me as Jude gathered me into his arms and hugged me to him so forcefully that I thought my back might crack. His face and nose were buried into the sensitive area between my neck and shoulder and his hands roamed my back, trying to pull me closer, as if to absorb me into himself.

"God. You slay me, Melody Carter," he murmured against my neck. The last bit of fight melted out of me and I buried a hand into the back of his shirt and held onto him as tightly as possible. "You've completely invaded me, Mel," he said gruffly. I pulled him gently until we were next to the bed.

"Lie down with me, Jude," I whispered. We laid in each other's arms for a while, my head on his chest, before I was able to speak past the lump in my throat. "I'm going to make love to you, Jude." He stiffened. "Not right now, not here," I said conversationally. "But once we get out of here, alive and well, I'm going to make love to you because I want to. I want you to be the first and last guy I sleep with in this new world, in this new life. The only guy who means enough to me that I would put my heart and my life on the line for."

Jude understood what I was saying. He understood what it meant to open yourself up to the possibility of love and living when everything could be ripped away from you at any moment. He knew it meant that I was in love with him and he let me know that he felt the same with a kiss that couldn't have been mistaken for anything other than an "I love you too" in *any* world.

It's All so Fucking Hysterical

We were up and following behind a guard who was toting an automatic rifle after a hard knock on our door a few hours later. Jude and I glanced at each other uneasily. There really was no telling what we were getting ourselves into. I could only hope and pray that whatever Tex had up his sleeve would be good enough to give us an edge for what was in store for us. When we passed through empty hallways and an equally empty rec room, I felt a stab of apprehension in the back of my skull. Where was everyone? What was worse was that we climbed the stairs that had led us into the base the first day, the ones that led back out into the toy factory and then out into the open city. Surely we weren't just going to be tossed out into the zombie fray? By the time we entered the toy factory, my uneasiness had tripled and I wondered if I should make a move to take the guard down. I glanced over at Jude and he shook his head once. *No.*

It took me a moment to realize that we were headed to the very back of the factory instead of the way we had entered. I didn't see what we were headed into, but I could *hear* something. When we went through the double doors in the back of the factory it took me a full minute to really grasp what I was seeing through the blinding sunlight, to understand what it was I was hearing. Jude sucked in a breath next to me and it was only his presence that made me feel grounded, like I wasn't dreaming or imagining the awfulness that was reality.

The scene in front of me made no sense, but then again, neither did a world chockfull of the living dead. We had walked out into what appeared to be a fenced-in shipping and receiving area for the abandoned toy factory. All of the semi-trucks had been arranged around in a circle, bumper to bumper, and on top of the trailers there sat tons and tons of people. They were screaming and cheering. I took a step out of the opening that I was standing in and realized they had lined the trucks up out of the shipping area in such a way that people could walk out of the factory and up a ramp, straight to the tops of the trucks. The guard that had led us out of the base nudged me and I took another step forward with Jude right beside me. When I reached the top of the first truck, I stopped, feeling dizzy from the view before me. Two semis divided the circle in half, parked with the back bumper of each one touching one another to make a bridge of sorts across the circle. Swarming the middle of the two half circles below us were no less than a hundred zombies. I immediately stepped away from the edge, my hand going to place that my knife should have been.

"What the fuck?" Jude hissed.

I glanced across the circle and spotted barbed wire poking out from under each truck. Large, wooden pikes pointed straight out toward the arena of undead to keep them corralled within the circle of semis. These people thought that made them safe, they thought they were in control of the situation. A small bubble of laughter worked its way past my lips.

"Finding something funny again, Mel?" Jessica's voice threw a bucket of ice-cold realization in my face as I turned to face her.

"Well, it kind of tickles me to think of all the arrogance the person who built this must be burdened to walk around with on a daily basis." I shrugged. "Yeah, I find that funny." I didn't see her hand whip out, but when I turned back to meet the hatred in her eyes, I wiped the blood away from the corner of my mouth and smiled. "Oh, that wasn't *you*, was it?" I asked, my eyes wide in mock horror. The second openhanded slap was well worth the look on her face. Besides, she still hit like a girl. I barely bit back another laugh. I didn't want to goad her into pushing me over the side of the bus too early in her day's planned festivities.

"What is all of this?" I asked, motioning towards the screaming and cheering people and down to the gurgling, moaning zombies right below us. Her smile told me everything I already knew, but didn't want to believe.

"This is just a little entertainment that I've prepared for our *guests*," she said loudly. Everyone nearby cheered at her words. The blood in my veins chilled.

"Let's go." The guard behind me gave me a shove and it took every ounce of self-control I possessed not to turn around and smash his nose into his skull. When we reached the center of the circle where the semis formed a bridge, Jessica and Jim were given folding chairs to sit on. Someone else set a third chair in between the two of them. "Come and sit by me," she purred from her throne.

I glanced over at Jude and then back at the chair. Jessica laughed loudly and then motioned for me to take the seat. Jude nodded at me. I took the seat in between *Tweedledee* and *Tweedledum*. When I sat down, I saw several more armed men headed our way. They also had a familiar face with them, the man who I'd threatened with a knife the day before. *What the hell?*

"We've been having troubles with Hosea here for a while now. After your little altercation yesterday, I decided to make an example of him and have him *punished.*" I narrowed my eyes and waited for the other shoe to fall. Jessica smiled when she spoke the next words. "I've decided to let Jude do the honors." She nodded over at Jude as if she were bestowing some great honor upon him. "A fight to the death," she finished.

I jumped to my feet only to find myself with Jim's hand around my throat and his knife biting into my jugular. He made a clucking sound of disappointment. It took three men to hold Jude back and even then they had a hard time.

"Stop fighting, or I will cut her throat," Jim spat. He dug his knife into my throat to make his point and I hissed at the sharp pain. Jude immediately stilled. Jessica laughed again. She stood up and walked over to Jude to run a hand up and down his chest. I stiffened, feeling an unreasonable amount of rage rush through my body.

"Ah, so that wasn't all a show, you *do* have a thing going on with Melody," she said gleefully. "That makes this so much more fun."

My hands balled into a fist at my sides and Jude mirrored the action. I almost smiled.

"You will fight or she will die, either by my hand or by the undead ripping her to pieces," Jim said against my temple and then placed a small lick there. Jude strained forward before catching himself. I shuddered.

"I'll fight," Jude said. His body was calm, but his eyes... his eyes were another story. Jessica nodded to the men holding Jude. They led him to the edge of the bus and one of them jumped down to the hood of the first semi. One of the guards shoved Hosea and he scrambled not to fall off of the top of the truck and into the nest of hungry zombies below. I closed my eyes when Jude was similarly shoved. He landed easily on the hood of the truck and then followed behind Hosea as he made his way to the top of the two truck trailers. One of the guards took Hosea all the way to the end of the second trailer and then handed him a knife before jumping down to the hood of the truck at the other side of the circle. Jude was also given a knife and left alone at his end of the trailer.

I stood at the edge of the arena, looking out at the two men, each grasping a knife, each standing on the roof of their truck trailer. Then, a shot landed near Jude's feet, a warning that he could be shot at any time if he chose not to play their little game. Jude glanced back at me for one second, but seeing me at the edge of the truck's roof with Jim's arm around my neck and the zombies below thrashing wildly to get at us was enough. Jude ran.

And my heart stopped.

Jude and Hosea met each other in the middle, both swinging their knives and trying to avoid the slashing of their opponent's steel. Jude ducked as Hosea slashed out high, aiming for his face. Hosea's leg caught Jude behind the knees and Jude rolled close enough to the edge of the trailer to cause the undead to writhe and moan at the promise of a fresh meal. I bucked against the restraints of Jim's arms, only to realize how close we were to the edge of the pit. If I did pull myself free, I would likely end up plummeting off of the trailer and right into the welcoming hands of dozens and dozens of zombies.

"Looks like Jude underestimated his opponent," Jessica said with her eyes still on the fight. "That's *so* like a soldier," she spat.

I turned my eyes back to the fight going on just in time to see Hosea's blade slice across Jude's stomach. I cried out while Jessica stood there and smiled.

"Why are you doing this? What happened to the girl I used to know?" I asked.

Jude stumbled to the side and drove Hosea back several feet.

"The girl you knew is dead," she said calmly. "The army made sure of that."

I shook my head, unable to take that for the truth. "You may wish the girl you once were was dead, but I know better. She's there somewhere, hiding in the recesses of your conscience. This person you've become isn't you, Jess," I said, my voice pleading, begging for her to acknowledge the truth. She turned her face to me and I shrunk back from the force of her gaze.

"Jessica is dead. Germain *is* who I am now." Her voice whipped across my skin, raising goose bumps along my arms.

I opened my mouth to argue, but the crowds cheered loudly, drawing my attention back to Jude. He was blocking Hosea's attack. Just as Hosea plunged forward, Jude moved to the side at the last second and pulled his knife across Hosea's stomach. Blood blossomed on Hosea's white shirt and he stumbled, lost his footing, and teetered over the edge of the trailer. It all happened so fast and yet it seemed like it all happened in slow motion at the same time. Jude leapt forward, reaching for Hosea, grabbing for his arm with his blood-covered hand, only to have Hosea's hand slip right through his as he plunged into the middle of the zombie mosh pit. The crowd held its breath for an extra-long second before they once again erupted into applause, cheers, and whoops of delight.

"Well now, that's a bit of a surprise," Jim said. "Hosea was one of our best knife fighters."

I shook my head, trying to clear the buzzing there. Jude was heading back across the tops of the semis, his eyes on me and Jim with a look of such calm and clarity that it was a hundred times more terrifying than his rage. When he reached the end of the semi, a guard was there waiting for Jude to hand over his knife. His eyes met mine, his hand clenched around the hilt of the knife. The guard visibly stiffened and raised his gun, and Jude threw the knife at the guard's feet with a sneer.

"That was a bit anticlimactic," Jessica said when Jude joined us. "I guess it's a good thing I have more fun planned for you both now isn't it?" Jessica took her seat once again and then nodded to a soldier still on the hood of the semi that Jude had just fought on. He ran across the bridge and continued back toward the shipping and receiving terminal until I lost sight of him. "Now that we've seen what Uncle Sam's finest can do, let's see what the offspring of Uncle Sam's finest can handle." Jessica smiled over at me, her eyes narrowed and pleased with herself.

Jude shouted out and only a gun to my head stopped him from morphing Hulk-style and kicking someone's face in. Jim gave me a slimy kiss at my temple before pushing me forward into the waiting arms of another armed guard.

I was prepared for the push when it came, but landing on a metal roof without sliding right off the side was not as easy as it looked, even with well-tread combat boots on. Still, the moaning and gurgling of a mob of undead was motivation enough for me to keep my wits about me. I found my footing and climbed to the trailer of the semi. The guard behind me tossed me the knife that Jude had finished with, the blood still fresh on the blade. I picked it up, wiping it off on my pants. Despite the situation, a sense of calm and rightness descended upon me. I smiled at the guard. His eyes widened fractionally and his hand tightened around the gun he carried. He *should* have been worried. I was pissed and I was feeling quite ready to tear someone apart with my bare hands. He had handed me my weapon of choice, and I knew how to use it—very, very well.

Movement out of my peripheral vision alerted me to the newest surprise that Jessica Germain had in store for me. The guard that left earlier led a rag tag group of men and one woman along the tops of the semis on the other side of the circle from Jessica, Jim, and Jude. I squinted in the sunlight, wondering if Jessica planned to make me fight all of them. Then, I finally realized something. These were the soldiers that Jessica had been holding captive. She was going to make me fight the soldiers we'd come to free.

How perfectly ironic.

One of the guards pushed an older guy forward and just by the way he held himself and his eyes raked over the guard, I knew he was probably the highest ranking soldier of the bunch. They shoved him until he landed on the top of the semi with a thud. I clenched my jaw and held myself as rigid as possible. Where was Tex and his big distraction when I needed it? I couldn't fight this soldier—an innocent man. I couldn't. I glanced back at Jude, noting the look of disgust on his face. He met my gaze and I knew what he was trying to tell me, but I didn't know if I could do what he would want me to. Even what my dad would have wanted me to. Survive. No matter the cost. Just survive. But what was the point of survival if you lost yourself in the process? I turned my head and met Jessica's gaze. Nothing in her face said she was human anymore. If I only had my rifle....

I turned back in time to see the soldier standing on the semi across from me. He held an identical blade to my own, a myriad of emotions crossing his face. Horror, hate for his captors, disgust for the situation, and... determination. I would've expected no less. My arm came up automatically. The eyes of the soldier widened and then cleared as I stood there and gave him the perfect salute. *Respect.* I heard the shot. I guess I expected it—expected it to land near my feet like it had with Jude. However, I didn't expect the explosion of pain to tear through my left arm. In a haze, I heard Jude bellowing in rage and saw the soldier move forward before a shot stopped him short of coming near me. I glanced down at my arm and raised my right hand with the blade still in it, hovering over the bloody wound on my bicep. Besides the moaning and gurgling of the undead in the arena, everything was eerily quiet.

I shook my head, trying to snap out of my shock and pain. I moved around slowly until I faced Germain, not the least bit surprised to see her standing there with a gun pointed in my direction. I stared at her until she lowered her gun and sat back down into her chair like nothing had happened. Like she hadn't stood there and shot her best friend. I nodded at her and made a promise with that nod. She was mine. She had to die, and I was going to be the one to make it happen. She smiled after a moment and nodded back. Jude was face down on the trailer with three guys holding him down and Jim's eyes were wide and unblinking, as if what had just happened had even shocked him. Well, la-de-fucking-da, that was only one of us.

I snagged the edge of my shirt and cut through the edge, ripping away a large piece of fabric. I wrapped the fabric around my wound and tied it tightly, hissing at the pain and wishing away the gray spots that danced before my eyes. The wound wasn't as bad as it looked. I was pretty sure the bullet had gone straight through. When I faced the soldier I saw his look. He was going to refuse to fight me, to put on the show they wanted. I met his gaze and jerked my head once to the side. Germain would put a bullet through his head. I was sure of it. I held my knife out and walked forward. He hesitated only a moment before jogging forward to meet me. The crowd around us went crazy and I was glad for the noise. I met the soldier at the end of my truck trailer and immediately struck out, catching his arm with the tip of my blade. His eyes widened.

"Sir," I gasped out, leaning in and pretended to grab him by the arm and hold off his attack, blade-to-blade. "I'm trying to get you and your men out of here." I grunted when he elbowed me in the stomach. I fell back on my butt with a thud. He was good at this. I scrambled back to my feet just in time to miss his forward lunge. This time, though, he knocked me off my feet and I found myself on the receiving end of a soldier's strength straddling me, his knife pressing down.

"If you have to kill me," he gasped out, "do it. Just try to get my men out of here." I nodded once and pushed up, trying to dislodge his body from mine. I was strong, but not strong enough. The soldier staggered off of me anyway. I quickly regained my feet, and so did the soldier. We were both weak, him from being held captive and me from my wound. We were both already breathing hard, and blood was soaking through the wrapping on my arm. I raised my knife and the soldier smiled a very small, understanding smile. He was ready. I gulped back my tears and hesitation and leapt forward. The soldier didn't try to dodge my attack. But right as my arm slashed forward, a series of explosions nearby rocked me off of my feet.

Tex.

Diversion Delivered

I stood up, my ears ringing, unable to hear what was going on around me, but I could see the utter chaos surrounding me, along with sheer devastation. I grasped hold of the soldier's arm and pulled him in close.

"That's our cue, Sir!" I shouted. "Let's get the hell out of here!"

The soldier smiled hugely at me and nodded. We turned to face where his men were, but the semi that led back to his men was mangled and dislodged from its normal spot. There was no way we could go back that way. I couldn't see through the cloud of black smoke to where Jude would have been and I felt fear; sharp and bitter. I knew he would want me to go on with the mission. I had to believe he was okay and we would meet up in a few minutes. Another explosion rocked us back down to our knees and the smell of burning, undead flesh permeated the air all around us. We both stumbled to our feet and I saw the only way we were going to be able to get out was to jump into the zombie horde. The last blast had punched a hole right in the middle of the undead. We only had a small window of time to take advantage of it. I pointed the spot out to the soldier and he nodded. He waved his arms to one of his guys and then waved them back toward the shipping area.

I could see the man trying to round up his group, to keep them moving, but in the panic of the grenades going off and zombies running free, people were panicking and trying to get back to the sanctuary of the base. That made them do stupid things. They were knocking others off of the trailers and into the arms of the undead in their frenzy to get to safety. Regular people, armed guards, and a few of the soldier's people fell off of the side of the trailers. We were helpless to do anything about it.

"Let's go!" I shouted and pulled roughly on the soldier's sleeve to tear his eyes away from the horrible scene. He snapped back to reality and we both jumped from the roof of the truck and into the pits of Hell. We ran full out and even being hurt, the adrenaline was pumping and the promise of freedom pushed us on. A lot of zombies had been clamoring near the edge of the trailers, waiting for hapless victims to fall into their laps. However, we still had to fight tooth and nail for every few feet that we advanced. My wound was a dull, throbbing pain in the back of my mind while I struck out time after time and ran my blade into the skull of as many zombies as were unlucky enough to get in my path. The older soldier beside me was holding his own, taking down nearly as many as I was. Shots echoed all around us and mass hysteria ruled.

We were within thirty feet of the shipping and receiving area when I tripped. I landed hard, my chin rebounding off of pavement hard enough to make me wonder if I broke my jaw. When I tried to stand, I realized that I hadn't tripped over anything, I'd been grabbed by a zombie that had been blown in half. The upper half of the almost-incapacitated zombie had a death grip on my booted foot and was pulling itself up my body, looking for a soft spot to sink its grotesque teeth into.

I kicked with all my strength, but I couldn't dislodge the zombie leech. Another zombie stumbled upon us and decided to get in on the action. With a scream of terror, I kicked the zombie holding onto my leg in the face until its head snapped back and cracked at such an angle that it twisted around and dangled from its neck. The second one was on top of me before I could blink and I held it off by sheer strength and a fist to its throat. I could feel my left arm weakening, my strength draining as my open wound began taking its toll. Just when my arm wavered dangerously, a bullet entered the right side of the zombie's skull and exited its left side, expelling a large portion of brain matter and bits of bone in the process. I shoved the body off of myself with the very last bit of strength I possessed. When a hand reached out to help me up, I took it and allowed myself to be pulled off of the ground. I found myself looking into a pair of familiar brown eyes. I cried out in sheer relief and threw myself into Jude's arms.

"Let's get these people to safety, huh?" he murmured against my hair.

The soldier handed me my blade and as I took it, I found a pair of eyes in the crowd near the place we were all headed fastened on me. Tex, his eyes guarded, a little bit hurt, but mostly understanding. He nodded to me before going back and barking orders out to some of the soldiers we were there to help. We made it to our destination and the chaos of people killing, people dying, zombies running about freely, and everyone trying to get back to safety made my head spin.

"Melody. I have a truck ready for you at the front of the factory. You're going to have to hurry though." He tossed me a gun and I tucked into the back of my pants.

"Thank you, Tex. We owe you big time."

"I plan on holding you to that debt," he said with a grin.

"Captain Parsons! Thank goodness!" a young female soldier hollered out as she joined us.

"How many?" the captain asked without preamble. The young woman's face fell when she answered.

"Four, Sir. Michaelson, James, Torres, and Astor. We are fourteen now, Sir." She stepped back and let the captain have a second to digest.

"We need to move," Tex said tersely. There would be time to reflect and mourn later. We had to get out of there fast. Tex turned to Jude. "What about Germain?" he asked.

Jude's eyes met mine as he answered. "I didn't see what happened to her in the chaos and smoke. I did make sure Jim wouldn't be bothering us ever again though," he said hollowly. I closed my eyes. Should I go back and search for Germain? Or should I just get the hell out of dodge? When I opened my eyes and found all the people I'd come to save watching me, I knew I had to deal with Germain later. I needed to make sure these people would be okay. That was the most important thing.

"Let's blow this popsicle stand," I said.

We all ran toward the one place no one else was headed, the front of the factory, where only a tall, barb-wire-topped fence stood between us and an open, zombie-infested city.

An eighteen wheeler was waiting for us when we reached the front of the factory, the engine running. A few of the soldiers with us immediately loaded up in the back. In front of the semi sat an Army tank outfitted with high powered machine guns. Jude whistled, taking it in.

"Riding in style," he grunted.

"Only a tank would do to get us out of this mess," Tex answered soberly. "What do you think, Melody? Would you like to ride in my tank? You can sit on my lap and..." Tex's voice faltered and he turned to face me.

I stood in the doorway of the factory, not daring to breathe or make any sudden movements. I cursed the gun at the small of my back. Fat lot of good it would do me in this moment. Jessica Germain stood barely three feet away, her gun pointing between my eyes, and blood dripping from a fresh bite on her exposed shoulder. I sensed Jude shift on his feet.

"Fucking move an inch and I will kill her before you get a round off," she hissed. Everyone froze, aware that my life was in the balance and that the balance was off her freaking rocker.

"Jessica, just let this go. Haven't we lost enough? Hasn't there been enough death and pain already?" I asked with a shaky voice.

She laughed and the sound sent a chill up my spine.

"What do *you* know about loss? Your father died—so what? He was military. Your mom died in a clean hospital with an IV full of medicine to help ease her pain." I flinched at the mention of my mom. "You want to know how *my* mom died, Mel? *My* mom died in a filthy city street after my dad bit into her jugular and ripped her throat out. Then he turned around and took a chunk out of my baby brother's arm. We got away though." She nodded her head and her finger twitched enough to make me flinch. "It wasn't until later that I realized he was changing into the exact things that were swarming all around us. I didn't even have a fucking gun to stop him!" Her scream tore through my heart and a sob escaped me. "No gun. I did find a crowbar though," she said calmly. "That's how I had to bring my sweet, gentle, little brother down. With a fucking crowbar." Her arm steadied and her voice calmed. "Tell me again, Mel. Tell me how *we've* suffered."

"I'm sorry, Jess," I said. "I'm so sorry."

Her lip curled up in a sneer, her hand steadied, and I knew it was the end.

"Oh, I have no doubt you're sorry, Mel. But not as sorry as you're about to be. Not as sorry as you'll be when you've lost *everything* like I have." Her arm shifted and I reached back to grab the gun from the small of my back.

Not quick enough, I thought as she swung around and aimed directly at... Jude. My mind screamed out as I pulled my weapon and aimed. *Not quick enough*. I pulled the trigger, but I heard her gun fire a split second before mine did. *Not quick enough*. My bullet hit her right in the temple. Hers hit him right in the chest.

Not quick enough.

Zombies vs. Tanks

I don't remember much of what happened next. My mind decided once again to click in and out of reality, saving me some of the details that I couldn't handle. I remember falling to my knees next to Jude and thinking that he couldn't possibly survive with so much blood pooling everywhere. I remember sitting there while people moved in slow motion around me. I remember someone slapping me and snapping out of my misery enough to help them apply pressure to his wound and load him into the back of the semi, so the young woman soldier, who was also a medic, could take care of him as we left. I joined Tex in the front of the truck, wanting to be useful, wanting to keep my mind off of the fact that Jude could be dead by the time we stopped somewhere safely. Tex never questioned me, he just handed me and automatic rifle and let me take out my misery on the zombies from my window. Three soldiers drove the tank and I recall the explosions and non-stop rapid fire of the machine gun wiping out swaths of zombies.

We cut a path of utter and total destruction through Charlotte, zombies fell before us en masse and blood and carnage rained down in sheets all around us. The only thing we had to worry about was following slowly behind the tank and avoiding the larger piles of bodies and abandoned vehicles. It was all relatively easy, but slow enough to make the ache of worry in my chest grow with every passing minute. What felt like an eternity later, but was more like two hours of non-stop driving, we pulled into the parking lot of the Toys-R-Us that Jude and I had stopped at a few days before.

"We'll stop here for the night, ditch the semi for something a bit smaller, and then head back to your base in the morning," Tex said in the silence of the cab of the truck. I smiled, but didn't face him. He sighed. "You love him." It wasn't a question, so I didn't answer. "He'll be alright," he said gently. I nodded and exited the cab after I saw the final zombie in the area meet its end by a soldier I'd yet to meet. My hand was shaking uncontrollably when I reached out to unlatch the back of the semi. Several people exited the semi as I climbed up into the back.

"How is he?" I asked the young woman with huge blue eyes who looked up at me as I approached. Her mouth thinned into a line and she glanced back down at Jude's ashen face.

"He's alright for now. The bleeding has stopped and there is an exit wound on his back, so no bullet to dig out. It looks like he was lucky and the bullet missed his heart." Yeah, lucky. "The sooner we get him antibiotics and clean bandages though, the better," she said.

I nodded and scooted aside when two guys came over to help move Jude inside the toy shop. I felt entirely and completely helpless.

"Let's set up shop inside," I said before jumping out of the back of the semi. The soldiers inside were already making preparations to hunker down for the night. Kiddie blankets and pillows formed makeshift sleeping areas and shelves were being moved to block the front, glass windows, and doors for extra security. It felt... *weird* not having any specific job to do.

"Tex, what do you need me to do?" I asked once he headed my direction. He searched my face and sighed. Surely he wasn't going to give me a hard time.

"To be honest, Melody, I don't need your help. I have a group of guys who are already on their way back to a few places we passed to scout for supplies for the night and the captain and I are taking the semi to exchange it for better vehicles for our group." My mouth popped open to argue, but Tex cut me off. "You're physically and emotionally drained, sweetheart. You need your arm looked at. You need to rest, and you need to be here for Jude in case he wakes up," he said.

I nodded and took a deep breath. He was right. "Okay," I conceded in a whisper.

Tex took charge of all the evening's preparations and I went over and allowed the female medic to clean and dress my wound. When she was all done, I walked over to where Jude was asleep on a kindy mat and covered with a SpongeBob fleece blanket. I knelt down and ran my hand across his forehead and whispered a small prayer against his cheek while I placed a kiss there. I snuggled close by his side, careful not to jostle him. I shoved a stuffed animal under my head and promptly fell into a restless sleep.

Tex

We drove in silence most of the way. Two soldiers thinking about everything we'd been through—everyone we'd lost and everything we would still face in the coming days. So much death and destruction. So much fucking insanity. I really didn't know how much more any man could be expected to take before he lost his mind and humanity completely. And then there was Melody Carter. My hands gripped the steering wheel tighter and I clenched my jaw harder. What was it about her that drew me to her? Sure, she was beautiful. She was also tough and smart, but most of all she stirred up feelings inside of me that I never thought I'd feel again. Not since Alison.

But Melody was falling in love with Jude. It was plain for anyone with two eyes to see. I was surprised I hadn't noticed it before. I knew that they *said* they were an item back in Charlotte, but I'd held out hope that it had all been an act. I don't think Melody had even known that she was in love with Jude, not until she thought she was going to lose him.

"We should check over there," Captain Parsons said, snapping me out of my thoughts. I nodded and pulled the semi into the parking lot of a Walmart Supercenter. I'm always surprised by the sight of an absolutely deserted shopping center, especially when the only signs of life come from those who aren't even living. How messed up is that? If it weren't for the zombies shuffling around in between abandoned vehicles and overturned shopping carts, the entire area would have been as silent as a tomb. I don't know which will eventually drive me over that super fine line of insanity, the absolute silence and void of life in the world or the fact that I sometimes appreciate the sounds of the undead. Any sort of noise is better than *nothingness*.

"Okay, let's do this quickly and get out of here. The other team should be getting supplies, so all we need to get are the vehicles."

Captain Parsons didn't reply.

"Captain?" He was staring out his window at the several zombies that were already making their way slowly toward us in the fading daylight. "You know it wasn't your fault, don't you, Tex?" His voice sounded far away and reflective. He turned his head and met my stare. His eyes were an eerie shade of blue, a shade so light that they seemed to look *through* you and straight to your soul. He looked tired and like he'd aged five years over the last several months. "No one blamed you for bringing Germain back to the base."

I sighed and ran a hand over my eyes. I was so tired.

"Any one of us would have done the exact same thing and taken her back to the base with us," Parsons droned. "We'd all lost someone. Every single one of us have something to prove. Someone we wish we would have been there for that first day."

His eyes searched mine and I nodded briefly in understanding. I knew no one blamed me, I even knew that any of the other soldiers would have done the same thing, but that didn't mean I still didn't blame myself. Soldiers died. People suffered. All because I wanted to make up for my past shortcomings.

"Ready?" he asked after a moment.

"Ready as I'll ever be," I answered.

The first several zombies were easily dispatched with knives driven into their temples. We immediately found a large SUV that was easy to hotwire and had half a tank of gas, so we left it running and circled the parking lot together, looking for another SUV or van that would hold six or more people. I soon spotted the perfect vehicle. An RV sat all by its lonesome at the back of the parking lot. I whistled to the captain and pointed at the vehicle, and started moving toward it. Two zombies were between me and the RV. The first one I took down without halting my stride. It was so swollen and slow that I was surprised it didn't self-combust into a pile of slushy zombie guts. It hadn't stood a chance. The second one brought me up short. It had been a woman, probably in her late twenties, and was wearing jeans and a black tee shirt when she turned. I blinked once, at first feeling unsure of why I even hesitated.

The closer she got the more I noticed how much of a resemblance the zombie had to Alison. Her hair was the same length, her build was the same, and this zombie had on the same type of dressy, decorative scarf that Alison had always worn. I stood there transfixed while the zombie came closer and closer, dragging one leg behind her because it had been damaged. I didn't move or breathe, I stood there and watched her, hearing the gurgling in her throat and the snapping of her teeth until she got within a couple of feet of me. Captain Parsons yelled and let out a string of curses. I heard him running in my direction and yet I stood rooted to that spot, unable to move.

It seemed so long ago that Alison had died, so long ago that I had put her and her parents down in their home. And yet, it was like it happened just yesterday. I had always been responsible for others, always taking care of family, civilians, and soldiers. I'd failed so many times. I didn't want to fail anymore. I just wanted the loneliness and failure to end.

The female zombie reached out and made a break for me, realizing an easy meal was within her grasp. Her hand reached my shoulder, and a shot caught her in the temple. The zombie's head jerked to the side and her body fell to the ground, pulling me forward. I stumbled over the corpse, but caught and righted myself before I landed on top of the undead woman. My heart was pounding so hard I could feel the extra blood pumping at each of my temples, could hear the blood rushing through my veins and past my eardrums. Time stood still as the realization of what I almost let happen came up to choke me. I stumbled again just as Captain Parsons reached me. His hands grasped me roughly about the shoulders and he jerked me until I turned to face him.

"Are you bitten?" he gasped.

I shook my head and swallowed. "No," I said roughly.

"Good." His fist caught me right in the jaw and I went flying to the ground like I'd been punched by a much younger and much larger man. I dragged myself off of the asphalt, spit out some blood, and wiggled my jaw. Not broken, but it sure felt like hell. "Pick up your knife, soldier," he barked. "Let's get the RV so we can get back to the group right now," he ordered.

"Yes, Sir!" I grabbed my knife and did what my commanding officer told me.

We pulled up to the toy store a few hours later with both vehicles and a few supplies we'd found in the trunks of cars around the Walmart parking lot. Much easier and less risky than entering the store. I'd done a lot of thinking on the way back by myself. I'd come to some conclusions and had made a decision that I knew I had to make. One that I knew some people probably wouldn't understand. I would break it to the group later though, after they were all safely deposited at the base. I got out of the RV and headed to the door of the toy store behind the captain.

"Sir, about what happened ..."

Captain Parsons stopped and turned to face me, his eyes sharp and discerning. "I've already forgotten about what happened," he said. "Just don't let it happen again, soldier."

I breathed in a deep, grateful, sigh and nodded my head. "It won't, Sir," I answered truthfully.

He watched me a moment longer before opening the door and going inside. I followed him in and found a spot I could crash for a few hours. The next day I'd be depositing everyone safely at the base and then be headed on my own separate way. I didn't really have a plan or even know where I would be headed, but I knew I had to go. Everyone would just have to understand.

Melody

My neck was horribly kinked and my arm was throbbing with pain when I woke up the next morning on the floor of the toy store. I wiggled my shoulders and rolled onto my back, blinking away the sleep and fuzziness from eyes.

"Thank goodness. I was beginning to think I was going to have to listen to you snore all day."

A pair of brown eyes, slightly bloodshot, stared down at me, and I reached up to run a hand along Jude's face. With a tiny sob, a tear escaped to roll down my cheek.

"You scared the shit out of me," I said. Jude smiled and then grimaced in pain. He rolled off of his side and back onto his back to get more comfortable. I sat up and placed a palm on his forehead. He didn't have a fever. I sighed in relief.

"I feel like I've been run over by a herd of angry elephants," he said gruffly. I smiled and ran a hand along his bare chest, and around the covered wound there where blood was seeping through the bandage. "I remember you promising me some *action* after we got out of that hell-hole. This wasn't exactly what I had in mind, you know." He waggled his brows and I laughed.

"There will plenty time for that later, soldier," I whispered and gave him a soft kiss on his cheek. Someone cleared their throat. I turned and saw Tex standing a few feet away.

"We should probably get going. The sooner we get to the base, the better. Everyone's exhausted and a few people still need some medical attention," he said. I nodded and got up from the spot next to Jude. The room spun slightly and Tex grabbed my arm to keep me steady. "Whoa there. You do remember that you were shot yesterday, right?" I scowled over at him and he laughed. He sobered then and looked at Jude. "You're going to have your hands full with this one," he said with a small smile. Jude blinked. I could tell he was a little confused. Heck, *I* was a little confused. "You'll take good care of her."

I wasn't sure if it was a statement or a question. The guys were staring at each other, some sort of male communication passing between them, mano-a-mano, that I couldn't decipher. Jude nodded, barely a movement, and Tex returned the gesture.

"We're ready to go when you two are." And with that, Tex turned on his heel and left.

"What was that all about?" I asked, my mouth still hanging open slightly.

"Nothing for you womenfolk to worry your pretty little heads about," Jude said with a wink and an exaggerated southern drawl. *Really*?

"I know you did not just refer to me as *womenfolk*," I said, narrowing my eyes. Jude laughed and immediately hissed out in pain and I knelt down beside him.

"Have pity on the wounded," he pled with big puppy dog eyes. I rolled mine and tried to look angry, but didn't quite succeed.

"How's my patient today?"

I looked up and found the young medic staring down us.

"I'm ready to take on the undead hordes. Where's my knife?" Jude said and she smiled. Jude smiled back widely at her and I found myself wishing the woman was a little on the ugly side.

A soldier came in to help Jude to his feet so we could get to the RV that Tex had secured for us the night before. When I got outside and made sure Jude was safely in the RV, much to his amusement, I walked over to Tex to see how everything was going. He watched me approach while he finished giving instructions to a Hispanic man who had been riding the tank the day before.

"How's everything looking?" I asked when I joined him.

"The guys were going to drive the tank to the base, but it is out of ammunition and only has fumes for gas. We can always come back for it later." He pointed to the tank where three guys were standing lookout for zombies. "We lost one guy on the supply run last night, a really young guy named Michael."

I frowned at him. I hadn't known we lost anyone last night. Of course, I'd been out cold until this morning.

"I'm sorry," I murmured.

Tex waved away the sentiment. "We have Captain Parsons driving the SUV with six passengers, and I'll drive the RV with you, Jude, the medic, and four of the others. We should be able to make it back in a little over two hours."

I nodded. Sounded about right.

"Look, I wanted to talk to you," I said tentatively.

Tex caught my gaze and held it. His eyes searched mine and then he smiled gently. "There's nothing to talk about, sweetheart. I understand. There's no hurt feelings," he said.

I felt a weight that I hadn't even known was there lift from my sore shoulders. "Are we good to go then?" I asked in relief.

Tex nodded and mumbled, "Yeah, we're good," as he walked away.

Something was off with Tex, but I couldn't place what it was. I guess there would be plenty of time to talk to him about it later, once we were at the base. Captain Parsons let out an ear-splitting whistle and we all jumped into our awaiting vehicles, anxious to be on the move.

Our trek home went without a hitch.

Zombie Bait

"I thought you two were zombie bait for sure."

Before I could respond, I was pulled forward by two muscular arms until I was completely enfolded in Ghost's embrace. I only flinched a little at the pain in my arm.

"Thanks for bringing him back to us alive," he said gruffly.

"I did my best, but I sure wish I could have brought him back without a bullet wound," I answered wearily.

Ghost lifted my chin with one long finger and made me meet his eyes. "You can't control everything, Melody. Jude's a big boy and he was lucky to have you with him on that suicide mission."

I smiled at him as Jude entered the room.

"I've been commanded to go straight to bed," he said grouchily as he joined us. I laughed and put arm around his waist.

"Well, let's get you tucked in, shall we?"

"Man, I'd take her up on that offer if I were you. A lot of guys would love to hear those words from her lips," Ghost teased.

Jude scowled over at him as I pulled him toward the exit.

"Wait, what did he mean a *lot* of guys?" Jude grumbled.

I sighed and threw Ghost a dirty look over my shoulder as we left the room. His laughter followed us all the way down the hallway.

After I tucked Jude into his bed, I went to check on how everyone else was doing. A few soldiers were being treated for minor wounds, several had already retired to their new rooms, and some were sitting in the small common area chatting amongst their new base-mates. I grinned at the young female medic, Maria, blushing while Big Ben flirted outrageously with her. I shook hands with Major Tillman and was about to head to my own room when Captain Parsons stepped in my path.

"Melody, may I speak with you a moment, please?" he asked. He looked serious.

"Of course, Captain. What can I do for you?" I asked.

He smiled at that and I marveled at how much he reminded me of an older version of my dad. I blinked rapidly and turned away from his gaze, not wanting him to see me get all girly and emotional. He cleared his throat.

"You have done so much for me, so much for my men already." He looked down at his hands and then back up again at me, his gaze sincere. "I hope I can help you some day, to pay you and Jude back for what you did for us." I was shaking my head the whole time he spoke. As if we would expect anything in return. "But for right now, I have to ask you for a small favor. Not for me, but for one of my men," he said uneasily.

"Captain, spit it out. I'd be *honored* to do anything I can for you or any of your men," I said gently.

"It's Tex," he said to gauge my reaction. "What about him?" I asked. I knew something was going on with Tex, I just wasn't sure what it was. Apparently the Captain had a better clue than I did.

"He's leaving," he said flatly.

I thought I misheard him. "Leaving?" I asked, as if it didn't make any sense. Where could he be going? Captain Parsons nodded his head.

"The darn fool has it in his head that he needs to be alone, so he's planning on heading out into...." His voice trailed off.

I knew what he was getting at. Tex was headed out into a world that we really had no clue about, a world full of misery and death, and he was going to do it all alone. I'd done that for two years and I wouldn't wish it on my worst enemy. He was an idiot and I was going to have to knock some sense into his honky-tonk-lovin' ass. I gritted my teeth and glanced over at the door that led topside.

"I'll take care of it," I said.

"Thank you," he answered.

I nodded and shook hands with him. "Now, *please* go get some rest, Sir," I suggested.

He smiled and walked away to check on the rest of his men. I left to tell the major I was going to be MIA for a few. He didn't question what I was doing, he just told me to be careful. I gave him a smart salute and pulled my knife from its sheath. He shook his head and sighed. A few minutes later, I found Tex sitting in an office, staring at a telephone like it might ring at any moment.

"You waiting on a call?" I asked.

He smiled wryly, his eyes never leaving the desk phone. "It's funny, really. I always hated to hear a phone ring. I despised my cell phone. I'd only gotten one in case Alison needed to reach me. So many people were caught up in their devices, their smart phones, laptops, and such. They tended to forget about *real life* going on all around them." His voice lowered as he stared at the phone. "I'd give anything to hear a phone ring again. To hear people bustle about, full of life and dreams." I took a deep breath, hurting a little for him and his pain. "How'd you know I was up here?" he asked a second later.

I shrugged and sat down on the edge of the desk. "What are you doing, Tex?" I asked after a moment.

He sighed deeply and raised his eyes to meet mine for the first time. "I'm doing what I need to do right now." My mouth flew open and I was ready to rip him a new one when he immediately cut me off. "I can't be here, Melody. Not right now. I know you think this is the absolute worst thing someone could do with the world the way it is right now," he said. "And normally I would agree with you. But I know what *I* need right now. I know where I'm at, what I've dealt with, and how much more I can take," he said vehemently. "I *need* this," he said, his eyes wide and pleading.

I stood up and walked over to the window, peering out through the blinds. Two zombies were lumbering around the small RV we'd picked up. I didn't want him to go. It wasn't good for anyone to be out there alone with the way things were. But I couldn't help but understand where he was coming from and kind of *get* what he was saying. Only Tex knew his mind and heart. Only Tex could make a decision like this for himself. He appeared to be making the decision with a clear head, so who was I to make him feel like crap for it?

"I don't like it," I said, as if it made a difference. I turned to face him. He grinned at me and got to his feet.

"I know you don't, sweetheart. And I know Captain Parsons doesn't either. But you'll both let me go, because you know it's the right thing to do."

I huffed out a breath and followed him to the door. "You better not get killed, Tex," I said angrily.

He smiled wider and reached for the doorknob. "I don't plan on it," he said with a wink.

"If it gets to be too much out there by yourself—"

"I'll pack up and bring my ass right back here," he finished for me. I crossed my arms over my chest and leaned against the wall. He turned the knob and cracked the door open.

"Tex, what's your real name anyway?" I asked when he stepped through the doorway.

He didn't turn or look back. "I'll tell you some other time," he said.

"Promise?" I whispered.

"Promise," he murmured and shut the door behind him.

I stood there leaning up against the wall for quite a while after I heard the RV start up and drive off. I thought about all I'd been through since that first day that the airplane fell from the sky to land in our neighborhood. I thought about all the time I spent alone in the woods, fending for myself and trying to survive day by day. I thought of all the things that had happened to me over the last several days, meeting other survivors, meeting Jude, almost dying a couple of times, meeting Tex, getting shot by my psycho ex-best friend and then having to kill her.

I thought of all that, all the horrible things and all the good things and I couldn't help but to have... hope. Hope that tomorrow would be a better day. Hope that the world could bounce back from the horrible, gaping wound it had suffered.

And hope that humanity would be able to find its way back from all the darkness, pain, and loss.

Holy Zombie Innards, Batman.

It had been over three weeks since everything had gone down at the Charlotte Army base and yet I still couldn't shake the overwhelming feeling of loss and betrayal surrounding me like a fog. I couldn't shut out the little voice of doubt every time I thought of Tex and how I had let him go out into the infested world all alone on a soul-searching mission or some such bull crap. Anger had been welling up inside of me so much lately that the guys had begun throwing around words like "hormonal" and "she-bitch" when they thought I couldn't hear them. For the past week I had pushed Jude away, holding him at arm's length for whatever screwed up reason my mind had concocted.

So here I was, squatting outside in overgrown weeds on the outskirts of the base, taking my anger and frustrations out on every single zombie I could find. It wasn't a difficult task and I'd convinced myself that we would be just *that* much safer if I thinned out the area several times a week, so that when we went out for a supply run, we'd have an easier time of it. Jude had stopped trying to convince me to stay inside. Everyone had.

I stood up from my hiding spot and rubbed the back of my neck. I glanced around the area in the fading light and squinted my eyes to scan the distant field. There weren't near as many zombies in the area as there had once been. Usually on any given day, even after I'd cleared them out a day or two before, I'd easily find a dozen or more zombies in our backyard. This time I had probably only taken out around six. And now that I thought about it, all the zombies I'd taken down in the past week or so had been a bit *too* easy. Maybe I was getting better at the killing. I wasn't sure if that was such a good thing, but one thing I did know was that it would keep me alive longer. There was that.

"I don't know about you, but I'm about ready to call it a day."

The voice came from close by and belonged to the young female medic, Maria, who we'd brought with us from the Charlotte base. I'd put my jealousy of her gorgeousness aside when I was sure she didn't have her eyes on Jude as anything other than a patient. We'd become pretty close since then. It helped that she didn't ask questions and was an amazing shot. I hadn't had anyone of the same sex to talk to since… well, in a very long time.

"Yeah, my shoulders are killing me. I could use some grub and a shower," I answered grudgingly. "You go ahead, I'll follow behind you in a few." She nodded and accepted what I said without blinking. She knew I needed my time alone and that I could handle myself out here.

"Okay, I'll see you inside. Be careful."

I smiled at her and started a final lap around the perimeter of the base. I took it slow, letting myself really enjoy the outdoors. I wasn't stupid. I knew the base, the underground safe house, was the safest place for anyone to be, but sometimes I missed the fresh air. I missed the outdoors, the open sky, and the sounds of nature. Because even though there were now unnatural sounds echoing all around the world, sounds that had no business haunting people's nightmares, I still missed the sound of a bird singing, the sound of the small river out in the woods trickling its way through the forest. Even in our most fucked up world, the good could still be seen and heard, if you were willing to look hard enough. I sighed deeply and slung my gun onto my back.

I sprinted across the property and skirted around a few buildings until I spotted a solitary zombie in between me and the door to the main office building. I slowed my pace to a brisk walk as I made my way toward the undead man. About the time he noticed me, I was within ten feet of him. Instead of closing the distance between us and dispatching the corpse like I normally would have, I stood and waited for him to come to me. The zombie opened its mouth to groan and gnash its teeth, but the sound that came from its throat was *off*. I couldn't put my finger on it, but it definitely didn't sound the same, it sounded… juicier.

The zombie's head also looked abnormally large, the cranium nearly double the size of what it should have been. Besides all that, an eyeball was hanging from one of its eye sockets and dangled back and forth as it stumbled forward. How attractive. I shuddered as the mutant zombie made an effort to come after me. He was slow. Very slow. Maybe it was because of the shape the corpse was in. Maybe I was overthinking it. Maybe. When he finally made it close enough to me, I didn't have to dodge him. I struck him once, right in the forehead. He didn't have a chance, and neither did my clothing. The zombie's head popped like I'd just burst a balloon that had been overstuffed with rank, rotten innards. The zombie-head-piñata burst and all its glorious prizes spewed forth in one huge *splash* all over me. I gagged and wiped some unknown substance off of my cheek and stumbled toward the door.

I was never going to live this down.

Risks and Rewards

I was scarfing down a protein bar and some nuts when Jude entered the mess hall and sat down at my table the next morning.

"So, I heard you were quite the sight when you came in yesterday." His lip twitched with the effort it took to keep from smiling.

I scowled and popped the last bit of protein bar into my mouth and watched him from beneath lowered lashes. "The freaking zombie just burst like I'd stuck a pin in an over inflated balloon. Blood, guts, and crap spewed all over me," I answered grumpily. The guys were still giving me crap about it this morning. My one-finger-salute and my very colorful vocabulary didn't sway their hilarity. I opted to ignore them from this point on. Jude, very wisely, kept his wisecracks in check.

"How was it out there?" he asked after a moment.

"I don't know. The same, but different. I can't put my finger on it, but something has changed."

Jude nodded and stood up from the table. "Well, looks like we are going to get a chance to check it out. Major Tillman wants us to lead a group out today."

I finished off my bottle of water and studied Jude's face. His face was resigned.

"You didn't want me to go." It wasn't a question.

He stared at the top of the table. "It's not that I don't think you can handle yourself. It's not that you're a female. So don't take it wrong. It's just that, well, I'd like to be able to go out like I used to."

I stood, pushing away from the table and came to stand in front of Jude with my arms crossed over my chest.

"And how did you go out when you didn't have me to tag along?" I asked.

Jude sighed deeply before answering. "With a clear conscience," he stated without apology. My arms fell to my side and I took a step back. "I was able to lead my missions, to go out there without any thought for myself. If I died, I died so that others could survive. If I die tomorrow, I'd feel the same. But when you're out there *with* me..." He shook his head. "I'll be worried about you and I might not be able to make the hard choices. I'll be worried that you'll get hurt. And if you got hurt—if you were to die, then nothing—none of this—will haven't meant *anything*."

I stood there with no idea what to say. I couldn't help how he felt and I couldn't just stay home and out of harm's way to keep him from worrying about me. That was part of the world we now lived in. I put a hand on his arm and waited for him to turn his face toward me.

"Jude, you can't keep the people you care about bubbled away from the harsh reality of the world. I could stay here this time, but the truth is that we put ourselves in harm's way now by just *living*. I could get hurt here on my daily rounds, we could have a breach, we could run out of food and water, or an illness could sweep through the base. That is our reality. No matter what happens though, no matter what we face, I would rather be by your side when it does. I would rather die tomorrow fighting with you then sit here twiddling my thumbs and wondering if you'll ever come back to me."

His eyes softened and his hand came up to caress my cheek. I closed my eyes and leaned my face into it.

"I love you, Melody Carter." My eyes popped open and I stared at his face, noting the crooked smile on his lips. "I think I've loved you since the moment you attacked me butt-naked and socked me in the eye." I grinned and felt my cheeks warm.

"I love you too, Agent Harrison," I said with a small smile. "Now, let's go round up the guys."

He nodded and grabbed my hand, entwining his fingers with mine and we made our way around the base, gathering our group to forage for food and supplies.

.*.

"Okay, so here's the thing," Jude said when we were all topside and gathered in the office building. "This won't be a regular supply run." I hadn't even known this. I glanced around the room and into the other dozen or so faces as they listened and immediately knew that no one else had known either. "Major Tillman didn't want to alarm anyone, but we are extremely short on supplies. Not only are we low on medical supplies, but we are dangerously low on food supplies too."

"How low?" Ghost asked, his deep voice booming off of the walls of the small office space.

Jude caught each of our eyes and then met Ghost's inquiring stare. "There is probably enough food to hold the entire base over for another two to three weeks if we drastically cut all our portions to the bare minimum."

A couple of guys muttered beneath their breaths and we all

understood what this meant. Higher risk for larger quantities of food and supplies. It wasn't easy to care for almost a hundred people in the middle of the zombie apocalypse.

"As some of you know, we also have another slight problem." He cleared his throat before continuing. "We have been doing supply runs in this area and surrounding areas for over two years now and the places we've scouted, the places we've foraged before have basically been picked clean."

"What does that mean?" The question came from a soldier we'd brought over from the Charlotte base.

"It means we are going to have to go into a larger city. It means this could be a very dangerous mission," I answered.

Jude nodded his head. "That's exactly what it means. We need to go out of our normal range and find larger quantities of food, larger quantities of supplies, which means going into zones that we haven't scouted before and probably running into a lot more of the undead while doing so." He glanced around the room once again. "If you don't want to do this run, we won't hold it against any of you and we won't think any less of any of you. The risk will be great." Jude paused. "If there's anyone who wants to stay, now would be the time to jump ship," he said seriously.

No one made a move.

"As if we'd let you and Melody go out and have all the fun," Manuel said with a smile. A chorus of "hell yeahs" sounded in agreement.

Jude grinned and stood up, pulling his knife from its sheath. "Well, let's get going then. We're burning daylight."

A Foraging We Will Go

The day was overcast and gloomy when we made our way slowly out of town in a small caravan of vehicles. The plan was simple, but everyone knew that simple didn't mean easy or safe. Safe was one of those words whose meaning had changed since the end of the world. Safety was really only a state of mind in our violent surroundings. Maybe one day that would change, but for now we could only help survivors until the world started getting back to normal—*if* it could ever get back to normal.

"So once we find supplies, how are we supposed to get it all back to the base?" a young man who went by the name "Z" asked.

"The plan is to find a truck big enough to haul everything back to the base. We have several guys who can drive semis on the team, so it shouldn't be a problem. I'm sure finding an abandoned eighteen wheeler or smaller won't be a problem either," Jude answered.

Z nodded at Jude and turned to look out the window as we kept driving. It was slow going where we were with a lot of abandoned vehicles and debris littering the road we'd taken to get to the city of Gastonia.

Jude pulled off to the side of the road a few hours later; the other vehicles followed his lead and pulled off behind him. I glanced around the area, spotting only a few zombies compared to the large number of deserted and overturned cars. Jude searched the area one last time and then turned to me. I nodded. This looked as good as any place. We were only a few miles outside of the city limit and needed to walk the rest of the way. Jude cut the engine to the SUV and we all waited for his command.

"Okay, let's do this."

We all exited the vehicles and continued our journey on foot into Gastonia, North Carolina, cutting down all the zombies in our way for the next two miles. There were plenty to go around. When we made it to the city limits we did what we had discussed and split into two groups. One group, with Manuel in charge, went in search of the two drug stores that were supposed to be only four blocks into the city and our group went to find the Sam's Club that was supposed to be nearly half a mile west of the pharmacies.

We made it several blocks in relative ease, but there was a tension in the air and I couldn't help but feel like something was wrong. I didn't voice my opinions though, I didn't want to spook our group. We ducked into a tiny bookstore about a block away from our destination when a larger group of zombies lurched around a corner and down the middle of the street. I took that time to really look at our surroundings through the glass doors of the bookstore while the zombies lumbered past.

"There's a lot of bodies in the streets," Ghost whispered near me.

I nodded. *Too many* bodies were in the street. The stench of the undead wafting off of the pavement was nearly toxic and definitely strong enough to make you tear up as you walked past. I searched the streets beside Jude and Ghost with my heart sinking further and further. Something just wasn't right.

"It's not only victims from those first days out there," I noted. "There are dozens and dozens of undead who look like they've been taken down recently, littering every single street." I shook my head. This couldn't be good.

"Damn it," Jude muttered darkly as we stood there and watched the majority of the larger group of zombies pass us by. "There has to be another group in this area."

Ghost muttered something darkly and backed away from the door, leaving me with Jude.

"Maybe they're not hostile." I tried to sound hopeful, however, the truth of the matter was that if there was a large enough group in the area to clear out hundreds of zombies at a time, more than likely they'd laid claim to all the supplies in the area or at least would make it very difficult for other groups to pilfer anything worth taking.

Jude swore again and we both stood, wondering if we should move forward or head back the way we'd come and find the rest of our group. We used the walkie-talkies we'd brought with us to tell the other group to be extra careful as they moved through the city. I pulled out the map and list of stores, hospitals, pharmacies, and such we'd made before we left camp.

I hunched down and spread the papers out on the ground, using my mini flashlight to look over them. I found what I was looking for and pointed it out to Jude when he squatted down next to me to look at my papers.

"That's where we need to go," I said, pointing to the scribbles.

"Ashbrooke High?" Jude questioned.

I smiled broadly and snatched the papers off of the ground.

"Think about it, Jude. The schools would have had hundreds of kids on a daily basis. Most schools have high fences for security and not many people would try to loot a school during a zombie outbreak."

Jude stared at me like he knew I was getting to a point, but he wasn't sure what it was. I rolled my eyes at him and sighed. "How much food do you think a regular sized school would have stocked up to feed hundreds of hungry teens at any given time?" I asked with a smirk.

Jude eyes widened and then he grinned at me. "I knew that," he said. "I was just testing you."

I chuckled under my breath and followed him over to the rest of the group and listened while he told them about our change in plans.

The road to the high school was paved with more bodies and even more of the undead. We tried to play it safe, only engaging the zombies when we had to, keeping to the buildings and ducking behind cars whenever possible. Sometimes, though, we had to fight tooth and nail for our lives, for the lives of our comrades, and to make it further into the city and closer to our destination. As careful as we were, we still lost one of our people on the way.

High School Still Sucks

Some things never change. The sense of apprehension that used to plague me every time I went to school certainly hadn't. Okay, so maybe it wasn't apprehension for quite the same reasons— like, who was dating who, what my friends would think of my new hairstyle, or wondering if Lisa Kasey was pregnant or had just gained a lot of weight— but there was some major stress involved in breaking into a high school, most of it having to do with the fact that we had no idea what lay on the other side of the barbed wire fence we were cutting into. Was the school completely deserted? Was there a mob of undead waiting for us, or had another group already thought of what I did and were inside the school? I could have led us straight into an ambush.

I adjusted my grip on my knife and wiped a droplet of sweat from my forehead as I fought off a few straggler zombies with Jude while we waited for everyone to get through the fence.

"Maybe this isn't such a good idea," I muttered darkly, ducking through the fence opening.

"It was a good idea, Mel. It'll be alright," Ghost said.

I still couldn't help but feel out of sorts. Nothing had really gone right since we'd started this mission and that was never a good sign of things to come. We made our way across the front of the campus and to the front doors of the school without running into a single zombie. So far, so good. The doors were locked tight. We didn't want to use our guns if we didn't have to. No reason to draw unnecessary attention to ourselves.

"Find another way in? Maybe break out a window?" I suggested.

Jude stepped away from the doors, motioning for Ghost to come over.

"It's all you, Ghost," Jude said.

Ghost approached the locked double doors and took out a tiny pack from one of his large pants pockets, pulling out a few tools. Not two minutes later, the lock popped and Ghost held the door open with a flourish. I grinned at him, wondering how many times Ghost's special abilities had come in handy over the past two years.

"I vaguely recall spending my teen years trying to sneak *out* of school," Ghost said wryly as we all entered the hallway.

I turned quickly, my knife coming up in defense at the sound of approaching footsteps—we were not alone.

"Relax, it's only us," Manuel said, his hands up and a smirk on his face.

I lowered my knife and relaxed a fraction and so did everyone else in our group. Ghost clapped Manuel on the back and they did some manly fist bump action.

"How did it go? Everyone okay?" Jude asked. Manuel lifted the long duffle bag off of his back and motioned to two others in his group. All three of them were carrying large, bulging duffle bags. Looked like their pharmacy run had been successful. "Good. Let's all move quietly and find the cafeteria," Jude said. "The quicker the better."

We moved through the eerily empty hallways with only the sound of our shoes echoing around us. I tried not to look at the bulletin boards, the award cabinet, and the depressingly empty classrooms we passed. But the fact that a place that was once so full of life and promise, a place that once held so many teenagers with dreams and aspirations for their future was now sitting abandoned like a ghost town wasn't lost on any of us.

We made a right turn down a hallway and saw what we had been searching for directly in front of us. A sign over the double doors read "Cafeteria". A door to the right of the cafeteria entrance led out into an open courtyard where tables and chairs sat, inviting kids to sit outside and enjoy their lunch in the fresh air. My heart felt pained by the reminder that I had been one of those teens sitting outside eating lunch with my friends, the majority of whom were probably dead now, just months before the outbreak. It felt like it had been a lifetime ago.

"Melody?" Jude was staring at me while I stood there with my thoughts in places they had no business being.

"I'm good," I said, approaching the rest of the group with a sad smile.

After Ghost worked his magic once again we all entered the cafeteria and made our way to the back, where supplies would have been kept. Ghost and three other guys decided to scout out the room and other doors that led into the cafeteria to make sure the room was as secure as possible. When Jude opened the back room, he let out a whistle. I followed behind him and Z when they entered the storage room. I couldn't stop grinning like a fool. Jude and Z shone their flashlights on the shelves that lined the rather large room. I spotted huge cans of peas, carrots, fruit cocktail, and tons of other vegetables all stacked in neatly organized sections.

"Holy shit," Z muttered. I walked over to where he stood rubbing his hand along a can like he'd found the Holy Grail. "Pulled pork," he whispered in awe, a man entranced.

Thirty minutes later, after everyone had oohed and ahhed over the storage room, the school had been well scouted, and everyone had sat for a few minutes to rest, I was itching to be on the move again.

"Now how are we going to get all of this out of here?" I asked. I was sitting with Jude, Z, and Manuel in the main room of the cafeteria.

"We need to find a truck," Jude said.

Right. Find a good sized truck with a decent amount of fuel.

"Bus," Ghost said, striding across the room.

"Bus?" Jude asked.

Ghost nodded and looked over at me. "According to our maps and the info we have, there should be a parking lot between here and the elementary school, probably half a mile further into the city. They keep the buses for all the surrounding schools there. They would be already gassed up and we could fill the entire bus with supplies and still have room for everyone to sit." Ghost glanced at me briefly before turning back to Jude.

Jude narrowed his eyes. "What's the catch?" he asked.

Ghost didn't flinch beneath his stare. "Looks like our luck has run out. I scouted out back. Around the school and from this block over, the undead are swarming the streets. It would be dangerous. It might be our best bet though. It looks the zombies are moving in huge packs, like some kind of *herd*."

I shuffled on my feet and stared uncomprehendingly at Ghost. *Herd*?

"That's nothing different than what we've dealt with before," Jude said.

Ghost rubbed a hand over his shaved head. "No, not this time. They're kind of moving across the city in a *wave*, like a flock of birds would." His eyes met mine and then he clenched his jaw and caught Jude's stare once again. "That wave is already headed this way."

I glanced out the windows and realized how late it was. The undead were making their way across the city and they were moving in our direction. No way we'd be able to get back out of town before they arrived, not without leaving behind all the supplies we'd found.

"If they're moving in waves during the day, maybe by morning they'll have moved past us or back the way they came?" I wondered out loud.

Ghost nodded. "That's what I'm thinking, but who knows? I've never seen them move together quite so in sync. When they do blow through, will they be able to get onto the school property or are we relatively safe here?"

"And there's still the problem of needing a way to get out of here with all of these supplies, so no matter what, we need some wheels," Jude stated.

Ghost nodded. He'd already figured that.

Jude sighed loudly. "What do you need?" he asked Ghost.

Ghost's lips tightened into a thin line. "I'll need two volunteers to come with me and I'll need Melody."

"Why?" Jude asked after a pregnant pause.

"You and Manuel will need to stay here with the others and organize all the supplies so we can load them when we get back, and you'll need Manuel to help if the herd comes through and the shit hits the fan while we're gone." Jude's eyes were on me while Ghost spoke. "Melody has the most experience besides the three of us in the group," Ghost went on. "She's fast, smart, and deadly with a weapon. She's the only person I know who can handle her shit under pressure besides you and Manuel. I need her backing me up."

My mouth dropped open quite unattractively when Ghost finished talking. I never realized he thought so highly of me. I shut my mouth and glanced over at Jude to see how he was taking it. He was staring at the ground, his jaw clenched so hard, I'm sure he'd have a headache later on.

"Alright." Jude looked at me questioningly. "Melody?"

I nodded. I was in.

"Let's see who else is crazy enough to volunteer," Jude said.

He broke the news to the rest of the group and told them our plan. Manuel and the majority of the group started organizing all of the supplies for easy and quick loading and then went to make contingency plans, just in case the shit did indeed hit the fan while we were gone. Z and a short guy with shaggy brown hair named Nate joined Ghost and me to go out into the city to find a bus and bring it back to the group.

M-M-M-Madness

Our small group headed to the back of the school. We only had a few hours of daylight left and we definitely didn't want to get stuck out in the middle of an unfamiliar city at night. Jude walked silently beside me as we approached the gate in the back of the school. I glanced over at him several times on our walk.

"Be smart. Don't take any unnecessary risks," he said instructed.

I smiled. Life *was* a risk, but I understood what he was saying. *Come back to me safely.*

"Will do, Sir." I snapped a salute and he smiled.

Lord, please, please let me come back to him, I willed out into the universe for good measure and ran to catch up with the guys.

Ghost turned to look back at Jude and tsked under his breath. I

"What?" I snapped.

He rubbed his hand over his chin like he was thinking. "I don't know, I guess I just figure if I was leaving behind the one thing that meant most to me in the entire world, I'd leave them with a little more than a nod and a *see ya later*," he said with a shrug.

I stared at him. His eyes were smiling at me, but he was one hundred percent serious and I knew he was right. What the hell was I thinking? None of us were promised tomorrow. I ran back to Jude. His eyes were wide and questioning, but when I launched myself into his arms, he didn't hesitate. Jude jerked me off of my feet and his mouth immediately found mine. His lips weren't gentle, they weren't patient. He seared me with his kiss, his lips claimed me as his own. And I did the same in return. I broke away breathless and stared up into his face.

"I love you, Jude Harrison. I will love you as long as I live and even after I'm gone I will still be yours."

Jude bent down and placed one more lingering kiss on my still-tingling lips. "Glad to hear it, Mel. I plan on loving you for a lifetime, so make sure you come back to me."

I nodded, removed myself from his arms, and ran back to the group waiting at the fence with huge grins on each of their faces.

"Now that's what I'm talkin' about," Ghost laughed.

My face flamed. "Shut it. Let's go and get this over with."

I was still grinning like a fool when we dipped through the opening in the gate. Our fight commenced immediately. We had to take down over a dozen zombies rapid-fire just to get away from the school. I ran with the group, pausing only to slide my blade through the emaciated neck of one zombie and then to stab through the bashed-in skull of another. I refused to look back at the high school. Jude and I would see each other again soon enough. We had to.

Avoiding the undead this time around was not an easy task. For one thing, they seemed more aware and more active since the sun was going down, for another, their numbers had tripled since we'd gone into the school. Zombies flooded the streets, sidewalks, and most of the buildings. There really was no "safe" zone as we moved through the city. We ducked behind cars, took out dozens of zombies, and tried to do it all while making very little noise. If the zombies were acting herd-like, then I didn't want to find out what a stampede of undead was capable of. I shuddered at the thought.

The only thing in our favor was that the zombies *were* moving slower than normal. I hadn't been going crazy back at the base. For some reason the undead were not moving as fast as they had been before. Ghost moved rapidly, driving his long sword through the skull of a female zombie before swinging it in an arc and splitting a large and extremely bloated one with dark gray skin from scalp to navel. The zombie exploded, its bowels splashing onto his pants and boots. I sighed inwardly. *Lucky.* Ghost's eyes were wide though, probably wondering how it was possible that so much rotten pulp could have fit inside of one undead man. I'd wondered the exact same thing the day before when I was unceremoniously showered in zombie entrails.

We all kept moving, knowing time was of the essence. We were within a block of the school bus parking lot and fighting our way towards it with our backs to busted-out storefronts, when the zombie population thickened right before our eyes. Each of us were downing two or three zombies at a time, not making much forward progress. Ghost fell in beside me, panting.

"Let's cut through that building and come up to the fence line from behind."

I glanced over at the store, which miraculously looked to have its front window intact, and nodded. I got Z's and Nate's attention and pointed to where we were heading. Z bobbed his head and took down another zombie before sprinting with Nate. I cleared the front of the store right behind Z and turned to make sure no zombies were closing in our group while Nate and Ghost made their way the last few feet to the store. When they cleared the front door, I locked it and leaned against it long enough to catch my breath. I wiped my hands on my jeans and pointed my knife toward the back of the store.

"We have to keep moving, the sun's about to set and then we will be fucked for real," I said between breaths.

We moved through the store, our breathing heavy and our hearts hammering. In retrospect, I should have remembered the barista from that Starbucks back in Midtown two years before. If I had, what happened next might have been avoided. We pushed open a door and entered the back room of the store we'd taken a shortcut through. Z stopped.

"Oh my god! Do you realize what store we're in?" he asked, his eyes bugged out in shock. I glanced around the room. In all honesty, I hadn't even noticed what it was when we ducked into the store. "We're in a freaking Dunkin Donuts," he groaned. I slapped the back of his head and shook my own. This kid was serious about his food. "Look over there." He pointed across the room at what looked like very dirty and old deep fryers. "They made their own donuts right here in the store too," he muttered in awe. Suddenly, I heard the banging on the front glass of the store, loud and frantic. The zombies were getting riled up.

"Sorry, can't stay and reminisce about the good 'ole days," I said, marching toward the back door. Nate and Ghost moved as well, but Z held back. I turned as Z squatted and put a hand out to touch a large bag of donut mix and icing on a lower shelf.

"Too bad we can't take a few—" His voice was cut off by a guttural cry of pain when a zombie that none of us had realized was in the room launched itself through the shelf from the other side and landed on top of a stunned Z and bit into Z's throat, ripping flesh with its teeth and tearing into an artery. Blood sprayed up in an arc across the room when Ghost jerked the zombie off of Z and decapitated it.

I ran over to Z and landed on my knees beside him. Blood pooled all around him. His eyes were wide and blood trickled from his mouth. His throat constricted several times, and his last few breaths came out in rapid pants as he laid there on the dirty storeroom floor and died. Ghost laid a hand on my shoulder a moment later. I wiped away the tears I hadn't realized I'd cried and stood unsteadily.

"I'm ready. Let's go," I said stiffly.

I turned away as Ghost did what he had to in order to make sure Z would never become one of the walking dead.

"Let's keep tightly together and get to the bus parking lot as quickly as possible," Ghost said when he joined us.

Nate and I both nodded. We came out of the store in a whirlwind of blades and good thing we did. Zombies—tons of them—stood between us and a line of buses not a hundred yards away. It was evident to me right away that we were fucked. No way around it. No way to sugarcoat it. We were going to die. And that pissed me off. I had promised Jude that I'd come back to him, dammit. I fought for all I was worth, but the moment Nate took out his gun, I knew there was no hope. His shots rang out in the city, drawing the attention of every zombie in the immediate area.

"What the fuck?" Ghost bellowed out. "Melody!" he shouted at me, drawing my attention to him just as a zombie sank its teeth into his arm.

I screamed in rage and ran my knife through the zombie in front of me, skewering it through an eye, heedless of the putrid juices that splattered my shirt. I ran toward Ghost, fighting off four... five... six undead before I reached him. He was still swinging his sword, his eyes blazing. He wasn't going down without a fight. When his eyes met mine, they were sorrowful. I think another small piece of my soul died in that moment. I heard a cry of agony come from behind me, but I didn't have the time or the strength to look back and see what was happening to Nate. When his high pitched scream pierced my skull and then... nothing, I knew it was only Ghost and I left.

"Melody!" Ghost bellowed.

I glanced up and saw him pointing his finger in the direction of the parking lot. I sliced my knife across the face of a short zombie and looked to where he was pointing. A small opening. Not much of one, but it was a spark of hope. We redoubled our efforts and moved in unison toward the break in bodies. Once I made it there, I started running, sure Ghost was right behind me, that he was going to make it. I ran in between buses, banging and pushing on the doors of a few, looking for one that was open. Surely one of them had to be open. I only stopped when a zombie stumbled into my path and only long enough to drive my knife into its skull and then keep moving.

When I got halfway down the line of buses I banged on another door, feeling like it was all quite hopeless. When the door gave beneath my pounding and I fell onto the stairs of the bus, I pulled myself off of the steps with a gasp and ran up onto the empty bus. I ran to the third seat and slammed a window down before pulling my gun off of my back and propping it up on the window frame. My hands were shaking by the time I spotted Ghost and started popping off the zombies that were hot on his tail. When he saw me in the window he ran for all that he was worth until he reached the bus, slamming the door shut behind him. I thinned the crowd of zombies that were closing in around the side of the bus, my shots never slowing.

"At this rate, I'll run out of bullets without making a dent in their numbers!" I shouted over the cacophony.

Ghost was sitting in the driver's seat, staring at the zombies banging their fists and gnashing their teeth on the bus door.

"Ghost?"

His eyes met mine and he smiled. "I'm dead, Melody," he said calmly.

I shook my head and slammed the window up into place. "No. There has to be something we can do."

Ghost chuckled beneath his breath and smiled at me sadly. "Not this time, beautiful girl," he answered matter-of-factly.

Tears ran down my face unashamedly. No. This couldn't be how things were supposed to be. I walked over to the first seat on the bus, close to Ghost, and sat down heavily.

The force of the zombies' bodies against the bus rocked it a bit. Holy hell. As long as they knew we were in here, they wouldn't quit. Even if we started the bus, we wouldn't be able to run over this many. We would never be able to get out of this mess. I closed my eyes and sank back into my seat. Jude's face flashed across my mind and I my heart tore in half. I heard Ghost ripping something and my eyes sprang open. He had ripped the hem of his shirt off. I walked over to him and took the fabric from him, wrapping it around the huge, bleeding wound on his upper arm. I took a bottle of water out of my pack, ignoring the frantic zombies on the other side of the glass door, and handed it to Ghost. He took it and downed a swig before handing it back to me.

"Put that back in your pack. You're going to need it," he said gently.

I did what he said even though I had no idea what he was talking about. He pulled his small pack out of his pocket and started working on the panel beneath the steering wheel.

"What are you doing?" I asked. "We won't be able to move, not with this many zombies surrounding us. We're going to die here."

"You're right, Melody. *One* of us will die tonight, but not both of us," he said through a grunt of pain as he jerked a large piece of metal off from beneath the steering wheel.

"What do you mean, Ghost?" I asked. "If you think for one second I'm going to leave you here, you got another thing coming."

Ghost yanked a bunch of wires out of the front of the bus. He didn't even look at me, but I could hear the smile in his voice when he said, "No, you won't be leaving. *I'll* be leaving, and taking a bunch of these undead bastards with me," he said like we were discussing whose turn it was to take out the garbage.

"I don't fucking think so," I growled.

Zombies were throwing themselves against the door even harder now and I flinched at the sound. I wondered how long the doors would hold before they broke through.

Ghost stood up from the driver's seat and swayed as he did. I put a hand out, but he waved me away.

"Sit down, Melody. I want to show you something." I did as I was told, too tired to question him. "You see these two wires?" he asked. He pointed out two different colored wires—one red and one blue—he'd separated from the others. I nodded. "Tomorrow morning, when you think it is safe, I want you to rub those two wires together lightly. It won't take much for the bus to start up." I frowned down at the wires. "Do you understand?" he asked, his voice weaker than before.

"Yes, but..."

Ghost knelt down beside me on the bus floor until our faces were even. His normally espresso-colored skin was ashen and a fine line of sweat dotted his brow.

"I'm going to die tonight, Melody," he stated. "The only way I can make it *mean* anything is to do it my own way."

I knew then that he had a plan, and that it was going to involve him sacrificing himself for me. I tried to jump from the seat, to talk some sense into him, but his hand landed on my shoulder and his eyes caught mine, begging me to understand. I wasn't sure I could. I'd come to love Ghost like a brother and I couldn't let him do this.

"Please, Ghost. Don't." My voice could barely be heard over the noise that the zombies were making.

Ghost smiled and brought a shaking hand to my face, tipping my chin up. "Ah, this won't be so bad. Dying for those I love. Plus, I'd hate to think of Jude being left all alone. Who'd watch his back and save his ass if both of us were dead?" he asked. A tiny burst of laughter left my lips. "That's better. Just don't forget me, Melody."

"I'd never forget you," I said truthfully.

Ghost smiled a huge grin, his white teeth shining in the final light of the day. "What else can a man ask for when he faces death?" he asked seriously.

My tears kept flowing while he outlined his plan. It was crazy. It was brilliant.

It was my only hope.

In the end, I didn't beg him to reconsider. I didn't make a huge scene or blubber all over him. I wanted him to have his final moments of glory, wanted to him to know how much I respected and loved him. I wanted him to know how much I owed to him for everything he was about to do. In the end, his death would be a death of honor for those he loved, and who was I to diminish his legacy?

Ghost got down on his hands and knees and made his way to the back of the bus where only a few zombies appeared to have figured out that they could see us from there. I crawled behind him, and when we got the back door, Ghost looked at me one final time.

"Until we meet again a very, very long time from now, Melody Carter." He kissed me on my forehead and then launched the back door open. I took out two zombies with my rifle to give him a little more time. I pulled the back door shut behind him, locked it, and then flattened myself against the floor as Ghost had instructed me. From where I lay, I could see him take out the few zombies in the back of the bus before he moved around to the side of the bus with a war cry. Even though I couldn't see what happened, I could imagine it all as I heard him.

He screamed his anger into the night while he ran. He took shots as he went, taking down more zombies than could be counted. When the pounding on the bus stopped, I knew he'd been right. The zombies had forgotten all about me, focusing in on him and the noise he was making. He bellowed his rage, yelling obscenities while he went, his voice growing more distant as he drew the zombie horde further away from the bus. My tears poured down my face and made a small pool on the floor where I laid impossibly still. And then, when he thought he'd led them far enough away and when he had them clawing at him and biting into his flesh, he dropped his gun and released two pins that he'd pulled from the grenades that he'd had strapped to his vest. The explosions rocked the city street, destroying the zombies closest to him and drawing the rest of the zombies to that spot.

Ghost's sacrifice would never be forgotten so long as I lived. I did what Ghost told me to. I was to wait until morning to start the bus. I stayed on the floor, crying until I could cry no more. Still, I lay there until exhaustion swept over me and I slept.

We All Live in a Yellow Submarine

I didn't sleep long, even with exhaustion plaguing my heart and body, I still had a job to do. I had to get the bus to the school. I moved from the floor to my knees and stretched until I could peer over the seats and out into the parking lot. The day was clear, the sun already rising, and the area was relatively clear of the zombie multitudes that had been surrounding the bus the night before. I moved quickly, not wanting to take a chance that I would lose too much time and the undead would take over the area again.

I threw my bag on the floor near the front of the bus and plopped down into the driver's seat. The bus was freaking huge and I'd never driven anything larger than an SUV. I gulped back my fears and took the two wires Ghost had pointed out the night before in my hands. The spark surprised me, but the bus didn't start right away. With a sinking feeling, I spoke to the bus in hushed tones, coaxing it like a lover would to make it turn on. I touched the wires together a third time, and finally the bus roared to life. My relief bowed my shoulders.

With a shaking hand, I put the bus in gear, pushed the gas gently, and pulled out into the parking lot. The dozen or so zombies in the area had already taken note of the moving bus. Time to get the hell out of dodge. I was pretty proud of myself when I got closer to the school. I'd only run over a few zombies, pushed a smaller car out of my way, and had done minimal damage to the ginormous yellow school bus. Very proud indeed. I circled the school two times, to make sure someone would see me, before driving to the loading area in the school. Someone would be looking out for me, of that I was positive. When I pulled up to the gates, several people were there to take out the zombies milling about while Manuel and Jude opened the gates wide for me to enter.

I parked as close to the school as I dared. Someone else could back it up to be loaded—I would have probably taken out a building if I'd tried. I opened the door to the bus and picked up my pack before exiting. When Jude, Manuel, and the others ran up, their eyes searching the bus for the others, the night before rose up again to slap me in the face.

Jude walked over to me. "Ghost?" he queried. A sob escaped my lips and he pulled me into his arms, shushing me and murmuring nonsense.

It was okay. Everything was okay.

Manuel led the others into the building to start bringing the supplies out and to stock up the bus. Jude grabbed my hand and pulled me along a sidewalk at the back of the school. I numbly followed him.

When we entered a locker room, I tugged on his hand. "Wait a sec, what are we doing?" I asked.

We went through another door and then we were facing shower stalls. Jude turned one on and miraculously, water shot out. I looked him, puzzled. He smiled shyly and walked over to me, removing my weapon from my shoulder.

"The school has a small backup generator. There's water."

I breathed in deeply, trying to feel good about that. Jude's hand ran down my arm until he caught my hand in his. He squeezed it lightly and then pulled me into his embrace. "Take your clothes off, Mel," he whispered into my hair. "Let me show you what you have left to *fight* for." He pulled my shirt over my head and then pulled his own off. "Let me show what you have left to *live* for," he murmured huskily. His mouth found mine and we both stumbled toward the showers, our hands seeking, our hearts and bodies joining.

I let him show me. I let him wash away my pain and sorrow with love and passion. I let him help me forget... even it was only for an hour.

.́.

When we emerged from the showers, clean and sated, with our hair still dripping wet, the group had already managed to remove four seats from the back of the bus. Supplies were being brought out in boxes and on a dolly the group had found at the school. I was told that it would take another hour or two to remove the four more seats and then to fill the bus so that we could leave. I kept myself busy by scouting the rest of the school for anything that we could use.

I didn't find much of anything that I thought we could use even though I walked through classrooms, offices, and the gymnasium. I did find a snack machine in the gym and considered shooting it to get the candy out. I was pretty sure that would have been a stupid idea though.

If only Ghost were here to pick the lock, I thought.

I took my anger out on the machine, punching it until I tired myself out and left smears of blood along the front of it. When I was ready and had myself under better control an hour had passed. I decided to head back and join the rest of the group. They were probably close to being ready to go.

I was looking at the ground while I walked when heard something that made me stop in my tracks. The sound of metal being crushed, and then a gunshot. My first instinct was to run toward the sound and to see what was going on so I could help the group, but then I heard the shouting. I pulled my rifle off my back and ran behind a huge cement pillar that blocked me from the view of the bus area.

"You stupid son of a—" I heard shouting again and then another shot. With my heart pounding, I knelt down and peeked from behind the pillar that I was hiding behind. An armed group of about eighteen men and women had the rest of my group at gunpoint, their huge trucks had torn down the back gates of the school. I scanned the group and found Jude alive, and he looked angry as hell. Manuel was also on his knees, his hands behind his head, while the man who appeared to be the leader of the group shouted a bunch of questions at them. I took a moment to breathe and to try and figure out what I could do to get us out of the situation without losing more people or having to kill the living.

I glanced back around the pillar and searched the group that had broken into the school, quickly realizing that only a couple of them were military or had probably ever used a gun before the outbreak. Several of them couldn't have been older than fifteen or sixteen. *Shit*. I couldn't kill a bunch of kids. I started thinking through all the possible ways I could get us out of the mess we were in when the decision was taken out of my hands. Someone screamed and a few shots sounded, echoing in the area, loudly ringing the proverbial dinner bell. I cursed beneath my breath and stood up. I raised my gun, pointing it at the head of the guy who had been doing the talking. No one noticed me at first, the morons had been making too much noise and had shattered an opening in our fence, letting dozens of the undead shuffle into the schoolyard.

"Hey, Jackass!" I shouted over the melee.

Jude swung his gaze to me as the man with his hair pulled back into a greasy ponytail and a goatee did. I held up my left hand in hope that he would see that I really didn't *want* to mean them any harm, but my scope remained trained on his head. His gun turned in my direction and he shouted at me.

"Stop fucking moving right now!"

I clenched my jaw. "How did you survive this long?" I asked loudly. His eyes narrowed. "I mean, how fucking stupid can you be?" I continued, fully aware he could pull the trigger at any moment, or maybe one of his teenage soldiers' shaking fingers could slip and I'd be a goner. "You not only let the zombies in, but you even ring the fucking dinner bell for them? Bravo!" I said with a sneer.

"You better watch you smart ass mouth, bitch!" he shouted, his face turning a very unattractive shade of red. Bullets were flying behind me; several of his soldiers were trying to keep the zombies from ruining his little raid, but I knew it wouldn't be long before we were overrun. And then we would *all* be dead. Without moving my gun, I jerked my head at the petite woman between me and the goateed dude.

"You okay with him killing a bunch of survivors just to take their supplies?"

Her face was full of doubt and she glanced between me, him, and our group on their knees. "He didn't say we were going to kill anyone. We just need the supplies," she said, indecision coloring her voice. She searched his face and I hoped she saw what I saw. He *was* planning on killing everyone. Even if we *did* give him our supplies. We were all dead to him.

"Shut your mouth, Nina," he practically growled. Nina took a step back.

He had followers because he'd probably helped them survive, but it was clear he abused the power he'd taken. None of them were following him because of his sterling personality and morals.

"I don't want to have to kill you, but I will," I said loudly, my eyes narrowing in on the guy. He laughed loudly one time, his gun moving away from me for a second and giving me the exact opening I needed. My bullet entered right between his eyes. When he dropped to the pavement, there was a moment of stunned silence and I ran over to his body and spun, training my gun on Nina. Her mouth was hanging open and she had already lowered her gun.

"I didn't see *that* coming," she said after a pause.

"We don't have to fight each other!" I shouted out into the crowd, secretly terrified to see so many zombies now pouring through the gates. "We'll be glad to take all of you with us. We have supplies and shelter."

I took out a zombie that had come within two feet of Nina and then lowered my rifle to jerk my knife from its sheath. Her eyes met mine. They were tired eyes, tired of seeing all the crap we had all been through.

Nina shrugged and nodded over to the body on the ground. "I never like that asshole anyway," she said, smiling at me.

I smiled back and winked at Jude.

"You guys might want to get your weapons. Shit's about to get real up in here," I said.

They jumped up and immediately ran to help the others fight back the wave of undead. Manuel closed the door to the bus before joining everyone else. We fought hard, we fought for those who had died trying to help the group. But we were fighting a losing battle. Thirty minutes into the fighting, Jude found my gaze, his face resigned. By shooting his gun and knocking down the gates, the man I'd killed had summoned an entire herd of zombies earlier than their normal routine. We were swarmed. Our only hope was to find a place to hole up and wait out the herd, hoping they'd stick to their routine and move on through the area later. Several young people from the group had already fallen and I was so sick of seeing people die.

"Melody!" Jude shouted over the noise to get my attention. "The cafeteria freezer!"

I nodded and ran over to Manuel. He whistled, a sharp ear-piercing sound to get everyone's attention. I caught Nina's eye and made a motion for her to round up her group and follow us into the school. Pretty soon all of us were making a run for it down the abandoned hallways of the high school. I was surprised when I reached the cafeteria doors to see the majority of our group and Nina's right behind me. When Jude brought up the rear, Manuel barked orders for everyone to move tables and chairs up against the doors and windows.

"Is that everyone?" Jude asked between breaths. "Is everyone accounted for?" he snapped.

Nina nodded, her eyes raking over what was left of her group. Besides her, only a dozen dirty and injured people remained.

"What about Mike?" Manuel shouted over the noise. Jude shook his head, frowning.

Manuel cursed. We were down to eight people ourselves. About that time a zombie ran itself into the window that faced the courtyard in front of the cafeteria. Several more immediately joined in. It would only be a matter of time before so many showed up that they broke the glass and got inside.

"Let's go everyone, let's get to the back storage room where the walk-in freezer is," Jude announced.

"That's your plan? To go and hide in the freezer?" a young girl with short, spiky black hair asked, her eyes wide in disbelief.

"As a matter of fact it is," Jude snapped, his eyes daring anyone to cross him.

"If you all had paid better attention to the zombies and the way they were acting around here, maybe you'd notice how they are moving herd-like," I said. "We figured it out in the first few hours of coming into the area. It's our best bet. We wait until the herd, hopefully, moves on after the sun goes down and the rest of the undead masses move through this neighborhood. And then we make a run for the bus and get the fuck out of here."

"Any other questions?" Jude asked sharply. No one said anything, but the sounds coming from the zombies were growing more desperate by the second, and I was sure the glass would be breaking sooner rather than later. "Good, let's go."

We all ran to the back room. When we got to the freezer and Jude opened it, the smell of two year old rotting food welcomed us.

Nina shook her head. "I get claustrophobic," she said.

I looked inside the freezer and had a moment of panic myself. It was a huge freezer, but with twenty people jammed into it for God-only-knew how long, it wasn't something I was looking forward to.

Manuel shocked the hell out of me and grabbed Nina by the hand. "We'll get through this together. All of us. Just like we all have survived everything since the beginning, well survive this too."

Nina gulped and nodded her head. Manuel and Jude entered first, jerked two shelves out of the freezer, and threw them into the storage room. They made quick work of shoving all the rotten food containers out into the storage room, and not a moment too soon. I heard a loud cracking sound and everyone froze in place, and then I heard the gurgles of the zombies who were filling the cafeteria.

They had arrived.

"Inside, everyone. Quickly!" Jude said.

We all obeyed immediately and once we were all inside, we shut the door behind us and bolted it from the inside. Manuel turned his flashlight on and shone it around the room. We had only enough room on the floor for all of us to sit. And no telling how long we were going to be stuck in the freezer. I just prayed our theory would be correct and the zombies *would* move on when the herd swept through.

"Are we going to be able to breathe long in here?" someone whispered.

Manuel shined his light up into the ceiling of the freezer. "There's a fan vent there where the cold air used to blow through. We'll have oxygen coming in from there. We'll be fine," he reassured everyone. "How many of us have flashlights?"

Jude, Manuel, James, and I all had flashlights on us.

"Good," Jude said wearily. "We'll turn on one for a few minutes periodically."

A boom from outside of the freezer rattled the door. The zombies were in the storage room. They started banging on the freezer.

We were in for a very long day and night.

Deafening Silence

Several hours later, we were all sitting on the floor listening to the constant sounds of the undead right outside of the freezer door. I felt like I was about to lose my shit in the dank, dark room, shut up with nineteen other filthy survivors and hoping the zombie wave would go through our area soon.

"Man, I'd give anything to be in my old man's beachfront condo right about now. Zombies or no, I'd sure like to hit some waves," a young man from Nina's group said, and the entire room groaned in agreement. "What about you guys?"

"Alaska. Might be cold, but that could mean fewer zombies," Nina answered hesitantly.

"A deserted island. No zombies," someone else chimed in. "Just me and wide open beaches, pineapples, and coconuts."

"Piña coladas," someone agreed with a laugh.

Laughter floated through the room and I smiled at that. A frozen beverage full of pineapple and coconut? Sounded like heaven to me.

"My grandmother's house," a young girl said. We all sobered up. "She made the best banana nut bread and pot roast."

I smiled into the darkness. The small things we took for granted from before would mean so much more to us now. Retrospect was a bitch.

"A fully functioning, zombie free, Mexican restaurant," I said into the silence. Everyone laughed. "Loaded tacos? Fresh homemade salsa?" I added for extra emphasis. "Am I right?"

"Margaritas," the same person who mentioned the piña coladas added in, and everyone laughed again.

Silence once again fell over the group and all that we could hear was the sounds of the zombies on the other side of the door, clawing and gnashing their teeth against it as they tried to get in.

Several more hours later, Jude switched his flashlight on to check his watch. It was late—really late. Darkness should have already fallen, and that meant we had to stay put and wait out the zombies. We were going to end up stuck in the freezer overnight and that prospect did not sound all that enticing to me. I scooted over next to him and laid my head on his shoulder. His muscles were tense. No matter what happened, he would feel responsible for this group, even if he couldn't have foreseen the other group attacking us, even if half the group weren't our people to begin with. Now we had to get these people to safety. I understood that; I felt the same way. A few moments later, his body relaxed enough for me to wrap my arm around his and doze off on his shoulder.

I'm not sure how long I slept, but I woke to the faint pounding and groans of zombies close by.

"No change?" I whispered.

"They're more sporadic now. Less *enthusiastic*," Jude explained.

I listened to the noises and I had to agree. They didn't sound quite as insistent and frantic as they had before. *This is good*, I thought.

"What time is it?" I asked.

"It's two o'clock in the morning," he answered.

Holy crap. I'd slept that long? I turned on my light and flashed it around the room. Almost everyone was asleep.

"So, what do we do next, Jude?"

He sighed and I knew he had to be exhausted. No telling how long it had been since he'd slept last.

"Once the sun is out, we make a run for it. No matter what, we can't stay shut up in here forever. We have to get to the bus and *pray* that at least half of the zombies have moved on."

I squeezed his arm and then entwined my fingers with his. "We have several hours then. Why don't you try to rest?" He immediately stiffened next to me. "You won't be any good to the group if you can't shoot worth a damn because you're dead on your feet. There's no way you'll oversleep," I said gently.

Jude's shoulders slumped and his body relaxed for the first time since we'd entered the freezer. Pretty soon his head was in my lap and I was stroking his hair while he snored softly.

I'm not sure how much time passed, but the next thing I knew, Manuel was kicking my foot and whispering loudly. I jumped, which caused Jude to jerk off of my lap, his body immediately ready for any threat.

"Do you hear that?" Manuel whispered loudly. I strained my ears. Jude's entire body was thrumming with adrenaline.

"What is it?" Nina asked from the back of the freezer.

I switched on my flashlight and shone around the room. Everyone was wide awake and listening intently.

"I don't hear anything," I said into the silence. I flashed my light back around to Manuel's smiling face.

"Exactly," he answered. "Silence."

There wasn't any banging or any gurgles, just the sweet sound of *nothing*. Jude flashed his light down at his watch. It was almost six thirty in the morning. We had to move. No matter what happened, this was our best chance.

"Alright everyone, let's get ourselves prepared to move," Jude whispered into the room. We all stood, grabbing our weapons and our packs, getting ready for whatever lay on the other side of the door. Whatever it was, we were all going to face it together. "I suspect that even if the wave of zombies has blown through and even if the area is pretty clear," Jude said, "there will be enough zombies left in the area to give us a fight to get to the bus. Don't do anything stupid. No guns. Only knives. Get to the bus so we can get the hell out of here." He paused. "Understand?"

We all answered the affirmative.

I gripped the handle of my knife and prepared for the worst case scenario, which would have been a horde of zombies right outside the doors, or in the cafeteria area. Manuel unbolted the door and the room took a collective breath in anticipation. I adjusted my grip and tightened my fist around the hilt of my blade. Manuel raised his hand and pushed the door. It didn't budge. I glanced up at Jude. His face was a mask of shock and "oh shit". Manuel and Jude put their shoulders to the door and heaved with all of their might. The door came open slowly, pouring light into the room and our sensitive eyes from the ruined storage doorway. I stumbled through the doorway and came up right behind Manuel and Jude, who were simply standing there.

"What is it?" Nina gasped in horror.

The freezer emptied out and instead of running for the bus like we'd decided while in the freezer, we all stood there in slack-jawed awe and confusion.

Bodies were everywhere. The undead lay in heaps and I'd never seen so much rotten sludge in my life. It was everywhere, coating the entire room. I walked forward and scanned the room, my head dizzy and disoriented.

What the hell is going on?

"Someone took them out?" the spiky-haired girl asked and the group erupted with questions.

"Who would do that?"

"Why would anyone do that and then just leave?"

"What the hell happened to their bodies? They look mushier than normal."

So many questions asked, but no one had any answers. I caught Jude's gaze and the look on his face told me he was land blasted like the rest of us.

"*Madre de Dios,*" Manuel muttered standing in the cafeteria doorway and making the sign of the cross.

We moved out of the storage room, pushing into the cafeteria behind him. The cafeteria was a slaughterhouse. We barely paid any attention to the two zombies when they charged. One of them slipped on the gunge that coated the floor. Manuel dispatched both of them without any help. There had to be close to fifty bodies piled in the room.

"No one touch any of the bodies and try to stay out of the mess if possible, we don't know what we're dealing with here," Jude said in the silence.

The carnage continued all the way out to the bus. Bodies and gore. Everywhere. We only had a dozen zombies near the school bus to take care of. It was all over in less than ten minutes and then we were piling onto our bus, everyone enveloped in the kind of shocked silence that follows massive devastation. I could see it on everyone's faces. They were scared. They were not used to the rules changing. We were used to knowing our surroundings, knowing who our enemies were, and how to defeat them. We'd all survived under the certainty that we knew how to beat the odds, how to adapt to our new environment. No one said a word when Manuel climbed onto the bus, shut the doors, and started the engine. No one said anything when we pulled off of the school property.

Even when we drove through the city where the bodies outnumbered the shambling zombies ten-to-one, no one said a thing. We were in shock. Was it possible that our world had changed again right before our eyes and without warning? Would it be possible for us to adapt again and to survive through more changes? We carefully made our way out of Gastonia.

"What's happening?" Nina whispered from a seat over as she stared out the window.

"Don't worry. We'll figure this out. It will be okay," I said, not sure if I was trying to convince her or myself.

Jude walked over to my seat and sat down heavily next to me and picked up my hand, interlacing my fingers with his. I looked up into his face with so many questions on the edge of my lips, so many fears of what we would have to face in the near future. I didn't voice any of it.

"We're going to be okay," I said matter-of-factly.

"Yes we are," he answered.

I took a deep, steadying breath. When Jude smiled at me and leaned over to place a kiss on my lips, I knew. I knew it would be okay. No matter what we faced, we would do it together. No matter how great the struggles we'd encounter on our journey, we would tackle them head on, knowing that our lives, however long— or however short— would be better because we had each other.

Epilogue

Eight Weeks Later

Exactly eight weeks ago, the undead corpses that had overrun the entire globe simply collapsed to the ground in droves, finally and truly dead in the most literal interpretation of the word. Many of them not only dropped, but their corpses, unable to contain all the putrid fluid their bodies had been hauling around, just *exploded*.

We're still trying to figure out what happened. I'm sure that there will be a more scientific explanation provided at some point, and by smarter people than I. Simply put, however, after exactly eight hundred and sixty-six days, the earliest parasite-infested zombies, who had not fed on enough humans after that first, horrific day, could no longer support the ever-multiplying and ever-feeding parasites inside of their corpses. The result was an unbelievably messy demise, which included the skin of the undead bursting and the mushy, putrid innards exploding from the inside out.

For four weeks we went topside to scout out all the surrounding areas and to keep an eye on what was happening. We were wary and concerned by what was occurring, scared that somehow the parasites would be able to survive on the outside of the bodies, or had even evolved, making it possible to take on a new, living host by means that were new and unknown to us. We wore face masks for the first time since the outbreak, hoping we hadn't been dealt an even shittier hand than before.

The fifth week, we decided to take our chances by collecting and burning a large number of the corpses in our area. We took precautions for our group, though, and stayed away from the base for days while we did so, just in case any of us became infected.

When it was clear that none of us had contracted anything by coming in contact with the bloated corpses, we initiated the long and exhausting cleanup process in our area. The cleanup was not without its risks. The world was not zombie-free by any stretch of the imagination. From everything we knew, we could only deduce that those zombies who were first infected had been the ones to drop off in scores in the previous weeks. But if the zombies had fed often or if they'd had been turned later, those were all still shambling around in search of their next happy meal, the next human they could sink their teeth into.

The population of the living was still devastated by the sheer numbers of dead and undead. The living were still in the minority. But I could feel it in my bones that we wouldn't be for long. Maybe I wouldn't see the day that we were once again the majority. Maybe it wouldn't happen in my lifetime, but it *was* going to happen. It was only a matter of time now.

The plan was simple: wait while the undead died off, play it smart, don't get killed, and take out as many of the bastards you could while you still had breath left in you.

Yeah, it was going to happen.

I helped throw another body onto the pile we'd made right on the outskirts of Midtown, thinking of all the things that had happened to us recently. We'd lost so many people that we cared about. We'd taken in more than thirty survivors since the day we came back to the base on the school bus from Gastonia. We'd cleared the entire area surrounding the base and had reinforced the perimeter fences. We'd also begun building brick walls around it; soon we'd be able to go topside just because we wanted to see the sunset and we wouldn't have to worry about the undead overtaking the base.

Earlier in the day we'd seen a very official group of soldiers enter the base and immediately shut themselves up in meetings with Major Tillman and Captain Parsons, another sign that things were changing for the good. We'd grown as a group and we'd caught a teensy glimpse of what the future could be.

The future didn't look quite as bleak as it had two months before.

I wouldn't go so far to say that any of us were naïve enough to think that the days of death and sorrow were completely behind us, but I would say that we were all firmly on the very difficult road to believing that we had a *chance*. A chance was really all that anyone could ask for.

We had so much work to do to make the world a safer place for our future, for our children's future. And the absolute truth was that the world would *never* be the same as it had been before. Humanity would never be the same. But humanity had survived overwhelming loss and damning odds to come out on top. I could only pray that we would continue to do so.

I wiped my brow and turned away from the pile of undead to stare at the "Welcome to Midtown" sign a few feet away with a smile on my face. Jude came up behind me and followed my gaze to the sign.

"What are you thinking, Mel?" he asked, rubbing his hand along the back of my neck, lifting the ponytail off of my hot and sticky neck to let the air hit it.

"I'm thinking how much has changed since the last time I saw that sign," I said. "I'm thinking about how much has changed since I walked into town by myself three days after my dad died."

"He'd be so proud of you," Jude said.

I glanced up to the blue sky above me and heard a bird singing a sweet tune in the distance.

"Yes he would be," I answered. "And he'd have loved you."

I looked over at Jude and he smiled at me, his eyes twinkling with love and happiness. I felt another one of the rips my heart and soul had suffered over the years mend itself. Oh, the scars would always be there, but they would be only a faded memory instead of a gaping wound.

We both got back to work making the world a little safer, a little more *worth living for*.

We were no longer a people without hope—a people without the promise of light at the conclusion of a seemingly never-ending tunnel filled with death and darkness.

We were beginning to have *hope* again.

Where there is hope, there is life.

And that's more than any of us had had in a very long time.

STATE OF RUIN
BOOK TWO

Hope, in reality, is the worst of all evils because it prolongs the torments of man.
~Friedrich Nietzsche

Prologue
Hell in a Hand Basket

Zombies here. Zombies there. Zombies everywhere.

I was tired of all the death and tired of all the killing, but what choice did I have when the entire world had gone to Hell in a hand basket? It was kill or be killed. A man-eat-man world now. And if that ain't screwed up enough, it's a living-take-advantage-of-the-living world as well. It's been two years since the world changed. Two years since a man on a trip to a remote South African jungle with the Peace Corps unknowingly brought a microscopic, organ-feasting organism into the US.

Patient 001, a cancer patient, and unaware of his deadly hitchhiker, went through a series of chemotherapy treatments, causing the parasite to mutate and spread. Fueled by the direct exposure to the chemo and helped along by the electromagnetic chaos emitted by technology on every city corner in Chicago, the organism spread out of control and killed off nearly eighty percent of the population. The worst was yet to come though. Once the host died, the parasites were able to act as a stimuli in the corpses' brainstem, causing the host to "reanimate", thus turning them into mindless, flesh-eating marionettes.

Some people would say this is the beginning of the end for humanity. That fighting a losing battle isn't worth the trouble. They'd be wrong. I might be from a tiny, Podunk town in Texas, but I'm smart enough to realize the odds of survival ain't so great for the living. That doesn't mean I'll go down without a fight. The world *might* end. Humanity *could* cease to exist. But if I'm sure of anything, it is that any life worth living is worth fighting for... and I plan to do exactly that.

That was back when I still had hope. When I still thought the world could be saved. Back before I lost so many people I cared about. Before I realized that death was a cruel bitch, not caring who or what she destroyed.

I miss the noise more than anything else. Funny how the one thing I absolutely hated and frequently complained about is the one thing I miss the most now that the world has come to an end. There wasn't a day that went by that I didn't wish for everything to stop, for all the useless noise to just... cease. And now that it has, I find the silence that has filled the void the noise left behind to be the most disturbing thing of all. Now that the world has ended, I miss those things. Those things that let me know *life* was happening all around me. Cars have stopped zooming, phones have stopped ringing, music has stopped playing, and children have stopped laughing. The only thing left behind is silence. Silence is not a good companion for the living.

Even more disturbing than the surrounding silence are the sounds that have replaced the echoes of life in this terrible new world: the macabre impersonation of the sounds of the living. Instead of an exhalation of breath, there is a sort of rattling of air. Instead of talking and laughing, whispering and singing, there is moaning, snapping teeth, and gurgling. Instead of walking, driving, skipping, and running, there is dragging and crunching, shuffling and scraping. There is movement and there are even noises, but there is no life. Where there is no life, there is no hope. I have found that my hope has all but deserted me. And without hope, what is there worth living for?

It was when I realized I had no reason left to live and no reason left to fight that I found myself wondering if it would be better to cease to exist entirely. It would be easier, certainly. Peaceful even. Then my mama's voice echoed inside my head telling me in no uncertain terms that she didn't raise no coward, she didn't raise her boy to give up when the goin' got tough. She didn't raise no quitter. I may have lost all my hope, but all hope was not lost. I may not have any hope left for myself, but I may have been someone else's last hope. I just needed to move on. I needed to get back to the people who inspired me. Back to the one place where I felt hope might still be alive.

I stepped back away from the ledge of the once beautiful two-story Victorian home and pulled the earplugs out of my ears. The sound of Johnny Cash's voice was immediately replaced by the sounds of the horde of undead that reached out to me from below the ledge that I stood on, waiting for me to take that step that I had moments earlier been so close to taking. The sounds of the zombies mingled with their putrid stench and wafted up to me. I took another step back, grabbed my bag, and pulled out my blade. Keep fighting it was then.

Thanks, Mama.

I pushed the earphones back into my ears and let the sounds of Johnny Cash's 'Folsom Prison Blues' drown out the moans, scraping, and gurgling. I made my way down the stairs of the building I'd gone into to die and cranked up my music full blast. Johnny came through for me once again as I listened to him ramble about *'the train a comin'*, '*rolling round the bend*' and how he '*ain't seen the sunshine since he don't know when,*' he was stuck in Folsom Prison and time kept draggin' on.

I let the music drown out everything; the sounds, the smells, and even the familiar feeling I'd get lately when I'd step out into the world with a knife in my hand and my jaw clenched in determination. That feeling that *this* was all there was left. Fighting. Killing. Surviving. Lather, rinse, and repeat.

This couldn't be all that there was left. I shoved a knife into a faceless corpse. *It couldn't be*, I sent out as a whisper into the universe.

Chapter One
Zombies in Dreamland

"Thirty-three bottles of Jack on the wall, thirty-three bottles of Jack. Take one down, pass it around, thirty-two bottles of Jack on the wall."

My off-key voice echoed through the truck as I drove down the deserted highway, the bottle of Jack Daniels that I'd scavenged from a convenience store about twenty miles back safely ensconced in the passenger's seat. Yeah buddy, me and Jack had a date tonight.

It had only been about three weeks since I'd left the group back at the Army base. Three weeks that I'd been on my own out in the midst of the infected. It felt like it had been an eternity. I like to think I was finding myself, that I was going to come out of this adventure and look back at see all the little things I'd learned about who I really am and used it to become a better person. The truth was that I was lonely and I hadn't learned a damned thing except the dead weren't good company. I felt like a complete jackass. So here I was headed back in the direction I never should have left. Back to the Army base and back to my group.

It was getting late in the day and if I had learned anything over the last few weeks, it was that I didn't want to be out and about, driving or otherwise, after dark. I drove twenty more minutes on the highway until I found a suitable turnoff. When I pulled into a gas station right outside of the nearest town, I was glad to find only a handful of zombies and a store that still had its windows in place. I didn't have it in me to clear out a bunch of undead before bunking down for the night.

Before the truck had even come to a complete stop, several rambling corpses lurched in my direction. I pulled my knife from its sheath and opened my door, instantly moving toward the decaying zombies. My arm swung in a killing arc, a movement as natural to me as breathing now. The blade caught the zombie in the left eye, stilling its reanimated body for good. When I yanked my hand back, the blade came free with a lot of crunching and sloshing, the sound of tiny bone fragments and decomposing organs coming free from the rotting layers of skin it had been a prisoner of.

"Son of a bitch," I growled beneath my breath. My stomach wanted to revolt, but I didn't allow it. I clenched my jaw and dropped two more of the zombies before I had too much time to think about the sounds and the smells. You think I'd be used to this shit by now. You'd be wrong. I hoped I never got used to it, I hoped my stomach would always revolt, and I hoped I always remembered how it *used* to be a little over two years ago. Some days remembering was easier than others. Today was not one of those days.

Three more dispatched zombies later, I pulled my pack out of my vehicle and shoved the bottle of Jack Daniels in it. The store was easy enough to break into seeing as how the door wasn't even locked. It had been ransacked long ago by the looks of it. I went to work immediately to make the building as secure as possible. I moved shelving against the glass door and large front window before cleaning out the space behind the register to sleep for the night. The back door to the store was still locked. It would be an easy way out if zombies somehow got into the store and things got hairy.

When darkness finally fell, I sunk down onto my sleeping bag behind the register area. I took off the black cowboy hat I'd taken to wearing since I'd been on my own and sat it on a shelf nearby. I didn't usually feel so sorry for myself and though I wasn't a big drinker, I could handle my liquor. Any southern boy worth his salt could. I took a swig of Jack Daniels, ignoring how it burned as it went down. Tonight I just wanted to forget. I just wanted to blur all the memories, all of the pain, and all of the death into a barely recognizable dream. I'd gotten a quarter of the way through the bottle before everything started getting fuzzy. I got halfway through the bottle before I was numb enough to nod of into dreamland.

Dreamland sure as hell ain't what it used to be.

*

It would be nice if a person could actually be aware that they were dreaming instead of becoming caught up in the panic and heart-racing events unfolding in front of their dream-self, unable to do anything to change them. It is especially hard when dreams morph different times, different people, and different events into one pulse-pounding nightmare.

My wife stood in front of me, her arms outstretched to me, beckoning me to come to her. She wore jeans and a white tee shirt with a pretty floral scarf around her neck. I smiled to myself. She looked as beautiful as the day I married her. I raised my hand to her, but instead of strong arms opened to welcome her into them, as I had done so many times before, my arms were dirty and battered. My fist clenched around a long, serrated blade coated in blood and chunks of rotting flesh. I was running to her, wanting to protect her from the undead and the horrors of the world, but as I moved, my adrenaline surged in anticipation of the kill and... it brought a grin to my lips. My wife's eyes widened in terror and her hands came up in a defensive pose, though not before a blade imbedded itself into her skull. I bellowed out my rage as her eyes went milky and blood poured down her face. I tried to reach out my hand to comfort her, to comfort myself, but it was already busy. I glanced up at the knife in my wife's skull and realized instantly why I couldn't move my hand to help her. It was my hand gripping the handle of the blade protruding from my wife's skull. It was my hand holding the weapon in a death grip and twisting it deeper into the place where I'd lodged it. I could feel the wet and sticky blood as it still pumped from the fresh wound.

"This isn't your fault." I dragged my gaze away from the scarlet wound that I'd created and found my wife's undead gaze on me. I flinched, keeping my hand around the blade I'd used on her.

"It's not your fault that I'm dead. It's not your fault that I turned, Tex." Her breath whispered across my face. Instead of the cinnamon flavored toothpaste she was fond of, the scent of putrid innards assaulted my nostrils. My eyes widened though I kept my emotions in check. I couldn't break down. Not now. Not ever.

"I failed you," I whispered. The blood oozed from the gaping wound in her frontal lobe. When I looked back down at her, she was no longer there. Instead, Jessica Germain stood before me. I glanced down at myself and barely recognized the clean uniform I'd worn on a daily basis while working with her dad. It seemed like another lifetime ago. Jessica was just like she'd been back before she'd become the hardened militia leader that had taken over the Charlotte Army base. Her hair was long and blonde, hanging down her back. Her face was as carefree as any teenager's should be and her clothing matched her girly demeanor.

"Everything could have been so different," she said as she, twisting her finger in her pale hair. My jaw hardened. I'd failed her as well. If I could've gotten her family into the base... if I could have snuck them in or if I'd had a little more time before the base had gone on lockdown, maybe I could have helped them.

"You couldn't have done anything, Tex. This is how it was all supposed to happen." Her eyes glazed over a bit just as a shot sounded and a bullet entered her forehead. I didn't move, only watched the back of her skull explode behind her and blood pour across her nose and down her body.

"I didn't want to have to do that." I turned just enough to see Melody Carter with a gun still pointed at Jessica approach me. "I never wanted any of this," she muttered in disgust.

"None of us did," I answered.

"It's the shitty hand we've been dealt." She looked over at me and grinned. "You look like hell, Tex." I grunted and glanced down at myself. I was back to wearing gore-splattered jeans, a tee shirt, and my black cowboy hat. A bottle of Jack Daniels was tipped over at our feet.

"I've felt better," I admitted.

She put a hand out and touched my arm. "Zombies and a bottle of Jack?" She raised a brow. "Probably not your best idea," she stated matter-of-factly.

I sputtered a laugh. "Probably not."

"You need to get your crap together, Tex. The world needs men like you more than ever."

I shook my head. Had she not been paying attention? I failed everyone. The world needed a whole lot better than what I had to offer.

"You're wrong, Tex. You're exactly the kind of man this world needs." She smiled again and took a step back. When I reached my hand out, she shook her head.

"Your problems, your journey. Your choice."

I frowned down at the bottle on the ground and reached for my head. Noises were beginning to filter through my groggy brain and a hammer was battering mercilessly on my skull. I flinched and glanced back up at Mel's retreating form.

"Wake up, Tex. Now!"

Her words were urgent, but I batted them away, willing the pain in my head to subside.

"Get your honky-tonk loving ass up RIGHT NOW, DAMMIT!"

Chapter Two
Pineville Welcomes You

I grunted, flinching from the force of the voice that yelled at me. The movement shot pain into every single spot on my head. I'm pretty sure even my hair was in pain. I rolled over and rammed my head into a counter.

"Shit!" I groaned, pulling myself up onto my elbows. The room swam around me. The store was bathed in sunlight and I realized with a jolt that the sun had come up long ago. Noise filtered into my alcohol-induced haze and I suddenly grasped the error I'd made by going on my Jack Daniels drinking binge. From the sounds outside the store, several zombies were moving around the area. Which meant they were surrounding my vehicle, which also meant I was going to have to fight my way through a group of zombies while dealing with my very own self-imposed version of death-warmed-over.

I made quick work of packing the contents of my bag and rolling up my sleeping bag. With a shaking hand and a swimming head, I popped the last few aspirin I had in my stash in my mouth and swallowed. Jack and I were no longer friends, the dirty rat bastard.

"As ready as I'll ever be," I muttered beneath my breath before standing up. Standing up should have been easier. Getting out of the store alive definitely would have been had I not slept away a good portion of the day. Zombies swarmed the front of the store. The sun was beating down onto the asphalt and the undead had taken refuge near the store to keep from baking. Even the undead had *some* sense of self preservation. I stood frozen for a moment too long, trying to decide what to do next. A bloated zombie who looked like he probably would make a sloshing sound when he moved spotted me and began banging on the window. Each hit on the glass not only left chunks of flesh and rivulets of rancid juices running down the window, it also hammered spikes of pain a bit deeper into my cranium. Pretty soon dozens of undead were banging and trying to push their way inside the little convenience store.

"If I live through this, I'm never drinking again," I said aloud. A promise I intended to keep. I hoisted my bag onto my back, sat my trusty hat as gingerly on my head as possible, and left the sleeping bag behind the counter. There was no way I'd be able to carry it as I ran and there was no way I'd be able to get to my truck. I was going to have to go it on foot for now. I sprinted to the back door. I had no idea how many undead were at the back of the store, but I was pretty sure I wouldn't luck out and find none. I was just hoping it would be a lot less than out front. Since the zombies were making so much noise out front, the sound might attract the zombies around the store to the front and give me an advantage. I was betting my life on that. Louder than what should have been possible, the sound of cracking glass echoed through the front of the store and reached me all the way in the back.

I reached for my handgun and closed my eyes for a second. I knew I had exactly six bullets left in the gun and that was it. I was going to have to make quick work of the zombies with my knife and then run like hell. I gripped the handle of the door and opened it slowly, slipping out of the building as quietly as possible. As soon as I was out and the door shut behind me, I knew my luck had come to a screeching halt. Zombies. Zombies *everywhere*.

The first corpse near me went down easily enough—all it took was a knife to the throat and when it fell, its skull gave beneath my booted foot like a rotten egg. Two more surrounded me before I'd even had time to lift my boot out of the rancid gunk. I swiveled and plunged my knife hilt-deep into the temple of one corpse while the other stumbled dangerously close. I tried to yank my knife free, but the blade was lodged deep into the zombie's head and stuck on a bone. In a panic, I grabbed my gun from my waistband with my left hand, pointed, and shot the second zombie between the eyes. As the zombie dropped at my feet, I used all my strength to shove the corpse that had become embedded onto my knife off of the blade.

The gunshot had sealed my fate. The zombies from the front of the store were showing up. Even if this was the end, I wasn't going to go down without taking as many undead as I could with me.

I steadied my shootin' hand and took my time as I pulled the trigger. Every shot took down another zombie and every shot counted. I smiled widely and tucked my gun back into its holster. I held my knife out in front of me as more than twenty decomposing corpses shambled their way toward me. Several were moving at a steady pace, but the majority were moving slower than I remembered. I chalked that up to the alcohol still coursing through my body. I met the four quicker zombies halfway and sliced and slashed until my world only consisted of rotten flesh and fetid viscera. My hands and arms had become slick with the fluids of the undead I'd taken down. I slid the palm of my hand down my jeans and then gripped the hilt of my knife tighter as I turned to the next group of zombies headed in my direction. The corner of my mouth tilted up in a half-smile, half-snarl.

"Ever dance with the devil in the pale moonlight?" I shouted. Maybe I was feeling a little maniacal. Maybe I had a reason to.

I lunged. Gnashing teeth and bloated bodies closed in on me. Corpses littered the ground all around me, though not enough to have made a difference. The death toll didn't matter; all that did matter was that I was surrounded, and unlike the living dead, I got tired. My arms were shaking and my legs felt like rubber from kicking the first zombies back into the crowd to gain myself a little more time. It had worked pretty well, but I couldn't keep up the pace, my body was about to give out on me. I shoved my knife into the neck of the next zombie, and I realized that I couldn't tell where my hand ended and my knife began. I kicked out and shoved the zombie back into the one behind him, though they didn't stay down for long this time. Two zombies charged me, ramming me back so far that my backside crashed into the brick building behind me. I had a hand around the thin neck of one gnashing and snarling zombie trying to break free and sink its broken teeth into my skin. My knife was deep into the throat of a second zombie and even though its insides were pouring out over my arm from the wound I'd given it, it was still snapping and gurgling. My arms were shaking and my knife hand slipped just a bit, bringing the impaled zombie even closer to his next meal.

Out of the corner of my eye I saw the final half-dozen zombies move in to make the kill. They were no more than a dozen feet away. It wouldn't be long now. I closed my eyes, blocking out the bleakness of the world around me. I thought of my wife and summoned a picture of how she looked on our wedding day. My knife slipped a little more and the sounds grew louder. I didn't open my eyes. I wanted to die remembering something good and beautiful. Something—anything—unmarred by the ugliness of the world.

Not my reality.

My eyes flew open when shots rang out all around me. Zombies were dropping and I suddenly found the strength to fight a little bit longer, a little bit harder. I shoved all my weight against the two zombies that were right on top of me, using the forward momentum and kicking out with a wobbly leg to dislodge the zombie from the edge of my knife. When he stumbled back in a daze, I rammed my knife into the eye of the zombie I still held by the neck. I spun, ready to finish off the zombie I'd stabbed in the neck, but a man stood there with an axe stuck into its skull. I blinked against the sunlight.

"You bit?" The man spat on the ground and pointed his axe at my chest. I blinked again, wondering if I was hallucinating.

"I asked you a question, son." I looked down at the axe and then back up into the face of the man who spat another wad of chewing tobacco on a corpse at our feet.

I shook my head. "I don't think so."

His eyes raked over me and I glanced down at myself. I was covered in guts. There wasn't a spot on me that wasn't covered in noxious zombie entrails. Two other guys wearing overalls joined the older man to stand there and stare at me like I was a museum exhibit. A tall, thin, blond man and a black-haired kid no more than fifteen stood in front of me.

"You got people?" the blond-haired guy with an unfortunate nose asked. I shook my head. The guys looked at each other, communicating without saying anything. Something niggled the back of my mind.

"Well, look, thanks for helping me out of this mess. I appreciate it." I stuck my hand out before I realized how ridiculous that was, considering it was coated in things I was more than ready to wash off. I put my hand back down to my side. "I should probably get going on outa here and I'm sure y'all will want to as well, so I won't hold ya up more than I already have." I grabbed my fallen hat off of the ground and put it back on. When no one said anything, I shoved my dirty knife into the sheath on my leg and took a step forward. My legs and back were so stiff I felt like an old man as I hobbled a few feet. I needed to get the muck off of me in case someone mistook me for one of the living corpses and put me out of my misery.

"Hey, wait a sec."

The blond guy stepped forward, what was left of his thinning hair hanging over his ears. "We got a secure place and we got people we take care of. We don't take in a lot of people and Michael has the final say-so, but we'd be glad to take you back with us. Ya know, to clean up and get ya back on your feet."

I held up a hand and winced. My body and shoulders were already stiffening up. "I really appreciate that, but I'll be okay on my own."

"Son, you ain't got a single bullet, have ya?" I met the stare of the older man with the axe propped up on his shoulder and clenched my jaw. "That's what I thought. You're in no condition to drive, no condition to run, and if ya get in another mess like this one, you'll be in no condition to protect yourself." The man did have a point. Plus, it'd be nice to meet other survivors and if their place were truly protected and secure... well, that'd be nice for once too. To sleep one night without looking over my shoulder, one night without worrying I'd be eaten in my sleep. Yeah, I'd sell my soul for that right about now.

"I'd be obliged to y'all if you'd let me go with you. I'll be better soon and I'll get off on my own as soon as possible so I don't use up too much of your resources."

"We'll talk about that later, let's get the heck outta here." Man of few words. I liked that. We walked up to a large black pickup truck. I climbed up into the bed of the truck and sat down without groaning in pain, which wasn't an easy task. After a few miles of being jolted around in the back of the truck, I craned my head to see where were headed. I couldn't be more than forty miles from the base, and probably a lot closer to Charlotte than I was comfortable with. A green sign on the side of the road read "Welcome to Pineville". I wondered what was in Pineville. Couldn't be much different than every other overrun town in the area. I rested the back of my head on the cab of the truck while we moved through the small town. I pulled my hat down over my eyes and nodded off before we made it to our destination.

I was the world's biggest idiot.

Chapter Three
Camp Victory

My head had been vibrating for a while now, and yet I'd been trying to ignore it. When the truck finally came to a complete stop after a bumpy ride on a gravel road, my head rebounded off of the cab of the truck with a loud *thud*. I moved my stiff body when the guys up front got out of the vehicle and slammed their doors. I got to my feet with most of my manliness still intact and glanced around the area. A densely wooded area surrounded us. We were at what looked like it used to be a campground out in the boonies of Pineville, North Carolina. I could see a few cabins and assumed there were several others on the property. I jumped down from the bed of the truck and joined the trio of guys who had saved my neck back at the convenience store.

"So, what's this?" I asked.

"This is what used to be Camp Victory," the teen replied.

"Now it is sanctuary to our group," the older guy added.

Sanctuary... That was an unusual term to use, but I got it. To feel safe from everything going on in the world now was worth its weight in gold and to have a place of safety and shelter from those horrors, well, that place was most definitely a sanctuary.

"Let's go. We'll show you where you can get cleaned up, then we'll take you to meet Michael."

I followed the men past a large building that looked like it probably was the place everyone would gather to eat or whatever. I caught movement out of the corner of my eye. Another young man, no older than the boy standing beside me, was perched up in a tree with a rifle pointed out past the wooden gates that surrounded the camp. A lookout for zombies? Likely. By the time I turned back to my group to follow them, I had already spotted three more lookouts. Once we passed the main building, we turned down a path that led to the right. Another path led to a set of cabins that were set a little apart from the main grouping of buildings.

"What's down there?" I asked.

"That's where the women and children stay," the blond, lanky guy answered without breaking stride. I raised a brow but didn't comment. They kept men and women in different areas of the camp? That didn't make much sense to me. If the camp ever got overrun, all the women would be at one end of the camp without any help.

"This here's the men's washhouse. Ain't no hot water, but a shower's a shower."

I walked over to the door of the washhouse.

"James will find you some clean clothes and bring 'em by in a bit. You go on ahead and get washed up. It's about time for lunch."

"Wait, I didn't even catch y'all's names."

The older gentleman grunted and pointed to the teenage boy. "That's James." James nodded in my direction. The man then pointed to the tall, thin man with the unfortunate nose. "That there's Clyde, and everyone hereabouts calls me Uncle Gus."

"I'm Tex. I appreciate y'all taking me in like this when ya didn't have to."

The old man, Uncle Gus, spat on the ground and gave me a tired, tobacco filled grin. "Don't worry about it, son, just get your shower and we'll see ya in a bit."

I went into the washhouse to try to scrape the caked-on muck off of my body. It wasn't easy. My ice cold shower felt like heaven and I never wanted to release the bar of Irish Spring. I probably scrubbed myself for a good thirty minutes before feeling like I'd gotten completely clean.

When I was done, there was a pair of jean overalls and a white tee shirt waiting for me outside of the shower stall. I eyed my dirty jeans, only considering for a second to wear the nasty things before discarding that idea. I didn't want to look like Farmer Bill, still fresh, clean clothes were something of a luxury and I didn't want to offend the people who'd helped me out of a sticky situation. I stuck my clean knife inside my boot and headed out of the wash room.

I didn't spot Uncle Gus, Clyde, or James when I stepped outside and after a good ten minutes of waiting, I started walking back the way we'd come from until I reached what I thought might be the mess hall. Nostalgia immediately took me back to my summer camp days as I entered the building, removing my hat. Picnic tables that were originally set up to feed hungry camp goers were now being used to feed hungry survivors. I glanced around the rustic cafeteria and found myself the center of attention. A few women were sitting at the other end of the room and as soon as my gaze caught theirs, they swung their eyes away from me to look down at their plates. I moved to the other end of the room and stood at a counter with a window that led into a kitchen area. The older woman there wore a white apron over her faded dress. She smiled warmly and handed over a tray with a bowl of piping hot stew and a chunk of crusty bread. My stomach grumbled loudly.

"Thank you kindly, ma'am," I said, taking the tray. She nodded in reply.

I looked for a place to sit in the large room. I didn't want to sit alone, but the few women who sat at a single table were sending off mean-girl vibes that I remembered all too well from high school. A dark-haired woman sat alone at a table near the wall. I hadn't even noticed her at first and she never looked up from her food. She just sat there blowing into her stew and ignoring everyone else in the room, lost in her own thoughts. I walked over to the table and sat down my tray across from her. The women behind me had become absolutely silent. I frowned when the woman's eyes rose to meet mine. She looked surprised to find me there and then a little panicked.

"Mind if I sit here?" I asked. When she didn't reply, I wondered if she was sitting alone because she preferred to instead of being snubbed like I'd originally thought. I smiled at her and picked my tray back up.

"I can find another seat," I said softly.

"No, you can sit here," she said, her voice husky with a Spanish accent. She motioned to the place I'd sat down my tray. "Please. I'm sorry, I was just surprised." I sat my tray back down along with my hat and took a seat across from her. I held my hand out.

"I'm Tex. Nice to meet ya."

She took my hand in hers and gave it a nice, firm shake. "I'm Maria," she said, her eyes flitting from mine to over my shoulder and then back down to her tray again. The women had begun whispering. My stomach growled loudly and Maria looked up with a smile on her face.

"Better get some food in you, Tex," she said, her dark brown eyes twinkling. I smiled back and dipped my spoon into the bowl of stew.

"Don't have to tell me twice," I stated, enjoying the first hot meal I'd had in weeks.

"You recently arrive?" Maria asked a few moments later.

"Just about an hour ago, actually."

Maria glanced around the room and then leaned in a little. "How are things out there?" she whispered from across the table.

Immediately, my back stiffened. She seemed like she was afraid of something, afraid of someone hearing her question. I set my spoon down in my empty bowl and studied her for a second.

"The same, I'm afraid." Maria sat back in her seat with a frown between her brows. "You were hoping things were getting better?" I asked. She nodded once, her jaw clenched and her eyes shining.

"You have safety here," I told her. "Hot meals, running water. A lot of people aren't this lucky."

Maria snorted and sat forward, tearing off a piece of her bread and forcing herself to eat it. "Yeah, you'd think that wouldn't you?" she mumbled beneath her breath.

"What does that mean?" I asked.

Her eyes met mine and her jaw was clenched. "It means things aren't always what they seem." I opened my mouth to ask more questions, but then Maria's eyes, staring behind me, widened. She schooled her face into impassivity before looking back down at her plate.

"You must be the new guy Clyde was telling me about." The voice whipped across the room, drawing the eye of everyone present. The entire room went silent once again. I stood up from my seat and turned to face the man who spoke.

"Tex," I said, offering my hand.

A man with a wide smile and closely cropped salt-and-pepper hair stood there. He was about the same height as me, on the slim side, with a presence about him that couldn't be ignored. He had a charismatic aura about him and I wondered for a moment if the man had been in politics before the world changed. The thought didn't set my mind at ease.

"Michael," he said, gripping my hand tightly, giving it a quick shake. Michael glanced over at Maria, who had resumed eating her lunch, not looking up at us during the introductions.

"It looks like you've met Maria," he mentioned offhandedly.

"She was kind enough to let me impose upon her and sit at her table," I said with a smile.

Michael's smile dimmed a bit, his eyes never leaving Maria as he spoke. "*Was* she now?" he said curiously.

"I wanted to thank you for the shower and clean clothes," I said to break the awkward silence. "Also for the hot food. It's been a long time since I've had such a satisfying meal."

Michael met my eyes, his smile once again at full watt. "We're glad to help out a brother in need," he said with a huge grin.

I smiled back, but something didn't quite sit right with me. Maybe it was the words he chose. Maybe the way his eyes told me a different story than what came out of his mouth. Maybe it was that his presence instantly raised my hackles.

Several men and boys came in through the side door of the cafeteria and immediately went to get the trays of food. Uncle Gus, Clyde, and James were among them. Uncle Gus looked even more tired than he did when I last saw him and his eyes widened when he saw our trio near Maria's table.

It was immediately apparent to me why the women had taken such an interest in me sitting with Maria. All of the men picked up their trays and moved to the opposite end of the room to sit together, leaving the women to their own area. They were segregated. I glanced over at Maria, who had watched me as I realized how things were. She smirked and then quickly looked back down at her tray before Michael could notice the exchange. What was going on here? The men and women lived in separate areas of the camp and they didn't even eat at the same tables. And then there was the way Michael eyed Maria... like he owned her, even though Maria had barely acknowledged his existence.

Michael chose that moment to clap me on the back and steer me away from Maria and her table, down to where the men were all congregated to enjoy their meal. I refrained from turning my head to say goodbye to Maria, I had a feeling it would have been a bad idea. And as much as everything seemed a bit off to me, I did owe this group my life and my gratitude.

Michael introduced me to the group of men as he took his seat. All of them were waiting for him, I realized. And then, as one, they all bowed their heads when he began praying over the meal. I bowed my head out of respect while Michael waxed poetic over the meal and all that the Lord had provided his humble servants. I clenched my jaw and just listened. I was a God-fearing man, my mama and my upbringing made sure of that, but I'm not gonna lie and say I hadn't been doubting an awful lot the past two years. I didn't blame God. At least I didn't think I did, however, with my head bowed and listening to the prayer Michael spoke over the food, my hackles were raised and I became more and more uneasy. When he finally finished and the men began talking and eating, the only thing I felt was relief.

"So, Tex, whereabouts are you from?" Michael asked from across the table. I met his gaze after glancing over at Uncle Gus. Uncle Gus seemed uncomfortable and that made me uncomfortable.

"Originally a little town in Texas out in the middle of nowhere," I said with an easy smile.

Michael broke off a piece of his bread and dipped it in his stew. "And more recently?" he asked. "Where were you when everything happened?"

I had a feeling I was being tested somehow, I just couldn't figure out how or why.

I shrugged. "I was stationed on an Army base out of Charlotte."

Uncle Gus glanced over at Michael and then turned back to his meal.

Michael pointed his spoon at me with a lopsided, carefree grin. I wasn't fooled. "I didn't peg you as an Army man. Thought you'd be more of a religious man."

My back stiffened. "Are the two mutually exclusive?" I asked, trying to keep my voice even. Out of the corner of my eye I saw Uncle Gus pause before resuming his meal.

Michael took another bite of his stew, regarding me as he took his time chewing and swallowing his food. "Many people don't think so. Some even think by defending their country, they were doing their God-given duty." He shook his head, making eye contact and including everyone at the table in the conversation. "We, however, know better now. Everything that has happened has only verified everything I've been teaching for years." He grinned at the "*amens*" that sounded around the table.

"What were you teaching that we are all now enlightened about?" I asked. I knew I shouldn't have asked. I even knew it would only likely enrage me, but I did it anyway.

"That the government and armed forces were for men and women who didn't have true faith in God. Men believed they were being patriotic, that they were protecting their country and their loved ones from threats, when in reality the threat has always been living among us. The ungodly were the threat and God has begun purging them from the true believers, from those that have always believed that the righteous will be the only ones left standing when this plague finally end."

I could feel a muscle jumping in my cheek. The entire table seemed to understand the threat in the room. If someone, anyone else, had said the things that Michael had just said to me, I'd have already thrown a punch to wipe the self-satisfied smirk right off of his face. However, I was a guest here, Uncle Gus and his crew had saved my life, and there were ladies present. Every God-fearing, patriotic bone in my body screamed for me to open a big 'ole can of Texas whoop-ass, instead I used what little control I still had left and stood from my bench at the table. A few of the men near me flinched visibly.

"It's been a long day and I'm a lot more tired than I thought I was," I stated. "I think I'll call it a day. I appreciate y'all's hospitality, I'll be on my way after a good night's rest, if that's okay with you," I said as civilly as I could manage. I even mustered a smile. Uncle Gus grimaced. Guess my smile wasn't as convincing as I imagined.

"No need to rush, we're glad to have you here. We can talk more in the morning," Michael said after a moment.

I headed out of the mess hall. It only took me a few minutes to realize I had no clue where I was going.

"Let me show ya to a cabin."

I turned to find Uncle Gus coming up behind me. "I didn't mean to take you away from your meal," I said.

He waved my concern away and caught up with me. "You didn't. Don't worry about that, son. Let's get you to a cabin so you can rest."

I walked silently for a few minutes before speaking again. "I appreciate everything you've done for me, helping me out of a tight spot when I was an idiot and got myself into that mess and all that, but this camp isn't for me."

We paused outside of a cabin and he faced me.

"I just wanted you to know that when I move on tomorrow it's nothin' personal."

"I know, and I realized right away you wouldn't be staying. I only thought you could use a decent meal and a good night's sleep before you move on. Those two simple things can mean a lot to a soul nowadays," he said gruffly. I walked into the cabin behind Uncle Gus.

"Ain't that the truth," I said with a smirk.

"Just be careful, ya hear?" He pointed over to an empty cot. I walked over and sat down on the edge. Every single bone in my body felt weary.

"I plan to," I said, reaching down to pull off my boots.

"I don't mean once you leave, you seem the sort of man who can take of himself... when you're not drinking like some idiot fool that is."

I rubbed the back of my neck and stared down at the wood floor, properly chastised by my elder.

"I mean while you're here. Michael is a religious man. He's also a man who has lost everything. A religious man who has nothing left to lose and who has a captive audience is a dangerous man." His eyes caught mine and they were deadly serious. "Michael Hatten is a very dangerous man."

I nodded my understanding.

Uncle Gus turned to the door. "Well, have a decent sleep for once. The camp is well fortified and we have patrols around the clock. I'll see you in the morning."

"Thank you," I said once again. He headed out the door.

I laid back on the cot. My feet hung over the edge, but I felt like I was on a king sized, pillow topped mattress. I pulled my hat down over my eyes. It wasn't long until I fell into a deep sleep.

Chapter Four
Not Again

I could see Danny's lips moving, but I couldn't hear what said he was saying over the sound of the music I was listening to. I pulled one of my earplugs out and raised a brow.

"You listening to that honky-tonk crap again?" he asked with a crooked smile. I knew he was full of it. I'd caught him humming some pretty familiar "honky tonk" tunes himself the last few days.

"You know me," I said with a shrug.

"Not really, man," Danny said. He let his head fall back just enough to rest on the wall behind him. His hand was moving in gentle strokes, petting the head of one of the mangiest dogs I'd ever clapped eyes on. Boy, as Danny had named him, had a limp and was in bad need of a grooming. Danny loved that dog more than anything in the world. Boy was usually found in the exact same place he was right then… in Danny's lap. Spoiled mutt.

"We've known each other for a couple days, but we don't really know a whole lot about each other." He wasn't accusing, only observing. I pulled my other earplug out of my ear and turned off the iPod I was listening to and shoved it into my backpack. It clanged against the twenty or so I had stashed there. I'd taken to looking for them when I was out scavenging for supplies in homes. Every once in a while I hit the jackpot with either a country music lover, or someone who, like me, had truly eclectic tastes in music, enjoying everything from REO Speedwagon to Frank Sinatra, and a lot of stuff in between. Those iPods I savored.

"I guess you're right."

"Let's play a little game to pass the time," Danny suggested.

"What you got in mind?" I asked. Anything to drown the sounds of the dead outside was cool with me.

"How about this?" Danny said after thinking for a minute or two. "How about I start out by asking you a simple question. And then you can only choose one thing as an answer. We'll call the game 'Only One'." Danny was grinning ear-to-ear, clearly pleased with his idea.

"Okay," I said. "Go ahead."

"Alright. One drink, any drink, can appear out of thin air. Which drink would you choose?"

"An ice-cold root beer in a glass bottle," I said immediately. Danny laughed and shook his head.

"Now your turn," I said. "Any movie playing in a nice movie theater."

Danny thought about it for a minute. "Trading Places," he said with a wide smile. That was a good one.

"One actress," he said with a raised brow.

"Jennifer Lawrence."

"One song on repeat as your theme song," I suggested.

"Bad Bad Leroy Brown," he said without hesitation. It was my turn to laugh. "One superhero as your sidekick."

"Batman," I smirked, as if there was any other choice. "One weapon," I offered up.

"A red light saber." Couldn't argue with that. "One book," he tossed out.

"My kindle," I said, grinning.

"Cheater." He laughed.

We went on like that for over two hours before we were tired and ready for bed. Danny was a pretty good guy. I'd been on my own for a week when we met, but it had seemed like months with only the dead to keep me company. I liked Danny. I even liked his ugly mutt too.

*

I woke up gradually, blinking the sleep out of my eyes with a strange feeling curling in my gut. Something wasn't right. I don't know how I knew it, but I did. I jumped up off of the twin bed that I slept on in the room and grabbed my gun and knife. I left the room and called out for Danny.

"Danny?" I whispered harshly. No sound. I walked through the apartment that we'd been camping out in for a few days. I'd met Danny right in the heart of Charlotte when, for reasons even unknown to myself, I'd ended up coming back after leaving the Army base. He was nowhere in the apartment. I started searching for Danny, checking all the places I knew he took the dog out to. Once I was sure he wasn't in any of his normal spots, I decided to take the stairs to the roof. Sometimes Danny liked to take the dog, Boy, up there to run around. I reached the top of the roof of our apartment building right as the sun was touching the building. It was a glorious sunrise and I stood there at the entrance to the stairs in awe for a moment. A sound dragged me out of my trance.

"Danny?" I said, my voice loud enough to carry across the roof. Danny didn't look up from where he crouched on the ground. He was on his knees, his hands clenched around something in front of him as he rocked back and forth muttering under his breath.

"Danny?" I tried again, moving toward him. When I got close enough to see him more clearly, I could hear him.

"Boy, Boy, Boy, Boy. Come here, Boy. Come here." He muttered it over and over as he rocked and rocked. I stepped forward carefully and put a hand out to touch his shoulder. His hands were covered in drying blood and he held what used to be Boy's homemade collar—fabric Danny had cut into strips and then braided into a collar to go around the dog's neck.

"Danny…." I whispered thickly. As soon as the words left my mouth, Danny leapt up suddenly. I stumbled back from surprise. Danny strode with purpose to the side of the building. As soon as he got there, he turned and looked directly at me. I shook my head and took a step forward.

"Not without my dog," he said harshly. He shoved his gun in his mouth as he took a step up onto the ledge and pulled the trigger.

My scream echoed loudly, mingling with the leftover sounds of a gunshot and the undead ten stories below as they ripped into Danny's corpse.

My breaths came out in harsh gasps and my heart raced a mile a minute. It took me several moments to remember exactly where I was. Luckily, no one else was in the cabin and from the looks of it, it was already well into the morning. I swung my feet over the side of the bunk and leaned over, letting my head fall into my hands. Nightmares again. Unfortunately, this nightmare was more of a memory. Another horrible memory I'd as soon forget. There was a lot I'd like to forget. I shoved my feet into my boots, ran fingers through my hair, and sat my hat on my head. Maybe a little food would help.

Chapter Five
Welcome to the 19th Century

Shocked was the understatement of the year. A plate of real eggs and real butter on homemade bread stared back at me from my plate and I had to pinch myself to make sure I wasn't dreaming. Especially after the previous night's trip into I-never-wanna-dream-again land. The moan of ecstasy was a real and justified thing when I bit into the bread, which I had thoroughly soaked in egg yolks. If I had been sure I wouldn't have scared the poor lady half to death, I'd have kissed the cook right on the mouth.

"Looks like you're enjoying that."

Not even Michael Hatten could ruin my good mood though. I smiled up at the leader of Camp Victory.

"Yes, sir. It's been a very long time since I had a plate of fried eggs," I said cheerfully.

Michael sat down with his own plate. After he prayed, he grinned over at me. "I was hoping you might want to take a look around the camp with me today." He shoved a fork full of eggs in his mouth. "I ain't gonna lie, we could use another able-bodied man such as yourself around here."

I finished off my bread, taking the time to sop up every little bit of eggy goodness before shoveling it in my pie hole. I regarded the man. Maybe I'd been a bit harsh in my judgment of Michael Hatten and his little sanctuary out here in the boonies. The world had changed and not for the good. People were learning to adapt and survive. Michael was clinging to what he thought he knew.

"I guess it wouldn't hurt to take a look around," I said amiably.

"Good!" He seemed genuinely pleased I was going to take a tour of the camp.

I sat there waiting for him to finish his meal, beginning to wonder if perhaps Uncle Gus finding me was a good thing, that perhaps it have even been meant to be. Maybe heading back to the Army base, back to Melody Carter and everyone else could wait a little longer. Maybe

Camp Victory was where I belonged for the time being.

Maybe I was being extremely optimistic.

When we headed out to begin the tour of the camp, I was feeling uncharacteristically hopeful. I guess a big plate of eggs and butter can do that to a man.

"How many people do you have here?" I asked.

"One hundred and twelve," Michael answered. I sucked in a breath. So many? "I'm responsible for one hundred and twelve souls here at Camp Victory." He smiled at me. "You'd be one hundred and thirteen," he added. We turned down a path and headed for the back of the camp, back past all the cabins.

"This is the garden and chicken coop," Michael said when we stopped walking. Several women were pulling weeds and tending to the garden. Another woman was bunching up what looked like fresh herbs to hang to dry. The garden was pretty large and well taken care of. I was amazed already. On the other side of the garden was a large chicken coop and yard. Two young girls were there. One was tossing feed to the chickens and one I could see was inside the chicken house gathering eggs. There had to have been over two dozen chickens.

"These are our laying hens," Michael explained." Around the other side are the birds we raise for meat."

"Where did you get them?" I asked.

"Uncle Gus. He had a pen of chickens. Only a few, but he only had himself to feed, so he used to sell off the eggs he couldn't use on his own. He didn't do it for the money, only to cover the cost of chicken feed. He also had his own small garden, so a lot of what we have now is a direct result of the plants and seeds that Uncle Gus owned."

Good 'ole Uncle Gus. These people owed him a lot.

"Uncle Gus is something else," I muttered.

Michael laughed. "Sure is. When everyone else was fighting and killing each other over the canned and boxed goods at Walmart, Uncle Gus had a group of us loading up supplies from the lawn and garden center and the local farm supply store. Nobody was fighting over Miracle Gro and chicken feed."

We walked along the fence line of the camp until we came to a building. Michael stopped and motioned for me to enter through the door. The room fell silent when we walked in and I immediately felt bad for interrupting. The room was set up with a round table and several desks. It was a classroom, currently filled with about eight children of varying ages from about four to ten. The woman teaching them was one of the "mean girls" from dinner the previous night. A woman of about thirty-some years, hair pulled back tightly into a bun. She would have been somewhat attractive if she didn't look like she wanted to murder me. That, and if she loosened her hair and ditched the dirt-colored clothing. She scowled at me then she noticed Michael coming through the doorway right behind me and her face then morphed into the perfect picture of grace and charm.

Just like Dr. Jekyll and Mr. Hyde, I thought.

"Ms. Yancy, so sorry to interrupt your class. I do hope you'll forgive us," Michael said with a grin and a wink. Ms. Yancy all but melted at his feet.

"It's no trouble at all," she said too enthusiastically. "Class, say hello to Mr. Hatten."

"Hello, Mr. Hatten," the children chorused.

"Hello, children. I'm showing Mr. Tex here around our camp and we thought we'd stop in to say hello."

The children turned their attention to me, all curious and whatnot. I tried not to fidget in front of the kids, it was just that they were beginning to freak me out a little. Hello? *Children of the Corn*?

"And what are we learning today?" Michael asked Ms. Yancy.

She turned to the children and tapped her yardstick on the chalkboard behind her. I hadn't noticed the writing on the board until then.

"Children, let's recite." Ms. Yancy pointed out the words on the board and the children began singing the exercise in unison with her to the tune of *Ring-a-Round-the-Rosie*.

The dead they surround us. But God, he protects us.

Ashes. Ashes. They all fall down.

The righteous will inherit the Earth. The unbelievers perish.

Ashes. Ashes. They all fall down.

I was standing there in horror, wondering if they were playing a joke on me, when Michal started clapping. Out of shock, I joined him.

"Very good, children," Michael said proudly. "Your teacher is doing wonderfully with you all here."

Ms. Yancy beamed. I felt ill. What the hell was wrong with them? I wondered if the parents of these kids knew what the teacher was filling their heads with. For some reason I was betting they actually did. And here I had been actually enjoying myself up until that little show. I couldn't get out the door of the classroom fast enough. As we walked away from the building, I heard Ms. Yancy tell the children to take out their math worksheets, so I guess they were teaching the children some academics along with their brainwashing techniques.

Once the bad taste of the classroom had been left in my mouth, I couldn't quite bring myself to appreciate the rest of our tour. A room dedicated to canning fruits and vegetables, drying and smoking meats, making candles and soap. Knowing what they were teaching the kids, how Michael felt about God's "will" being done through the zombies, it all just put a different spin on everything I was seeing. Surviving, thriving even through gardening, canning, and all other old-school methods of living was all wonderful... just not when you expected people to live and think like they were in the nineteenth century.

Now I noticed what I hadn't before. Young girls who should have been in the classroom doing manual labor; women kept segregated in sleeping quarters, during meals, and about everywhere else I could see; women doing all the work that you would think women in the eighteen hundreds would have been doing— teaching, sewing, canning, cleaning, and cooking; men doing manly things around the camp. None of the men preferred cooking over hunting? None of the women preferred going on supply runs for clothing and necessities rather than making them by hand? I knew firsthand that some stuff was still plentiful out there— soap, shampoo, tee shirts, etc., and yet the women at Camp Victory were slaving over a boiling pot to make old fashioned soap. If they enjoyed it, that was great. Doing it just to keep women doing womanly things? Not so much. And that wasn't the only thing that had begun to bug me.

All the women wore drab dresses or long skirts, no bright colors, no fitted tops even, no jeans. And no matter what anyone would ever say, I knew that every single woman and young girl in the camp couldn't prefer to wear the clothes they had on if they had a choice. The truth was, I knew they didn't have a choice. And that's when my rose-colored glasses fell completely away. Take away the little farm in the back, the hot meals, and the showers and beds, and you would be standing in the center of a cult.

Even with that realization crashing down around me, still, who was I to say anything? No one was really doing anything wrong. No one was murdering people. No one was held here against their will so far as I could tell. And no one was complaining. People were healthy. Safe. Happy. I had no business judging.

I had no business being in Camp Victory at all.

When I got back to my borrowed cabin, I was convinced that after one more day of resting here at the camp, I'd be on my way again and headed toward the Army base. I could stomach these people for less than twenty-four hours.

At least I hoped so.

Chapter Six
Cult Mingle.com

I decided to skip lunch and clean my jeans and tee shirt on an old washboard a woman who was older than Methuselah grudgingly let me borrow. The tee I could have done without since I had two others in my pack, but the jeans were the only ones I owned and I was not going to leave camp the next day wearing these overalls. When that was finished and I set them outside the cabin to dry, I worked out for a good hour in the cabin. I then cleaned and sharpened my knife, and reorganized my pack. I kept myself busy and out of the way like that for as long as I could. When I thought dinner might be coming close to an end, I decided to head to the mess hall hoping to snag some food without having to run into Michael or really anyone except for Uncle Gus.

The mess hall was pretty empty when I got there, and I realized that not only had I misjudged the time since the kitchen looked like it was closing down, but also that I'd managed to show up right when something else was about to begin. I stood in the middle of the doorway, unable to decide what to do. With a sigh, I turned to leave and head back to my cabin. At least I knew there would be a hearty meal in the morning to fill me up before I headed out of the camp. Michael Hatten was approaching the mess hall right as I was stepping out.

"Tex, haven't seen you around in a few hours," he said loudly. "You get some dinner?"

I shook my head. "My own fault. I didn't realize what time it was. I'm going to head back to the cabin and catch breakfast in the morning," I said, taking a step in that direction.

"You can't go to bed without eating."

"I don't want to trouble anyone," I said, still moving.

"Nonsense! I forgot to mention to you earlier today that on Tuesday nights we eat earlier. Come on in. I'm sure we have something you can make a sandwich out of or something in the kitchen." Michael walked over and slapped me on the back like we were buddies. Clyde and a few other guys were walking with him into the mess hall and I couldn't make any excuses or leave at that point without offending someone or looking like an unappreciative ass, so I followed him back into the building.

"So you guys eat early on Tuesdays?" I asked as we walked over to the kitchen area.

"Yes, every Tuesday we close up the kitchen an hour early for our Tuesday evening mingle."

What the hell was a "mingle"? "A mingle?" I asked after Michael finished asking the women who were cleaning up the kitchen area if there was a meal he could grab for me.

"Just a little time we set aside each week for those of us who are single and would like to spend some quality time with the opposite sex."

"A dating service type of thing?" I asked, suddenly uncomfortable.

Michael grimaced. "We like to think of it as courting in a controlled, Christian environment. *Dating* is such a loose and worldly term."

I was saved from having to comment by the lady I normally saw working in the kitchen during meal times. She gave me a brown paper bag and I thanked her. She waved away my thanks graciously. I sat at one of the empty tables and hoped Michael Hatten would disappear.

I pulled a bowl of bean soup out of my bag and set it on the table in front of me. The bowl was still warm when I took the lid off. There were a few chunks of homemade fried bread in the bag as well. My mouth watered.

"What is it you're looking for, Tex?" Michael asked me.

I tried not to scowl and shrugged nonchalantly. "Hope. Something other than just surviving," I answered truthfully, taking a spoonful of soup.

"We have that here," Michael said.

I didn't disagree with him. They did indeed have *something* here at Camp Victory, though I was pretty sure I didn't want anything to do with it.

Glasses of what looked like lemonade were set out on a table along, with some bowls of pecans. Michael left the table to "mingle" with the people of the camp. Everyone stayed away from me and for that I was glad. When I was finished with my food I sat back and watched everyone interact. To say the whole thing was awkward would be putting it lightly. Men stood feet away from the women they were talking to. When couples were sitting, they still had at least a foot between them. There was no privacy, no intimacy. It was uncomfortable even for me and I wasn't even participating. I tuned out the weirdness of the scene in front of me and wondered how soon I could make an exit without offending anyone or getting cornered by Michael again.

"Come on now, you're not mingling? You're the talk of the camp... the big news," a voice from nearby said.

"Am I?"

Maria rolled her eyes.

"Of course you are. New guy. New, *young* guy, walking around with Michael like some esteemed guest," Maria said with a sidelong glance toward Michael, who stood near two people who were talking more to him than to each other.

"Esteemed guest, my fanny," I snorted. "He just wanted to show how big his was."

Maria sputtered out a surprised laugh. She glanced around quickly and came to sit down next to me, careful to keep some space between us. I gave her a questioning look. She knew exactly what I was asking.

"We have rules here about all this kind of stuff," she said waving a hand around to include the room. "We don't touch the opposite sex. No mixed swimming, hand-holding, mixed cabins, etc. We keep at least six to twelve inches between us at all times, to safeguard our *sexual desires*," she said with a smirk.

"Wow," I said after letting that sink in. "Is it optional?" I asked.

Maria's eyes were twinkling. "I'm afraid not, cowboy," she said with a grin.

"You here for someone in particular?" I asked, unable to resist. Maria stiffened and I was sorry I brought it up.

"I'm required to attend," she said after a moment ticked by.

A muscle jumped in my cheek. *Required*. Got it. Cult.

"What do you usually do when you come on Tuesday night then?" I asked. "Guys probably line up to, um, court you," I said with a grimace.

Maria snorted. "No they don't, actually. Not when they know Michael is interested."

I turned to her, careful not to lean too close. I didn't want her to get in trouble on my account, even though she was a damned grown woman with a mind of her own.

"Why don't you tell him you're not interested?" I asked.

She sighed deeply and smiled sadly. "If that were going to deter him it would have worked months ago," she said softly.

So Michael didn't know how to take a hint. Good to know, and another ugly mark on his character.

"What do you do besides wish you were anywhere except for here on a Tuesday night?" I asked. "Recite poetry in your mind?"

Maria chuckled under her breath. "You really wanna know?" she asked in a hushed whisper.

"Yes I do."

"I do bad lip readings of the couples here in my head to pass the time."

I sat back with a grin spreading across my face. I thought for a moment Maria might have blushed under my scrutiny. A woman who was funny and pretty. My weakness.

"Show me," I said, indicating a couple across the room from us.

"I can't, Tex." Maria looked scandalized. "I usually only do it in my head."

"Aw, c'mon now, sweetheart," I begged. "This is the kind of entertainment you can't withhold from a poor, mortal man. It's inhumane! Withhold sex, yes. But comedy?"

Maria shushed me with a giggle, glancing around to make sure no one heard my scandalous words.

"Alright," she said.

The short guy with a shaggy haircut talked and then dipped his head to look at his lap every few seconds. The woman, probably in her late twenties and bored out of her mind, wouldn't even look up at him except when he was looking down. It looked like she answered his questions in single syllable words. Maria cleared her throat. She deepened her voice in an exaggerated southern drawl for the guy and raised her voice in a sheepish, girl whisper for the woman.

"These pants are the most comfortable pair I own."

"Okay."

"My mama made 'em for me. Said the ladies would like 'em."

"Okay."

"Yeah. They're real soft. The softest pair I own."

"Nice."

I'd already begun chuckling under my breath. Maria's lip reading with the way the two kept talking to each other, avoiding meeting each other's eyes, and his head bobbing down toward his crotch was a hysterical combination.

"They'd feel good to the touch, ya know?"

"Yeah."

"Soft enough for even the womenfolk."

"Okay."

"You can touch 'em if you like."

"Um..."

"You can come over here and sit on my lap if ya wanna."

"Um... I—"

"What are you two whispering and laughing about over here?"

Maria froze next to me.

"I was just telling Maria how absolutely clumsy I am," I said easily.

Michael stared at Maria as I spoke. "My mama used to keep a fully-stocked first aid kit on the kitchen table when I was growing up because of how often I was falling down and takin' lumps on the head." I chuckled. "Probably why my head is so lumpy now and I forget so many things," I said with a wide smile.

"Could be," Maria agreed. "A lot of childhood head injuries could cause forgetfulness in adulthood."

"What about you, Michael?" I asked, drawing his gaze away from Maria. "What kind of kid were you?"

Michael glanced between the two of us, clearly not comfortable with us spending time together and wanting to say as much, yet he was torn. He'd have looked a little too overbearing and domineering for the image he'd built up for himself here at the camp.

"I was the careful type," he said. "The kind that knew how and when to pick his battles," he said with a glint in his eye. "I almost always won all of my battles by being patient and careful, knowing when to put pressure on and when to back off." He wasn't just talking about his childhood any longer and all three of us knew that.

"Well, I was known to win a battle or two myself," I said, standing from the table. "Despite all the lumps, I mean." My smile matched his and so did my mood. Fortunately, the female sex is usually more levelheaded than the cavemen of the world.

"Well, I was a rambunctious, feisty child who liked to have time to herself once she got tired of company," Maria interjected. "If you two will excuse me, I've got to be getting back to my cabin."

Michael held her chair out for her to stand. I nodded and murmured *ma'am*, and she took her leave of us. She didn't spare either of us a glance as she left the building. I did my best not to grin.

I liked Maria a whole lot.

Michael clearly wanted Maria and this was his camp. Another reason to be on my way first thing in the morning.

Chapter Seven
Little Chapel of Horrors

"Hey, Mister?" I swatted away the pesky voice and turned over. "Mister, you need to get up, we've got chapel in a few minutes and everyone's required to attend." I cracked an eye open and spotted the kid with the annoying voice.

"It's morning?" I asked in a gruff. Man, my throat was parched.

"Yup."

My brain hadn't caught up with everything, but I didn't think I'd slept more than eight or ten hours. It wasn't Sunday, was it?

"What day is it, kid?" I asked, opening both my eyes and swinging my feet off the edge of the bed. I realized there were several others in the room— an elderly man and two other men around my age, watching the kid and me with interest. The boy had the brightest head of red hair I'd ever seen and so many freckles on his face, I imagined he'd been picked on ferociously in school. Well, when there had been regular school.

"Wednesday"

I grimaced. "Y'all have chapel services on Wednesday morning?" I asked, grabbing my boots.

"Sure do. We have chapel on Sunday, Sunday night, Wednesday morning, and Saturday mornings." I stood up and stretched.

"Well, that seems a bit excessive," I muttered beneath my breath. The little boy giggled and one of the men who had been watching stood up and walked over to us.

"Get on outta here, Kyle. Don't be late for chapel," he admonished. When Kyle lit out of the cabin, the man turned his angry gaze on me.

"Chapel is the most important part of our week here at Camp Victory. It'd do you good not to forget that," he snarled and then headed out of the cabin himself.

"Well, hell," I mumbled a few seconds later. "Guess I'd better head to church and repent then." I heard a snort from the older gentleman in the room as I walked out of the cabin.

I followed the people I found outside, assuming they were all headed to where the chapel services were to be held. Sure enough, everyone was entering a wooden building, quite a bit smaller than the mess hall, but a little larger than the regular cabins. When I got inside I found a plain, old fashioned church set up. Wooden benches were lined up like pews and a walkway went down the middle of them, leading to the front of the church where a wooden platform and pulpit sat. I glanced around, taking note of how all the women sat on the right side of the church. I made sure to choose a seat on a bench on the left and in the back of the room.

Pretty soon the room was filled and I was surprised to see so many survivors in one room. It was a shock to the system. There were a couple of children in the bunch, though none younger than the boy who had been given the unfortunate job of waking me up. The women all wore long skirts and sat stiffly on their side of the room. There were a few older women, no more than four or five though. All the rest were probably younger than thirty, and several were teenagers. I spotted Maria sitting in the back of the room as I was. She made no move to acknowledge my presence and I didn't want to put her in an awkward spot once again. The men's side was fuller than the women's, though that was no surprise. A few men had come in with their rifles on their back and it seemed a little odd to me. I guess nothing could really be qualified as *odd* now that the dead walked among us and the world as we knew it had ended. I was curious though.

"Why do some of the men have their guns in here?" I whispered to the older man sitting near me. He eyed me up and down before answering.

"Those are the men who are on patrol right now."

I blinked several times before asking the question that seemed ludicrously obvious. "If they're in here, how can they be on patrol? Do you mean they just got off of patrol or they're about to begin their patrol?"

The man smiled, revealing a golden front tooth. "Those are the men who are on patrol right now. Everyone is required to attend chapel. Even those who are supposed to be on patrol and protecting the camp."

I blinked stupidly at the man several times until his smile dimmed. "Then who is protecting the camp during chapel?" I asked, afraid I already knew the answer.

"God protects his own when they obey his commandments," the man said seriously.

I shifted in my seat and searched the back of the room, considering how the entire camp would be completely unprotected while everyone sat in chapel, expecting God to do their work for them, to suddenly protect the people from the horrors of the world, when from my point of view, He'd allowed all of the horror to be unleashed upon the Earth in the first place. I was about to stand up, to take it upon myself to watch the walls, even if all I had was my empty gun and my knife. I couldn't sit there and do nothing. Just as I rose from the bench, Michael Hatten walked through the back door and strode by me to take his place behind the pulpit at the front of the church. The doors were then shut and two men stood there in front of them. I wasn't sure if they were there to keep the undead from getting in or the living from getting out. Either way, I didn't like the position in which I'd suddenly found myself.

"Good morning, everyone," Michael said. The men all responded cheerfully. The women's side was quiet. I sat stiffly, hoping he would get on with whatever they did during chapel times. I felt more and more uneasy as the moments ticked by. Michael went through a few announcements and much to my dismay, he picked up a hymnal and told everyone to turn to page thirty-two and to stand with him. Everyone obeyed immediately. I joined them and flipped my own hymnal to page thirty-two. *Nothing but the Blood.* I cringed. How very fitting.

While people around me sang cheerfully about the blood of Jesus, I surveyed the room and the people. Most of the women sang softly while the men bellowed out their song. Maria looked like she was singing, but I was certain she was only mouthing the words. After a moment, I turned to find Michael watching me. His eyes had been hard and calculating. He quickly covered the look with a smile and a curt nod. I nodded back, my jaw already aching from keeping it clenched for so long.

After several more verses, Michael led everyone in a long-winded prayer and then bid us all to sit. He pulled out what appeared to be a very large bible and set it on the top of the pulpit with a resounding *thud*. No one else took out a bible like they had whenever I'd gone to our little country church back in Texas. My unease tripled before he even opened up his mouth. Then he began speaking and I knew right away that everything Uncle Gus had told me, the warning that Michael was a dangerous man, was the understatement of the century.

Michael wasn't only dangerous, he was delusional. A dangerous man could be dealt with easily enough. A man who was not only dangerous but also thought he'd been called by God to lead survivors to the narrow road of salvation was someone everyone should be terrified of. Hearing him talk, I knew that Michael thought of himself as some kind of chosen prophet or something. He hadn't just survived the apocalypse, he'd flourished in this horrible new world, assured that God had spared him for some magnanimous reason.

"God has chosen the righteous to inherit the Earth," he intoned a few moments later. "He has cut down all the unrighteous, all the wicked-doers from the face of the Earth, just like He did back in Noah's day." Sounds of agreement and *amens* echoed throughout the room. My stomach knotted hearing those words. Had Michael not been out there when everything had happened? Had he not seen that innocent women and children had died and turned? How could he infer that they had deserved what had happened to them? How could he stand there and say to all these people that their loved ones had been taken from them as a natural and righteous act of God? I clenched my fist in my lap and glanced around. No one seemed angry. As a matter of fact, everyone seemed to be in complete agreement, watching Michael as he spoke fervently from the front of the room. Everyone except Maria. Maria had her head slightly bowed and her hands clasped tightly in her lap. Her entire body was tense.

"Zechariah 14:12. *And the Lord will send a plague on all the nations.... Their people will become like walking corpses, their flesh rotting away. Their eyes will rot in their sockets, and their tongues will rot in their mouths. On that day they will be terrified, stricken by the Lord with great panic. They will fight their neighbors hand to hand.*" Michael glanced up from the passage he'd read and glanced around the room in the silence that followed.

"As we already know, our God is a just God. He knew, even back when the Bible was being written, that He would one day have to send a plague upon the Earth to rid us of unbelievers, to rid us of the apples that looked shiny and sweet on the outside and yet were as rotten, dead, and full of worms on the inside as they now are on the outside. We now see the unbelievers for what they truly are, their outer shell reflects the contents of their hearts. We know who God has chosen to remain upon the Earth, who he has decided will repopulate the Earth and live out their days according to His word and His commandments." Michael's eyes had been on Maria for several moments, but hers never raised to meet his. She sat there stiffly, surely aware that he directed his stare in her direction. I imagined he did that a lot and I chafed at the thought.

"We have to accept it as truth before it's too late and God deems us as unworthy as those unbelievers who still roam the Earth, dragging their rotting corpses around and doing God's will by ridding his new world of those who still might not have put their faith in His will and the words of His chosen messengers."

I flinched. By chosen messengers, I took it he meant himself. Maria's head popped up, her eyes wide as she met Michael's glare. He had meant that last specifically for her and I once again wondered how she had come to be at such a place. She didn't seem the religious nut type and she didn't act like she really even wanted to be anywhere near Michael. Would he not let her leave? Had he threatened her?

As abruptly as the sermon had begun, Michael, sure he had gotten the point he wanted to make across, rounded out the morning with a few Bible verses about virtuous living and admonishing the women to make sure they gave the men no reason to make sexual advances outside of marriage. My mind tuned most of his final words out. I was conscious of the fact that I was nearly the only person in the room who was astonished by how backward and absolutely medieval the entire camp operated. How two years of death and horrors had turned back time for women and civil rights for hundreds of years. Just like that, with one man and one book, women were once again being treated like property and the Bible and religion were being used to control the masses. I felt ill.

"Let's bow our heads in prayer..."

I bowed my head, not in prayer, but in thought, wondering how fast I could get the hell out of Camp Victory and put the entire sickening place far behind me. When chapel service was dismissed, I was the first person out the door and I didn't stop until I was back in the washhouse so I could splash my face with cold water and take a few moments to let my blood pressure lower. I could hoof it from where I was back to what was left of civilization, but it would be so much easier to get back to the base if I could get Uncle Gus to drive me into town. Besides, I really had no idea where I was exactly, nor how far back into the woods. Had to be back far enough that all the zombies from the neighboring towns weren't a threat to the camp, but how far back was that exactly? Maybe Uncle Gus could at least get me a map or an idea. I'd been in worse situations.

With my mind made up to find Uncle Gus and to get on my way as quickly as possible, I left the washroom and wandered through the camp. I needed to put miles between myself and Camp Victory, and soon.

The more miles the better. The sooner the better. For everyone.

Chapter Eight
Run. Run. Fast as You Can.

Out of only a hundred or so people, you'd think one older man who spat chewing tobacco wouldn't have been a problem to find. You would be wrong. No one seemed to know where Uncle Gus had gotten off to and I found myself ready to strangle some folk just to get a straight answer. I'd been circling the camp for a half hour questioning people when I realized with a jolt that I'd wound up in the women's section of the camp. I stopped mid-stride and took two steps back the way I'd come when someone called out to me.

"You look like you are a lost little puppy." I turned to find Maria smiling sardonically at me from between two cabins. She was hanging clothes on a line. "Which shouldn't even be possible, seeing as how the camp is pretty small, but yeah, I'd say you're definitely lost."

I let out a sigh and walked over to Maria at the clothesline. She glanced around before she spoke again.

"You don't belong here, Tex," she said simply, her smile gone as she reached down to grab a white shirt to hang on the line with old fashioned clothes pins.

"I know I don't." I breathed in deeply and met her tired brown eyes. "I was just looking for Uncle Gus so I could talk to him about leaving. I thought maybe he would be willing to give me a ride into the nearest town or even provide me a map so I can get going on my own."

Her eyes searched mine before she clenched her jaw and went back to her task of hanging laundry. "Uncle Gus will be around in a little while. A few of the men have a meeting with Michael every Wednesday right after chapel." Maria shrugged. "It usually takes about an hour, so you have a few minutes before you need to head back into the other section of the camp. Uncle Gus will be near the chapel then," she said brusquely. After a moment of silence, with nothing except the breeze and the scent of clean linen on the air between us, I spoke up.

"You don't belong here either," I said gently. Maria's hand stilled above the line, a wet skirt and pin in her hand. "Some of these people might. Some of them might even believe all that garbage Michael was spouting in chapel, but not you."

Maria snapped out of her stunned silence and continued her job, pushing her basket with her foot further down the line.

"You don't know me, Tex."

She was right. I *didn't* know her. I didn't know her story or all that she'd been through, I only knew what I'd observed since I'd been at Camp Victory.

"I reckon you're right about that," I said. "I don't know anything about you, Maria. But I've known women like you. Smart. Strong. Fighters. Women who would've ripped into the Michaels of the world a little over two years ago." I smiled at her. "Tell me you haven't wanted to tell him to go to hell at least once," I goaded.

She tried to stare me down and she almost succeeded until a tiny grin lifted the corner of her mouth.

"I've wanted to tell him a whole more than that," she confided. Immediately her eyes hardened again though, and the smile disappeared from her lips almost as quickly as it had appeared. Maria had been through a lot. I put a hand out and grasped hers.

"Why do you stay here? Won't they let you leave?"

A deep sigh sounded from the woman standing in front of me and her head bowed deeply. After a second she removed her hand from under mine and raised her head. "They would have let me leave, I think, *before*. But where would I have gone? This is the safest place I've found and I can't go back to being on the run every single night... I can't do that to... myself again. And now... now I don't think Michael *would* let me leave," she murmured, turning her face away from me. There was something else that she wasn't saying, but I didn't want to pry. I did the only thing I could, given the situation.

"I know of a safe place," I said quietly. Her eyes widened and she glanced around us nervously. I did the same. I really didn't want Michael knowing there was a functioning safe house at the Army base. I didn't trust him and I didn't know any of his people enough to trust them.

"I've been there, it is safer than even here and I know without a doubt that they'd take you in." Something very close to hope lit in Maria's eyes and I found that I was extremely glad that I'd been the one to put that look there. "It's Army. I was headed back there when I got myself into a messy situation. That's when Uncle Gus and the guys picked me up." Maria wet her lips with her tongue nervously. My gaze followed the movement. Ashamed that I suddenly realized how beautiful Maria was and how perfectly kissable her lips were, I took a step back and ran a hand through my hair.

"This Army base... do you think they'd be okay with two more besides you?" she asked cautiously. I must have taken too long to answer because she added an explanation. "I... I have someone else I'm responsible for."

Ah, of course. Maria would never have stayed in a place like this if she had only herself to think of. She wasn't the type. She didn't though, she stayed to keep someone she knew safe. Not a husband. Maybe a sister or brother. My mind recalled a young man, maybe twelve or thirteen, with Maria's light brown coloring and chocolate brown eyes. They definitely could have been related.

"Of course they would," I said with a smile. "They would take in anyone, I've no doubt of that."

Maria searched my face and after a moment smiled in return. "Michael wouldn't let me leave. He's got it in his head that I'm meant to marry him. He thinks God told him that I am meant for him, meant to be his helpmeet during these days of purging," she spat. "If he only knew...."

Michael would be a problem. If a man like him truly thought Maria was his and that she was destined to stand by him and his little religious reign, well, he wouldn't give her up so easily. I frowned.

"I need to think of a plan before I commit to taking you out of here," I said. "I think you're right about Michael, which would mean sneaking you out of here, and that would mean we'd have no help and we'd be on our own, on foot, facing the zombies. I'd be putting you and your brother in a lot of danger. I won't be responsible for getting you killed."

Maria looked confused. And then her eyes widened in surprise. "No one would be responsible for my actions except me, Tex. I'd never allow you to take that kind of responsibility onto your shoulders."

"You wouldn't, but I would. I wouldn't be able to forgive myself if I took you out of here only to die under my protection. I'd never be able to live with myself." Voices came from a short distance away and Maria snatched her basket off of the ground.

"We can talk later," she threw over her shoulder. "Right now you need to get out of here." I turned to make my way out of the women's camp as quickly as possible. I only had to explain that I'd gotten turned around twice before returning safely to the main part of the camp. I found Michael and Uncle Gus close to the chapel just like Maria said I would.

"Ah, there you are, Tex. Uncle Gus and I were just talking about you." I raised a brow as I joined the two men.

"Only good things I hope," I said with an easy smile.

"Of course. Uncle Gus seems to think you'd like to be on your way as soon as possible. He was thinking of giving you a lift into town if you'd like," Michael offered.

I felt my smile stiffen on my lips and knew I should just take the gift that had been dropped in my lap. To take the easy way out and jump in a vehicle and get on my way to back to the base right then and there. However, that wasn't what kind of man I was. Even knowing I'd failed so many, knowing that people had died and suffered because of me, I still couldn't turn my back on someone who needed my help.

"Actually, I was thinking I might like to stick around a while longer, if that's okay," I said enthusiastically. Uncle Gus's eyes bugged out of his head and a crease appeared between his rather shaggy brows.

"After the chapel service I did some thinking. A lot of what you said made sense, but I just need another day or two to think everything through before I make any decisions."

Uncle Gus looked like he was about to have an apoplectic fit. Michael beamed at me and cuffed me on the shoulder.

"Take all the time you need, we could use a few more strong and able bodies like you here." I smiled tightly.

"Perhaps you'd like to even go hunting with us tomorrow morning," he offered. "To keep busy, earn your keep and all that."

"Absolutely. I'd be glad to."

And suddenly I was staying in Camp Victory until I could come up with a plan to help Maria and her brother escape from Camp Cuckoo Kazoo.

Chapter Nine
A Huntin' We Will Go

When I woke the next morning and got ready for the hunting trip, I had a little time to think over the previous day. After speaking to Michael, wandering around the camp, and having a few nice meals and a clean bed to call my own, I realized why people were so willing to swallow all the bullshit Michael Hatten had been feeding them. Not only was the camp relatively safe, but they also had supplies, shelter, food, and medical attention. They had built a new life for themselves right in the middle of the apocalypse. The camp was removed enough from town and the rotten stench of decay that you could almost pretend it wasn't even happening elsewhere in the world. Only the occasional sound of a gunshot which signaled that the men had taken care of one of the undead who'd wandered too close to the camp reminded me that the world was still a dangerous place. I had a feeling a lot of people had convinced themselves exactly that. If they couldn't see it, couldn't hear it, couldn't smell it, then it wasn't happening.

I hadn't spoken to Maria again since the previous morning, and I was second guessing my decision to help her escape the camp. I'd be taking her out of a place of safety and back out into a world of death and horrors. What if I couldn't get her to the base? What if I got her killed? If I didn't, however, she'd eventually end up having to give in to Michael and if she married him out of fear and not out of choice, well, I wouldn't be able to live with myself then either. I almost wished I'd never set foot in Camp Victory. Almost wished I never met Maria. Almost.

A knock on the outside of the cabin told me the men were ready to get on with hunting before the early morning hours wasted away. I grabbed my hunting knife and went out to meet them. I glanced around the group standing. Only six of us, Michael among the men present. Uncle Gus was missing though. I spotted only two lookouts as we left the camp and I hoped the old man and the young boy were decent shots. My instincts screamed for me to stay and protect the inhabitants of the camp, instead I quickened my stride without looking back.

"You know, Tex, I'm glad you decided to stick around a little longer. Once we get back to camp, I want to show you something that might even convince you further that it was always God's will that you become a part of Camp Victory."

I gripped the rifle that he had given me in my hand and ducked down to squat near Michael, who had found a spot that we could blend in and wait to see what animal might come across our area. We bagged several rabbits before we stopped once again in a good place to wait for more game.

Rustling nearby alerted us that our next game was much larger than a rabbit and I only hoped we might be lucky enough to find a nice sized deer. The sounds grew increasingly louder and I knew without a doubt that no deer made that much clumsy noise, no animal made those unnatural sounds at all. Only the undead made the sounds that had grown increasingly closer. And sure enough, a few seconds later, a corpse shuffled into our line of sight, drawn to the sounds of our gunfire and the scent of our rabbits' blood.

I waited a breath to see what Michael might do, if he wanted to take care of the dead man himself, but he made no move to raise his gun. In fact, he acted like he hadn't even noticed the zombie at all. I glanced over at the severely decomposed body that stumbled closer. A man, still dressed in a suit and a tie, on his way to work, maybe on his way home from work when the world ended. Someone going home to a wife perhaps, or maybe someone just heading home to a cold beer and a movie. Still, someone who never deserved what had happened to him. I raised my rifle, ready to put the poor soul out of his misery, ready to eliminate a threat.

"Don't," Michael whispered. He put a hand on the gun I held and pushed it down and away from my target. My instinct told me to jerk away and finish the zombie off before he stumbled right on top of us, and my gut told me to knock some sense into Michael and do what needed to be done. I lowered my gun and met Michael's gaze.

"He isn't why we're here. We aren't why he's here."

I jerked my head back toward the sound of the zombie's moans and gurgling as he drew closer. I readied to take the zombie down with my knife if I had to. Just then, a gunshot close by rang out through the forest and the zombie abruptly turned toward the sound, then jerked away as if the strings of some twisted, master puppeteer had orchestrated the entire encounter. I wiped the back of my hand across my forehead, swiping the sweat that had beaded there away.

Michael was insane. Insane men get people dead. A lot of people.

We did eventually take down a deer, yet it didn't bring me out of the foul mood I'd slipped into since seeing the zombie in the woods earlier that morning. We started back to meet our group around lunchtime. I was more than ready to get back to the camp and get a bit further away from Michael. My patience had begun to wear very, very thin. We joined two of the guys who had been grouped together and sat down to wait for the last duo to join us when a gunshot and shouts echoed around us.

I took off at a run. I heard the men behind me running as well, though I knew I would be the first to find the source of the screams. I reached a clearing at a dead run and nearly bowled over one of the younger men who'd gone with us to hunt. He was on his knees crying, his hands dug deeply into the earth and his gun thrown uselessly on the ground beside him. Not six feet away was a zombie feasting on the insides of one of our men, oblivious to his audience. He ripped into the soft flesh and tissue of his meal, enjoying the fresh and still warm smorgasbord.

"My... my brother!" the young man wailed. He'd been hunting with his older brother. His brother who was now dead at the hands of the very zombie I'd seen earlier, the one I'd wanted to take down out in the forest with Michael. Michael and the rest of the group reached the macabre scene. I pulled out my knife and walked over to the zombie. I met Michael's gaze as I drove it into the top of the zombie's skull and yanked it free. The zombie slumped forward over the body he'd been devouring, dead for the second time. Dead for good. My eyes never left Michael's. Not even when I wiped the gunk off of my knife on the leg of my jeans. He broke eye contact and walked over to the young man on the ground, placing a hand on his shoulder.

"I'm sorry, son," he said loudly. "We have to trust that God's will has been done." The kid didn't answer Michael, then again Michael hadn't said it for his sake, he'd said it for mine. His eyes challenged me, and in that moment I understood him perfectly.

We left the dead body in the forest right where it lay, per Michael's instructions. They didn't bury the unbelievers; they were left to decay with the world as God had intended. I knew beyond a shadow of a doubt that I despised Michael Hatten and I was beginning to realize the error I had made by not killing him when I had the chance when we were alone out in the woods.

We walked in silence for about a mile when Michael motioned for the guys to start setting up a fire and camp site. I glanced around at everyone, wondering what was going on. We'd gone hunting and had quite a bit of success. We'd lost one of our own to a zombie. Surely it was time to start heading back to Camp Victory.

"What are we doing?" I asked.

Michael threw a bunch of firewood into a pile. "We do this once a week. After we've gone hunting, we set up camp and celebrate the Lord's generous bounty."

I shifted from foot to foot. I had to tread carefully here. I knew that, but the more time I spent with this bozo, the more likely I was to shove a knife in his skull.

"Even if you lose one of your men during the hunt?" I asked, motioning toward the young man who was still visibly upset over the loss of his brother.

"Especially then," Michael replied. "God is good and just in all of His dealings with us. Paul will understand that. He'll realize that his brother was not meant to survive, that he must have harbored unbelief in his heart or the Lord would have spared him like he has all of us." I stood there, unable to even articulate a response. It was probably a good thing too.

Michael spread his arms to encompass the camp and the men working together to set up the fire and to prepare a few rabbits to roast over the fire.

"We are here as believers and each one of us has inherited the Earth." Michael smiled broadly. "God has provided for his faithful children. You included." Michael turned back to his task and I walked away. I started skinning rabbits, preparing them for a meal, trying not to think too much and trying hard to keep my hands and mind busy. It wasn't long before we had a good fire with rabbits laid across to cook for our meal. One of the older men brought out a pot and emptied mixed vegetables from a can into the pot to heat up. He took out a cast iron skillet and heated up some of the fat of the rabbits. He mixed up something in a bowl and before I knew it he'd prepared and poured his mix into the piping hot grease. He sat back to let it cook with a smile of satisfaction on his face. I peered into the skillet. Looked like cornbread batter. My stomach growled in appreciation. It'd been a long while since I'd had homemade cornbread.

The men gathered around the fire to talk and joke around as they waited for the food to cook. Even Paul, who had recently lost a brother, perked up a bit as the smell of cooking meat wafted around the site and Michael kept including him in conversation.

"So, we know you were in the Army when the apocalypse began," Michael said a little while later. "What else is there to know about you?" he asked.

The men all stopped chattering and turned to look at me. I shrugged. "Not much, really," I said

"Well, what's your real name and how'd you get the nickname 'Tex'?" Paul asked.

I leaned back into the trunk of the tree I was sitting in front of. "My real name is Jeremiah Jackson," I replied.

"Jeremiah. A biblical name," Michael said with a wide smile of his own. I let him assume that's where I'd gotten it from. Truth was, I'd gotten it from my great, great granddaddy who'd been a womanizing moonshiner.

"Tex I picked up in college right before heading into the Army. Not really because everyone knew I was born and raised in the good state of Texas, but mostly because I wore cowboy boots, drove a big truck, and have always been madly in love with Shania Twain," I admitted.

Paul guffawed and few of the other guys chuckled. Michael didn't like my nickname story as much as my real name one.

"You have a family?" one of the men asked.

I guess we were getting personal here. It was almost like a written rule or something, *not* to ask about the loved ones everyone had lost in the last two years. I turned my gaze back to the flames of the camp fire. "A wife," I replied gruffly. I cleared my throat and looked across the fire to Michael. "What about you?" I asked. "What were you doing? Did you have a family?"

The men glanced from me to Michael. At first I didn't think he was going to answer. He stared at me for the longest time before speaking. "I was an assistant pastor at a church in the town over. Reston, North Carolina. I had a wife. We'd been married three years," Michael said without looking at anyone. The men were riveted. It must have been unusual for him to open up to strangers like that. "Some of the men here at Camp Victory knew me from before," he added. "Most didn't. He met my gaze, his eyes defiant and angry. "I found out a week before the dead swallowed the Earth that my wife had been having an adulterous affair with someone from the church." He smiled. It wasn't a sad smile or even a happy smile. It was a twisted smile. "She even told me the baby she was carrying wasn't mine," he said. "When the undead started walking and ripping into the living, I went looking for my wife, hoping to find her alive. To tell her I forgave her for her sins and that God would forgive her."

My mouth was suddenly dry. Maybe this hadn't been such a good idea after all.

"You know where I found her?" he asked, not really expecting anyone to answer. "She was supposed to be dropping off canned goods to the church and instead she was meeting her lover there in the church parking lot." He reached out and turned the rotated the meat on the fire. "The church was in town and the entire place had become overrun. The undead ripped my pregnant wife and the man she was seeing to shreds, and I saw it happen." Michael sat back down and shrugged nonchalantly. "I knew immediately that God was punishing the sinners, the unbelievers. Why else would he have spared me and taken both of them even though we were all at the same place at the same time? After that, I got as many believers and supplies together as I could and headed to Camp Victory. I'd been out here with a church group, ironically enough, to learn some survival skills. Candle making, curing meat, canning food, even sewing. Stuff like that." Michael smiled at the memory. "Sure came in handy."

"Sure did," I said after a pause of silence.

After his story, I understood where Michael Hatten was coming from. I got why he was the way he was. Kind of. He was clinging on to his beliefs, seeing God's hand in things that there was no way it could be. I kind of understood. I still didn't like him though.

"Looks like the food is done," the older guy, whom I'd found out was named Bobby, announced. Good. Something to keep us all occupied. I'd had enough of the heart-to-hearts. After Michael prayed over the food, we all dug in with gusto. The food was good and the silence was a blessing.

When we were all full and rested, we tore the camp down and preparing to head back to Camp Victory. Michael clapped me on the back in companionship as we started off.

"I'm glad you came with us, Tex," he said. "I think you fit in nicely here with our group." I smiled and nodded. On the inside, I was cringing and giving him the bird.

Chapter Ten
No Other Way

"Meet me in the chapel in an hour," Michael said to me when we entered the safety of the gates and had dropped off our load. I nodded even though I couldn't summon a smile in reply.

An hour later I entered the chapel, still distracted by my thoughts of what had happened earlier in the day. A man was dead because Michael thought he could play God, thought he knew the mind of God. I still hadn't calmed from the rage that had been building inside of me.

"I'm glad you came," a voice called from the front of the chapel. I closed off my thoughts and turned a high watt smile on my host. Michael stood at the front of the church with a huge grin on his face. My back stiffened and I went over to him to shake his extended hand. It was then that I noticed a figure in the shadows, standing quietly by. I glanced over and Michael followed my gaze. His smile widened and I felt the urge to knock out a few of his perfectly aligned teeth. No one had ever been able to enrage me quite as fast as the man standing in front of me.

"What was it you wanted to show me?" I asked politely, dredging up the years of southern hospitality my mama had instilled in me. Michael crooked his finger to the person standing just outside of my peripheral vision. A young girl, maybe fourteen or fifteen, stepped forward. I thought I'd seen her in the chapel the day before. The day before her hair had been pulled back in a bun, and was now loose and hanging down to the middle of her back in a thick, golden cloud. Her eyes were crystal blue and they looked up at me shyly and even a bit afraid.

I met Michael's twinkling gaze. "Am I supposed to know her?" I asked, dumbfounded.

"Not yet you're not," he said with a wink. I stood there uncomprehending. Michael took the girl's hand and brought it to his lips, placing a kiss there. She blushed and looked down. He took her hand and placed it in mine and then turned his gaze back to me.

"I wanted you to see that God is not just smiting down his enemies from the Earth. He's also rewarding his followers and given them an edict to replenish the Earth with children of true believers." He picked up a strand of hair from the girl's shoulder and rubbed it between his fingers.

"This is Amanda. Amanda will be sixteen in a week and then she'll be eligible to marry one of our men here at Camp Victory during the purity ceremony we've begun preparing for. I think she'd be good for you... that is, if you decide to stay."

His smile turned my stomach and the girl's hand in mine felt like lead. The girl standing in front of me should be in high school worrying about fashion and which boy might have a crush on her, but she stood here in front of me, her head bowed as a man paraded her in front of me like a brooding mare for sale. She was still just a girl. A child.

I stood there for a moment, pretending to consider the girl, her beauty, how much she would please me, instead, I was trying to get the red that blurred the edge of my vision to abate. I was trying to strengthen the last, fraying thread of self-control I had before I pulled my hunting knife out and lodged it deeply in the skull of the man who still stood smiling at me from only a foot away. After a moment, I squeezed the girl's hand and then let it go gently.

"Amanda is beautiful," I said. "She would, I'm sure, make any man happy," I added, even though the words stuck in my throat and I wanted nothing more than to be there if any man dared touch her. I turned to Michael and grinned crookedly. "You've given me even more to think about," I said. "But for now, can I grab a shower and some sleep? I'm ornery when I'm tired."

Michael threw his head back and laughed, the picture of an unburdened conscience. I turned to Amanda and said, "You go on and head out to grab some lunch with the womenfolk, okay?"

Amanda smiled up at me and let out a relieved breath, nodded, and left the chapel. I excused myself from Michael and told him I'd meet him over at the mess hall for dinner once I got a quick shower and some sleep. I left the chapel with one thought in my mind: I needed to get the hell out of Camp Victory that night and I was going to take Maria with me.

There was no other way.

Chapter Eleven
Escape Plan

I showered and made sure I stopped and made small talk with the men while Uncle Gus eyed me like I'd grown two heads. He was right about that, and because I had no idea what type of loyalty he had to Michael, I avoided his gaze and kept to myself. I couldn't risk Uncle Gus telling Michael that I planned to break out of the camp and take Maria with me. Too much was riding on the fact that I need to move quickly and without being noticed to give us a good head start before Michael would realize that we were gone. A while later, I made my way to my cabin, aware the Uncle Gus was following not far behind. Maybe his cabin was close to mine; maybe he was keeping an eye on me. Either way, he knew I was up to no good. The old man had far better senses than Michael and that made me realize I had very few hours left in which to act. I waited until I was certain he wasn't watching the cabin. Luckily none of the men I shared the cabin with were back yet or my plan might not have worked.

I slipped out of the cabin, weaving my way in between the cabins and buildings, making sure I wasn't seen heading to the women's side of the camp. When it was all clear, I ducked in between the two cabins where Maria had been hanging clothes. A large tree sat near the back of the two cabins and I was able to slip behind it unnoticed. I squatted down and waited.

It wasn't long before a young woman left the cabin. I wasn't sure if I should have tried to peer inside and then risk going in to speak to Maria, or wait it out even longer and risk being seen out in the open. Both options were risky. Then the back door to the cabin opened again and I saw Maria's dark hair appear. I acted quickly, grabbing her from behind, my hand over her mouth, and jerking her behind the tree with me. Maria fought, and she fought hard. I was grunting when I finally wrestled her into a safe place.

"Shh shh shh! It's me, Maria!" I whispered near her ear. Her hair had come undone from its bun and her wild black curls tickled my face.

She immediately stilled, her breathing heavy and her heart racing next to my chest.

"I'm going to remove my hand now so we can talk. Understand?" She nodded once, stiffly. I slowly removed my hand and loosened my grip on her. She turned so fast that if I hadn't been leaning against the massive trunk of the tree I probably would have lost my balance. Now that would have been embarrassing, especially since she couldn't have weighed more than a buck twenty soaking wet and she stood easily six inches shorter than me. Her eyes narrowed dangerously and her chest rose in anger. She stabbed her finger to my chest.

"What is *wrong* with you? You nearly gave me a heart attack!" she growled.

I shrugged and tried not to smile. "I'm sorry, I didn't know how else to talk to you without someone seeing or hearing me." She crossed her arms over her chest and stared up at me. She raised a brow when I smiled like an idiot.

"What?" she snapped.

"Nothin'," I replied. "Nothin' at all."

"Well what did you want to talk about?" she asked, her anger fading a bit.

"If you still want to go with me, I'm leaving tonight. I'm going to see if I can get a hold of some ammo and supplies. I can't stay any longer."

Maria searched my gaze and sucked in a breath.

"What did you see?" she asked.

"A young man was killed today. Michael wouldn't let me take a zombie out when we were hunting and the zombie ended up killing one of our group later." I clenched my jaw and turned my face to hers. "He said it was God's will."

Her eyes hardened and her mouth thinned into a straight, angry line. "What else?" she asked after a moment.

"How do you know there's more?" I asked, surprised. She raised a brow, but didn't answer. I blew out a breath. "He said he wanted to show me how he knew God had chosen me to join everyone at Camp Victory... one of the *benefits*," I spat. "He brought me a girl, Maria. A girl who isn't even sixteen yet." Maria's eyes widened. "Said I could have her as my own during some purity ceremony they're planning soon. She's a *child* and he's going to give her to someone to use," I said, my voice shaking with the rage I'd been bottling up since I'd entered the camp. Maria put a hand on my cheek and the contact took the edge off of my anger.

"I know they have been talking about such things for a while, but I thought they'd all see reason. I never thought they'd actually agree to something so horrible," she mumbled. I covered her hand with mine.

She glanced up at me, her eyes tired and frightened.

"I'll get you out of here, Maria, but it has to be tonight and we have to move quickly. I'll do my best to get you to the Army base. I can't make any promises." Maria stared up at me for a moment and then closed her eyes. When she opened them, I saw new resolve and determination there. She stood on her toes and placed a kiss on my lips.

"You're a good man, Tex," she whispered. I shook my head, but she just smiled. "You can deny it all you like. I know the truth. I can see you for what you are," she said gently.

I didn't know how to respond. Though I didn't want her to think I was some kind of hero, deep down I realized Maria wasn't the type of woman who needed a hero, she was more than capable of saving herself... she just needed a little push was all.

"I'll gather all the supplies and ammo I can find," I said.

"And I'll make sure we have water and food," she offered.

I smiled. Sounded like a plan.

"After dinner, then," I said. "We don't want to leave before, our absence will definitely be noticed if we're not in the mess hall for a meal." She took a deep breath, worry creasing her brow for a split second. Then she shook her head and squared her shoulders. She'd made up her mind.

"Good. Let's meet after most of the camp has gone to sleep, around eleven, near the mess hall. We should be able to sneak out of Camp Victory from there."

"Alright. Tonight at eleven then."

"Tonight at eleven," I confirmed. Maria stepped back and made sure the coast was clear.

"Be careful, Tex," she threw over her shoulder. She sprinted across to her cabin.

"You too, Maria," I whispered after her.

Chapter Twelve
Final Supper

I stuffed a large rucksack that I'd found and filled with supplies behind a thick line of shrubs near the mess hall. It was on a side that no one used and I was confident no one would see. Gathering supplies had been too easy. I'd found extra wool blankets, a compact tent, a first aid kit, waterproof matches, two boxes of bullets for my handgun and plenty of other hiking gear that would help us stay alive and survive in the woods for a few days if we had to. If we could get out of the woods, we'd be able to find a vehicle and get to the base quickly. I just needed to keep us alive until then.

The first hours would be the most important for us to put as much time and miles between us and the camp as possible. I only hoped tonight went without a hitch.

"Tex, there you are," Michael called from across the mess hall when I entered. I raised a hand in greeting and then moved to the window to take my tray from the kind lady there. For a brief second I found Maria's gaze and held it. She nodded once curtly, an almost imperceptive movement, but it settled my heart and I breathed a little easier. Maria was ready. We'd be skipping camp in less than five hours. I wondered if her brother was ready, if she'd even told him, or if she'd spring it on him later in the evening. I hoped the kid was smart and would understand the danger that his sister was trying to get him away from.

I sat close to Michael, taking care not to sit directly in front of him or too close to Uncle Gus. I didn't need either of them sniffing out my secrets. Our plates were heaped with meat and white rice. A brown gravy had been generously spooned over the whole thing. Even for the camp, the portions were a bit extravagant. I glanced around the tables, aware that the men and boys there were in high spirits, the hearty meal and infectious enthusiasm making the atmosphere seem even more homey than normal. I caught Michael's stare out of the corner of my eye as I'd been laughing at something one of the guys had been saying.

Another point for Michael; he knew how to play on weaknesses. One of mine was missing my home, missing my mama's home cookin', and missing the feeling that everything was going to be alright. Damn him. And damn me for being so utterly transparent.

Right about then, my luck ran out. Uncle Gus came over and sat down next to me. I hardened my jaw, trying to play off my unease. The man was highly perceptive and even though I owed him my life, I still didn't know him well enough to trust him.

"So, Michael seems to think you'll be staying on permanently," he said, his voice low so as not to be heard over all the loud chatter. I sat my fork down on my empty plate and took a drink of water before answering.

"Does he now?" I asked.

"He does. He seems to think you made up your mind after your little chat in the chapel this afternoon." I whipped my head around and met Uncle Gus's scrutiny, my blood pressure rising at the thought that I could be swayed to stay for such a despicable reason. He searched my face and then grunted. He turned to watch the guys at the table near us messing around. All the women had already left.

"That's what I thought. You're not that kind of man." Uncle Gus clucked his tongue and sighed deeply.

"And you are?" I asked.

"No. I'm not, son, but I hope I can be of some use here. I've brought people in here who would be dead out there on their own. I don't agree with anything Michael does here, but what is the alternative? Leave the survivors I find out in the world to die? Or bring them here to live, even if it means things like that disgraceful purity ceremony take place?" His eyes met mine and I realized how much he really had thought it all through, how much guilt he was carrying around on his shoulders. He was saving lives only to bring them into the mess at the camp. And yet... he *was* saving lives.

"The world we live in is chaotic, the decisions we make are hard ones," I said after a moment. "With death all around us and hope disappearing more and more every day that passes, people desperately need something to believe in, something to hold on to. I just wish it wasn't all the crap Michael has been shoveling."

Uncle Gus grunted at that. "So do I, son. So do I," he agreed wearily. "So, what are you doing, Tex? What are you planning?" I met his gaze for a second before turning my face away. I still couldn't trust him. I'd be wagering Maria and her brother's lives on a hunch that Uncle Gus was a good man, a good man in an impossible situation. I still couldn't take that chance. It wasn't my call. He sighed deeply and then stood up from the table.

"I could really use a drink right about now," he muttered beneath his breath. "Whatever it is, Tex, please be careful. You know what Michael is capable of. I don't want to see anyone hurt."

I nodded my head once and glanced up into Uncle Gus's all-knowing gaze. "I'll be careful," I promised.

He shook his head and smiled sadly. "Good. Godspeed, Tex. I have a feeling I won't be seeing you again."

"Godspeed, Uncle Gus."

A few minutes later, I left the mess hall and headed to my cabin.

It was almost time.

Chapter Thirteen
One Bad Mother

When the time came to sneak out of my cabin, everything was eerily quiet. My cabin mates were asleep, some of them snoring loudly, and it only took me a second to sneak out the door and to make my way across the camp and back to the side of the mess hall. I found the rucksack right where I'd stashed it. I pulled out my loaded gun and stashed it in my waistband. I hauled the bag on and attached my knife to the front strap for easy access. I drew back into the shadows of the building when one of the men who patrolled the wall of the camp strolled into view. He didn't have his weapon at the ready. They were very casual since they didn't have more than a few zombies to dispatch each night. They only rarely had a large group come through this part of the woods from what I'd been told. I told Michael and the other men that they needed to be more vigilant. Eventually a large mass of zombies would come through. Drawn to the sounds and the smells of the camp, it would only be a matter of time and they needed to prepare for that here, though I had a feeling my warning had fallen on deaf ears.

I turned, warned by a sound that someone was coming up behind me. I yanked my knife out, but Maria stood there with a backpack on and a large bundle in her arms. I breathed a sigh of relief and put my knife away. I glanced behind her looking for her brother, except no one was with her.

"Where's your brother?" I whispered, pulling her arm gently to bring her more fully into the shadows like I was.

Her eyes met mine and her lips thinned into a straight line. She raised her chin. "I don't have a brother."

I frowned, my forehead creasing in thought. "I don't understand. That teen boy wasn't your brother?" I asked. If he wasn't, then who did she mean when she asked about the base taking two people in? Maria's mouth popped open to reply right as the bundle in her arms moved, revealing a small head of hair at the top of the bundle. Maria's mouth closed with an audible snap and she covered the head with the blanket.

My heart thudded painfully in my chest and my mouth dried out. I reached over, my hand surprisingly calm. Maria stiffened, though didn't object when I removed the blanket and pulled it down far enough to reveal the tiny, sleeping face of a child.

So many emotions and thoughts ran through my body that I nearly staggered from the onslaught. I hadn't seen a child so young in over two years. Not a live child, anyway. Not much older than a baby, I even wondered how well the child could walk. Then it all came crashing in. My eyes widened and I took a step back.

"I can't, Maria. I can't take a baby out in that," I said harshly, pointing to the gates.

"We have to," she insisted. I shook my head and set my jaw. No way in hell. "This isn't up to you, Tex," she hissed.

"Like hell it isn't," I replied, my anger barely controlled. "I will not be responsible for getting a baby killed." I ran a hand through my hair and pulled roughly on the ends. "You can't ask me to do this," I said without looking at her.

"I can, Tex," she replied. "I have to. Don't you see? I can't allow my daughter to be raised here. Have her growing up believing in Michael's teachings. To be his daughter?" she asked roughly. "And then when she turns sixteen to be handed over to a man twice her age to further the propagation of the *true believers*? I'd rather die first."

"What about her?" I asked. "Would you rather her die than stay here?" I asked a little softer this time. She glanced down at the face of her baby and wiped a gentle touch across her brow before covering her head once again with the thin blanket.

"I'm willing to take this chance. For her. For her future. What point is there to survival if you're only surviving to live a life with no hope?" Her eyes met mine full of unshed tears. Her words echoed inside my skull. Not so long ago I'd thought the same things. Not so long ago I was ready to die rather than go on with no hope. Maybe she was right. Maybe I had survived this long to be her source of hope for her child.

"This isn't going to be easy," I murmured, searching the area. Maria snorted softly, drawing my questioning gaze back to her.

"Tex, I survived the zombie apocalypse during my last trimester all alone. I delivered my own baby in a deserted pharmacy in Charlotte, and I nursed and protected an infant who could scream at any moment for months before Uncle Gus found me and brought me here to Camp Victory."

My mouth hung open. Maria had survived against horrible odds. Maria was one tough mother.

"I think I understand the risks," she said with a half-smile. Knowing all of that, knowing she was making the choice she felt best for herself and her baby, still I hesitated. I ran a hand through my hair and over my face roughly.

"Okay then. Let's do this."

She blinked rapidly before turning her eyes down to the bundle in her arms.

"I'm ready," she whispered.

We waited for the front gate patrol to pass by before we made our move a few heartbeats later. We both knew he'd walk the entire length of the front fence line and then head back toward the gate. We only had a few moments to slip through the gates unnoticed. I pulled up the bar on the gate while Maria slipped through easily. I slipped through after her and when no one shouted out and no shots flew past us, I moved quickly away from the camp, making as little noise as possible. Time was our only hope. We had to put a lot of ground between us and the camp before everyone awoke and before Michael noticed we were gone. I had no doubt he'd come looking, I just hoped he would give up if we made it too difficult for him to find us. If we made the risks not worth the reward.

We walked for two hours before stopping to rest for the first time. Maria sat down on the ground and laid the child in her lap, taking a moment to stretch her arms.

"How long do you think it will take us to clear the woods and to get to the nearest town?" she asked after she took a quick swig of water.

"Probably all morning. We might be able to clear the woods about the time everyone realizes we're missing," I answered. "I'm hoping maybe to even be in town at that point. It will be harder to find us if we have buildings to hide in. If we're caught out in the open though...."

Maria frowned. "Yeah, we don't want to be caught out in the open," she agreed.

"We should get moving," I said a few minutes later. Maria shifted the baby in her lap, snuggling the sleeping child into her before trying to get up. I came over to help her. She smiled gratefully.

"She weighs a lot more than she did a year ago," she whispered. I stood there for a moment, gazing down at the sleeping child. The world shifted into rightness for a blessed second. Hope was a tangible thing in the form of an innocent child sleeping in her mother's arms. I vowed that I would get that hope to the Army base come hell or high water. I wouldn't fail. I couldn't. Maria searched my face and I wondered if she saw the determinedness there, the hope she and her child had rekindled in me.

"What's her name?" I asked softly.

Maria smiled up at me. "Rose," she said. "Her name is Rose."

We continued on walking in silence after that, both of us lost in our own thoughts.

Both of us determined to get little Rose to safety.

Chapter Fourteen
Zombies Go Splat

We walked straight through the early morning hours, only pausing to catch our breaths and to drink a little water before moving on. I'd been worried about Maria carrying the baby, and yet she never once complained even though I knew she had to be getting tired.

"Tex," Maria breathed out in a whisper, "look."

I turned in the direction that she was staring. The tree line thinned there and I could see the sun shining off of a sign. A sign meant a road and a road meant we were closer to a town. I looked up into the sky. The entire forest was getting brighter and brighter. Morning had already come and people would soon realize we were gone.

"We need to hurry," I said.

We both picked up our pace. We had to find a place to hole up before Michael came looking. The baby would wake up soon and we both needed to rest. We cleared the tree line cautiously, making sure we hadn't miscalculated and would find Michael already waiting for us if we chanced coming out into the open. Nothing moved. Nothing living, that is. It only took us another half hour before we found the undead waiting for us.

"It's been a long time since I've had to fight," Maria whispered at the sight of the first zombie approaching us.

I wasted no time, not wanting to risk the corpse getting too close to Maria and the baby. The zombie splatted on the pavement in front of us, its brains nearly bursting from its cranium before I even got my knife free. We both stood there in stunned silence for a moment, staring down at the explosion of gray and black matter.

"Well, that's new," I muttered beneath my breath, trying not to inhale too deeply.

Several more zombies met their demise like the first. They couldn't move very fast, so they were easily taken down one by one. I wondered what was wrong with these particular zombies. Were they sicker than the hundreds of undead I'd fought previously? Were they more contagious? My head spun from what it all could mean.

When we spotted the town of Pineville, Maria and I both heaved a sigh of relief. Oddly enough, the town didn't look like it was in too bad shape. It didn't even look too badly overrun with the undead.

"Michael will come here first thing," Maria said. I nodded. I'd thought that too. We needed to find a car and move away from Pineville as soon as possible. Several cars littered the streets. Two had been wrecked. One looked like it had been in bad shape even before the apocalypse. Then, at the other end of town, I saw a car parked in front of a bookstore. I was betting that car might have had the keys in the ignition. If not, maybe the owner had worked at the bookstore and the keys were there.

"There," I said. "You stay behind me and I'll take down as many as get in our way. If things get ugly, you make a run for that bookstore and I'll meet you there."

Maria pulled a knife, holding it in her right hand and the baby in her left. Rose stirred in her arms.

"Just a little longer, mama. Sleep a little longer," she whispered sweetly to the sleeping child. I began moving. I didn't look back. I knew she was following closely behind.

We moved swiftly through the little main street of town. Zombies fell around me and though the town was by no means overrun, it did have a plethora of corpses looking for a meal. We were only two storefronts away when I heard Maria gasp. I turned right as a zombie stumbled out of a broken store window we'd passed. I'd been so busy taking down the threats on the street, I hadn't noticed that one inside the store. I moved quickly, but not before the zombie got to Maria. She didn't hesitate though, her arm moved out to the right and swung in an arc until her knife was embedded in the left temple of the badly decomposed zombie. The jarring movements woke the baby abruptly, scaring her into crying. I reached Maria while she tried to remove her deeply lodged knife.

"Hand me the baby," I said. Maria handed Rose over to me hastily so she could pull her knife free. More zombies were headed our way and Rose had begun to wail. I shushed the baby gently, murmuring absolute nonsense to her as we ran the rest of the way to the bookstore. We reached the store and threw ourselves inside, opting to take our chances inside than outside with a crying child and shambling corpses headed our way.

Maria reached out for Rose as soon as we had the door secured.

"Stay here, I'll check out the store." Maria already had the baby calmed down when I set out to make sure the store was zombie free.

"Looks like someone stayed here before," I said from around a few bookshelves. "There's a couch over here."

Maria came around the corner with a very alert Rose on her hip. The baby eyed me curiously, not looking like she trusted me for one second. She had her mom's dark brown eyes and her skin was the same pretty shade as her mom's as well. Maria walked closer to stand in front of me.

"Look, Rose. This nice man's name is Tex," she said sweetly. I smiled at the baby, meeting her very serious gaze. Maria raised her hand and placed in on my chest. "Tex," she said again gently. Rose put out a small hand and her mom leaned in, bringing her closer to me. Her tiny hand patted me twice on the chest and then she grinned. And just like that, I was done for any other woman. Rose would have me wrapped around her tiny little finger for life. Then she blinked and lost interest in me altogether. Maria took her over to sit on the couch. I held out a colorful board book I'd picked up a few minutes earlier. Maria beamed at me and the baby instantly cooed over her new prize.

"I'm going to see about finding keys to that car and I'll also see about clearing out the zombies we attracted to the front of the store," I said after watching Rose play with her book for a few minutes longer.

"I'll feed her some snacks while you do that and we'll be ready to go as soon as you are," Maria assured me. I turned to leave.

"Tex?"

"Yeah?" I threw over my shoulder.

"Be careful," Maria said softly.

"I will."

Ten overly-bloated zombies later, I had cleared the front of the store. Unfortunately, that meant that the entire area was now covered in putrid innards, by far the largest mess and most stomach-curdling stench that I'd encountered since the first day the dead began to walk. I stood outside for a while looking over the bodies of the zombies, careful not to get closer than necessary. My boots, jeans, and arms were covered in their entrails, but I didn't want to take the chance it would get in my face or on me any more than necessary. Something was going on, though it was yet unclear exactly what. What that meant for us survivors was anyone's guess. Was the virus adapting? Evolving? I grimaced. I didn't like the implications.

The car was unlocked and the inside was clean. I didn't find any keys, but if I had to I could get it started with some effort. First, I needed to check on Maria and Rose. I found a half empty bottle of water and a tee shirt in the back of the car and used them to wash up before I went inside.

"How is it out there?" Maria asked when I entered.

"We'll be able to leave through the front without any problems."

Maria studied me over the top of her daughter's head. The tiny girl, no older than nine months or so, was happily and quietly playing with her book.

"Something has changed." I glanced away, not wanting to scare her, especially since I had no idea what the change in the zombies could even mean.

"Yeah, something *is* different. Maybe it's just these zombies though. Maybe they were all sick before they died or maybe they were exposed to something after they died that made them this way. It's nothing to worry about since we have no idea what the circumstances are."

Maria sat there for a moment in thought and then heaved a sigh. "Alright. We should get out of here. The camp must be awake now. People will be heading to breakfast," she said.

And then they would know we were missing. Yeah, time to move.

"I couldn't find the keys to the car, so I'm going to have to hotwire it," I told her. "It's been a long time since I've had to do it, but I think I can manage."

Maria grinned hugely and shook her head.

I raised a brow. "What?"

She tossed me a set of keys. "They were in a purse under the cash register area," she laughed.

"Guess I won't get to show off my mad car theft skills then," I grumbled.

"No, but you can help me for a moment if you don't mind." She held out the thin blanket she'd had Rose wrapped in. "I'm going to wrap Rose onto me. That way my hands can be free while we're on the move. I don't want to get caught like I did earlier unable to use both hands."

"I'll help however I can."

"Just help me get her wrapped securely to my back like a baby carrier. Pull the fabric around us both, I'll guide you which way to wrap it and then tie it securely at my waist."

We maneuvered surprising well seeing as I had no clue how a baby wrap was supposed to work. However, Maria did, and after a moment the baby was strapped snugly onto her back. I finished up tying the long fabric around Maria's waist.

"Rose doesn't mind traveling like this?"

"I think she rather enjoys it," Maria said. "She feels comforted and safe like this, and I think she remembers all those months that we were on our own. I wore her a lot like this then. Of course, she was a lot smaller then, so it was easier for me to wrap her myself and I usually wore her in front."

I tugged on the knot that I'd made and then ran my hands along the baby and Maria, making sure they were completely secure. My hand came up to the straps on Maria's shoulder and she put a hand on mine, stilling my perusal.

"Tex," she stated, "we're good, I promise."

I took a deep breath. I had to get them to the base as quickly as possible. I couldn't let anything stop me. Maria's eyes searched mine, hers confused and then wide.

"I'm going to get you there safely," I said gruffly.

"Whatever happens, we made the right choice leaving Camp Victory," Maria said. "It was my choice, not yours. If we...." I shook my head and tried to pull away, but Maria held tightly to my hand on her shoulder. "If we die, Tex, you are not allowed to feel guilty about it."

She had no idea. I already felt that guilt, that burden.

"Tex, you're a good man and you deserve peace. Whether you die today or are the last man standing, you need to know that none of the stuff that has happened is your fault."

I glanced away. Maria put a hand on my cheek and moved my face toward hers, making me meet her gaze.

"You don't know me, Maria."

She smiled sadly, her eyes showing the pain and the uncertainty she had felt, that all of us had felt since that first day over two years ago. She reached up on her tiptoes and placed a gentle kiss on my lips. I closed my eyes and kissed her back. Not out of passion, not even out of love really. Mostly out of a mutual need to feel like we weren't alone, to feel alive, and to feel hope.

"Ma-ma," Rose cooed. I pulled back and gazed over into Rose's perfect little face.

"Don't worry, niña, you'll always be mama's number one," Maria cooed to her daughter.

I placed a gentle hand on Rose's head. She glanced up at me and giggled. The pain around my heart chipped away just a bit.

"Well, ladies, shall we?" I asked.

"Yes," Maria said and we turned to the door.

With our bags thrown in the back seat and Maria and Rose sitting next to them, we set off from Pineville, planning to reach the Army base in a few hours. Hoping to leave Pineville, Camp Victory, and Michael Hatten far behind us.

Hoping for a future for Rose.

A future worth surviving for.

Chapter Fifteen
It Could Be Worse, Right?

The roads were even worse than the last time I'd driven down them. Vehicles littered the highway and zombies lurched in groups throughout all the wreckage. I didn't dare turn off on side roads. Not only did I not know the area very well, but odds were the narrower roads would have led to small towns, and I'd been in small towns alone the past several weeks. They were little pockets of zombie lairs. It seemed that everyone there thought they could just hunker down and wait out the apocalypse. And that made for entire towns that were wiped out and infested with the undead. Not an hour later of thirty mile per hour driving, we had to pull off of the side of the road. Too much debris and two overturned semis made passage by vehicle impossible.

I glanced back into the review mirror and caught Maria's worried gaze.

"We can do this," I reassured her. She lifted her chin.

"We have to," she affirmed. I took everything out of Maria's backpack and added it to my bag. I discarded anything that wasn't absolutely essential and exited the car, pulling on the one and only bag we were taking with us. Maria followed. She pulled her knife and a gun she'd brought from the camp. Several zombies were already headed our way. Without a word, Maria and I started off, cutting down every corpse that got in our path. Maria was surprisingly effective and quick, even with Rose strapped to her back. Rose was quiet, as if she knew how important it was and how much danger we were all in.

"Tex?" Maria asked as we walked down a particularly quiet part of the highway.

"Hmm?"

"Why were you out on your own when Uncle Gus found you if you knew where a safe haven could be found?" I searched the highway, making sure I stayed alert. Zombies had way too many places they could be lurking. Letting our guard down would have been a big mistake.

"There were a lot of reasons," I said after a moment.

"Like?" Maria insisted with a questioning gaze.

I sighed deeply. How much did I want to share with her? Would she second guess her decision to come with me if I told her the truth?

"For one thing, I couldn't stay at the base because there was this girl...."

Maria smiled widely. "Isn't there always? Every good story begins with a girl and a boy," she said with a soft sigh.

"So does every tragedy," I muttered.

Maria rolled her eyes. "And this girl... she broke your heart?"

"No and yes..."

Maria walked and waited, letting me gather my thoughts. "I didn't really know Melody enough to say that I loved her. So, really there was no way she could have broken my heart."

"And yet...?" Maria prompted.

"And yet my heart was broken when I left. Not really because I knew I had no chance with her or because I realized she was in love with someone else," I said. "It was because I had let myself hope for and fall in love with what *might have been*. Even though the world was shit, my dreams haunted me, and I blamed myself for my wife's death, I had let myself believe that it was possible to have all the things I'd once had and never truly appreciated. Hope. Love. Happiness." I shook my head and walked up to a zombie that had stumbled onto the road from the woods ahead of us. My knife cut through its skull like a hot knife through butter.

"And now? Maria asked when I joined her on the highway again. "Do you still not believe it is possible to have all those things once again? To have love and hope and happiness in the world the way it is?"

"I believe it's possible to have those things," I said carefully.

"But?" Maria wasn't going to let it go. She was going to make me say it.

"But I think it's fleeting, the feeling of love and contentment. The illusion of happiness and hope. Here for a moment, gone the next. Snuffed out as easily as a life is in this new, terrible world of ours."

We walked in silence for a moment before Maria spoke again.

"I guess that's all the more reason to hold onto love and hope and the things that make us happy while we can. To cherish it all, even the little things, more than ever." Her eyes met mine. "Now, more than ever, those things matter." I glanced back at the baby on Maria's back. She'd fallen back to sleep, content to be carried like a sack of potatoes while her mother and I walked and talked and killed. I turned to keep a vigilant look out as we moved. Maria was right and I didn't want to admit it. Not to her, and especially not to myself.

I breathed a sigh of relief when the toy store came into view. I'd been there before, weeks ago with the group that had left the Charlotte Army Base. I knew it would be relatively safe, knew that we'd fortified it for an overnight stay at one time. Hopefully not much had changed since I'd been there.

"Head for that toy store," I said to Maria. She pulled her blade free from the top of a zombie's head and glanced over at the building, panting from the exertion of our walk and fighting her way through several tight groups of the dead. Fueled by our need for a rest and to get out of the open with the baby, who must have been hungry and tired as well, we moved out.

The inside of the building was darker than the outside where the sun was shining right down on us. It took a moment for our eyes to adjust to the semidarkness. The store looked much the same as it had when I'd last been there, but it looked dirtier and a stench that also hadn't been there previously permeated the space. After bolting the door, I stiffened, aware instantly that there was at least one zombie in the room with us. I grasped my blade, flexing my fingers, ready for whatever came around the corner of the toy store shelving. A single zombie, a woman missing most of her torso and wearing filthy, ripped yoga pants, struggled around the corner, dragging a leg behind that was missing the majority of a foot. Maria and I both moved forward, glad we'd lucked out and only found the one zombie in the store. I moved a little more quickly than Maria, intending to take care of the limping zombie myself. Just then, a flash of movement from the far side of the room drew my eye.

The second I took my eyes off of the zombie I'd moved in on, she found her footing and heaved herself, teeth snapping, toward me, knocking me off balance. I landed on my back with the surprisingly strong zombie on top of me, her rot filling my nostrils at close proximity and her hands clawing at me. My knife bounced off of the tile floor next to me right out of reach. And then I heard Maria cry out, her voice pure agony as she muttered the same Spanish phrase over and over again. *Madre de Dios, por favor... no.*

I reached out a hand and struggled to reach the hilt of my knife, holding the zombie away from my neck. I grabbed the corpse's hair and yanked as hard as I could to dislodge it from on top of me. Instead of jerking her back, the hair and a large portion of the dead woman's scalp ripped away from her head, leaving me holding the wad of matted hair and rotted flesh in my palm and bringing the zombie's face terrifyingly close to sinking her rotten teeth into my chest. I held her only inches away with my left hand as my fingers finally found my knife. A scream from Maria nearly stopped my heart and I shoved my blade beneath the zombie's chin, the tip exiting the top of her skull. I didn't even have time to register the gunk that instantly drenched my neck and chest. I shoved the body off of me and leapt up from the ground. I swung around to where Maria was with Rose still strapped to her back. They were in a far corner of the room. What had them cornered was a thing out of a person's worst nightmares.

Maria had her knife in one hand and I could tell it was shaking before I even started running toward them. In the other hand, Maria held onto a fist full of dirty, pink tee shirt. Gnashing its tiny teeth inches away from Maria was an undead toddler. No older than three when it had died, it was one of the smallest and most terrifying zombies I had ever seen and it was just as ferocious and deadly as its much larger adult counterpart. Maria was crying, her hand out to make the kill, but she just couldn't do it. I reached her right as her grip on the miniature demon loosened. My knife sunk into the small skull just as the zombie lunged. Maria sunk to her knees, tears streaming down her cheeks and her eyes wide, staring at the lifeless body of the toddler between us. I put a hand on her shoulder.

"It's okay," I murmured. Her eyes, red and wide, met mine... they told me she knew I was lying. Nothing about having to put down a toddler, a once-innocent child, was okay. Nothing about the world we lived in was okay. And maybe it never would be again. I took both of the bodies out of the toy store and laid them out near the back. I placed a dirty blanket over them. I imagined the mom had been staying in the toy store with her little girl when the child had probably turned. The toddler had killed her mom and then both were there waiting for us when we'd arrived. I walked the perimeter of the building, making sure it was still secure and then headed back inside to see how Maria and Rose were holding up.

"Do you think life will ever return to normal?" Maria asked when I came up to her and Rose. Her hands were working the knots I'd tied at her waist for the wrap. I stepped closer and gently pushed her still trembling fingers away. I began loosening the knot as I spoke.

"Normal?" I asked. "No, I don't think it will ever return to the normal we knew." Maria stilled and lifted her face to look at me. I shrugged beneath her gaze.

"So you think the world will always be like this? Death and killing. Running and dying." The knot finally came undone and I helped Maria unwrap the fabric from her and Rose. She pulled the baby to her hip and placed a gentle kiss on her cheek.

"I believe that one day things will get better. I think there will come a day when people won't be living in constant fear and that there won't be death on every street corner." She rocked the baby back and forth and Rose wound her tiny fingers into her mom's hair.

"I don't think the world will ever be quite the same as it used to be, and yet I hope and pray it will be the kind of place where Rose can grow up safely." I smiled down into the big brown eyes of the toddler that had already changed my life and smiled. "I pray that when she is all grown up, the world will be a better, safer place and that she'll only be reading about all the death and devastation in her history books."

And that was where I'd placed all my hopes. On the head of this tiny child who wasn't even mine. On the promise of new life and new beginnings and what the future could possibly hold for her.

"Me too, Tex," Maria said.

"We can rest here for a while. There are things we can use to sleep on and we are relatively safe. Once we get a little shut-eye and Rose is fed and rested, we'll move again. The base isn't far from here. If we can find another vehicle, we'll be there in a few hours."

We ate in silence, the only sound was Rose's nonsensical chattering filling the space. A little while later Rose was yawning and Maria was nodding off. They snuggled into a pile of stuffed animals and cloth kindergarten mats and fell asleep together. I sat there for a while watching them sleep. Eventually I got up and walked through the building, too restless to sit down for long. I wandered up and down what was left of the original aisles of the store. A place that normally would have been overflowing with cheer and laughter was only a macabre reminder of all that we would never have again. I walked down another aisle and found the shelves completely empty—except for a single toy at the end of the long shelf. I reached out and picked up the stuffed elephant with large, embroidered eyes. It was made of some super soft, light gray material, its ears huge and floppy. The inside of its ears were made from a silver, satiny material. I noticed the logo on the tags of the elephant and smiled. A tiny, yellow rose. I stuffed the elephant in my pocket and went back to watch over Maria and Rose.

Chapter Sixteen
We Do What We Have To Do

"Maria, wake up." She groaned and after a moment her eyelids fluttered opened.

Her eyes widened. "What time is it? Did I sleep too long?"

"No. I hated to bother you. You both looked so comfortable," I said, waving over to the baby snuggled into Maria's side.

"We need to be going, right?"

I nodded and stood back up.

"If we want to get to the base by nightfall, then yes, we need to go soon."

Maria sat up, moving away from the baby gently, careful not to wake her. She stood and stretched.

"Tell me something about you," I said.

Maria took a drink from her water bottle, eyeing me over the rim. "Like what?" she asked.

"I don't know. Anything. There are so few moments left where we just get to know people anymore," I replied. "I'd like to know you better. You and Rose."

She came over and sat back down near the baby. "There's not a lot to tell really. I wasn't anything special. A normal woman living a normal, boring life."

"What I wouldn't give for a normal, boring life right about now," I murmured.

"I guess you're right about that. Okay. Well, I lived in Miami most of my life. My parents owned a Mexican restaurant there for years." She smiled, lost in her memories. "Best homemade salsa in the state. I have three brothers, all older than me. They were overprotective jerks, but I loved them, and they'd have loved to have met Rose."

"Sounds wonderful," I said. "What about your life? What were you doing when everything happened?"

She sighed. "I was working full time as a waitress in a fancy restaurant trying to pay my way through art school."

"Really?" I said, surprised. "What kind of art?"

Maria pulled a sketchpad out of her bag. "Pencil sketching mostly. I enjoyed painting too."

I flipped open the book she placed in my lap. There were all types of sketches. Some of random people from Camp Victory, some of places that had been bombed or burned out after the dead began to walk, and some of Rose. Rose sleeping, playing, smiling. And then there was one of me. I stared at the drawing for a long while. I looked full of life. Full of determination and hope. I never saw myself that way before.

"They're amazing," I said sincerely. Maria blushed. I handed the sketchbook back to her.

"What about you?" she asked softly.

I shrugged. "My family is... *was*... all in Texas. I was an only child. Spoiled rotten." Maria snorted. "I was in the Army when it happened, on base, and on lockdown. I wasn't allowed to leave. My wife was at home."

Maria breathed in sharply. "I'm sorry," she whispered.

It really seemed like so long ago now. We sat in silence for a few minutes. I stood and walked over to the windows, taking a look outside. Maria followed behind me.

"Tex, I've been thinking..." Her voice was serious and immediately I felt the hairs on the back of my neck rise.

"What is it?"

"I know I have no right to ask this, I know I even promised you that I wouldn't, but being back out here in the middle of everything... I just have to be sure of something."

"Ask me," I said, my jaw tight.

"If anything happens to me...." I flinched and took a step away. Maria put a hand on my arm to still me.

"No. Please let me finish," she pleaded. I tamped down my own fears, my own insecurities, and nodded briskly.

"If anything happens to me out there, I need to know if you'll do everything in your power to make sure Rose gets to the base." She tightened her grip on my forearm when I flinched and continued on. "I meant what I said about you couldn't possibly be held responsible for my actions or for mine and Rose's lives. But I need to know that you'll at least try to get her safety, that you'll make sure she's got a fighting chance at life if anything were to happen to me between here and the base," she finished thickly.

"Nothing is going to happen to you, Maria."

"You can't promise that, Tex, and I don't expect you to. I came into this with my eyes wide open. I need to know that if I fall my baby girl will have a chance. No matter how slight."

I growled deep in my throat and pulled Maria roughly to me. She was one of the strongest and most intelligent women I'd ever met. I held her tightly as I whispered into her ear.

"Of course. I give you my word that I'll protect Rose with my dying breath if anything happens to you. I'll fight every zombie between here and the base with my bare hands if I have to. I won't fail you. I won't fail her," I vowed.

She released a long breath of relief. "Thank you, Tex."

"Thank you for coming into my life, Maria. You and your little girl gave me a reason to keep going. A reason to fight another day. I owe you everything."

She pulled back a little to look up into my eyes. "I wish our circumstances were different," she said.

I smiled sadly, knowing exactly what she meant. "I'd loved to have been able to show Rose the horses my parents had on our little farm back in Texas," I said.

"She'd have loved that," Maria said. "*I'd* have loved that," she added after a moment. I ran my hand up her back and cupped it behind her head, angling it just so. I brought my lips down to hers, savoring the way her eyelids lowered in desire and her lips parted in anticipation. I kissed her slowly and thoroughly, telling her without saying a word how much I wished we'd met when the world was a different place. How much I was going to fight for her and Rose.

After we kissed as if it would be the last time either of us would enjoy the simple pleasure, we went over together to wake Rose up and to get her strapped on her mama's back once again. When Rose was securely in place, I pulled the little stuffed elephant out of my pocket and held it out to her. Her huge smile and immediate love of the stupid toy put an idiotic grin on my face. Maria wiped at her eyes and glanced away. I pretended that I didn't notice the few tears she shed. Maria cleared her throat.

"Ready?"

"I am," I stated.

Chapter Seventeen
We All Die In the End

We exited the building, ready to be on our way and find a car that would take us to the Army base. The zombies were sparse, but we took down three of them before we'd even left the front of the toy store.

"Let's head on around the building and see if there are any good cars on the other side," I suggested. We took off in that direction, skidding to an abrupt halt when we made it around the corner.

"Where the do you think you're going?" A kid stood there. No older than thirteen, his tall lanky frame standing defiantly in front of us with his dirty brown hair hanging down over his ears. More importantly, he was pointing a shotgun directly at us, his finger already on the trigger. Maria and I both froze in shock.

"Look, kid, we ain't lookin' for any trouble. We're just moving through the area on our way somewhere safer."

The kid's blue eyes hardened as he stared at us. "There's no place that's safe," he said calmly. His voice didn't waver, his hand pointing the gun at us was calm. This kid had to have been through a lot to have survived this long. He had to have seen a lot of horrible things the past two years.

"Well, being just about anywhere would be better than being out in the open," I said, keeping my voice as even as possible. The gun was making me jumpy. I hated it being pointed at Maria and Rose.

"Inside or outside, we all die in the end," he said. It was then that I realized the kid was more than likely even younger than I'd originally thought. His eyes were the eyes of someone who'd been through a lot, seen too much in their short life time.

"That's true enough, yet we'd like to fight as long as possible," I said. I still held my knife in my right fist, but Maria and I both were acutely aware of the fact that our guns were going to be of no use to us right then. This kid would have blown us away before we ever had a chance to pull our weapons. I was certain he wouldn't have blinked doing it either.

"That's going to be hard to do without all your gear," said a voice from behind us.

Maria sucked in a sharp breath and I turned to the sound of the voice. Another kid, a boy who was about ten years old, stood there with a frown on his dark brown face. Behind him stood two more children even younger than the first two boys... a little girl and another little boy, all dirty and all carrying weapons with homemade silencers. When I turned back to the boy with the shotgun, I found a second kid had joined the first. He was the oldest of the group, a teenager, but not old enough to have been mistaken for a man. He grinned at us and I realized immediately that he was the leader of this little ragtag group of children.

"We'll take your weapons and your bag," the boy with the shotgun said.

I stiffened and took a step back.

"Don't move. I *will* kill you!" the boy behind us yelled.

"If you take our weapons and our pack, we won't survive," I said through clenched teeth.

"Not our problem," the kid with the shotgun said blandly.

I tamped down my anger and said to the children behind us, "If you do this, you're killing us."

The little girl glanced over at Maria and the baby and then back over to the leader of the group.

"If you do this, you're killing the baby," I added. The boy who stood next to the girl flinched and glanced around his group. Neither of them dared to say anything though.

"Hand over your gear," shotgun boy said without emotion. I hardened my jaw and started calculating all my options. Could I get to the shotgun before the kid fired? Would he fire if I moved? Just then the kid shifted his shotgun enough to have it pointing at Maria and Rose instead of me. I tensed and shifted, my heart thumping wildly in my chest.

"I said to hand it over," he growled. I glanced over at Maria and met her wide eyes. I nodded once. She dropped her knife and kicked it out of her way. I did the same.

"Now the bag. Take it off and sit it on the ground at your feet," he commanded. I pulled the bag off of my back and did as he had instructed. His gun was still pointing at Maria and the baby. Inside I was screaming for him to point it back at me, to keep it far away from them. On the outside I waited for the opportunity to help them.

"Max, Alexis, check them for more weapons." Shotgun boy nodded over to the younger of the two children and they immediately did as he asked. The little girl pulled my gun out of the back of my pants and the little boy removed the gun from Maria's. They both backed away and waited for their next orders.

"Now that you've taken everything that would have given us a chance at survival, can we go?" I asked harshly. My mind was spinning as it tried to think of where we could find anything we could use as weapons. We only needed to get to a decent vehicle, only needed to make it back to the base before dark. Surely, even without our weapons, we had a slim chance. Our odds weren't good, but I'd seen worse. The two younger children took down two zombies as we stood there facing the leaders of the children of the zombie apocalypse. The boy holding the shotgun lowered it just a fraction and nodded to me.

"You can go," he said. I clenched my jaw and turned to walk back to Maria and Rose.

"No."

The word stopped me dead in my tracks and a tingle of unease dripped down my spine. I turned back and faced the teenager who was standing near the boy pointing the shotgun. He had a grin on his face and his eyes were... dead.

"What do you mean?" the boy with the shotgun asked, his voice rising above the sounds of the few undead heading our way.

"I mean that *they* aren't free to go, Carter," he said evenly. I glanced back to the shotgun toting kid named Carter and saw for the first time a flicker of uncertainty cross his face. His eyes narrowed.

"We are supposed to strip down any survivors we find of their gear and weapons and then let them go. That's the way it's always been, Nick, so what makes you think we should listen to you and change the way things are done this time?" Carter snapped.

Nick stepped closer to Carter and brandished his knife in front of his face. He moved the blade down his cheek and then pressed into the flesh there until a drop of blood appeared, trickling down Carter's face.

"Because I'm in charge when Warren isn't here, because it has been over a week since we've found any other survivors, and because my orders are Warren's orders."

I flinched from the malice in Nick's voice. The teen was barely holding himself back. He wanted nothing more than to rip into Carter right then and there.

"You got a problem with that?" he spat, his face close enough to Carter's that I could see the hair around the boy's face move with the rush of Nick's breath. Carter clenched his jaw, still stiff and unyielding, still making no move to draw a weapon or jerk away from the tip of the blade digging into the flesh of his cheek.

"No," he answered finally. Nick smiled widely, clearly pleased with himself.

"Good," he said after a moment of staring Carter down. "I'd hate to have to tell Warren you didn't obey his orders." He pulled the knife back. "You'll be going with us," he said, his eyes lighting up with glee.

"I don't think we will," I ground out.

"Really? Then how about I blow a hole through your friend and her baby."

I flinched and held up a hand.

"Why would you want more mouths to feed?" I asked, taking a step back.

His smile calculating, he raised his handgun, which had a makeshift silencer on the end.

"Who said we were going to feed you?" His eyes sliced through whatever he looked at. I couldn't find even a sliver of humanity there. "And if you keep moving without me telling you to, I'm going to kill all of you here and now," he said as casually as if he were talking about a baseball game.

"Okay," I said, fully aware that we had been bested by a bunch of kids who wouldn't hesitate to kill us where we stood if it meant their survival.

"Alright, let's get going. We need to get back to the rest of the group before it gets much later," he said to Carter. Carter nodded, bringing his shotgun back up to point at us. He walked over and placed the barrel of the gun at the center of my back.

"Don't try anything. Just move when we say move," he said stiffly, giving me a little shove. I caught Maria's gaze out of the corner of my eye. She had realized a while back that we were really up a shit-creek without a paddle.

The kids took care of zombies with eerie accuracy and efficiency on the move. We came upon a plain white van a few blocks away and were unceremoniously shoved inside with Carter watching our every move and most of the other kids sitting in back with us, all of whom seemed uneasy that they had gone from pillaging supplies and weapons to kidnapping in the space of a few moments. Whatever this Warren had planned for us, I knew it couldn't be anything good. I just prayed that I would eventually have the opportunity to keep my word and get my chance to get Maria and Rose to safety. No matter the personal cost, I had to get them to the base.

I was their only hope.

It was my mission.

It was *my* only hope.

Chapter Eighteen
Apocalyptic Kiddie Brigade

We didn't go far by my estimation. Maybe four or five miles at most before we came to a stop. When the doors to the back of the van were yanked open and we were pushed back outside, I had a fleeting question as to why the kids hadn't blindfolded us to keep us from knowing where to find their hideout, but the question flitted away as quickly as it had entered my mind. There was no reason to blindfold us if we were never going to leave this place. The kids' hideout was an elementary school. An elementary school completely surrounded by a secure, chain link fence. Sitting on the outskirts of town, it was in a prime location from the zombies that probably had overtaken the town just down the road and within our line of sight. With the town within spitting distance, I expected to see more zombies surrounding the chain link fence that separated the school from the undead, but there were only a few stragglers in the area and as soon as they came within two to three feet of the fence, a muffled shot would sound and the zombie would drop to the pavement with a hole in its head, truly dead at last.

"Quickly," Nick said. "We don't have all day."

I walked next to Maria, my eyes scanning the school and the fence line, trying to come up with a viable way out if we could get free. I spotted several shooters on the top of the school and two on the ground outside of the main building. They were there to watch the perimeter and to keep the area surrounding the fence clear of zombies. Most of them were children, though a few of them had to be eighteen or nineteen, maybe even twenty None were older than that. I counted six outside and then five in the crew who had picked us up near the toy store.

When we entered the school, we walked quietly down hallways with the crew who had grabbed us at our backs and Nick leading the way. When we passed the gym, both Maria and I stopped, our mouths opening in shock. There were probably more than twenty kids of varying ages in the gym. Some of them were working out, some were playing basketball, and some were practicing their knife skills on a set of mats nailed to the wall with human outlines drawn on them. I hadn't seen so many children in one place since before the dead reanimated. We stood there almost in awe despite our circumstances.

Rose picked that moment to cry and the noise echoed down the hallway all around us. The entire gym of children paused at once, instantly turning their heads in our direction. I was reminded once again that our world had changed into something twisted and ugly. Some of the kids looked surprised, some looked curious, even more looked wary. *All* of them looked at us with distrust and shuttered glances. These children were killers. Every single one of them, whether they had only killed the dead or whether they had to do worse things to survive, had all been touched by darkness and death. They were all a threat to Maria and the baby.

"Shut that kid up and keep moving," Nick barked at Maria. We moved down the hallway and the baby thankfully quieted. We walked a little while longer until Nick stopped outside of a door at the end of a corridor right off the main hallway.

"Get in," Nick commanded. Maria entered in front of me and I followed, making sure I kept Nick in my peripheral vision. Everything about the kid put me on edge and I didn't want him anywhere near Maria or Rose. The room was tiny and bare except for a dingy mattress near the wall and a plastic chair in a corner. The single window in the room was not only high up, but also way too small for any sort of escape plan to work.

"How long do you plan on keeping us here?" I asked.

Nick and Carter stood in the doorway. I could also see the face of the little girl, Alexis, a little beyond them but no one else.

"That will be up to Warren," Nick spat. He turned to leave.

"The baby will need her bottle, it has water in it, and a little food. Just a little," Maria pleaded. Nick sneered at her, but Carter reached behind him to a boy who stood out of my line of vision who must have been holding our bag.

"I didn't say that was okay," Nick growled at Carter. Carter clenched his jaw and ignored him, handing me the baby's bottle and bag of snacks. He also handed Maria the washcloth and rags that she used for diapering.

"Did you fucking hear me, man?" Nick yelled. "I said I didn't say it was okay to give them stuff." Carter pushed Nick back out of his face, the muscles at his neck bulging as he held in the violence and the rage that was simmering just beneath his surface.

"I'm not going to starve a baby. Not even Warren would want that. If you've got a problem with it, you can tell him. Until then, I'm going to assume he wants to keep these people alive for now and that means not letting them die from dehydration and starvation." Nick wanted to argue, oh he wanted to do much more than argue. He smartly reigned himself in, realizing the truth in Carter's words. How would he explain to this Warren that he let a baby go hungry on his watch, especially if Warren wasn't the type to harm children? Nick nodded over to one of the other kids outside in the hall.

The post-apocalyptic kiddie brigade left us a few minutes later and locked the door behind them, leaving Maria and I in the repurposed supply closet. I helped Maria unwrap Rose from her back and then slid down the wall to sit on the floor in defeat.

"Well, this was unexpected," Maria said with a sigh after a few moments of silence. The sarcasm dripping from her voice took me by surprise and a bark of laughter escaped before I could stop it.

"You could say that again," I said with a huge grin. Maria started laughing and I joined in. We both sounded a little hysterical and a lot insane, but we couldn't stop ourselves. The whole situation was ridiculous. Ridiculous or not, however, we were in a world of trouble. It didn't take long for both of us to sober up. Rose sat on the mattress playing with her stuffed elephant, oblivious to the dangers that now surrounded her. In reality, danger would always surround her in some form or another. The thought was sobering.

"What do you think this guy Warren will want with us?" Maria asked after a while.

I turned my gaze away from the baby to look at her. "I'm not sure, but nothing good."

"I noticed that there aren't any adults here. Not any that I could see anyway."

I nodded. I'd noticed that too. "No and I bet that isn't an accident either. Warren apparently has built himself an entire army of children."

"Why do you think that is?" she asked.

"If I had to guess, I'd say it's because children are not only loyal, but they are also trainable."

Maria let her head fall back on the wall behind her. "An army of children willing to do anything for you, to die for you, because you helped them survive when everyone else had died or abandoned them," she murmured.

And she was exactly right. Whoever this Warren was and whatever his motivation, he was brilliant. And ruthless.

We had spent several hours in the tiny room when I was ready to tear my hair out in frustration. The hours passed, the room gradually got darker, and I knew we weren't going to be going anywhere anytime soon.

Chapter Nineteen
Warren... Peace?

When I finally heard footsteps coming down the hallway toward the room we were in, I was still deciding the best course of action. If there were only one or two guards, should I try to overpower them, using the element of surprise to try and gain the upper hand? Or would that be too much of a risk with Maria and the baby in the room with me? My mind spun and my body tensed up, ready to make a move one way or the other. When the door opened, however, I took a step back to look less threatening than I felt. There were four older kids there along with Carter, and they all had their weapons drawn. Too much of a risk, I couldn't take the chance that a stray bullet would hit Maria or Rose. Carter eyed me up and down before he entered the room with his buddies. I had the overwhelming feeling that he'd been ready for me try something, that he'd actually expected it. Smart kid.

"Warren would like you both to join him for dinner." I glanced over at Maria and saw the surprise I felt reflect back at me in her gaze. What kind of game was this Warren playing at?

"And if we refuse?" I asked, crossing my feet out in front of me as I leaned back against the cement wall.

That's me, the picture of ease.

Carter's eyes met mine.

"You really don't want to find out," he said matter-of-factly. He didn't say it with a sneer or even to sound threatening; it was a statement of fact and I took it as such.

"Okay then, let's go have dinner with your boss." I placed a protective hand on Maria's back and led her and the baby out of the room. We silently followed Carter and a second kid down the hallway with the other two child-guards following close behind us.

We were led down the same hallways we'd taken when we first got to the school, except once we passed the gymnasium, we were led down a different hallway until we reached a set of doors that led outside. Once outside, we kept following a sidewalk that headed straight for another school building. I could hear the dead not so far away, moaning and moving about. We heard a few shots as well. Warren had his children work around the clock to keep the dead clear of the school fences. We entered the new building and were ushered into what once was an elementary school cafeteria. I squinted against the brightness of the room, no longer used to the harshness of the UV light bulbs that hung overhead.

"Sorry about that," a voice from further inside the room announced. "I usually don't use these lights except for special occasions. I thought using up a little of the gas from the generator for dinner tonight would be worth it for our guests."

Maria and I stood in the center of the cafeteria, facing the only other person in the room. He was tall, around the same age as me, but with a gruff exterior, unshaven and a little unkempt. The way he held himself to me he wasn't military, just a guy with survival skills and a way with manipulating children to do his bidding.

"Warren, I reckon," I said after a short pause.

"Indeed. And you must be Tex," he said, then turned his gaze to Maria. "Maria and little Rose?" he asked like he didn't already know.

Maria nodded stiffly. Rose was sound asleep in her mama's arms, her little brow relaxed in a sweet sleep and her dreams still uncorrupted by the horrors of the world. Oh how I wanted to keep them that way for her.

"Please, come and join me. I've had a nice little meal prepared so we can eat and chat."

Maria looked up into my face. I had about as much of a clue as she did, and that was none at all. With no real choice to be made, we walked forward to the table that Warren stood next to and sat down once he took his seat at the head.

"Would you like someone to take the baby so you can eat?" Warren asked. A girl came forward and put her hand on Rose. My chair hit the floor as I surged forward. The girl, shock and anger plain on her face had moved quickly, pulling her gun to point it right at my forehead.

"No one will be taking the baby," I growled. The kid's eyes widened a bit, just enough for me to know that she was smart enough to realize I could be a real threat.

"Alright, no one will take the baby. It was just an offer so Maria could eat without having to keep the baby in her lap," Warren suggested too reasonably. I glanced down at Maria's wide eyes and blinked. What was I doing? Maybe Maria would've liked to not have to hold Rose while she ate. I hadn't even asked her.

"Maria?" I asked.

She met Warren's gaze with a tilt of her chin. "The baby stays with me at all times."

"Very well then." Warren waved his hand and the girl standing in front of me with the barrel of her gun inches from my forehead lowered her weapon and walked over to a counter. I righted my chair and sat back down. A moment later a teen brought all of us a plate of food and a glass of water.

Warren lifted his fork to his mouth. Two of his teenage soldiers stood behind him, one of whom was Carter.

"Enjoy," he said, motioning toward our plates.

Maria and I both sat there for a moment. She was probably thinking exactly what I'd been thinking. Why go to all this trouble of kidnapping us, just to feed us well? Did that other boy, Nick, make a mistake in thinking his boss wanted the next people they stole from to be taken prisoner? I studied Warren for a moment. No, that wasn't it, though I wasn't sure what exactly his game was yet. One thing I was pretty sure of was that he didn't mean to kill us right then. He had other plans for us. If he only wanted us dead, he'd have had his kiddie brigade shoot us in the back of the head earlier. I nodded my head at Maria and we both picked up our forks. It wasn't anything fancy... some beans and chunks of canned chicken over a bed of rice, but it tasted good and both Maria and I needed the sustenance.

"So, why have you taken us against our will like this?" Maria asked.

Warren's eyes met her accusing ones and he finished chewing the food he had in his mouth. He wiped his mouth on a napkin and sat back in his seat.

"We have a problem, something we've been trying to accomplish for a long while now, and we think you two can help us," he said nonchalantly.

"You're telling me you kidnapped us because you needed a little help with some kind of... of stupid *project*?" she asked, befuddled.

"I assure you, it's no little or stupid project," Warren said with a tight smile.

"Then what is it?" I asked.

Warren looked at me and smiled. He was clearly more at ease speaking to me. It seemed Maria made him a bit nervous. At any other time, in any other place, I may have found that a bit amusing, seeing as Maria stood only about four inches over five foot and Warren had to be nearing six feet. As it was, I just filed the information away for later.

"We've been trying to raid the high school about a mile away from here, to clear out all the canned goods and supplies that have been untouched since the day the old world died, but we can't get close enough to the fence line to get inside without losing a lot of our people or risk letting the undead inside the perimeter with us, which would make getting all the supplies back out that much more difficult."

I sat back in my seat and listened to him while he spoke. Behind Warren I'd noticed that Carter's eyes had widened in surprise before he schooled his features back into passivity. Even the girl who was refilling Warren's glass with water had paused with the water pitcher frozen over his cup. She snapped out of it as quickly as Carter had, though not before shooting an anxious glance in Carter's direction.

"You couldn't have just asked for our help? Instead you had to take our weapons, our supplies, and bring us here like prisoners to get us to help you with your *project*?" Maria shot out.

"Would you have come if I'd asked nicely?"

Marie tightened her jaw and shot daggers at the man sitting across from us. We all knew the answer to that. No way would we have gone off our course, especially not with the baby, just to help someone else and their group. Still, there was definitely something else I was missing, something Warren wasn't saying.

"What exactly do you expect us to be able to do if your entire crew hasn't been able to get through the crowds of the undead to raid the high school? We're only two people," I said. "Unless you are holding more people against their will that we don't know about?" I added.

"No, you two and Rose here are the only guests we have right now," he answered without answering the most important question. "As to what you can do to help... I'll share that with you a little later on. First, I wanted to show you around the school a little. Let you see what I've accomplished here and what plans I have in store for the children that I've taken in before we talk about business." Warren smiled broadly. Now he was pitching it as a business transaction.

Maria snorted beside me and I grinned widely, matching Warren's air of ease and complacency.

"Sounds like a plan," I agreed.

Chapter Twenty
Loot, Shoot, and Scoot

"These are a few of the classrooms that we've converted into sleeping quarters for the children," Warren said half an hour later.

We peered inside one of the six classrooms in the short hallway. Children were milling about, some freezing when they saw us, others ignoring us entirely. The rooms were small, but comfortable. Cots and some homemade bunk beds lined the walls. There wasn't much left behind of what you'd expect to find in an elementary school. No brightly colored artwork hung on the walls, no little cubbies filled with backpacks and homework, and no play centers to welcome children. Instead, basic survival gear was spotted throughout the room. Kids sat on the floor and on their beds, cleaning guns and sharpening knives. Some kids wrote in dirty, beat up notebooks, while others hung plain, wet clothing up along a rope pulled taut across the room to dry. The entire scene was surreal.

"Who teaches them? Who helps the younger ones do the things they can't do for themselves?" Maria asked after a moment. Her eyes were on a little girl no older than seven or eight who sat on the edge of her bed holding a worn copy of *Goosebumps*. Warren laughed, making Maria and I both jump.

"No one has to help any of these children do anything," he said, walking back through the classroom door. We trailed behind him, with our ever-present armed guards following in our footsteps.

Warren showed us the few rooms that had been set aside for entertainment and fun. He said the children had fixed them up themselves, that they knew if they wanted a space to hang out or do whatever, they had to take it upon themselves to make it happen. There was only a handful of children in those rooms though. A few were playing a board game and a couple sat in overstuffed chairs reading or sketching.

We made our way back to the gymnasium, fully aware that that was where most of the children spent their free time. We could hear yelling and cheering before we turned down the hallway that led to the entryway of the gym.

"This is the activity hub of our little camp," Warren said proudly as we entered. A hush fell over the room the further we went inside. Kids stopped what they were doing and all stood... waiting.

"Everyone form a line," Warren barked out. Without even the slightest hesitation, a line of children formed in front of us, taking up the entire width of the gym. Everyone looked forward; no one raised their eyes to us. They moved automatically, like they'd done so many, many times before.

"Each and every one of these kids was alone when they came to join our camp," Warren told us. "Some of them, like Nick over there, were alone for the better part of a year when we took them in." I glanced down to where Warren motioned and saw the dead-eyed boy who had been the leader of the group who'd snatched us up. He didn't acknowledge Warren or us.

"Some, like Mike and Jeffrey over there, were together, but not doing so well."

The boys he pointed to this time had to have been barely out of kindergarten. I glanced up and down the line of children. My heart ached for what they must have been through the past two years. A lot of them were so young that they shouldn't have even had a slim chance of surviving out in the world of the undead alone, and yet, here they all were alive and thriving. Maybe Warren was right to teach them this way, to help them become tougher. The weak got eaten by zombies. The weak got preyed on by the strong. The weak couldn't survive in our new world, only the strong could. And yet, I still couldn't bring myself to fully appreciate the army of kids standing in front of me. Its unnaturalness didn't sit right with me. Children should be protected, not only their lives, but also their innocence. Children no longer existed in this harsh world, only the dead, their victims, and survivors.

"None of them have any family left?" Maria asked. Her eyes were filled with compassion as she gazed at the line of children.

"Every child here either saw their families get eaten by the undead, had to kill their own family once they turned, or worse, were abandoned by their family so they wouldn't slow them down," Warren said without inflection.

Maria flinched, wrapping her arms around Rose a little more snuggly.

"So, out of the kindness of your heart, you took them all in and showed them how to become survivors and became their family?" I interjected sarcastically.

Warren smiled, and it wasn't a fake smile, it was the genuine deal.

"I tell every kid I bring in here the exact same thing," he said. "I'm not your mommy. I'm not your big brother or your best friend. I'm a survivor, and if you want to be a survivor you have to do tough things and make tough choices, otherwise, you're just another dead kid living on borrowed time."

"Charming," Maria muttered beneath her breath.

"So what exactly do you teach these kids then?" I asked.

"Besides how to kidnap," Maria added.

"I teach them how to toughen up, how to take care of themselves, and how to survive against the odds," he said simply. Despite our circumstances, and even though I knew Warren couldn't have brought us to his camp to show off his accomplishments and to "help" with his high school project, I had to admit, I wasn't fully against what he was doing here with these children. He was missing balance, yet no one would argue that these kids now had a fighting chance of making it.

"Survivors!" Warren bellowed out, rousing the baby out of her sleep.

"Yes, Sir?" the children chimed in unison.

"What is the first thing all survivors must learn to do?"

"We must learn to forage, to take what we need. We *loot*!" they chorused perfectly.

"And what is the second things survivors must learn to do?"

"We must learn to fight, to wield a knife. We *shoot*!"

"And what is the final thing all survivors must learn to do?"

"We must run, we must move, we keep going. We *scoot*!" they shouted.

"One more time!" Warren commanded, his booming voice bouncing around the gymnasium.

"We *LOOT*! We *SHOOT*! We *SCOOT*!"

"Who are we?" Warren roared.

"Survivors 'til the end!" the children chanted.

I stood there in awe and horror. A child army of survivors, indeed.

"Warren?" Nick chimed up from across the room. I narrowed my eyes at the boy. Of all the living I'd come in contact with over the past two years, Nick had to be one of the worst for making my skin crawl.

"Yes, Nick?"

"Will is ready," he said with a sure spark of excitement. An excited Nick made me nervous.

"Oh, good. Let's see him off then, shall we?" Warren said, walking toward the back of the gym. Once we started moving, the kids in the line began dispersing, but a large group of them followed in the direction where we were going. Near the back exit there stood Carter, the teen girl from the lunchroom, and a young boy.

Nick handed Warren a backpack. Warren opened up the bag and

inspected the contents. He nodded and then handed it over to Carter, who helped secure it on the little boy's back.

"What's going on?" Maria asked.

"Tonight, Will here, is going through his final phase of testing," Warren said over his shoulder.

My stomach immediately knotted. This wasn't going to be good. Maria shifted on her feet and the baby stared over her shoulder and up at me. Not thinking, I held my finger out to her. She immediately wrapped her chubby little fingers around it and smiled.

"Each child who comes into the camp goes through a lot of different exercises to better prepare them to take care of themselves out in the dead-infested world. Then they go through three phases of testing, with the final phase being the most rigorous."

Every word Warren uttered began to make me more and more uneasy.

"And the final phase is?" I asked, not really wanting to hear it, yet needing to know despite myself.

"We give the child a bag filled with a few necessary items. Water, a little food, matches, and a knife. Three days prior we pick a location and stash a bag of loot, usually a new weapon, a pack of rare goodies, etc., there." Warren was checking over the boy, looking at the weapon he carried, making sure everything looked ship-shape. "Then, when they feel they are ready, we send them out alone one night to retrieve the pack and bring it back to camp."

Holy shit, I thought, but then I heard kids nearby me snicker. It took me a moment to realize Maria had said exactly what I'd thought out loud.

"How long does it usually take them to do this?" I asked.

Warren shrugged. "Sometimes a day, sometimes up to three," he said.

"What do you do if they don't make it back?" Maria asked, watching the little boy prepare to head out into the zombie infested dark alone with only a knife and a small bag of supplies.

Warren shrugged again.

"You don't go out looking for them?" she asked.

Carter shifted on his feet and the teenage girl near him wouldn't look us in the eye. They both looked a little uncomfortable.

"No. If they can't make it to the loot and then back without getting killed at this point, they're as good as dead anyway," Nick said harshly.

Maria moved to argue. I put a hand on her shoulder. We weren't here to liberate these kids, they were all there on their own accord, just like the people back at Camp Victory.

Kids came by to pat little Will on the shoulder and to wish him good luck. Then he was led through the back door of the gymnasium by Carter and the teen girl, all of them swallowed up by the darkness before the door swung shut.

"He's going to do it. He'll be fine," a little voice said from nearby. I turned to the girl and saw her big, blue eyes riveted to the closed door. She was about ten years old, maybe a few years older than Will.

"He has a good chance with all the training he's received," I agreed to soothe the anxiousness I saw in her gaze.

"He will be," she said matter-of-factly. "My little brother is tough," she added softly to herself. Maria sucked in a breath through her teeth. The little girl's eyes raised to mine and Maria's.

"If he doesn't make it back, then he isn't a survivor and he never would've made in this world anyway," she said vehemently and then walked away.

Warren started moving back toward the front of the gym and we fell in step behind him. After only a few minutes, I knew where we were headed.

"Here we are," he said after stopping outside of the door of the room we'd been held in earlier that day.

"So, when were we supposed to discuss whatever it is you want us to help you with?" I asked impatiently.

"And if we decide to help you, will you let us go free?" Maria added in.

"We'll talk about that tomorrow, Tex. And yes, you will be allowed to go ," he said to Maria.

Maria entered the little room first and we found two mattresses and fresh linens waiting for us. Rose was cooing, rubbing her eyes, so I imagined she'd be getting tired soon. It looked like we were going to have to bed down in the cell for the night.

"We'll talk tomorrow," Warren said as the door was shut and secured with locks.

"Yes we will," I muttered to no one in particular.

"At least we have the night to think everything through," Maria said, sensing my darkening mood. "I don't think he means to kill us," she said optimistically. I walked over and helped her get the mattresses covered so Rose could play until she wore herself out.

"I don't think he does either," I said, mostly to reassure Maria, to let her sleep somewhat peacefully for one more night. I knew, however, Warren was up to something. Two more people wouldn't make that much of a difference in taking over an overrun school. Warren didn't want us dead... not yet at least, but he definitely didn't just want an extra set of hands for a day. He had something up his sleeve, and I was very sure we weren't going to like it.

"We should get some rest," I said to Maria.

She lay down on her mattress, pulling Rose over to play in the circle of her body. Rose jabbered softly, chewing on the ear of her stuffed elephant. I lay down on my mattress and pulled my hat down over my eyes.

"I hope that little boy makes it back safely," Maria whispered into the tiny room.

"So do I, sweetheart, so do I."

Chapter Twenty-One
Welcome to the New World

"We don't know much beyond what has been told to us at this point,"
Captain Parsons told the crowd gathered around him. "What we do know
is that the virus is spreading rapidly, it is killing fast, and it is allowing
the dead to reanimate."

We'd been hearing talk all day. Some said that the outbreak that had
happened over the past twenty-four hours was multiplying out of control.
Some said the end of the world was here, others that it was just a scare
tactic to keep everyone quarantined so we could keep our world leaders
safe until it all blew over. I didn't know what to think. All I knew was that
when I'd tried to leave an hour ago armed soldiers were telling everyone
no one was permitted to leave and that we were to remain at the base
per official orders. That made me extremely nervous. Military didn't
quarantine their own unless some serious shit was going down. All I
could think was that I needed to get out and to get to my wife.

"Reanimate? What does that even mean?" a soldier braved to ask,
speaking out even though it was against protocol.

Captain Parsons looked out at us, clearly trying to decide how much
to let us know. I wondered how much he was even allowed to let us know.
That uneasy feeling in the pit of my stomach tripled.

"The dead are coming back to life, killing and... eating the living," he
said gruffly. A cry went up throughout the room.

"Why aren't we being allowed to leave?" someone else asked over the
murmurs.

"We are under orders directly from the President to keep all military
personnel that are currently on base under quarantine. No one leaves
and no one enters."

"What about our families?"

"What about the soldiers off base?"

Everyone was hurling questions, but I only had one.

"Captain," I said loudly, capturing my commanding officer's
attention. "How bad is it here in Charlotte?"

The crowd hushed, waiting for the Captain's answer.

"The city is already overrun," he said loudly. Gasps and cries echoed in the building followed by horrified silence. "People are panicking, city streets are clogged, and the dead— the infected— are multiplying faster than anything the CDC has ever seen before."

"Surely we'll get this under control," Sergio suggested from beside me. "Surely we have protocol for this type of thing."

I watched Parsons' face and realized the truth before he even spoke it.

"All protocol we have in place doesn't come close to being prepared to deal with something like this."

I knew better. I knew what it was he wasn't saying. The only protocols we've ever had as a nation, as the human race, was very simple: Drop bombs, wipe out the threat, even if it means the lives of innocents have to be lost in the process. The very fact that after only twenty-four hours of an outbreak all military were on lockdown instead of gearing up to face the threat was a clue. The military weren't going to try to contain the spreading virus, they were going to try to burn it and everything it might have come in contact with, living or dead, away.

"What do we do now?" Sergio asked.

"We wait. We work. And we pray." With that, the captain held the mini microphone out to his second in command.

"We need everyone who has been off base in the past twenty-four hours to go with us. Anyone who has been on leave, had physical contact with anyone off base, or might have been in direct contact with anyone who may have been sick or showing signs of illness, please report to the medical wing of the base right now."

Several soldiers started heading out of the room toward the medical wing. I felt an itch at the base of my skull. I needed to get home. There was nothing I could do here. They weren't sending us out to face the threat, they were only keeping us here to make sure we didn't contract whatever it was that was spreading. Fucking dead coming back to life and killing people? I was suddenly living in a George Romero flick and it wasn't nearly as cool as it should have been. Real life rarely lived up to Hollywood hype.

Sergio was agitated, and I mean more agitated than usual. I'd known him since I'd joined the Army, since that first day in basic when I thought I was going to die from the pressure and the physical stress we were under. Sergio was always hyperactive. Constantly moving, constantly going and fidgeting. At first I wanted to knock him out and make him relax a little. His edginess made me edgy, and I was usually a laid back sort of guy. But I'd grown used to it. He was out of control agitated right then though.

"Hey, man. You okay?" I asked when we entered our assigned bunks. Sergio didn't even act like he'd heard me.

"Yo, Sergio." I whistled loudly, trying to snap him out of his little quivering bubble of energy. He jumped, startled by the sound of my voice.

"Yeah? What?" he snapped.

"You okay? It's going to be alright, you know that, right?" I asked. Sergio's eyes weren't really focused, but he nodded anyway.

"Yeah. I guess."

"You going to head to the medical wing?"

"What?" Sergio asked, his eyes wide.

"You were off base yesterday. You going to medical now?" I asked, raising a brow.

Even for Sergio, this was a little crazy. Dude needed to calm down. We couldn't do anything until they opened up the doors for us. Nothing except sit and wait and hope, just like the captain said. Sergio sat in a chair a few feet away and ran a hand back and forth on his closely-shaven head. His knee bobbed up and down, a nervous tic I'd gotten used to after a while.

"I'll go in the morning," he said after a minute.

"You sure that's a good idea?" I asked. "They seemed to want everyone to go right away."

Sergio relaxed back in the chair and shrugged. His knee stopped bouncing. "They'll be busy all night with all the people who headed there right now. I'll get there in the morning and I'll still probably have to wait," he said, looking up at his bunk. "I just need some rest," he added softly, almost to himself.

Made sense. The medical wing was going to be a madhouse.

"Alright. I'm bushed. Let's call it a night. I'm sure there will be more news in the morning. And we both know how early morning starts around here," I said.

Sergio didn't answer. He just sat there staring at his hands. I lay there a long time thinking of my wife and the house she was in... her parents' house. How many windows were there? Was it close to a main city street? Were the neighbors dangerous if there was chaos surrounding them? Of course they were. Everyone was dangerous if they were trying to survive. Everyone was in danger. No matter what, I had to get to her the next morning. A long time later I fell into a restless sleep.

Moaning. I turned over and put a pillow over my face. Sergio must be dreaming. He talked in his sleep sometimes. Even when he was supposed to be asleep, the bastard was moving and talking. I kicked the bed above me.

"Shut it, Sergio," I snapped. I needed some rest. I needed to be clear headed for whatever was going to happen later in the day. A deep gurgle bubbled out of Sergio's throat and I froze where I lay. That didn't sound right. Sounded like he might be ill. If he was, I needed to get him to the medical wing.

"Hey. You okay, Sergio?" Sergio didn't answer, only more gurgling and raspy breathing. I sat up and pushed my sheets back, right as Sergio fell from the top bunk. The loud THUD was followed by more sounds that I'd never thought I'd hear. Something of a mix of the death rattle and liquid insides all pushing forth from a deep hollowness of the body. The hairs on my arms stood on end. I ignored them and jumped out of bed to help Sergio free himself from the tangle of sheets and blankets that he was thrashing around in. The stench hit me about the time I registered how soaked the blankets were. Was that all sweat? Had he wet himself in the night? So many thoughts and questions slipped through my mind as I removed the last of the blankets. None of it mattered though. I needed to make sure Sergio was alright.

Once free from the encumbrance of his bed clothes, Sergio lunged for me.

"Sergio!" I shouted as he crashed into me, knocking me off my feet and onto the floor. A lamp, a laptop, everything on our desk went crashing to floor along with us. Sergio was on top of me. I held him off with all of my strength, trying to keep him from wrapping his hand around my neck. His teeth were snapping and as he struggled to get free from my grip, he thrashed his head from side-to-side, liquid dribbled out of his mouth and landed on my chest.

My arms tired rapidly, and still he pushed and lunged, trying to...was he trying to bite me? I reached a hand out frantically, searching for anything I could use against the crazed soldier on top of me. My hand finally found the smashed lamp. I wrapped my hand around the base, ignoring the broken glass cutting into my hand. I swung out, bringing the heavy metal base of the lamp against Sergio's left temple. I didn't want to kill him, just stun him. Get him off me until I could get help. The thwack of metal against his skull would have put a man of any size down, but it didn't dislodge him. He didn't even seem to notice that I'd hit him. It only enraged him more, making him try step up his efforts to rip me apart.

My next swing caught him in the exact same place, and the blow, much harder than the previous one, caught him just right and he stumbled back off me, stunned. I backpedaled on all fours until I hit the door to our room. Sergio was already getting back up and heading in my direction when I stood and reached for the handle. He was in front of me so fast all I could do was swing the broken lamp again. I threw the door open right as Sergio lunged a third time. I hit him with all my strength and heard the bones in his skull give way with a sickening crunch. And still he didn't stay down.

I stumbled out into the hallway, unaware that people were running *in our direction. When Sergio made his fourth appearance, we were in the hallway and bathed in the florescent lighting. When he came at me the final time, his head was smashed in on one side, the left eye was protruding from its socket, and it looked as though his body been dead and decaying for a week. I clenched my teeth and swung at him, putting out of my mind all the time we'd spent together as Army brothers. Putting aside all the laughs we'd shared, all the pranks we'd pulled. And putting aside all the family I knew he had waiting on him at home. This wasn't the real Sergio any longer. My weapon of choice, a broken lamp from Ikea, smashed into his already broken skull and he dropped to the ground in front of me. Still he gurgled, still his arms moved, reaching out for me. I brought the lamp base down again and again until the corpse no longer moved and until I was sure that the monster who had once been one of my best friends would never get up.*

I sat roughly in the floor of the hallway with blood and bits of bone and other stuff I ignored splattered all over my boxers and tee shirt. I sat there with my back to the wall while people came and asked me questions I didn't hear. Until they moved the thing that I'd put down, and until they took me away to the medical ward.

"Welcome to the new world" was the only thought I had that morning.

Chapter Twenty-Two
What Comes Next?

Fucking sandman won't leave me alone lately, I thought, jolting awake with a pounding heart and a throbbing head. Too many memories all coming back to haunt me in my sleep. As if I didn't have enough nightmares to deal with when I was awake. I got my breathing under control and sat up. Maria and the baby were still asleep. I watched them sleep for a long while, glad to have a simple pleasure to brighten up the darkness in my life. I was an idiot to have brought them out of the safety of Camp Victory.

"Tex?" Maria's eyes fluttered open and it took her a moment to focus on me. "How long have you been awake?" she asked.

"Not that long. I was just sitting here watching you two sleep and wondering exactly what the hell I was thinking when I took you away from Camp Victory."

Maria's gaze softened. "You were thinking you were helping me do what I would've attempted to do on my own eventually anyway," she said. "At least this way I have you to help me, and I didn't have to take Rose out on my own. I never would've made it."

"Fat lot of good that did ya," I grumbled. "Here we are shut up in a room as prisoners, waiting for Warren to show up and feed us a few more lines of bull crap until he reveals what he really wants us for."

"It could have happened to me, whether I was with you or not," she countered. I snorted. "Or maybe I never would have even made it this far. I could have been killed, along with Rose, long before making it to this point."

I let my head fall back onto the wall behind me. She was right, of course, yet it didn't make me feel like everything that was happening was any less my fault.

"Warren's got something planned for us and whatever it is, it isn't going to be good," I said after a moment.

"I know," Maria replied. Rose wiggled around, her eyelids twitching, trying hard to bring herself out of a relaxing slumber.

"Whatever it is, we'll face it together." Maria's gaze was fierce, protective. She was a mama tiger.

"I'll die protecting you and the baby." My voice was low, but Maria heard and understood. We both realized that whatever Warren was planning, he wasn't planning on us liking it or even surviving. Why else would he not say it outright last night? He had paraded all of his "accomplishments" in front of us proudly, took the time to treat us to a nice dinner, and made sure he planted the seeds that we actually were going to have a choice in "helping" him. Maria and I both knew better, we both had our eyes wide open, the only way you can see your enemy's next move. With eyes wide open, even if you didn't like what was headed your way, at least you could prepare yourself.

The baby had played, eaten, and fallen back to sleep for nap before anyone came to get us out of our cell. By then, we were packed up and ready to go. We knew we wouldn't be coming back to the elementary school once we left it... one way or the other.

"Do you need anything for the baby?" This came from the girl that followed us with a gun to our backs as we marched behind Carter and a few other armed children. It was the same girl that served us in the cafeteria the previous night.

"We could use a few more old cloths for diapering and something soft for her to eat," Maria said after an awkward silence. "We ran out of her snacks last night."

From the corner of my eye I saw the girl nod once before breaking away from the group and heading in a different direction. The two other kids behind us stayed and kept their guns trained on us.

We were led back into the cafeteria where breakfast was provided by Carter. We ate hot oatmeal with cinnamon. Warren was curiously absent.

"So, you know what Warren has planned for us?" I asked nearly half an hour later. Maria and the baby were finishing up her oatmeal and I'd caught Carter watching us, sometimes his features softening just a smidge until he'd catch himself and force a scowl.

"I'm not permitted to say," he said, uttering his first words since escorting us to the cafeteria.

"But you *do* know."

"We just want to be left alone," Maria said gently, her tone soft and motherly. "We want out of here, we'll never come back." She ran a hand over Rose's tiny curls. "We just want to get the baby to safety." Maria's eyes pleaded with Carter to let us know what was going on. Carter's jaw tightened and I thought that there was no way he was giving up an info, but he breathed out and his shoulders sagged in defeat.

"Look, all I know is that Warren wants you to help with the high school. It has been overrun and we've had no success getting through the dead to loot the supplies there. The cafeteria canned food will feed our camp of kids for a long time." His eyes begged Maria to understand.

"What can we do that you all haven't tried already? What would only two more sets of hands do to break through so overwhelming a mass of dead outside the school?" Maria sounded flabbergasted.

I felt frustrated. Carter looked sick suddenly.

"He doesn't want you to help us break through the undead," Carter said.

Maria looked at me, an obvious question on her face. I was afraid I knew the answer to her unasked question. I turned and asked Carter anyway.

"If he doesn't want our help breaking through the horde, what does he want us to do then?" I asked through clenched teeth.

Carter met my eyes, shutters beginning to slam down once again, to protect himself from the ugly truth.

"He wants you to distract them," he said.

Air rushed from my lungs and I found myself on my feet. Every gun in the room was instantly on me, except for Carter's. Carter knew I would not try anything that might end up unintentionally hurting the baby.

"What does that mean... distract them?" Maria asked sharply. She stood slowly, aware of the tension coursing through the room. Then she gasped. *"Bait,"* she whispered beneath her breath, trying the words out on her own to see if they meant something other than what we both suspected.

"He plans to use us as live bait, so that while the zombies are distracted by their hot, fresh happy meal, he can take a crew of foragers into the high school and loot the cafeteria. He might even be able to eliminate enough of the distracted zombies to make a second trip possible," I said, rage building up inside of me. My fists clenched and a noise deep in the back of my throat rumbled out, making a few of the child-soldiers nearby antsy.

"You should've killed us," Maria said, and Carter flinched.

I turned to her, my gaze landing on a woman, a mother, who had suddenly realized exactly how precarious our situation was. Our odds of surviving this were so slim that they bordered on nonexistent.

"You've killed us," Maria accused. Carter's eyes widened. The teen girl had just walked up to Carter, she had an Army issued bag in her hand, her eyes widening when she let Maria's words soak in.

"Carter?" she asked, looking at him.

"You've killed us. You've killed my baby!" Maria screamed. Carter stumbled back. The girl near him flinched, glancing between all of us. She had no idea what was going on. She probably didn't know about

Warren's plans.

"Now, now, let's not be overdramatic." *Warren*.

We all turned to the sound of his voice. He stood in the doorway, dressed in Army fatigues. Maria's body hummed in aggression as she stood next to me, holding Rose on her hip. If Maria thought she even had a chance, I know she would have launched herself at Warren and scratched his eyes out.

"So, this is your little *project*," I spat. "Feeding people, including a woman and an innocent baby, to the undead just so you can scavenge a school. You're disgusting."

Warren walked further into the room.

"I'm not proud of this, but I'm also not going to deny it. I've tried a lot of different things to get through to that school. I have over forty children here I need to take care of, to provide food and supplies for. That high school will help us survive for *months*," he said.

"So you're willing to kill three people that easily... to *survive*?" Maria asked.

Warren looked at her like she'd lost her mind.

"I'm not going to *kill* you," he said, seemingly offended. "I'm going to give you a bag of supplies, weapons, and everything any of my children would need to make it seventy-two hours alone in the infested world." He sounded so very sure that he wasn't doing anything wrong.

"And then?"

"And then I'm going to let you go."

"Right next to the high school," I said sarcastically. Warren nodded. Oh sure, he was going to be letting us go and giving us weapons and gear, but only before driving us to a zombie hot spot and dumping us, veritably ringing the damn dinner bell. He knew what our odds were. He knew we would be overwhelmed and ripped to pieces within minutes, yet he'd convinced himself he wasn't *killing* us because he had equipped us with survival gear. Well, la-de-fucking-da.

"I'm going to kill you," I said, not bothering to raise my voice. Nick, who stood next to Warren, moved to lunge forward. Warren put a hand out to stop him.

"I hope you get the chance to try," he said as if he really meant it. I stared at him. If he came anywhere near me, if I even got the slimmest of an opportunity, Warren would die. He saw it in my eyes and he nodded his head. Just so long as we were clear.

"Get them ready to go," Warren barked and turned to leave the room. Nick and a few other kids trailed after him. I turned to Maria and put a hand on her shoulder. She searched my face, looking for answers that were nowhere to be found.

"We have a chance," I said. "Not much of one, but it's there."

She nodded and then sank back down into her seat. I sat down next to her, feeling the weights on my shoulders grow even heavier.

"We have a chance," she echoed.

Her voice was hollow and so was my heart.

Chapter Twenty-Three
Hope Against the Odds

"I put a box of baby cereal in the bag for you and a few things of applesauce, along with a pack of diapers I found," the girl said softly, not meeting Maria's eyes. "I also brought this," she said, her hand outstretched with her offering. I took the black contraption from her and held it up.

"It's a baby carrier," Maria said after I stood there like an idiot for a few minutes. She didn't thank the girl, she was way past that point. The girl didn't appear to take offense, though.

"I found some of this stuff in a nursery about a block away from here a long time back. I stashed it away just in case we ever had someone show up here who might need it," the girl said, showing me how the carrier worked. I could tell right away it was going to make carrying Rose a lot easier, a lot safer.

"Thank you," I said. The girl still didn't look up at me.

"Don't thank me," she said harshly. "I wish it could be different." She cleared her throat. "I also put a bottle of baby fever medicine and allergy medicine in the bag. I thought maybe you could give the baby the medicine before..."

Maria smothered a cry of distress and bowed her head over Rose's. I nodded my thanks to the teen. We would give Rose some medicine in her bottle to help her relax and sleep. If we survived, she'd be knocked out during most of the struggle. If we didn't... well, maybe she wouldn't be awake when it happened. I tightened my jaw.

"Jenna, you need to go now," Carter said, glancing toward the doorway. "Nick will be back here any second and I don't want you in any kind of trouble with him or Warren."

Jenna paused as she reached the door, glancing back at us, her lips parting to say something. She thought better of it though and clamped her lips closed and strode through the door.

"There isn't much time," Carter said as soon as Jenna had gone through the door. He walked over and spoke in a hushed voice. "You both will be given knives right before they let you go. I stashed a loaded gun inside your bag, hidden in the diapers that Jenna gave you. There is also a second magazine to reload. You have about forty-eight bullets total. Make them count."

Maria perked up, listening intently to what Carter had to say.

"Why are you doing this?" I asked him.

"Really? We don't have time for all that right now. I never wanted any of this to happen, so I want to help you guys have a fighting chance."

I nodded. No arguments from me.

"Not far from the high school, about three blocks south, there is a street with a bunch of cottages, Buck Street. All of the houses are empty. We've been there, it's as close as we've gotten to the high school without having to pull back. Head there and go to the white house with green shutters. The house is secure from the dead and I have a secret stash hidden there in a toy box under a bunch of stuffed animals in a pink bedroom. Enough food for a few days, hurricane candles, water, and another gun with ammo."

"A secret stash?" I asked.

Carter shrugged. "I started preparing it a few weeks back just in case I ever needed to get out or if things ever went south," he explained. "Anyway, there is also a car in the garage, it worked a few days ago and has a quarter tank of gas. I wouldn't take off in it until you're sure Warren and the rest of our crew isn't in the area after looting the school. If they see you, no matter what Warren says, he *will* kill you."

"Got it."

Carter stepped back so as not to look quite as suspicious if anyone were to walk in. "I wish I could do more," he said.

"You did more than anyone else. You gave us hope," I said honestly. A gun. A plan. I could work with that. Our odds were still bad, but I now had hope and sometimes hope could outmatch any odds. The baby started fussing. It was time for her bottle. Maria opened up the bag and took out the allergy medicine and added some to the baby's bottle. She hesitated only a moment before giving it to her. She rocked the baby and sang softly to her until her bottle was empty and she fell into a deep sleep. Maria met my stare and raised her chin.

"I won't let her die," she said with all the conviction she possessed.

"We won't let her die," I promised. I meant every word of that promise.

Just then, Nick came through the cafeteria doors with two other kids.

"Time to go," he announced cheerfully. I ignored him and stood, picking up the black baby carrier.

"Put the baby on my back," I said to Maria. Maria's eyes widened and she tightened her hold on her daughter. She had always been the one to carry her, to keep her safe in the circle of her arms.

"Tex..."

"Sweetheart, I'm stronger. I can carry her weight and hold my own in hand-to-hand combat. You'll tire faster and that can make it more dangerous for you and for Rose."

She looked torn. I knew she trusted me, but it was hard for her to put her baby in someone else's arms when she knew what lay ahead of us.

"I'll protect her with my life," I vowed.

Maria smiled and kissed Rose's tiny head one last time and then stood. "I know you will, Tex."

Maria helped me place the baby in the carrier, snuggling her in tightly with the fabric from the wrap Maria had used to carry the baby before. Once she was on my back, we made a few adjustments until we were sure the baby wouldn't be jostled too easily and that she was absolutely secure in the carrier. We tucked her little hands into the fabric so they wouldn't be hanging out. The only thing visible of the baby on my back were her little legs hanging down in back. Maria kissed her daughter's tiny face and then pulled on the backpack Jenna gave us. She had her game face on and we both knew that in this game it was win or lose it all.

"You two ready now?" Nick said with a smirk. Neither of us answered him, or even looked at him, we just followed him out the door and toward our uncertain future.

Chapter Twenty-Four
Into the Belly of the Beast

We were brought out into the front of the elementary school where Warren and a band of almost twenty children waited. All of the kids, including Nick and the young girl whose brother went out into the dark the night before, were armed with guns and knives.

"You six will be going in the van with Nick. Roger will be driving. Pull around the front area of the school as quickly as possible and drop these two off right in the middle of the street. Once they are cleared of the van, haul ass out of there and swing back the opposite way around toward the side of the school. Once the zombies start going after them, we'll be ready to make our move on the side of the school, near where the buses picked up and dropped off." Everyone nodded. Not a single child looked at us. We weren't even there as far as they were concerned, we were just a means to an end. We could have been cattle for all they cared.

"I hope you guys make it, for your baby's sake," Warren said.

Without warning, Maria spat in his face, throwing Spanish curses at him. Some I understood, some I'd never heard in my entire life, but one little Spanish kid standing nearby looked scandalized, and terrified by what he heard coming from Maria's mouth.

"She says 'fuck you'," I translated in summary when she was finished.

Warren wiped his face on the arm of his long sleeve. The entire group froze; the only sounds came from the dead in town and a few gunshots. Even Nick was surprised into immobility.

"Let's go," Warren said, turning toward the vehicles that awaited us. And just like that, we were loaded into the back of a van and heading right into the belly of the beast.

I grabbed Maria's hand and leaned into her so I could whisper in her ear.

"As soon as we are clear of the van, you get the gun and ammo out of the bag. I'll cover you until then," I said as quietly as possible. Maria nodded once. She removed one of the backpack straps, allowing the bag to hang from one shoulder. It would make it a lot easier for her to get the bag off and to get reach the gun. Nick sneered from across the van. He thought she was an idiot. Carrying a bag like that was risky. I was content to let him think we were incompetent.

Maria reached over and touched the baby's head gently, whispering a prayer as she leaned up to kiss her brow. I wanted to reassure her, to tell her everything was going to be alright, but I didn't want her to think was going to be easy, that our odds were any better than she thought, because it wasn't and they weren't.

The van was moving fast, faster than anyone usually dared to drive when there were shambling corpses everywhere, ready to stumble out in front of you and cause an accident.

"One minute!" the kid from the front yelled. Maria's hand tightened in mine.

"Here are your weapons," Nick said, holding out two nice looking recon blades.

I reached out and grasped the hilt, noticing how the other three kids in the van all tensed and made sure I knew I had guns trained on me. Maria also took her blade firmly in hand. If I were those kids, I would've been nervous too. Maria looked like she would have gladly plunged her knife through the throat of anyone in the van.

"Thirty seconds!" the kid shouted from the driver's seat.

The van shifted and thumped along loudly when the kid sideswiped several objects in the street. I could only image those objects were the dead who'd walked into the path of the vehicle. As fast as were flying through town, the van came to an abrupt halt, nearly throwing everyone onto the floor. Two boys threw the van doors open and opened fire on the dead nearby. There were a lot of them.

Nick grabbed Maria and gave her a shove toward the doors. She barely kept her grip on her knife and the bag on her back slipped awkwardly on her arm. A large, silent kid pointed a shotgun at my back and then gave me a shove as well. As soon as my feet hit the pavement, Nick kicked his leg out and connected with Maria's lower back, sending her sprawling into the pavement below. I shoved my blade in the first zombie to reach us, keeping myself close to Maria and the van at the same time. Nick planted his blade in the skull of a zombie that had gotten close enough to reach the van's door. As soon as he jerked it free and reached out with a hand to close the door, I knew the van was one second away from speeding off. I reached up and grabbed Nick's leg and jerked with all my might. No one anticipated the move and before they could react, the van was already speeding away and the dead were moving in. Nick's head had ricocheted off of the bumper of the van, knocking him out cold onto the road. I spun around, not sparing a glance for the kid. Maria and I moved several yards away from the unconscious Nick, hoping the zombies would go for him as an easy meal.

My knife stopped a zombie merely a foot from Maria as she grappled with the backpack to find the gun. The undead had found Nick and were tearing into him, his screams and the scent of fresh blood drawing a crowd of the zombies in his direction. Not all of them were enticed away from us though. Several groups of the undead were still headed in our direction, and many more were coming from the area of the high school. Warren's plan was working. My survival instincts took over and I cut and slashed my way through half a dozen walking corpses.

As the sound of moaning and gurgling rose, so did my apprehension. We needed to get out of here, let the zombies feast on Nick, and make every effort to get to Buck Street. The longer we were in the middle of town, out in the open, the higher our odds of getting ourselves killed. It seemed like an eternity passed until Maria pulled the gun out of the backpack and handed it to me. Her fighting arm began moving as soon as she handed the gun over. Rotten zombie parts littered the ground around us and rancid fluids slushed along the streets.

We stood back-to-back, keeping the baby between us and slicing our way south toward a side street. We heard bones cracking and flesh ripping as the dead tore Nick into little bitty bite-sized pieces. I was still using my knife when we turned a corner and found an opening large enough in the horde to try and make a run for it.

"Run, Maria!" I shouted. "There!" I pointed to the rapidly closing space. We ran full out, dodging more than a dozen zombies that lurched into our path and killing several others, hoping against hope that we could get ahead of the zombies that teemed in the streets. We made it past several streets before we turned a corner. The horde of zombies was thicker here. I pulled the gun Carter had given us and started taking them down with single shots to the head as rapidly as I could and still they kept coming. For every zombie Maria plunged her knife into, I took down three more with the gun. And yet, they seemed to be multiplying.

"We could break into a house and wait it out!" Maria shouted as she plunged her knife into the eye socket of a thin zombie still wearing a McDonald's uniform.

"We can't, not with this many surrounding us. They'd box us in and we'd have no way out to get food or supplies. Our best bet is to try and make it the house Carter told us about." I lunged forward and brought my knife down into the top of the skull of a corpse that had gotten way too close for comfort.

"We have to move then," Maria grunted, pushing a huge zombie back into the fray of bodies pressing our way. I jumped up on the porch of a house we were fighting in front of.

"Let's go through here. We can go back out the back door or a window on the other side of the house."

As soon as Maria got up on the porch, I wiggled the handle of the door. To my relief, it was unlocked. I swung the door open after shooting the three zombies that had already climbed onto the porch after us. We slammed the door shut once we were inside and did a brief search of the house. Nothing dead or alive was inside. We ran to the back of the house and I sent up a prayer that the back of the house, the yard, and area surrounding would be a little better than the front. To my relief, the backyard had a privacy fence and was completely empty. Maria and I both were breathing heavily, but I knew now was not the time to rest. We had to keep moving and get to Buck Street.

"There's a gate over there that leads into the backyard," Maria said in a rush. She wiped her gore-splattered hands on her jeans and then tightened her grip back around the handle of the recon blade.

"We should be close to Buck Street now, maybe another block. We'll move fast, making as little noise as possible." I checked my gun. Six bullets left. I shoved the gun in my waistband and pulled my knife back out. It was going to have to be hand-to-hand the rest of the way. We didn't want to draw any more dead toward us if at all possible. We'd lucked out so far, no need to make stupid mistakes at this point.

When we got to the gate, I stood there trying to figure out if all the noise in the area was from the dead in the front of the house, or if we'd be walking out into even worse conditions in the back. Unfortunately, there were so many moaning and gurgling undead moving about in the area, it was impossible to tell.

"Ready?" I asked. Maria's eyes flicked to Rose on my back and then back to me. Her jaw tightened and her eyes showed her resolve.

"I'm ready," she said.

I opened the back gate enough for both of us to squeeze through. We walked right out into a tiny back alley, just large enough for a single car to squeeze through. Instead of a car blocking our way, we found dozens of zombies standing on idle, just waiting for something to snap them out of their inactivity. Even with the promise of fresh meat, though, these zombies were slow, their skin nearly bursting with fluids so near the surface that a single cut or poke of our knives would result in fetid liquids bursting forth like an unholy geyser.

We didn't have time to contemplate the nearly liquefied state of the zombies though, even slow and sloshy, they still had numbers and teeth on their side. We moved fast, taking advantage of the fact that the undead in this specific area were having a hard time lifting their arms and moving. By the time we'd sliced our way through the tight space, the back alley looked like a small river. A river comprised of the most noxious smelling liquid zombie guts on the planet. We moved further away from the scene that could have been straight out of a horror movie with a nonexistent budget. If I hadn't been there myself, I never would have believed it had happened.

We ran for all that we were worth, cutting down however many zombies got in our way. When we crossed a street in front of a boarded up Baptist church, I saw the sign that signaled we were coming up on Buck Street only two streets away. Our goal. We were going to make it. Just as the thought came to me, a low buzzing sound filled the air, almost like an odd white noise, but nothing natural, nothing that sounded like it belonged in this once picturesque little southern town. It was a sound I knew all too well and it was the sound that I had only heard when I lived in Charlotte... the sound of hundreds and hundreds of the undead packed together.

Chapter Twenty-Five
Never Have Been Lucky

"*Madre de Dios*," Maria uttered, crossing herself.

Zombies flooded the street in front of us, pouring out of the street that ran next to the church and the street between us and our goal. Hundreds of them staggered, some slowly, some quicker than the others. The quicker ones were on us before we could formulate a game plan. After taking down several zombies, we backed up, intending to go back the way we'd come. But the street we'd just been on, the one that had only had about two dozen zombies when we moved through it, also had dozens issuing out. Where were they all coming from? It was like someone had opened up a flood gate and let them out at the worst time possible. If I didn't know that Warren was at the high school, taking advantage of his well laid plans, I would have thought that he'd somehow orchestrated the whole thing. But, the truth was we were just un-fucking-lucky. Several groups of the undead had converged and then happened to meet up in the exact same place we were headed.

"What do we do?" Maria gasped, shoving her knife in the right temple of an elderly female zombie wearing a dress and a string of pearls.

I didn't know what to tell her. I didn't know what to do next, how I could get her and the baby to safety.

"Tex!" Maria shouted. "What do we do now?" Her voice was panicked... just like I felt. Only, I didn't know our next move. The baby on my back was a constant reminder of everything that was at stake. The undead making their way toward us from all directions were going to win. My life had to mean more than this. It had to have meaning, even if that meaning was to die so that Rose would be able to live. With that thought, I pointed to the old church behind us.

"Follow close beside me!"

Maria nodded, ready to do anything so long as we were taking some kind of action. I sliced through the undead as I ran. Each swing of my knife hit a zombie that led up to the church's front steps. If I could get us there, just get us out of the mass of lumbering bodies that were quickly closing in on us, maybe we'd have a chance. Just maybe.

We made it up to the step, but dozens of zombies, squishy and slow or not, made it at the same time as us. We fought for what seemed like an hour only to keep the zombies far enough from us that they didn't trample us or get between us and our target. When we finally got to the front door of the church, I don't know. I guess I thought it was going to be open just like the house we'd ducked inside was. But it wasn't. It was locked and closed up tight. The windows were also boarded up. Mara took down three zombies while I beat my booted foot against the front doors, cursing them as I did. The doors were solid and there was no way we'd be getting through them. In an instant, all our hopes of surviving were dashed. Zombies were flooding in from every direction around us and all we had was a locked, impenetrable church door at our back. I was out of bullets, out of time, and never had luck on my side to begin with.

"It can't end like this!" Maria shouted, tears streaming down her face as we fought the zombies who staggered unsteadily up the steps of the church. We were both becoming fatigued and that meant we wouldn't be able to hold out much longer. Something had to happen. If I only had some way to distract the zombies, some way to get them headed in another direction so Maria and the baby could get free.

"Maria, you need to take the baby. I'm going to lead the zombies away, cause a distraction so you can have a chance," I said over the noise. She whipped her head around briefly, meeting my eyes, her own wide in understanding.

"You'd sacrifice yourself for me?" she asked. "For Rose?"

"Without a doubt," I replied, shoving back two zombies with a foot to their midsections, knocking them back into the fray trying to push their way up the church steps.

"We just need to figure out how to get the baby off my back and onto yours without letting these meat bags gain ground on us," I said gruffly. My knife penetrated the temple of the zombie in front of me and I once again used his body to knock back the undead behind him.

"No," Maria said.

I thought I heard her incorrectly.

"What?"

"I said no, Tex. It has to be me," she said kicking her own zombie back down the steps, adjusting her stance to play the same game over again.

"No, Maria. No way in hell. Rose will need her mother!" I shouted, angry she even said such a stupid thing. Maria's wide smile took me by surprise.

"Rose needs someone who is strong, someone who has the best chance of keeping her alive. Someone who is willing to die for her." Maria's strength seemed to renew as she spoke, her arm moved quicker, her kicks were harder, and her entire body poised in focus of her goal.

"Maria... don't," I warned, my own voice shaking from fear. Fear of losing her as soon as I'd found her and fear of being the person she'd entrust her most precious cargo to. She didn't turn back around, she didn't look at me or at Rose.

"Kiss her for me, Tex. Tell her every day how much I loved her. Let her find the good in the world," she said with a broken sob. Before I could move to stop her, before I could form the words to beg her not to, Maria threw her backpack over to me, sliced her knife across her arm, and then leapt over the side of the balustrade of the church and right into the middle of the undead fray.

I bit back a shout, not wanting to draw even more attention to myself. I moved as fast as I could, shoving my blade into the eye of the zombie nearest me. I heaved the rather large dead man with all of my strength, watching him take down several of the zombies closest to him. I scanned the crowd for Maria and tracked her to the spot where zombies had already begun to turn, where they already decided their next meal would come from. Her blood was pulling even the slowest zombies in her direction. She screamed and I died a little inside. It should have been me out there. I grabbed Maria's bag up and let it hang on one arm.

I saw her from the corner of my eye, bloody and swinging her knife with all her might, drawing hundreds of the animated corpses in her direction. She had been bitten several times, and still she pushed through the crowds, still on her feet and pushing even after they had ripped into her. She parted the crowd, but I knew she wouldn't last much longer, and I had to get Rose to safety. I couldn't let her sacrifice be for nothing. I pulled my gun from my waistband and took aim at the zombies that now stood between me and my goal—safety for Rose. With most of the zombies heading toward Maria, I now had a decent shot at making it to Buck Street. I charged the lumbering corpses, swinging my knife with my left hand and taking shots with my right. Just when my gun clicked empty, I saw the street sign ahead of me, only a few feet away, Buck Street.

I turned around in time to find a zombie right on top of me. If I hadn't turned to get a glimpse of Maria, to see if the zombies were still heading that way or not, the zombie would've been right on top of the baby on my back. A cry of distress and pure heartache was ripped out of me as I slammed the butt of my gun into the skull of the zombie over and over again, even when it was no longer moving, even when the cranium had given way beneath my blows into a pile of brain mush, blood and bone fragments, still I rained blows down. It wasn't until I saw zombies turning back in my peripheral vision, turning to the sound of me acting like a wild man did I snap out of my rage. I turned onto Buck Street and ran with all the energy I had left.

Stepping onto Buck Street was like stepping into the Twilight Zone. Nothing moved, not even a zombie. It was like stepping into a soundproof room. I could still hear the zombies merely a street over, and a few had straggled on the street after me, but if I hadn't just seen the hundreds of dead, if I hadn't seen Maria have to sacrifice herself to give me and her baby a chance, I would've thought the apocalypse had never happened here. It all looked so *untouched*.

Now I understood what Carter had said when he mentioned never making it past Buck Street without having to pull back... he must have run into that mass of zombies like we had. Except, Warren had a little army with him and he had vehicles. Warren would pay for this. I clenched my jaw in order to keep my anger in check. I just needed to make it to the green-trimmed house for now. Then we'd have supplies and transportation. It was only little Rose and I. I still couldn't wrap my head around that, so I shoved it out of my mind for later.

I immediately found the house with green shutters and trim. The door was unlocked and the zombies that had been following us were of the slow, smushy variety, so they were several houses back when I closed the door behind me. I double bolted the door and shoved a bookshelf in front it. I went from room to room, checking out the windows and doors before heading upstairs to the pink bedroom that Carter spoke of. It had been a baby's room, complete with crib and everything. I didn't think about what had happened to the infant that had once slept in the room, I just shoved all the toys out of the toy box until I found Carter's stash.

With two duffle bags from the toy box in hand, I went into the main bedroom and dropped them on the dusty bed. I was going to go through them when I felt the baby shift gently on my back. I did my best to remove the baby carrier without waking up or dropping Rose. Once I got her free, I laid her in the center of the bed and stared at her little face, still asleep, even though we'd just been through Hell, her and I. I used a shirt out of a dresser and a little water from the bags to wash my arms and hands. I was bone weary.

I sat down on the edge of the bed and ran a hand through my sweat-matted hair. I sifted through the bags on the bed. Water, candles, some canned goods, a can opener, a nice gun with plenty of ammo, and several other random items. Maria's bag had our gear and stuff for the baby. I took out a clean bottle and got it ready. I laid a clean diaper on the bed. The baby would be hungry and need to be changed when she woke up. While I sat there staring at the baby, I noticed that zombie gunk had been splattered on the feet of the button up pajamas Maria had her dressed in.

I went into the pink room and found a few pajama outfits that looked about her size, along with a soft, fluffy blanket. I sat everything on the bed, ready for her when she awoke. Would she somehow know what had happened? Would she cry for her mama, not understanding why she wasn't there? I worried over all of that and everything else in between before I laid down on the bed next to her, waiting for her to wake up. It wasn't long until I drifted off to sleep, my exhaustion winning out over my worry.

Chapter Twenty-Six
Midtown, North Carolina

Little hands touching my face, little *slobbery* hands, is what I woke up to. I blinked, trying to remove the sleep from my eyes. I looked around the room, noticing the way the sun was starting to light up the space. Had I slept the entire day and night away? I jolted fully awake, startling Rose. She stuck out her bottom lip like she was going to cry.

"Hey there, little lady," I said gently. "How long you been awake?" I glanced over at the bottle on the bed, completely empty. Her pajamas look soaked, so I imagined she'd wet straight through her diaper.

"Let Uncle Tex take care of you, honey," I cooed at her. Rose stared at me like she didn't know what to think, but at least her lip wasn't quivering anymore. I changed her diaper and her little pajama set, taking entirely too long to figure out the snaps that went up the front. When I finally got all the snaps lined up, she mumbled in baby language, "*Mama.*" A fist squeezed around my heart as I gazed into her big brown eyes. Her mama was gone. I was all she had. I picked her up and sat her on my lap, handing her the little gray elephant from the bag Maria had carried. She grabbed it excitedly, immediately stuffing the elephant's ear in her mouth.

"Your mamma loved you very much, Rose," I said. "She made sure you were safe and she said she always wanted you to look for the good in the world, even if it seems hard to find." Rose smiled and chattered away in her baby gibberish. I smiled down at her.

"We're going to get through this, kiddo," I said more to myself than to Rose. "We're going to make your mama proud." Another set of baby words was her only answer. It sounded like an affirmative to me.

"Alright, let's get a move on then, little miss," I said. "We've got some people to meet. Your new Auntie Melody is going to love you." I sat the baby on the bed and handed her the blanket I'd found. She played with it while I condensed all our supplies into a single backpack. Enough to last three days. Everything else I added to the duffle bag. I'd put that in the car, but if I had to ditch the car at any point, I'd leave the duffle bag behind. I'd only be able to carry the baby and a single backpack. I loaded the gun I'd found in the toy bin, tucked it in my pants, and added the two extra clips of ammunition to the pockets of my jeans.

"Okay, Rose, it's time for us to go. We'll take your little elephant with us and your new pretty blanket, okay?"

Mostly I just talked to hear something, anything to block out my own thoughts. It was reassuring to hear myself sound so confident even though Maria was gone and I had no idea what to do with a baby. I picked Rose up along with her carrier and our two bags. When I got downstairs, the sun had risen even more and I was ready to put miles between us and the infested town. The map I'd found the previous evening in a kitchen drawer told me that we were about thirty miles outside of Midtown, North Carolina. Old bills on the kitchen counter told me the small town we were in was called Palatka. Midtown was right outside of the Army base that Rose and I were headed to. It could take an hour or two to drive that thirty miles with the way the world was now.

Inside the garage I found a tan Hyundai. I stood there with the baby and all our bags in my arms, wondering how I was supposed to do this. Should I strap the baby to me while I drove? That could be dangerous. Should I strap the baby in the back seat? But what if I had to get to her quickly to make a run for it? So many scenarios rolled through my mind and I felt even more unsure of myself than ever. I opened the back door of the car and there was a baby car seat. I took that as a sign and put her in it. The straps looked complicated, so I opted to pull the seat belts across the car seat instead of taking the chance that once I strapped Rose in I wouldn't be able to get her back out if I had to. I threw our bags in the seat beside her and climbed in the front seat. I set my gun in the front passenger seat and turned the key in the ignition. The car started on the first try and just like Carter had said, there was a quarter tank of gas. I owed that kid a lot.

I backed out, shutting the garage as soon as we were clear. I didn't want to take the chance that Warren or anyone in his group would notice that something was different in the area. It was best that Warren thought we all had died the day before. I put the car in drive. Some of us *had* died the day before. And Warren would pay.

When I turned off of Buck Street, I didn't even glance in the direction of the church. I ignored the masses of zombies still wandering the streets there and I drove away with nothing on my mind but getting Rose safely to Melody and Jude at the Army base. There would be time to mourn Maria later.

It took us almost two hours to reach the outskirts of Midtown. The baby had to be fed and changed after an hour of driving and we had to make three minor detours to get around roads blocked by abandoned vehicles or the dead. We were running on fumes by then. When I saw the "Welcome to Midtown" sign, I let out a relieved breath. Once we made it into town, I knew we were going to be only a couple miles from the base. Only a few miles from absolute safety. I'd been hoping to make it on what was in the tank, but the car ran out of gas half a mile before we made it into town.

"Looks like we'll be hoofing it from here," I said to the baby. She just stared at me from the rearview mirror.

"You can pretend Uncle Tex is a big 'ole horsey," I said with a grin. Rose smiled and clapped. Maybe she understood more than I gave her credit for. I tucked the gun in the waist of my pants and began the daunting task of putting the baby in her carrier. It wasn't as difficult as I thought would be. I tried to remember everything Maria had done. With the baby securely in place on my back, I loosened the straps on the backpack enough to wear it on my back around the carrier and so that it wasn't too tight or awkward around the baby. I'd carried heavier loads in the Army. We headed into town.

Midtown looked like any other insignificant small town in North Carolina. It wasn't without its charm, but these towns tended to have big secrets and hidden surprises, and I found that after the undead began to walk over two years ago that this was doubly true and seldom a good thing. I just wanted to get into town, find a new set of wheels, and then to get back out of town as quickly as possible. That should have been more than easy, since the town was filled with abandoned cars, many with their keys still hanging in the ignition. The problem was, someone else had gotten into town before me.

The gunshots were my first clue. I ran to the side of the building I'd been walking around and hid myself back from the view of the main street. I could hear the dead lumbering around and I also heard shots coming from very close by. I was up shit creek with no paddle in sight. I needed a car, but the people shooting up the town might not be the types I wanted to run into with Rose on my back. I couldn't stay out in the open this close to town without taking shelter, not if I didn't want to end up a meal for the zombies. I clenched my teeth in frustration. I had not come this far to fail. I would have to backtrack a bit, take the long way around town, and walk the few miles to the base. Better safe than sorry.

I took several steps back, my eyes on the main road in town, when a zombie behind me grabbed my arm. There were two of them on top of me before I could say skedaddle. I yelled out, startling the baby, who immediately started crying. My knife stilled the first zombie before it could do any damage. I grappled with the second one, trying with all my might to keep it from biting into the baby, to keep its extremely aggressive, snapping teeth away from Rose. I grunted, taking the full force of the zombie's attack. I finally managed to shove my knife into its temple, slumping against the wall when the corpse finally quit moving. Rose was pretty shaken up. I shushed her and talked nonsense to her, and she eventually she quit crying, but not before the undead started flooding the side street. The way we had come was already filling up with walking corpses. I had no choice. I ran toward the center of town, hoping that whoever was there wouldn't have heard the commotion and hoping they wouldn't see me.

I cleared the building and stepped right out onto the main street in town where I was immediately noticed. Just like the zombies we'd been running into the past few days, these zombies too looked like something was wrong with them... and I mean more wrong than the fact that they were walking, rotten corpses. They were slower, their skin waxy and nearly translucent from the liquid that pushed the skin so taut that it threatened to burst with the slightest touch. A barefoot zombie reached me and its feet were nothing but bone. The flesh had shredded away and a constant stream of rancid fluids poured out of the wounds there. The rest of its skin hung on the skeleton like the zombie had lost hundreds of pounds and all that was left was skin over bones like melted, sickly white candle wax.

I was so taken aback by the state of the zombie who lunged at me that by the time I forced my knife into its skull, several others had surrounded me. I pulled my gun out. No time to care if anyone would hear. I took out the half dozen zombies that had managed to sneak up behind me before positioning myself so that Rose wasn't exposed. With my back to a storefront window, I planted my feet and began putting a dent in the number of dead that were closing in on us. It wasn't until I rammed my last magazine of ammunition into the gun that I realized more zombies had arrived.

When I was almost on empty and ready to pull my knife, another gun went off and the undead started dropping like flies all around me. I yanked my knife free and began taking down all those that were nearest me, hoping that the people helping me out were decent shots, even so, I didn't want bullets getting too close to Rose. When bullets stopped flying, I glanced up from the carnage that surround me and found Uncle Gus standing there, his gun drawn and looking at me with a shocked look on his face. I'm sure I had the same look on my own. He jumped down from the back of the truck he'd been standing in and ran over to help me fight off the last few zombies with his metal baseball bat. The waterlogged zombies didn't stand a chance.

"What are you doing here, boy?" Uncle Gus hissed as he neared me.

"I could ask you the same, old man," I grunted, pulling my knife from a zombie's throat and then spearing it through the eye.

"He's here with me," a voice I never intended to hear again said. I swung around and sure enough there stood none other than Michael Hatten. Michael walked over while Uncle Gus took down a few more zombies, striding toward me like he was invincible, untouchable. When he finally realized what it was I carried on my back, he froze, his eyes widening then narrowing in white-hot fury.

"She's dead then?" he asked.

I gritted my teeth, and stared at him. I didn't dare say anything for fear that the rage I was once again experiencing would spill over and I'd lose control like I had the day before. Uncle Gus shook his head sadly.

"God found her unworthy then," Michael said heatedly. He pulled his gun and before I realized his intent, he pointed it right at me.

"Michael... don't!" Uncle Gus gasped.

Michael didn't even spare him a glance. "Give me the baby," he commanded.

My grip tightened on my weapon. "It will be a cold day in Hell when I let you have her," I growled.

"I *will* shoot you," he said calmly. "What if the bullet accidently hits her instead?" he asked as if he were asking me what my favorite color was.

"If you truly want her, you wouldn't take that chance," I said.

He cocked his head, like he was studying a fascinating specimen under a microscope. "Wouldn't I?" he asked after a few seconds ticked by. "If it's God's will that I take her to raise as my own, he will protect her."

"Don't!" I said raising a hand in surrender. "I'll hand her over."

Michael cocked his head again. "No. I don't trust you. I do trust God though." Michael raised his arm again, his intention written clearly on his face. Uncle Gus yelled out and I saw movement from the corner of my eye just as Michael's gun went off. A bullet struck Uncle Gus right in the chest as he threw his body in front of me. It all happened so fast that I barely had time to register my surprise or my anger. I pulled my gun and shot Michael Hatten, still staring down at Uncle Gus on the pavement at my feet, in both of his kneecaps. Michael hit the ground and his gun flew across the pavement where he lay screaming in agony. Uncle Gus was dead before his body hit the ground.

I walked over to Michael, now writhing in pain in the middle of the road, vaguely aware that all the zombies that were left in town were beginning to show up to see if any food was available. I picked up Michael's gun from the pavement, tucked in my pants, and stood over him, staring down.

"Please kill me. Don't leave me here like this. Let me die righteously," he begged.

His words made my stomach turn. Even in death the man thought he was some kind of big deal to God. I took my gun out of my pants and pointed it directly at his forehead. After a moment, when the zombies were closer, and when the gun hadn't yet discharged, Michael opened his eyes to stare at me questioningly.

"Naw," I said, tucking my gun back in my pants. "I don't think it is God's will that I kill you."

Michael's eyes frantically scanned the area, noticing the zombies that lurched in his direction. I threw my backpack in the still-running pick-up truck and climbed in. The zombies fell on Uncle Gus. I was sorry it couldn't be different, but at least he was already gone. I waited until the last few zombies reached Michael where he was trying— unsuccessfully—to crawl away on his belly.

I watched as they tore him apart and I felt *nothing* but relief.

Rose would never have to worry about Michael Hatten again.

Chapter Twenty-Seven
Auntie Melody Carter

Something strange happened as Rose and I made our way out of town. We were just about a mile outside of the Army base when we stopped in the middle of the road. Ahead of us there were three undead making their way down the back road. Normally I would have sped up and dodged the trio, yet something in the way they looked, in the way they moved, caught my eye. I sat there for a moment watching the zombies, trying to figure out what it was that had caught my interest. I shook my head and put the truck in drive, ready to pass them up.

I must have been imagining things.

As soon as my foot left the brake, one of the zombies, a large man, so severely bloated that he could barely raise his foot to take a step, just... exploded.

At first, I was in such complete and utter shock, that I convinced myself I must have misunderstood what I'd just witnessed. That perhaps one of the other zombies had somehow attacked the undead man, but they didn't usually attack one another. Had someone shot the zombie and I'd been too distracted to notice? Not likely, and that wouldn't explain how the corpse had quite literally erupted all over the street like a deranged piñata. The other zombies, unperturbed by the sudden demise of their rotting companion, continued their painfully slow progress across the asphalt. While I stared at huge mess of guts and decaying flesh and bones that was once one of the undead, like rapid fire, two of the other zombies also met their end in a similar fashion. It was so sudden and random that I burst out laughing. Rose began giggling and clapping, encouraged by my inappropriate bout of hilarity.

I glanced around the area, into the surrounding forest, and the mostly-empty highway. I almost expected to see a cameraman somewhere filming the whole thing, some kind of post-apocalyptic documentary where they go around punking people. As unlikely as it might have been, it still would've made more sense than zombies randomly and violently bursting apart in the middle of an empty country road. Whatever was going on, it might not have been a good thing. Who knew what was inside those zombies? If the parasite that started the whole outbreak could live outside of its host and what spewing insides could mean for what was left of humanity? Yeah, time to get Rose to safety. I put the truck back in drive and took off, avoiding the now major mass of carnage in the center of the road.

When we finally pulled up to the Army base, I had so many emotions flowing through me that I was unable to sort through them. Relief, happiness, grief, and sorrow. Those and so many others. So much had happened since I'd left this place, and yet here I was again. I'd made it. I'd gotten Rose to a true sanctuary like I'd promised her mom. I cut the engine, aware of the quietness in the area, most definitely a sign for concern. Where were all the undead? Had they been more vigilant about cleaning out the area since I'd been gone? I got out of the truck, grabbed the baby and our backpack, and turned toward the doors of the office building that led to the underground Army bunker. To my left I saw what was left of a zombie. It looked like it had met its end recently and similarly to the ones I'd recently encountered.

I hurried up to the front of the office and went inside. Nothing was moving. The hidden door in the back office swung open effortlessly. I walked down the steps, holding the baby tightly to my chest. My arms were aching and sweat was beading on my forehead. I was so tired after days of being on the run, fighting hundreds of the dead to survive another day. It had taken its toll on my body. I felt like something someone had scraped off the bottom of their boots. I punched in the code and sighed in relief when door creaked open. The code still worked. I stepped inside, keenly aware of a flurry of activity coming to a complete and screeching halt. Then Melody Carter was standing in front of me. She looked about as rough as I felt. Her eyes bugged out of her head when realized what I was carrying.

"Tex?" Melody gasped.

"Hello, sweetheart," I said with a grin. "Ya miss me?"

She walked over to me, her hair pulled back in a messy ponytail and smudges all over her face and clothes. She looked like a mess.

"You look like you've been outside," I said to break the awkward and deafening silence.

She glanced down at herself and waved a hand in dismissal. "We just got back in from a supply run," she said, her eyes never leaving the baby, who stared back at her in equal fascination. "What about you?"

"I got a new sidekick since I've been away," I said with a grin. I tucked Rose's toy elephant into her arm and she rewarded me with a smile and the incoherent baby talk that I'd come to love.

Melody walked closer, reaching a tentative hand out to Rose, only to be treated to a smile. She smiled back and ran a hand over the baby's head, clearly in awe. There were no babies in the Army base.

"Her mother?" Melody asked softly. The question was a painful one to answer.

"Maria died yesterday trying to make it here," I said gruffly, swallowing down the lump that had formed in my throat.

"Come on, Melody, don't keep the poor man standing there all day. He looks like he could use a shower, some food, and a good rest," Major Tillman's voice cut through the silence, effectively breaking everyone out of their daze.

I nodded my thanks to the Major, who nodded back and turned on his heel to bark orders out to people still standing about stupidly.

"Sorry about that, Tex, I don't know what I was thinking," Melody said in apology.

"It's alright," I said. Yet the truth was, I was tired and I needed to get a shower as quickly as possible. I still had a lot I wanted to do before the day wasted away and one thing I'd learned over the past few days was that you had to get while the gettin' was good, or you might miss out. I had a lot of gettin' to do.

"Tex, glad to see you, man," Jude said, walking up. He too looked tired and ready to drop, but there was excitement in the air as well.

"You guys know what's been going on with the eruptin' dead?" I asked.

"Probably about as much as you," Jude said. "While we were in the city doing a big supply run, we were about done for until a lot of the zombies just started self-destructing."

"The damndest thing I've ever seen," I agreed.

"You want me to get someone to watch...?" My hand immediately tightened around the baby when Melody spoke. I was going to have to relax a little now that were safe.

"Rose," I said.

Melody and Jude stood in front of me. I saw them share a worried glance. I cleared my throat.

"Her name is Rose. And yes, I'd like someone to take her while I get cleaned up." I handed Jude her bag and her elephant. I held Rose out to Melody. I stood there a moment feeling an overwhelming need to snatch the baby back, but knowing I couldn't. I had things to set to rights.

"Just you, Melody," I said roughly. "Just you and Jude. No one else." It was a plea and Melody and Jude, both aware now that I was asking them to care for the baby personally, looked concerned and surprised.

"Okay, Tex," Melody said. "We'll gladly watch Rose for you."

I nodded my thanks and headed away from the trio.

I had to get my head clear. A cold shower would help that. And then... then I would do what I thought might be the hardest thing I'd ever done in my entire life, but the truth was, it was going to be the easiest.

Chapter Twenty-Eight
Untethered

I could smell the salty water and hear the waves crashing upon the beach. I smiled widely and leaned back, digging my toes into the damp sand. Was there anything better than this? A carefree laugh drew my attention away from my sandy feet and the feeling of cool water misting my face as I sat close to the ocean. Jessica Germain was there, and beside her was my wife, Alison. They were talking and walking along the beach, the picture of ease and contentment. Further up on the shore Maria was playing with Rose, building a sand castle complete with a moat and shovel draw-bridge. I got up off the ground and walked over to Jessica and Alison.

"What are you ladies up to?" I asked. They didn't seem to hear me and didn't turn to me. They just continued walking and occasionally splashing the water at each other with their feet. I wondered why it was that they didn't have anything to say to me, why it was they couldn't hear my question, but I didn't let it bother me. They seemed happy enough and I was relaxed and enjoying the beautiful day. I walked over to Maria and Rose and sat down beside them in the sand. I laughed when Maria screamed after a piece of seaweed tickled her foot. I never thought she'd be such a girly-girl.

"Make it any higher and the baby won't even be able to play with it," I said with a laugh.

Maria didn't listen to me either, she just kept building, kept making the walls to the sand castle thicker and bigger. She was done playing with the baby after a few minutes and instead focused all her energy into building the sand castle. Rose played nearby by herself, looking up to watch her mom every few seconds. Maria dug frantically around the castle, making the moat around it deeper and deeper until I became concerned that the baby might tumble in and hurt herself.

"You know, that's probably deep enough," I said to the back of Maria's head. She dug, using the wet sand she removed to fortify the walls of her castle. The walls to the sand castle had to be at least a foot

thick and the castle itself was big enough to play inside of like a fort. The more frantic Maria became, the more uneasy I felt.

A boom of thunder sounded in the distance over the ocean, pulling my attention away from the sand castle and toward the darkening sky. Nasty looking storm clouds were beginning to roll in insanely quick. I turned back to Maria to tell her we needed to get Rose off of the beach and to safety, except Rose wasn't where she'd been playing. I felt horror and panic wash over me before finding her sitting in the center of the enormous sand castle. The sand castle was now built up and reached over five feet or more off of the ground and Rose was crying as she sat up at the top, looking down at the beach.

I swung around to look for Maria to tell her to grab the baby from the castle so we could all get to safety, but Maria was still digging her moat, which was now at least two feet wide and getting deeper and deeper. A huge wave roared from behind me. I turned, thinking that I had to warn Alison and Jessica when the wave hit the shore with a resounding crash. The waves left a mass of red, foamy water upon the once sparkling white sandy beach. Bodies littered the beach in different stages of decomposition. Some of the people I recognized. Friends and loved ones, soldiers and civilians. Some I didn't know, not while they were alive, but they were the hundreds of walking dead that I'd come across and put down over the past two years. The ocean ran red with the blood of the dead. Vultures circled overhead and swooped down to feast upon the corpses. The beach looked like a massacre had occurred. And it had. Jessica Germain was slumped over the bodies of her fallen family. Her open, dead eyes blamed me. My wife was among the corpses as well, along with her mother and father on the beach.

Another wave crashed upon the shore and the water, murky with blood and floating bodies, washed up around my legs. I stumbled back only to fall into the moat that Maria had been diligently digging. The muck reached my waist here. I whipped around to find a way out of the mess, to find a safe haven, but there was none. The baby was crying from atop her sand castle and Maria was no longer there to comfort her. She was like everything else on the beach. Dead and decaying.

I held my hands out to Rose, telling her to come to me and let me hold onto her. The baby came willingly into my arms, but she wouldn't stop crying. The waters rose up and threatened to swallow us whole as we stood at the tip top of the unstable sand castle. Someone was calling my name. Someone was shouting for me to turn around. I dragged my gaze away from the shore, away from the danger long enough to see that further up upon the shore, further inland was... safety. If I had just turned around, just looked past the shore, I might have seen it sooner. Melody Carter was there, yelling for me to run, yelling for me to get off of the beach. I couldn't. No matter how much I wanted to and no matter how *much I needed to for Rose, I couldn't take the step that would've brought me off the beach and out of death's reach.*

Jude walked up behind Melody, put a hand on her arm, and whispered into her ear. Melody nodded and with a sad smile, held her arms out to me. I could feel tears coursing down my cheeks. No shame in crying. No shame in wishing it could be different. I kissed the top of the baby's head and held her out. As soon as I did, Melody was there to scoop her up safely into her arms and move back from the chaos of the shore.

As the bloody waves crashed around me, pulling me further down into their murky depths, I stopped fighting. For the first time in over two years, I felt like it was okay to just... let go. When the waves swallowed me whole, I didn't have a single thing keeping me tethered to the shore. The thin thread that had kept me there for two years was snapped long ago, and even though the responsibility and love I felt for Rose would never diminish, I knew as I watched her be carried away in Melody's arms that she would be safe. She was going to be fine. And that's all I cared about. The murky waters of death be damned.

I coughed and choked, water sputtering out of my nose and throat. I rubbed my hand over my face roughly, shoving my sopping wet hair out of my eyes. Water poured all round me as I stood in the shower stall like an idiot trying to regain my composure. I guess it wasn't enough to have nightmares and vivid memories haunting me while I slept at night, now I had to have them while I was semiconscious and taking a shower as well. I turned the shower handle until the water turned off completely and grabbed a towel off of the hook on the wall nearby. No time to contemplate the screwed up dream. I had things to do.

Chapter Twenty-Nine
To Die is Easy

I sat at a round table finishing up the last few lines of what I was writing when Jude and Melody walked into the conference room. Even though I'd requested for them to meet me in the room, they still looked surprised to find me there in clean clothes and with papers spread out in front of me on the table. I folded the papers carefully and put them in an envelope, sealing it.

"Where's Rose?" I asked.

"She's out like a light," Melody said, a smile softening her lips.

"Good," I said. Poor baby was probably exhausted. They both came in and took a seat across from me at the table.

"What's this all about, Tex?" Melody asked after a moment.

Leave it to Melody Carter to cut the crap and get to the bottom of the matter. I pushed the envelope I'd sealed across the table toward Melody and Jude.

"That's for Rose. One day she's going to want to read it."

Melody looked at the envelope with Rose's name scrawled across it in my chicken scratch and then back up at me. "I don't understand," Melody said. "Why don't you give it to her yourself when you're ready?" she asked, looking to Jude for agreement. Jude's eyes were on my face though and I knew that what I was asking was probably starting to set in.

"I can't, Mel," I answered. "And I'm not only asking you to give that to her when the time is right, I'm asking you two to take her in, to love her as your own,." I said, aware that my voice sounded rough, like the pain I was feeling was seeping through to my words. "To love her like her mother loved her and gave her life for her."

Melody moved her hand to push the envelope back toward me on the table. Jude's hand stopped her and his fingers found hers, giving them a gentle squeeze. Melody glance down at the envelope, at me, and then at Jude. Finally her eyes found mine again, full of understanding and grief.

"I only ask you guys because you're the only ones I trust to love her and to care for her as much as I do." I cleared my throat again and wiped a hand across my warm forehead. "To give your lives for her... like I have."

"Tex," Melody choked out.

I grinned crookedly at her. "Don't tell me you're regrettin' the way you blew me off *now*," I teased her.

She smiled through her tears. "You wish, cowboy," she said.

I smiled at that. "I realize you need some time to talk about it, that it is a lot of responsibility," I said. "I just don't have a lot of time to wait. I have something I need to take care of before...." I shrugged. I didn't want to make a big deal of it. Dying was going to be the easiest thing I'd done since the end of the world. Living... living was so much more difficult.

"We don't have to talk about it. We'll love Rose as if she were our own," Jude said confidently.

"Jude?" Melody questioned softly. She had a smile on her lips and determination in her eyes.

"Besides, I've seen her with the baby and I know there is no way anyone will ever be able to part them," Jude remarked.

My heart lifted. It was as it should be. "Good, then it's settled," I said, standing.

Melody and Jude both stood with me. I could tell Melody wanted to say more, but for once I was actually glad that I was on a deadline and I couldn't waste even a few precious minutes. Jude took the letter from the table.

"You'll see that Rose gets the letter when she's older?"

"We'll make sure," Melody promised.

"There's a camp not too far from here called Camp Victory," I said as we walked down the hallway. "It was run by a man who thought himself a prophet or some such bullshit." Jude snorted. "It's where Maria and Rose were when I found them," I said. "The leader is dead now, but there are some things going on there that are wrong."

We turned a corner and someone bumped into me. I winced and put a hand over the spot where the zombie had bit me on my shoulder back in Midtown. Blood had begun to seep through the bandage and my gray tee shirt.

"Tex, you want us to take a look? We have pain pills and...."

I smiled over at Melody. She knew as well as I did that I wasn't going to let anyone make a big fuss or to use up any resources. I'm pretty sure I heard her mutter something about *big, stupid, hardheaded hick* beneath her breath, but I couldn't be sure. Nah, I wasn't about to let people poke and prod me during the last twenty-four or forty-eight hours I had left to live. I had a lot more important things to do… like say goodbye to Rose. And after that, to kill Warren. I waved away her concern.

"This camp is pretty well fortified, out in the middle of nowhere and such, but I hope you guys will go there if and when you can. Just give people a choice to go with you or to stay behind. Maria didn't have a choice and she didn't want that for Rose."

I knew if they could do anything at all, they would. I handed Melody a map of the surrounding areas.

"I marked where you can find the camp on there," I offered. "There's also another camp, a school filled with children."

"Children?" Melody asked in surprise.

"They aren't just kids anymore though, they've been turned into a small army. They all have done terrible things to survive. Some of them are broken," I said, thinking of Nick.

"Who's leading them?" Jude asked, his eyes hard, his jaw clenched. No one liked the thought of children getting hurt, but worse was having to kill a kid to save your own life.

"A guy named Warren," I said through gritted teeth. "You won't have to worry about him though. Not after tonight."

Melody put a hand on my arm. "Your unfinished business?" she asked.

"Yes."

"Okay, and once Warren is out of the way, what is it you want us to do for these kids? Bring them here?" Jude asked.

I shook my head. "No. Most of them won't want to come anyway, but a few might. There's a kid, an older boy of maybe twelve, named Carter. If it weren't for him…." I trailed off. "Well, I wouldn't be here and neither would Rose. Carter is the kid you'll want to contact if you can. Just don't treat them like children. Don't go in thinking you're Army and they're just a bunch of snot-nosed brats, because believe me, those kids will not hesitate to put a bullet in your head and leaving you for zombie bait."

"Jesus," Jude whispered beneath his breath.

"Here we are," Melody said when we reached their room where Rose was sleeping.

"Can I have a few minutes alone?" I asked, staring at the door.

"Of course," Melody said. "We'll meet you back at the front when you're ready."

*

"Hello, Sweetheart," I whispered to Rose. She was sleeping on her tummy, cuddled into a pillow on Melody and Jude's bed. Melody had given her a bath and changed her into pale pink pajamas. Her stuffed elephant wasn't far away. I picked it up and tucked it under her arm, then rubbed a hand lightly over her head and down her back. She was so tiny, so fragile, and yet I had a feeling she was going to be a strong kid. I had no doubt she was going to live a long and full life. My only regret was not being around to see her grow and bring new life and new hope into a tired and scary world.

"Your mama loved you so very much, Rose," I whispered to the sleeping infant. "She knew what I know and that was as long as there are blessings like you in this world, there will always be some hope left." The baby shifted a little, turning her head over to get more comfortable. I smiled.

"You and your mama came into my life when I needed something to believe in, when I needed to find that one thing that would give me hope once again, hope to keep moving forward," I explained to her. "You were that one thing, Rose," I said softly. "You are the hope I needed. Now I can walk out of here knowing my fate and yet not resenting it, not regretting anything." I sat back away from the bed and watched the baby sleep for a few more minutes.

Rose would be safe with Jude and Melody, of that I was sure. They would teach her to be strong and to fight. They would teach her to love and to hope. That's all I could ask for. The rest was up to her. I leaned forward and kissed Rose on the head.

"Don't be afraid to kick ass and take names, little girl," I whispered. "And don't forget to look to the good inside yourself. Hold on to that goodness and life will always be worth living."

I set my black cowboy hat, her mom's sketchbook, and an army green backpack filled with my iPods next to her on the bed before I walked out.

I left the Army base a dying man. A man with absolutely no hope of survival and no hope for living. And yet I left with a smile on my face, a heart that felt lighter than it had in years, and true hope. Hope for a real future for humanity, a future worth fighting for... even if I wouldn't be there to enjoy it.

Hope is a powerful thing.

Chapter Thirty
The Hard Part

So this is what it must feel like to die, I thought. My bones ached, my body shook from chills and I felt so drained of energy that I could have just stayed in the truck and gladly let myself slip into death's embrace. Death would be the easy part. Killing Warren without killing any of his little followers was going to be the challenge. I glanced at myself in the rearview mirror and chuckled even though it hurt to. I'd gone Rambo. Dark camo pants, long-sleeved black shirt, smudged charcoal on my face, and even a piece of black fabric tied around my forehead. If I was going to die anyway, I might as well enjoy myself a little bit before I met my untimely demise. Besides, I'd always wanted to be Rambo when I grew up. This was my chance.

My new weapon, fitted with a silencer thanks to Jude, lay on the seat next to me. I picked it up and turned it over it my hands. I grabbed the backpack I'd gotten ready for this little field trip. Time to take care of business before I became too sick. I opened the door to the truck and slipped out into the darkness a whole lot less worried than I normally would have been. It's amazing how freeing it is when you no longer have to worry about your own survival. My only concern was to make sure I fulfilled my promise to myself and to Warren. He was going to pay for what he'd done to us... what he'd done to Maria. And for Rose having to grow up without her mama. Warren wasn't allowed to live after that.

I crept stealthily along the dark streets, ignoring the pain shooting through my body. I took down a few zombies here and there with my gun. Mostly I avoided them. It looked like this area also had had its fair share of exploding corpses as well. If any of us had known the zombies were going to do that, if Warren had known, would he have still led us out to the slaughter? In the end it didn't matter, I guess. All that mattered was that he *had*, and Maria had paid the ultimate sacrifice because of it. Warren would die.

I stopped close enough to the elementary school that I could see the fences and the kids that were posted as lookouts on the roof of the buildings. Only two kids from what I could see. Maybe Warren figured fewer were acceptable because of the way the zombies were dying off so suddenly. Or maybe there were other kids and I couldn't see them. The only way to be positive was to scout around the whole school perimeter. A shiver shook my body and a wave of dizziness reminded me that I didn't have a ton of time. Soon I would be in no shape to run around acting like Rambo. I'd be incapable of doing much of anything.

I decided to take it on faith that there were indeed fewer lookouts posted. I kept to the shadows and waited until I knew I was out of the sights of both the kids and ran to the fence line of the school. I pulled a pair of wire cutters out of my backpack and cut through several pieces of the chain link fence. Once I was done, I squeezed through, and then secured the fence with several zip ties. They'd be easy to cut through when I was ready to make my escape. Even though I was there to take out Warren, I didn't want the dead to get inside. I didn't want any children getting killed by zombies, even if they would shoot me between the eyes without blinking.

Getting inside the school was a lot easier than I imagined it would be. I guess not having a shotgun poking you in the back or someone threatening to shoot a woman and infant made a huge difference. At the sound of a group of people approaching, I ducked into a dark classroom. I peeked out through the crack in the doorway, holding my breath.

"I don't know, man. Sometimes I'd rather be out there on my own, ya know?"

"Shhh! Don't be saying that shit out loud or to other kids. Half of them would rat you out to Warren before you even finished talking."

"I know. I won't. Let's get outside and take over for John and Dalton so they don't get pissed."

"Yeah, they're going to want to join everyone for the party in the gym before it's all over."

Their voices faded as they walked away, going out the door I'd just come in through. Party in the gym, huh? So, Warren was celebrating and that's why there were fewer lookouts posted outside. Guess I was going to be crashing a party.

I got as close to the gymnasium as I could without being seen. There was a lot of noise coming from that general direction and I knew that they wouldn't be unarmed, even at a celebration. There were no side entrances to the gym, only the front doors that led into the hallway and the back door that led out onto a school playground. No way I'd be able to get inside without being seen. Even if I could get inside the room, I probably wouldn't be able to get a shot off without one of the kids putting me down first. I actually didn't care if they shot me at this point, hell, they'd be doing me a favor. I just didn't want to meet my maker before I sent Warren to the afterlife.

My best bet was to wait it out and see if I could get to Warren after everyone headed to bed for the night. The problem was, I didn't know where Warren slept. If he slept in the same area that the children did, I'd be able to narrow it down, but I was pretty sure he didn't sleep near them. The way I figured it, he probably had a space to himself. He struck me as the type of guy who would need to feel a little removed from the grungy community sleeping quarters of his child-soldiers.

I was contemplating my next move from my hiding spot inside an administrator's office when—lo and behold—a voice I recognized froze me in place. *Carter.* I peeked through the crack in the door and saw him standing right outside of it, speaking to a kid who was a lot younger than him, giving him tips on hand-to-hand combat. Carter's back was to the door I was hiding behind, but I could see the face of the kid he was speaking to.

"You're small now, and that isn't always a bad thing," Carter said to the kid. "It means you're weaker, but it also means you're faster and you can fit into spaces larger kids can't. Into places the dead can't reach. Just keep practicing and you're going to do great."

The kid beamed up at Carter. "Thanks, Carter! I'll work harder, I promise!" He lit off down the hall, not pausing to glance back. Carter was still looking down the hallway in the direction that the kid had run when I reached out, putting my hand over his mouth, and yanked him back into the room with me. Caught off guard, he was in the room before he processed the danger, which was good for me. Unfortunately, his surprise didn't last long and he began fighting back after his survival instincts kicked into overdrive. His head cracking into the bridge of my nose was the least of my worries. He had a knife pulled and at my throat before I could recover. He stood face-to-face with me in a rage, his eyes glints of steel.

"Damn, kid. I'll be sure to send a message first next time," I sputtered through the blood pouring down my face. His eyes widened and he took a step back, blinking until his eyes focused more fully on my face.

"Tex?" he asked. He glanced around the room, completely closing the door I'd jerked him through.

"Your head is hard as a rock," I grumbled, mopping my bloody nose with the back of my sleeve.

"Yeah, so I've been told," he said with a smirk. "So, you made it." He glanced around us, realizing suddenly that I was alone. "The baby?"

"The baby is safe."

"Maria?" he asked after a pause. I gritted my teeth and turned my face away.

"I'm sorry," he said sincerely.

"I know." It was all I could manage.

"So why are you here?" he asked after giving me a moment.

"I made a promise to Warren," I said.

Carter studied me closely, not surprised, but not enthusiastic either. "Is it worth it?" he asked.

"Worth what?" I asked. "My life? Because I don't have a life left to worry about," I added gruffly. I pulled back my shirt, exposing my bandaged wound to Carter. "I'm not here for me."

"I know," he said understandingly.

I believed he did understand. I didn't care that I was going to die in the next twenty-four hours. I knew I was going to die for over two years now, it was just a matter of when and for what cause. Maria and Rose had been my cause. Warren had fucked with my cause.

"So, what is your plan?" he asked.

"Well, getting in here was about it," I admitted. "Other than killing him, that is."

"It's going to be hard to get to him without being seen," Carter said.

I knew that, but that wasn't going to deter me.

"His room is a building over from this one. If you can get there, your best chance is to snag him while he's on his way to bed. He's been relaxed all night, feeling kind of invincible, I guess."

I clenched my teeth. Yeah, he would be. Carter told me the layout of the building where Warren slept. After I thought I had it down, I glanced over at the boy, who was really more of a man than a kid.

"I told some friends about your group here." Carter stiffened beside me. "They're good people from an underground Army base. They won't force you to come with them. It will be up to each one of you to make that choice. Once Warren is gone, these kids will need someone to look up to," I said.

Carter shook his head. "I'm not the oldest. Not even close. There are some older boys who will want to be in charge."

I put a hand out and placed it on his shoulder. "You're a good kid, Carter, and a natural leader. People will follow you if you want them to. It's a lot of responsibility to have people look to you for their survival though, so I understand if you're not ready for that. Just keep your head up, make smart decisions, and if things go bad, get out of here."

Carter nodded. "I will. Thank you, Tex, and... good luck."

I shook hands with him and then turned to the door.

"Good luck, Carter," I murmured as I left the room while the coast was clear. Time to get this over with.

Chapter Thirty-One
Promises, Promises

I watched Warren enter his room. I purposely waited until I knew he'd be asleep. I waited until most of the school camp was asleep. And I waited until I couldn't wait anymore. My body was starting to feel too heavy, my eyes too hard to keep open. I couldn't wait much longer. Dawn was rapidly approaching and I planned to see one more sunrise before I died.

I entered Warren's room quietly, fighting off the waves of dizziness that had become my constant companions. It didn't matter though. Warren was snoring so loud, I could have tripped and come through the doors playing a trumpet and it wouldn't have woken him. He had passed out, fully clothed, on top of his bed. For some reason the ease in which he slept, the way he was so clearly free of any sort of nagging of conscience, ate at me more than anything else. I had planned to just shoot him in the head and leave the way I'd come in through the fence. Instead I found myself pointing my gun in his face and kicking his booted foot with my own.

"Get up, you piece of shit," I hissed. Warren, moved once, but didn't wake up fully until I kicked him again, harder than before and calling him all kinds of names my mama would've been scandalized to hear. Or maybe she woulda been proud... I couldn't be too sure. It was a toss-up with southern mamas sometimes.

He jerked awake, his eyes widening once he realized he had a gun inches from his face. When he finally realized who was holding the gun, there was a moment of pure shock and disbelief that I found quite satisfying.

"Bet you didn't think you'd see me gain, huh?"

"How...?"

"Am I still alive?" I finished for him. He nodded. "I'm not."

"How...?"

"How did I get in your little camp?" I completed his question once again. "Easily enough."

He held up a hand, but immediately put it back down when I shoved my gun even closer to his face. He knew I'd blow a hole in his face without the slightest provocation.

"Tex, we can—"

"Work this out?" I suggested. He nodded his head, swallowing the lump that had surely formed in his throat. "Naw. We can't."

Warren looked ready to argue. I didn't give him a chance.

"Stand up," I ordered. "Slowly."

He moved cautiously, sliding off his bed and standing a foot in front of me. I held my gun to his back and shoved him toward the door.

"We're going on a little trip," I said cheerfully, hiding the pain I felt behind gritted teeth.

"Where?"

"Oh, you'll love this place, don't you worry your little heart about it," I answered with a smile. I cracked the door open and glanced up and down the hallway. "You make one wrong move, one noise outside of your feet walking on the ground, and I'll put a bullet in your head so fast you'll be dead before you hit the ground. And don't think otherwise. I've nothing left to lose, you understand?" I asked.

Warren's eyes searched mine and he found exactly what I wanted him to find there. The absolute truth of my words.

I stood behind him as we left the room. My gun was pressed between us, pointed directly at his heart. The hallways were empty and we easily slipped out into the schoolyard. If I was lucky, there would only be two lookouts on the roof still.

I grabbed Warren by the shirt and pulled him into the shadow of a building. We were only a few yards away from the fence. I stood there trying to decide what to do. The kid that was posted would see us and I'd have to kill him to keep him quiet. Was I willing to do that just to make sure Warren got what I promised him?

"Hey, John!" I heard the shout right as I was ready to make my decision. I pulled back further into the building.

"Hey. What are you doing up here? I thought I had a few more hours until someone came up to relieve me."

"I couldn't sleep, man. I figured I'd go ahead and do something instead of just staring up at the bunk above me, ya know?"

A smile spread across my face.

"That's really cool of you. There's nothing going on out here anyway. I'd love to catch some extra z's," John replied to the unseen newcomer.

"No problem. Make sure you check out on the chart and grab some food."

"Will do. Thanks, man.

"No problem."

I waited a few minutes until I was sure that John had plenty of time to get back to the main building before I gave Warren a shove. We moved quickly, but not before a light shone down on us from the roof above. We both stopped dead in our tracks. I saw Warren's grin from the corner of my eye. I raised a hand and gave a short wave and the light blinked a few times before going out.

Thank you, Carter, I thought.

Warren's look of absolute astonishment hadn't faded even after we pushed our way through the fence line and secured the opening behind us. We reached the truck a few minutes later.

"Where are we going?" Warren asked as he drove us through the dark streets. I could tell he was already getting nervous. I would be too, considering we were heading toward the high school in town.

"A little place I found the other day," I answered. The pain in my body had reached a level that I didn't think possible and I thought for a moment I might black out. Sheer force of will and anger made me push myself back from the brink. When we were a street over from Buck, I had Warren pull off the side of the road and kill the engine.

"So what, you going to drive me out here and then put a bullet in my head?" Warren snarled. "You could've done that back at the elementary school."

"Yeah, I could've," I agreed. "And I'd actually planned to, but then I changed my mind at the last minute."

"So what are you going to do then?" he asked, his eyes wandering around the darkness. I was sure he knew about where we were. He had had his boys and girls scout this area previously, trying to find a way to get to the high school. Without success, of course. He knew the area was crawling with the undead.

"I'm going to give you the same chance you gave me," I said after we'd sat there in silence so long that I could see the area around us begin to gradually lighten in preparation for the sunrise. Long enough that zombies had spotted us and were headed our way. Oh, there were still a lot of them. Not as many as what were there when Maria and I had been here, but enough to make my point.

"What do you mean?" Warren asked gruffly, watching the dark figures shambling in our direction.

"I mean exactly what I said. I'm going to give you the same chance you gave me and Maria. A knife and your survival skills. If you can make it on that alone, you'll live," I said conversationally. "Now start the truck back up and slam on the gas," I ordered.

Warren's face swung around to mine, his eyes panicked. "You don't want me to do that!" he shouted. "It will mean your death too."

I smiled widely and the truth hit him in the face.

"That's right, Warren, old pal, I couldn't give two shits whether or not I survive this little field trip of ours." His hand tightened on the steering wheel. "But if you don't do what I say right this second, I will put a bullet in both your kneecaps and then push you out onto the pavement."

I promised. Whatever he saw on my face convinced him that I meant business and he turned the truck on.

I reached into my bag and pulled out the same knife that had been given to me by Nick. Warren took two deep breaths before gathering the courage to put the truck into gear and gun the gas. We flew through the street, hitting at least a dozen overripe zombies before the truck sideswiped another vehicle and we flew up and over a sidewalk and into the same balustrade that led up to the church that Maria and I had been trapped on. The truck was totaled. Warren had hit his head on the steering wheel and was bleeding from a gash on his forehead. The back of my head had bounced off of my window, but the pounding and stickiness that I found there was nothing to alarm me. I didn't have a lot of time left anyway. I pointed my gun at Warren and held out the handle of the knife toward him with a huge smile. The zombies were already closing in and if the sounds echoing all around us were any indication, there were still a shit-ton of them.

"Better make a run for it," I said with a deep chuckle. Warren snatched the knife from me, rammed his shoulder into the truck door to jump out, and took off. I opened my own door and pointed my gun at Warren's back. He didn't get far before he had to fight and fall back. Zombies were already swarming him when I abandoned my backpack in the truck and walked away. Armed with a single gun and ammo, I headed across the street. Warren was yelling like a crazed maniac, drawing the dead toward himself like a meat magnet. I kept moving, cutting down every zombie that hadn't already headed toward Warren, every zombie that was standing in between me and my goal. A silencer was a beautiful thing.

By the time I made it across what felt like a never ending street and was standing beneath the street sign I was looking for, I could hear Warren's screams echoing throughout the entire town. Seems old Warren hadn't been much of a survivor after all. I turned and walked toward my destination.

There wasn't a single zombie on Buck Street.

Chapter Thirty-Two
Texas Pink, Texas Tough

I stumbled into the house, closed the door behind me, and then trudged up the stairs. My feet felt like lead and my body felt a hundred years old. I walked into the pink bedroom and sat down roughly in the floor next to the window. My heart was racing so fast, I wouldn't have been surprised to learn that the parasites that turned people into walking corpses first attacked the heart, causing cardiac arrest and then eventually death. I sure felt like my heart was working in maximum overdrive. It felt like it was about to burst right out of my chest. I set my knife and gun on the floor next to me and worked for a while trying to get my boots and socks off. If I was gonna die, I was going to be comfortable, by God.

Michael Hatten was dead. Warren was dead. Rose was with Melody and Jude at the Army base. Everything was in place. Everything was taken care of. I had nothing left to accomplish before I died. No one left to get to safety. Nothing left to prove. I sat there with my bare feet buried in the dusty tan carpet and thought back over the past two years. I'd lost just about everyone I loved. I'd had to kill people I'd loved after they'd turned. I'd lost all hope at one point. I'd lost the will to live more times than I could count. I'd kept fighting despite everything and as a result I'd met Maria. I was glad I'd met her and Rose. Even knowing how everything had turned out with Maria dying and having to say goodbye to Rose for good... I still would have made the same choices.

I'd like to say I would have made different choices, especially knowing what I knew now, what was going to happen and all that, but I'd be lying. And if there was one thing I wasn't, that was a liar. Even knowing the sacrifices that were going to be made, even knowing both Maria and I would lose our lives, still I would have helped Maria take Rose out of that camp. I would have cherished all those moments, as short as they were, that I'd had with Rose. I would have wanted her anywhere but at that camp and with the likes of Michael Hatten and his cult-like teachings.

Death was the only thing any of us were certain of. Death was the only thing any of us were promised after we were born. It was just a matter of when, where, and how. In my opinion, the *how* wasn't so important. Not anymore. The *when* was a surprise to most of us, but the *why*... the *why* was what had kept me from giving up long ago. The *why* had to matter didn't it? Had to mean something?

I'd like to think the reason I was about to put a bullet in my own head so I wouldn't turn meant something. That because of mine and Maria's sacrifices, Rose would have a real chance at a life that was worth living. I was going to cling to that. In my final moments, I was going to cling to the thought that my death meant life for a little girl. That little girl was the future. Life was the future. Hope was the future. And for the first time since the fall of the human race, I had true and unwavering hope for the future of mankind. I was going to die in peace. It's all any of us could wish for. My wish was going to come true. Everything around me became fuzzy as I wavered in and out of consciousness.

Pink walls.

At least I thought they were pink walls. I couldn't be sure. My body felt like it was on fire. I glanced around the room, at the walls, the girly toys and baby clothes. No flames. Then I remembered. I was in a baby's room in a house on Buck Street. Not Rose's room though. She was safe with Melody and Jude back at the Army base. Is it odd that on the brink of death, I took comfort in a pink baby's room? That I wanted my final moments to be surrounded by the things that reminded me of little Rose and what she meant to me and to... the world? If it was, I could care less. I'd gladly die here in this room being reminded of everything I held dear.

Reminded of Melody and Jude. Of Maria and her sacrifice. Of Rose and the hope she embodied. Of the world, though overflowing with death and violence, of the promise it still held. Of hope. Just an insignificant little word, and yet so powerful an emotion. Yeah, I'm happy in my pink room with everything it reminds me of.

I doubled over in pain, unable to stop the moan that left my lips.

My body knows it's time.

My mind knows.

My heart knows.

It's time.

Suddenly I felt... *alive.* Truly alive, and not waiting for death to knock at my door. No flames were licking at my body. No pain was shooting through my skull, bones, or joints. No fevered delirium made me second guess everything I saw and thought. No thoughts of becoming one of the undead if I misjudged how much time I had left weighed down my mind. Just peace. Peace isn't something I've felt in so long that it took me a moment to adjust to the feeling. My shoulders felt unencumbered. There were no weights there anymore. How many had I been carrying all this time to feel so... *free*?

I remembered then. The pink room. The pain. The gun in my hand. The moment of absolute clarity and the moment I pulled the trigger.

Living in the world after the dead began to walk the Earth had been hard.

Death... death was easy.

THE END

State of Spoil (Book #3) will be in bookstores in October 2015!

About the Author

Peggy Martinez is a full time Author who has over a dozen published works, including the Time Warper Series, the State of Decay Trilogy, the Contradiction Series, the Reapers Grimm Series, her middle grade Super Zero Series, and various novellas and serials.

When not writing, Peggy can be found homeschooling her teen son and four daughters. You may also find her packaging hundreds of boxes for her monthly box subscription business she founded just for readers! (Lit-Cube) She could also be spotted reading, making soap, dabbling in aromatherapy, watching gangster movies, prepping for the zombie apocalypse, or downing insane amounts of Twizzlers and Kazoozles. Oh yeah... and day dreaming about owning a small homestead or taking a dream vacation to Greece, Scotland, & Ireland. She could totally be doing that.

www.peggy-martinez.com